HALO®

EVOLUTIONS

DON'T MISS THESE OTHER THRILLING STORIES IN THE WORLDS OF

Halo: Renegades
Kelly Gay

Halo: Silent Storm
Troy Denning

Halo: Bad Blood
Matt Forbeck

Halo: Legacy of Onyx
Matt Forbeck

Halo: Retribution
Troy Denning

Halo: Envoy
Tobias S. Buckell

Halo: Smoke and Shadow
Kelly Gay

Halo: Fractures: More Essential Tales of the Halo Universe (anthology)

Halo: Shadow of Intent
Joseph Staten

Halo: Last Light
Troy Denning

Halo: Saint's Testimony
Frank O'Connor

Halo: Hunters in the Dark
Peter David

Halo: New Blood
Matt Forbeck

Halo: Broken Circle
John Shirley

THE KILO-FIVE TRILOGY

Karen Traviss

Halo: Glasslands

Halo: The Thursday War

Halo: Mortal Dictata

THE FORERUNNER SAGA

Greg Bear

Halo: Cryptum

Halo: Primordium

Halo: Silentium

Halo: Evolutions: Essential Tales of the Halo Universe (anthology)

Halo: The Cole Protocol
Tobias S. Buckell

Halo: Contact Harvest
Joseph Staten

Halo: Ghosts of Onyx
Eric Nylund

Halo: First Strike
Eric Nylund

Halo: The Flood
William C. Dietz

Halo: The Fall of Reach
Eric Nylund

EVOLUTIONS

Essential Tales of the Halo Universe

BASED ON THE BESTSELLING VIDEO GAME FOR XBOX®

GALLERY BOOKS

New York | London | Toronto | Sydney | New Delhi

G

Gallery Books
An Imprint of Simon & Schuster, Inc.
1230 Avenue of the Americas
New York, NY 10020

This book is a work of fiction. Any references to historical events, real people, or real places are used fictitiously. Other names, characters, places, and events are products of the author's imagination, and any resemblance to actual events or places or persons, living or dead, is entirely coincidental.

Copyright © 2009, 2019 by Microsoft Corporation. All Rights Reserved. Microsoft, Halo, the Halo logo, and 343 industries are trademarks of the Microsoft group of companies.

All rights reserved, including the right to reproduce this book or portions thereof in any form whatsoever. For information, address Gallery Books Subsidiary Rights Department, 1230 Avenue of the Americas, New York, NY 10020.

This Gallery Books trade paperback edition April 2019

GALLERY BOOKS and colophon are registered trademarks of Simon & Schuster, Inc.

For information about special discounts for bulk purchases, please contact Simon & Schuster Special Sales at 1-866-506-1949 or business@simonandschuster.com.

The Simon & Schuster Speakers Bureau can bring authors to your live event. For more information or to book an event, contact the Simon & Schuster Speakers Bureau at 1-866-248-3049 or visit our website at www.simonspeakers.com.

Manufactured in the United States of America

10 9 8 7 6 5 4 3 2

Library of Congress Cataloging-in-Publication Data is available.

ISBN 978-1-9821-1173-1
ISBN 978-1-9821-1174-8 (ebook)

CONTENTS

INTRODUCTION *Frank O'Connor* 1

BEYOND *art by Sparth, words by Jonathan Goff* 3

PARIAH *B. K. Evenson* 5

STOMPING ON THE HEELS OF A FUSS *Eric Raab* 53

MIDNIGHT IN THE *HEART OF MIDLOTHIAN* *Frank O'Connor* 78

DIRT *Tobias S. Buckell* 101

ACHERON-VII *art by Sparth, words by Jonathan Goff* 156

HEADHUNTERS *Jonathan Goff* 158

BLUNT INSTRUMENTS *Fred Van Lente* 197

THE *MONA LISA* *Jeff VanderMeer and Tessa Kum* 228

ICON *art by Robogabo, words by Jonathan Goff* 355

PALACE HOTEL *Robt McLees* 358

HUMAN WEAKNESS *Karen Traviss* 385

CONTENTS

CONNECTIVITY *art by Robogabo, words by Jonathan Goff* 427

THE IMPOSSIBLE LIFE AND THE POSSIBLE DEATH OF PRESTON J. COLE *Eric Nylund* 429

THE RETURN *Kevin Grace* 507

FROM THE OFFICE OF DR. WILLIAM ARTHUR IQBAL 536

ACKNOWLEDGMENTS 541

INTRODUCTION: WHY SHORT STORIES?

Because the Halo universe is almost as vast and boundless as the real thing. And because Halo fans enjoy a broad spectrum of flavors and moments from the games and the extended canon. In fact, no two Halo fans are quite the same. We have hard-core fans who only enjoy one game type, on one map, with one weapon. We have fans who are enthralled by the tactical exploits of UNSC commanders. We have fans who wish to explore the deepest mysteries of a forgotten civilization. We have fans who want to drop from orbit with the ODSTs. We have fans who view the entire canon through the lens of the Master Chief's faceplate.

Moreover, we have fans who can't wait years between novels to get their next fix, that next glistering nugget of data about their favorite part of the worlds Halo has created. Short stories allow us the luxury of sampling those flavors and moments. Like a box of chocolates, to borrow a Gumpian phrase.

We can dive in, visit the bridge of Admiral Cole's latest command, or hide in an abandoned spacecraft with the life ebbing out of us. We can wander the desert of a distant world in the cloven shoes of an Elite. We can explore the ravenous appetites of the

Gravemind through Cortana's tortured gaze. And we can do all this in a single book.

The first anthology I ever read was called *Great Space Battles.* It assembled short stories built around completely unrelated illustrations, and wove together a universe from the art it represented. I remember thinking what a wonderful way to read: in bite-size chunks. We have the luxury of an already established fiction and a vast range of characters and worlds at our fingertips.

Some of these stories are short and sweet and will melt in your mouth. Others are heartier fare, but they'll taste like a perfectly cooked chateaubriand. They'll all add ingredients and menu items to the Halo table, and they'll all taste remarkably different.

The iron chefs catering this affair are a mixture of masters. We have stories from the Titans of Halo Fiction: Erics Nylund and Raab, Tobias S. Buckell, Robt McLees, and Fred Van Lente. And we have newcomers too: Karen Traviss, who has left an indelible mark on *Star Wars* fiction; Tessa Kum and Jeff VanderMeer collaborate across an ocean and an international dateline; and B. K. Evenson, Jonathan Goff, and Kevin Grace bring some new ingredients. Even I've been in the kitchen, cobbling together something partway edible. I hope.

This anthology is certainly a smorgasbord and may be a lot to consume before we move back to the main course of novels, starting in 2010 with Greg Bear's new Forerunner trilogy. But you guys have the intestinal fortitude.

Bon appétit.

Frank O'Connor
Redmond, Washington
September 2009

BEYOND

There is majesty here
Beyond reason
Beyond understanding
Vast in its implications
What wonders; offered around each new corner—
Over every skyward peak—
Or hidden deep; within in the shadows of each sunken valley
The questions raised
In astonishment;
In fear—
If such glories can be divined, yet forgotten
Lost to time;
Strewn about the entirety of stars
What then are we—
Be us man,
Or be us monster
In light of knowledge, so vast—
So far beyond
Superior; even to our dreams
What matter, then, our petty confrontations
When weighed against the sins we sow
What matter, then, our fate amongst the cosmos, eternal
In light of the Halo; its luminous glow

PARIAH

B. K. EVENSON

PROLOGUE

"Will you tell me your name?" asked Dr. Halsey. She made no move to squat down in front of the boy, to smile, to do anything at all to come down to his level. Instead she remained standing, her posture neither friendly nor threatening, but simply as neutral as she could make it. Her gaze was steady, interested.

The boy looked at her from across the room. He was only six but the boy's gaze was just as steady as hers, though there was perhaps a trace of wariness in his eyes. *Completely understandable*, thought Dr. Halsey. *If he knew why I was here there'd be more than just a trace.* He held his body just as noncommittally as she held her own, though she could tell by the tightness in his neck that that might change any moment, without warning.

"You first," the boy said, and then moved his mouth into something that could pass for a smile.

His voice was calm, as if he were used to being in charge of a situation. Not afraid, then. Not surprising, thought Dr. Halsey. If the report she'd read was correct, he'd managed to survive on his own, in the Outer Colonies on the planet Dwarka, on an illegal farm in the middle of a forest preserve one hundred kilometers from nowhere, for nearly three months after his parents had died. Surviving under normal circumstances on a harsh world still in the process of being terraformed was hard enough. But for someone who was barely six years old it was inconceivable.

"I already know your name," Dr. Halsey admitted. "It's Soren."

"If you knew, why did you ask?"

"I wanted to see if you'd tell me," she said. Then she paused. "I'm Doctor Halsey," she said, and smiled.

Soren didn't smile back. She now saw more than a trace of suspicion in his gaze, suspicion that sat strangely in his face alongside his straw-colored hair and his pale blue eyes. "What kind of doctor?" he asked.

"I'm a scientist," said Dr. Halsey.

"Not a sigh—, not a sigh—"

"No," she said, and smiled. "I'm not a psychiatrist. You've been seeing a lot of psychiatrists, haven't you?"

He hesitated just a moment, and then nodded.

"Because of your parents' deaths?"

He hesitated, nodded again.

Dr. Halsey glanced at the holographic files displayed discreetly on the interior of her glasses. His mother had apparently succumbed to a planet-specific disease. Treatments were readily available, but a family living off the grid wouldn't have been aware of that. Instead of reporting immediately to the planetary officials as was required by law, the boy's parents had dismissed the symptoms as those of a cold and had kept working. A few days later, the mother was dead and the stepfather sick. Soren, perhaps because his younger immune system had adapted more readily to Dwarka, had never become ill. He had, according to his stepfather's dying wish, buried the bodies of both of his parents, then continued to live on in their farmhouse until supplies were almost gone, finally setting out by foot to cross 112 kilometers of blue-gray forest and arrive at the beginning of authorized farmland.

Was she right to consider him for her team of Spartans? Certainly he was bright and resourceful. He was tough and clearly wouldn't give up easily. But at the same time, what would it do to someone to go through that experience? Nobody knew how traumatized he was. Nobody knew for certain what it had done—and might still be doing—to him. Probably not even him.

"Why are you here?" he asked.

She looked at him and considered. There was no reason to tell him anything; she could simply do as she and Keyes had done with the others and make the decision for him, flash-clone him and kidnap him for, as she'd started telling herself, the *greater good.* But with the other children she'd in part assumed they wouldn't understand. Here was a boy without parents who, despite being only six, had had to grow up fast, much faster than her other recruits. Could she tell him more?

"The truth is," she said, "I came to see you."

"Why?" he countered.

She returned his even gaze. Suddenly she made her decision. "I'm trying to decide if you're right for something I'm working on. An experiment. I can't tell you what it is, I'm afraid. But if it works in the way we hope it will you'll be stronger and faster and smarter than you could ever imagine."

For the first time, he looked slightly confused. "Why would

you want to do something like that for me? You don't even know me."

She reached out and tousled Soren's hair, was pleased when he didn't flinch or shy away. "It's not *for* you, exactly," she said. "I can't tell you much more. It won't be easy; it'll be the hardest thing you've ever done—even harder than what happened with your parents."

"And what have you decided?" he asked.

"I've decided to let you be the one to decide," she said.

"What if I say no?"

She shrugged. "You'd stay here on Dwarka. The planetary authorities would arrange a foster home for you." *Not much of a choice*, she thought. *He's between a rock and a hard place.* She wondered again if she wasn't being unfair putting the choice on the boy.

"All right," he said and stood up.

"All right what?" she said.

"I'm coming with you. When do we leave?"

LATER, BACK on board, when she spoke with Keyes, showed him the vid of her conversation with Soren, he asked, "You're sure about this?"

"I think so," she said.

He just grunted.

"As sure as I am of taking any of them," she said. "At least he has a notion of what might happen to him."

"That's an awful lot to lay on a child," said Keyes. "Even one who's grown up fast."

She nodded. Keyes was right, she knew. The terms for the test subject known as Soren were different from those of the others—he was coming into the program in a different way from the very beginning. She'd have to remember that and keep an eye on him.

ONE

What neither Doctor Halsey nor Lieutenant Keyes knew—and what they would never find out, since Soren, though only six, was smart enough not to tell them—was what really happened to him during those three months alone. That was something that Soren, or Soren-66 as he would come to be called, didn't like to think about. It had been terrible when he realized his mother was dead and that the reason she was dead was because his stepfather had been too worried about going to jail for his illegal farm to take her to a doctor when she got sick. By the time his stepfather was convinced there was no other choice, it was too late; his mother was already gone.

But his stepfather had refused to face it. He moved Soren's mother's body into the box room and locked the door, telling Soren that it was not possible to see her, that she was too sick and needed to be alone to recover. That had lasted a few days until finally, late one night, his stepfather had had too much to drink. Soren stole the key and crept slowly through the door to see her there, lying on a pile of flattened boxes, the skin of her face tight and sallow. She smelled bad. He had seen and smelled enough rotting animals in the woods to know that she was dead.

He cried for a while and then sneaked back out of the room, shutting and locking the door behind him, returning the key to his stepfather's bedside table, and then sneaking out again. In the kitchen he sat brooding, wondering what to do. His stepfather was responsible for his mother's death, he sensed, and as far as he was concerned he should have to pay. Just thinking about it made him tremble.

Thinking this and things like it led him to get off his chair and take the sharpest knife off the counter. He knew it was the sharpest because his mother had never let him use it without her help. He had to stand on his tiptoes to reach it. It was big, heavy. He stood staring at the low flicker on the blade in the half-light and then slowly made his way to his stepfather's bedroom.

His stepfather was lying in bed, still asleep, groaning slightly. He stank of liquor. Soren pulled the chair closer to the bed and stood on it, looming now over his stepfather. He stayed like that, clutching the knife, trying to decide how to go about killing the man. He was, he knew, small, still a child, and he would only have one chance. *The neck*, he thought. He would have to jab the knife in quick and deep. Maybe that would be enough. He would fall onto his stepfather and stab into his neck at the same time and then before his stepfather could do anything he would start running, out into the forest, just in case it didn't kill him. Fleetingly the thought crossed his mind that to do something like this might be wrong, that his mother would not approve, but having grown up off the grid on the edge of the civilized universe, living under a man growing illegal crops and possessed of a mistrust for the law, it was hard to know where wrong ended and right started. He was angry. All he knew was that his mother was dead, and that it was the fault of this man.

Years later, when he thought back to the situation, he realized there were nuances to it that at the time he had no chance of understanding. There was something seriously wrong with his stepfather, an inability to face up to his wife's death, that had let him simply block the death out. Yes, he'd been wrong not to take her to town at the first sign of illness, but his behavior afterward had been less maliciousness and more a sign of how deeply troubled he was. But at the time, all Soren knew was that he wanted whoever was responsible for his mother's death to pay.

He waited there poised on his chair for what seemed like hours, watching his stepfather sleep, until light started to seep in. Then he waited a little more, until his stepfather stretched and rolled over in his sleep to perfectly expose his neck.

He leaped forward, bringing the knife down as hard as he could. It turned a little in his hand as it struck, but it went in. His stepfather gave a muffled bellow and flailed around him but Soren was already off the bed and running out the bedroom door. He was just opening the outer door when his stepfather appeared, red-eyed and swaying in the bedroom doorway, the knife jutting out between his neck and shoulder a little above his clavicle, his shirt already soaked with blood. He cried out again, a monstrous sound, like an angry ox, and then Soren had the door open and had plunged out into the crisp morning air, vanishing into the forest.

He was well-hidden within a clump of bushes by the time his stepfather came out, the knife out of his flesh now and in his hand, the wound sprayed with biofoam. The man was grimacing, clearly in pain.

"Soren!" he cried out. "What's wrong with you!"

Soren didn't say anything, pulling himself deeper into the bushes. His stepfather came in search of him. Whatever was wrong, the man claimed, could be sorted out if Soren would just come out and explain it to him. He passed very close, so close that Soren could hear the ragged sound of his breathing. His stepfather nearly stepped on his hand, and then he continued on deeper into the forest, occasionally stopping to call out his name.

THAT WAS as far as Soren's plans went. He couldn't, he felt, go back into the house, not now that he had tried to kill his stepfather. And yet, where was he to go? They were in the middle of nowhere, miles away from anything.

The first night was difficult, the air cold enough in the dark that he kept waking up shivering, his teeth chattering. He kept hearing things, too, unsure whether it was his stepfather or the animals of the forest—and, if the latter, whether they were just small rodents or something larger that might be carnivorous. His mother had always warned him not to go far into the forest. "It's not like the parks back home," she had claimed. "It's not safe."

He awoke at dawn, hungry and bone tired. He crept to the edge of the clearing and watched the prefab house from the safety of the brush, wondering if he could sneak in and get some food. He was getting ready to do so when he caught a brief flash of his stepfather through the window, standing just inside, waiting for him.

He slunk back into the forest, stomach still growling. He wanted to cry, but the tears just didn't seem to come. Had he done the right thing stabbing his stepfather? He wasn't sure. In any case it hadn't worked, had only made things worse. He should have had a better plan, he thought, or at least figured what to do next. This was no time for crying, he decided. He had to figure out what to do next.

The first thing was to have something to eat. He couldn't get into the house for the food in there—he should have thought of that before stabbing his stepfather, should have taken some food out of the house and cached it in the woods. But it was too late for that now. He would have to make do.

At first he tried to catch an animal, one of the toothless squirrellike creatures that slid silently as ghosts around the trunks and boles of the trees. But after only a few minutes he realized they were much too fast for him. Next, he tried to sit motionless to see if they would come to him. They were curious and got close, but never quite close enough for him to grab one. Maybe he could kill one by throwing rocks? He tried, but mostly his aim was off, and the one time he hit one it simply gave an angry chitter and scuttled off. *Even if I catch one*, he suddenly realized, *how am I going to cook it? I don't have anything to start a fire.*

What could he eat, then? Some of the plants were edible, but which ones? He wasn't sure. His family had never harvested from the forest, sticking instead to their prepackaged provisions.

In the end he stepped on a dry, rotten branch and heard it crack, an eddy of bugs pouring out of the gap and quickly vanishing into the undergrowth. He heaved the branch over and saw, along the underside, pale white larvae, worms, large-jawed centipedes, and beetles spotted orange and blue. He avoided the beetles—if they were that brightly colored there must be something wrong with them—but tried both the larvae and the worms. The larvae had a nutty taste and were okay to eat if he didn't think too much about them. The worms were a little slimier, but he could keep them down. When a few hours had passed and he didn't feel sick, he turned over a few more fallen logs and ate his fill.

Before night fell he started to experiment, moving a little farther away from the house and making several beds out of the leaves and needles of different trees. One type of leaf, he found, raised a row of angry, itchy red bumps along his wrist when he touched it; he made a mental note of what it looked like and from then on avoided it. He tried each of the other beds in turn until he found one that was soft and a little warmer. He was still cold during the night, but no longer shivering. He was far from comfortable but he could stand it, and even sleep.

In just a few days, he had started to understand his patch of forest. He knew where to go for grubs, when to leave a log alone for a few days and when to turn it. Watching the ghost squirrels, he learned to avoid certain berries and plants. Others he tasted. Some were bitter and made him sick to his stomach and he didn't return to them. But a few he went back to without any ill effect.

He watched his stepfather from the bushes. He was there to see him in the morning, when he came out of the house and went to the crops or to the processor that refined them into a white powder, and there to see him as well at night. Each time his stepfather left the house he carefully locked the door, and though Soren had tried a few times to break his way in, the windows were strong and he wasn't successful.

Maybe I'll make a trap, he began to think. Something his stepfather would step in or fall into or something that might fall on him and crush him. Could he do that?

He watched. His stepfather took the same route to the field every day, a straight and straightforward line along a dirt track his own feet had carved day after day. He was nothing if not predictable. The path was clear enough that there was little chance of hiding something on it or digging a hole without his noticing. Nor were there trees close enough to drop something from above.

Maybe it had been enough, he tried to tell himself. Maybe he could just forget about him and leave. But even though he told himself that, he found himself returning, day after day, to stare at the house. He was growing stronger, his young body lean and hard, nothing wasted. His hearing had grown keen, and his vision was such that he could now see the signs of when something had passed before him on the paths he traveled. When he was sure nothing and nobody was listening, he told himself stories, mumbled whispered fables, versions of things his mother had told him.

Several years later, thinking it over, he realized that he had become trapped, neither able to go into his house nor leave it behind completely. It was as though he was tethered to it, like a dog chained to a post. It might, he realized when he was older, have gone on indefinitely.

And indeed it did go on, Soren growing a little more wild each day, until something suddenly changed. One morning his stepfather came out and Soren could see there was something wrong with him. He was coughing badly, was hunched over—he was sick, Soren realized with a brief shudder of fear, in the same way Soren's mother had been. His stepfather went to the crops, weaving slightly, but he was listless, exhausted, and by midday he had given up and was headed back. Only he didn't make it all the way back. Halfway home, he fell to his knees and then laid there, flat on his stomach, his face pushing into the dirt, one leg jutted to the side. He was there a long time, unmoving. Soren thought he must be dead, but then as he watched his stepfather gave a shuddering breath and started to move again. But he didn't go back to the house. Instead, he crawled his way to the truck and tried to pull himself into it.

When he failed and fell back into the dust, there was Soren, above him and a little way away, his face expressionless.

"Soren," said his stepfather, his voice little above a whisper.

Soren didn't say anything. He just stayed there without moving. Watching. Waiting.

"I thought you were dead," said his stepfather. "I really did. I would have kept looking for you otherwise. Thank God you're here."

Soren folded his arms across his tiny chest.

"I need your help," said his stepfather. "Help me get into the truck. I'm very sick. I need to find medicine."

Still Soren said nothing, continuing to stand there motionless, waiting, not moving. He stayed like that, listening to his stepfather's pleading, his growing panic, followed by threats and wheedling. Eventually the latter passed into unconsciousness. Then Soren sat down and stayed there, holding vigil over the sick man, until two days later his breathing stopped and he was dead. Then he reached into his stepfather's pocket and took the keys and reclaimed the house.

IT WASN'T easy work to drag his mother out of the house and bury her, but in the end, his fingers blistered and bleeding from several days of slow digging, he managed. His stepfather he buried less from a sense of obligation and more because he wasn't sure what else to do with the body. He liked to tell himself in later years that he had buried him to prove that he wasn't like him, to prove he was more human, but he was never sure if that was the real reason. He buried him where he had fallen, just beside the truck, rolling him into a hole that was just deeper than the body and mounding the dirt high around him.

He stayed in the house for a few days, eating and building up his strength. When the provisions began to run low he finally managed to shake the house's grip on him, walking out into the forest, making his way slowly in the direction that he thought a town might be. He was in the woods for days, maybe weeks, living off berries and grubs. Once he even managed to kill a ghost squirrel with a carefully thrown rock and then slit the fur off with another rock to eat the spongy, bitter meat within. After that, he stuck to berries and grubs.

And then, almost accidentally, he came across a track that he knew wasn't made by an animal and followed it. A few hours later he found himself standing on the edge of a small township, startled by how the people stared at him when he emerged from the underbrush, his clothing tattered, his skin covered with dirt and grime. He was surprised by the way they rushed toward him, their faces creased with concern.

TWO

With such experience under his belt, life on Reach in the Spartan camp seemed less of a challenge to Soren than it did to many of the other recruits. After living in the woods alone, he felt he was ready for anything. He was quick to figure out the best way through an obstacle course. He could fade quickly into bushes and undergrowth when on mock patrol. Camouflage was a way of life for him: He faded into the background too when in groups, wanting neither to come to attention as one of the leaders of a group nor to be seen as an outsider. He stuck to the anonymous middle.

But despite that, there were times when he noticed Dr. Halsey standing at a deliberate distance, watching him with an expression on her face that he could not interpret. Once, when he was nearly eleven, she even approached him as he ran through an exercise with the other children, standing at a slight remove, as he hesitated, wondering which team to join. He couldn't decide if he was having trouble because she was scrutinizing him, or if he always waited until the last minute to make his choice and it just took her presence to make him realize it.

"Everything all right, Soren?" she asked him, her voice carefully modulated. Officially he was now Soren-66—a seemingly arbitrary digit for recruits, decided by the Office of Naval Intelligence for reasons they kept to themselves—but the doctor never called him by the number.

"Yes, sir," he said, then realized she wasn't a sir, or even, for that matter, a ma'am and blushed and looked guiltily at her. "Yes, Doctor?" he tried.

She smiled. "Don't get distracted by irrelevant data," she said to him, and then gestured idly past him, at the two teams already running for the skirmish ground. "And above all don't let yourself get left behind."

DON'T LET yourself get left behind. The words echoed for him not only through the rest of the exercise but for a long time to come, haunting him long after he was sure Dr. Halsey had forgotten them. There was, he slowly came to sense, something different about him, something that the other recruits either didn't have or didn't care to show. For that matter, he didn't show it either: as he grew, he was very careful not to let anyone see anything that would make him different, would make him stand apart.

When he was very young, six or seven, he had been less careful. He hated sharing his room, found it exceptionally difficult to sleep hearing the sounds and the breathing of his fellow bunkmates. In their breathing he heard his stepfather. Sometimes he waited until they had fallen asleep and then slipped slowly out of his bed to hide under it, sleeping in the damp, musty space near the wall. He felt safer there. But when one morning he had slept late and hadn't returned to his bed before the others had started waking up, the way they looked at him made him feel less safe. No, he would have to play along, would have to learn to go through the motions that all the others seemed to make so naturally. He wanted not so much to *fit* in as to *fade* in.

But after a while, it didn't seem like an act anymore. He liked many aspects of the life of being a recruit. He enjoyed the challenge of it both mentally and physically. Having grown up off the grid, he had never been around people who were going through the same things he was; at times, particularly when they were darting through the forest together or crawling their breathless and silent way through a ditch full of mud, it was like being surrounded by many other versions of himself. It was comforting. Indeed, he felt closer to the other recruits than he had to anyone but his mother. Dr. Halsey, too, was the next best thing to a mother to him, though often distant, often preoccupied. But there was something about her that he found some strange kinship with.

He still needed time to himself, still found himself figuring out ways of being off on his own or, if not on his own, of creating a kind of momentary and temporary wall between himself and the others as a way of trying to think, to breathe, to be more fully himself. He realized very early on that he was never going to be a leader. He was not very communicative, but his instincts were honed and good and he was willing and able to follow orders. The others knew they could count on him. He felt in this the beginnings of a sense of meaning and purpose to his life, and he felt better than he had ever felt. He was keeping up. He wasn't letting himself get left behind.

And yet he was still haunted by the past. Sometimes, particularly late at night, in the dark, he couldn't help but think about what had happened when he was younger. He knew that whatever it was that made him different from the others came from that. At first the past was something he tried to push away, tried to forget, but as he grew older and smarter his thoughts about it became more and more conflicted. In his early teens, he began to see his stepfather less as a monster and more as someone who was scared and confused, somebody disastrously flawed, but someone who was also human. He fought against that realization, kept pushing it away, but it continually surged back over him. He had watched his stepfather die—it had been so quick, almost no time at all between the first symptoms and that strange transition from life to death. Which made him wonder, with a disease that moved that quickly: could his mother really have been saved?

All in all, he was neither the best nor the worst. He was a solid recruit and trainee, someone who, though haunted by his past, was doing his best to move beyond it. Perhaps, he thought, for the moment that was all he could ask for. Perhaps for now it was enough.

THREE

He was fourteen now, and standing at attention on the other side of Dr. Halsey's desk. Her face, he noticed, was drawn and tight, her responses a little jerkier than usual, as if she hadn't been getting enough sleep or was overworked. She hid it well, but Soren, himself an expert on hiding things well, saw all the cues he was learning to suppress in himself.

"At ease," Dr. Halsey said. "Please take a seat, Soren."

"Thank you, ma'am," he said, and sat, a single fluid movement, nothing wasted.

She was whispering quietly to herself, scanning a series of electronic files. The files were holograms whose contents were visible to her but which he saw only as an image of a small brick wall, an image of CPO Mendez on the other side of it with his finger pressed to his lips. *Someone has a weird sense of humor*, he thought.

"Do you mind if I ask you a question?" she asked.

"Of course not, ma'am," he said.

"Dr. Halsey," she said. "No need to make me sound any older than I am. Do you remember when we first met?"

"Yes," said Soren. Hardly a day had gone by without his thinking about that meeting and everything it had led to.

"I wonder, Soren, do you remember what I said, how I gave you a choice?"

Soren wrinkled his forehead briefly, then the lines cleared. "You mean whether to come with you or stay on Dwarka? Or was there something else?"

"No, just that," she said. "You were young enough that I didn't know how well you'd remember. How do you feel about your choice?"

"I'm glad I made it," he said. "It was the right choice, ma'am."

"I thought we already talked about your calling me that," she said, smiling. "I wondered at the time whether I was right to give you a choice. Lieutenant Keyes wondered too. Whether you weren't too young to have that burden placed on you."

"Burden?" he asked.

She waved the implied question aside. "Never mind," she said. "The reason I've brought you here is to give you another choice."

He waited for her to continue, but for a moment she simply stayed there, staring at him, the same unreadable expression on her face that he'd noticed before, when he had caught her watching him during exercises.

"You're still very young," she said.

Soren said nothing.

Dr. Halsey sighed. "You've trained well, all of you. But training is only the first step. We're on the verge of the second step. Would you like to take it?"

"What is it exactly?"

"There's only so much I can tell you," said Dr. Halsey. "There's only so much the bodies that we have can do, Soren. So we want to augment them. We want to modify your physical body and mind to push it beyond normal human capabilities. We want to toughen your bones, increase your growth, build your muscle mass, sharpen your vision, improve your reflexes. We want to make you into the perfect soldier." The smile that had been building on her face slowly faded away. "However, there will be side effects. Some of these we know, some we probably can't anticipate. There's also considerable risk."

"What sort of risk?"

"There's a chance, a nontrivial one, that you could die during the augmentation. Even if you don't die, there's a strong risk of Parkinson's, Fletcher's syndrome, and Ehlers-Danlos syndrome, as well as potential problems with deformation or atrophy of the muscles and degenerative bone conditions."

He didn't understand everything she was saying, but had the gist of it. "And if it works?"

"If it works, you'll be stronger and faster than you can imagine." She tented her fingers in front of her, staring over them at him. "I'm giving you an option that the others won't be given. I am offering you a choice, while your classmates will simply be told they are to report for the procedure."

"Why me?" asked Soren.

"Pardon?"

"Why am I the one who gets to make a choice? Why not one of the others?"

She turned her gaze to the desk in front of her, her voice distant now, more as if she were speaking to herself than the boy. "What the Spartans are is an experiment," she said. "In every controlled experiment you need one sample whose conditions are different so as to be able to judge the progress of the larger group. You're that sample, Soren."

"We're an experiment," he said, his voice flat.

"I won't lie to you. That is precisely what you are, and you—an experiment within the experiment. An exception to a rule," she said.

"Why me?" he asked again. "You could have chosen anyone."

She shrugged. "I don't know, Soren. It just turned out that way."

He was silent for a long time, staring straight in front of him, sorting it all out in his head. Finally he looked up.

"I want to do it," he said.

"You do?" said Dr. Halsey. "Even knowing the risks?"

"Yes," he said. And then added, "I don't want to be left behind."

STRANGE, DR. Halsey thought after he had left. What had he meant by not wanting to be left behind? Where had she heard that before?

She shook her head to clear it. "Déjà," she said. "You were listening in, I take it?"

"Of course, Dr. Halsey," said the AI's smooth voice. Her hologram flickered into existence on the desk beside her. Created specifically for the Spartan project, her self-chosen construct was that of a Greek goddess, barefoot and holding a clay tablet.

"Any thoughts?"

"Is that a rhetorical question?" asked Déjà. When Dr. Halsey didn't respond, she continued. "You didn't tell him everything," the AI said.

"No," said Dr. Halsey. "I didn't."

"I would be remiss not to point out that, as the individual responsible for the intellectual development of the Spartans, you've given him faulty information about how a control generally works in a scientific experiment. The control group generally is the group that does not experience the conditions of—"

"I know that, Déjà," said Halsey, cutting her off.

Déjà nodded curtly. "I would also be remiss not to point out that Soren-66 himself is precociously intelligent and has almost certainly realized that the reasons you gave for allowing him a choice were false."

"And what were my real reasons?" asked Dr. Halsey.

"I don't know," said Déjà. "I have a feeling, however, that I'm as confused about that as *you* are."

Dr. Halsey nodded.

"But if I had to guess," said Déjà, "knowing you as well as I do, I would say that it was a way of easing your own conscience. You just wanted to tell him. You wanted to tell one of them. You wanted to see if just one of them would make the choice for himself."

Dr. Halsey sighed. "Yes," she said. "You may be right. Thank you for being honest with me, Déjà."

"No need to thank me. I can't help it," said Déjà. "It's in my programming."

Dr. Halsey brushed her hand through the hologram and it disappeared. She leaned back in her chair. *I've given him a burden to live with*, she thought. *I've let him make his own decision, but Déjà's right. I've shifted the burden of responsibility back to him if anything goes wrong. A child. Carrying my sins.*

Let's hope nothing goes wrong.

FOUR

He was dreaming but even in the dream it was as if he couldn't wake up, as if he had been asleep for days and days. In the dream he was back in the forest again, but in addition to the cold and the hunger there was also something stalking him, a strange creature, almost human but not quite: deformed somehow, its mouth cast in an odd leer, its body lumpy and irregular, dragging one of its feet behind. It was always just a little way behind him, never quite catching up with him, but he couldn't seem to shake it, either. He could hear it there crashing through the woods behind him. Every so often it would give a cry of pain that was so piercing that it was all he could do to keep going. How long had he been walking? He ate what he could grab from the ground around him and kept going, dead on his feet, half-asleep, until suddenly he took a wrong turn and found the path before him blocked. And there the creature was, just behind him and on him before he could escape. It plucked him up off the ground like a toy and hurled him. He smashed through limbs and branches and came down hard, the forest around him fading to white as he died.

Only he wasn't dead. What he saw, all around him, was a blank, uneasy whiteness, filled with a slow buzzing. And then the whiteness slowly resolved into a piercing light. To either side of him, dim shapes began to take form, resolving into heads, the heads themselves covered with white cloth caps, the faces hidden behind breathing masks. Beneath these heads, he saw, the clothing that covered the bodies was spattered and stained with blood. It took him a moment to realize the blood was his own.

One of the heads was speaking, he realized, a low rumbling coming out of it, though he couldn't understand what it was saying. It stopped and one of the other heads started to make a similar sound. *What's wrong with them*, he wondered. And then, *What's wrong with me?*

Then a set of fingers waved itself over his eyes. He tried to follow them but could do so only at a slight remove, his eyes moving always just a little late. A head dove down closer to his eyes, suddenly becoming crisply, painfully defined.

"Is he supposed to be like this?" the head asked, its voice muffled through the mask. Then other heads were there, suddenly looming toward him, crisp and almost as if too close. There was a flurry of movement, too, shouting, and then everything became too slow, everything moving oddly and slowly, as if underwater.

This is real, he suddenly realized. *This is really happening.* Then abruptly the buzzing increased and the thought slipped through his mental fingers and was lost, to be replaced by another dream, another nightmare.

IN THE dream he was sitting in a chair but couldn't move. There was nothing restraining him, nothing blocking his arms or his legs; he simply couldn't move. No, wait, he could move a little, could move his eyes very slowly back and forth. At first the room was indistinct, as if the chair were simply sitting in the middle of a vast pool of darkness, but, very slowly, it began to take form around. Not a chair, he suddenly realized, but a bed: He was lying in a bed—how had he ever thought he was sitting upright in a chair? There was a blanket he recognized, but he couldn't quite place it. The shape of the bed was familiar as well, the shape of the room familiar, too, but he was unable to place where he was until the door at the far end of the room opened and his stepfather, impossibly large, stooped and shouldered his way in.

I'm in my mother's room, he thought. *In my mother's bed.*

And upon thinking that, he began to realize that he wasn't the only one in the bed, that he wasn't alone. But he couldn't turn his head to see who the other person was. His stepfather stood in the doorway, more shadow than man, a strange piping noise coming from him—something with all the structures of a language but impossible for him to even begin to understand. He appeared to be pleading, exhorting, but maybe it just seemed that way.

And then suddenly the other person in the bed moved, began to speak in the same birdlike piping, and though he still didn't understand a word of it he realized, by the sound and tenor of the voice, that it was his mother. She moved and he saw just the edge of her hand, the skin gray and beginning to rot, to come apart to show a thin strip of bone below. He wanted to scream, but all he could do was let his eyes dart frantically about in his sockets as she slowly shifted in the bed, her hand carefully feeling his face. She gave a low hiss and began to pull herself up.

He was just beginning to see her face when a sudden intense pain washed over him, as if someone had worked broken glass into his veins. The dream wavered and spun and reduced itself to a small white dot on a black field and then, with a hiss, was gone, leaving nothing but darkness behind.

How long did that last? Impossible to say. He had no sense of time passing, no sense of anything but that limitless void, a vague sense of himself as part of it, but even that seemed to be blurring around the edges, any sense of himself as an individual being threatening to slip away.

And then, very, very slowly, the darkness was broken by a small white dot, a dot which grew larger and larger and in the end swallowed everything around him.

And then it swallowed him as well.

HE AWOKE to find himself screaming. He was restrained, tied down to some sort of table or bed, and he felt like he was on fire, his skin itching and burning. The veins on his arms stood out and pulsed and felt as if they were being torn slowly out of his skin. He flexed his wrist and pulled and the strap around it started to tear. It felt like a series of plate-glass windows were shattering beneath his skin, the muscles quivering and contorting over and into one another.

There were men and women in white coats all around him, but keeping a little distance, except for one, trying to approach him from just behind his head, almost out of sight, with a raised hypodermic. They were all moving slowly, too slowly, as if something was wrong with them, as if they were underwater. He tugged at the strap again and it tore like paper, and then he tugged at the other wrist and both hands were free.

He was still screaming, couldn't stop. He reached out and grabbed the hand with the hypodermic in it and squeezed, was surprised how quickly his fingers reacted and even more surprised to hear the bones in the man's wrist cracking like dry wood as they snapped. The sound the bones made was uncomfortably loud. He caught the hypodermic before it hit the floor, jabbing it into the neck of a man on the other side of him, who went down without a sound. The other hand was already tearing the straps off his legs. Some of the others had started to turn now, turning to flee the table, but they were moving so slowly—what was wrong with them? The pain was making it hard to think. He lashed out, struck the nearest one in the back with his fist, was surprised to see the man's body slam into the far wall and then collapse, leaving a blot of blood on the wall where he had struck.

Then he was out of the bed and running for the door, but something was wrong there, too—he was having a hard time keeping his balance. The whole world seemed to be coming at him at an angle, and his legs weren't working in the way he expected. He was loping more than running, one shoulder close to the ground, steadying himself against the floor every few meters with an outstretched hand. He seemed to have stopped screaming, though sounds were still pouring out of his mouth, a kind of intense glossolalia, a language without meaning. He barreled through the remaining white-coated figures and they scattered at the slightest touch, thrown to the floor, screaming and groaning. And then he was out into the hall.

Which way? he wondered for the slightest fraction of a second and then darted left. Where was he? It looked familiar, it was somewhere he knew, but the pain was still making it difficult to think. What had they been doing to him?

He reached the end of the hall sooner than he'd expected and slammed into the wall, crumpling the panel with his momentum before turning left again and continuing on his way. Was the wall that weak? Yes, he thought, he knew this place, he knew where he was, the Spartan compound, and then a wave of pain burned through his head and he stumbled and went down screaming.

Almost immediately he was up again. To the end of the hall, he remembered, then right, and then the outer doors. Then he'd be out and free, somewhere where he—where *they*, he corrected himself—could never find him.

An alarm was going off somewhere, the halls strobed with a red light, but the strobe too was moving too slowly. Again he didn't stop in time, running into the wall at the end of the corridor and skittering off it before turning right and making for the outer doors.

But between him and it was a line of five or six Marines, kneeling, pointing their weapons at him. And there, standing just behind them, hands on his hips, was CPO Mendez.

"Stand down, soldier!" the man's voice boomed out. And for just a moment Soren-66, hearing the command from the man he'd been taking orders from for more than a half dozen years now, slackened his pace.

But the pain and the confusion, the sensation he had of being trapped, of being hunted, quickly took over, and he sped up again.

"Stand down!" Mendez called again. Soren was almost on them now. He saw the muscles in the forearms of the Marines tighten slightly as they prepared to pull the trigger, and he suddenly found himself galloping on all fours, like a dog. As Mendez gave the order to fire, he leaped.

He heard the shots, oddly muffled. It wasn't bullets they were firing, he realized as he saw the blur of red flash by his elbow, but tranquilizer darts. They passed harmlessly below him except for one that he felt stinging in his ankle. He came down and smashed into the line of Marines and was through them, tugging the dart loose as he made for the doors.

He rammed into the doors, found them locked. He hit them hard with his shoulder and they gave a groaning sound, starting to give. He hit them a third time and at the same moment felt the stinging of tranquilizer darts in his back and legs.

He bellowed in pain and frustration and turned to find himself confronted again by the row of Marines, Mendez standing in front of them now, giving every impression of being in control of the situation.

"I asked you to stand down, solider," stated Mendez. "Will you comply?"

The tranquilizers were starting to take effect. His tongue felt heavy in his mouth. The pain, which had been so visceral, so intense, was now receding into the background. He took a step, found his legs threatening to go out from under him. He started to turn back to the door, stumbled. The hallway lurched, righted itself. He turned back and found now, just behind the line of marines, an out-of-breath Dr. Halsey.

"Don't hurt him!" she was shouting. "Please!"

"Dr. Halsey!" he cried when he saw her. "What have you done to me?" Arms outstretched, he took a single step toward her and collapsed.

FIVE

When he woke up he was in the brig, his wrists now in titanium wristlets, each of them hooked firmly by a titanium chain to a ring in the wall. He tested them. They were too strong for him to break out of easily.

When he stood, he realized there was something wrong with his legs. They were strong, the muscles differentiated and much larger than before, but the muscles had done something to the bone, twisting them, curving them in the odd directions. One leg was more or less normal, just a little bit bowed and twisted. The other, though, was gnarled and a good six inches shorter, and seemed more comfortable when folded up. That leg's ankle was rubbery and left the foot flopping. He could still stand but only at an angle, leaning far to the side, and he was more comfortable, he realized, if he used a hand for balance as well.

His arms, too, were rippling with muscle and seemed almost impossibly strong. They were for the most part fine: They were hardly deformed, relatively straight. But the fingers of one hand had become twisted and bowed, functioning now less like individual articulated digits and more like a single pincer or claw. *I've become a monster*, he thought.

HE WAS still trying to take in his new body when the door opened and Dr. Halsey entered, an armed Marine to either side of her.

"Hello, Soren," she said.

He stood motionless, watching her. She in turn looked him over, both of them waiting out the other.

Finally, she turned to one of the Marines and said, "I don't think I'll need you."

"According to CPO Mendez—" the Marine started.

"This is a science facility and here, I outrank Chief Petty Officer Mendez," she said. "I want you to leave." She turned to the other Marine. "Both of you," she said.

"Is that an order, ma'am?" asked the second Marine, his voice calm.

"Yes, it is," she said.

The second Marine quickly saluted and went out. The other, after a moment's hesitation, followed.

"There," said Dr. Halsey. "That's a little bit better. I'm sorry about the restraints. They weren't my idea, but even I was over-ruled on that point. I'm afraid I don't have any means to remove them." She came closer and sat down on the cell floor, deliberately within easy reach of him. If he'd wanted to, he could reach out and break her neck. "Let's just do our best to pretend they're not there," she said.

Soren stared at her a long moment, then slowly sat back down, gathering his body awkwardly under him.

"How are you feeling?" she asked.

"I don't know," he said. His tongue felt awkward in his mouth, as if he was using it for the first time. "Not very good. I'm having a hard time thinking."

"That's probably the medication," she said. "They had to give you something for the pain."

He closed his eyes, remembering how his body had felt like it was being torn apart from the inside. "Is that normal?" he asked.

She shrugged. "We're still figuring out what normal is. Some people seem to have pain. For some of them it goes away. For others, it's always there."

He nodded.

"We thought you were going to die," she said, and reached out to touch his arm. He let her touch him for a moment then slowly pulled the arm back and out of reach. "You've been comatose for nearly three months. Again and again they thought you were going to die. It reached the point where we decided to disconnect life support. You flatlined for almost four minutes and then your heart started beating on its own again."

"I wish I had died," he said flatly.

She shook her head. "You may feel that way," she said, "but your body doesn't. It could have let go at any time, but it never did."

He tried to think that over, shook his head. He gestured at his legs, his gnarled hand. "What happened to me?" he asked.

"Your body reacted badly to the muscular enhancement injections and the thyroid implant," she said. "Basically your muscles grew in ways and directions that we couldn't predict and then tried to crush or twist the bones beneath them. We were able to use the carbide ceramic ossification process to stabilize and strengthen the bones and to stop it before it became too severe, but as you can see we had better luck with some limbs than others."

She watched him and waited for him to say something. When he didn't, she went on.

"Unfortunately, what that means is that there's a constant tension between your muscles and bones. It's like your body wants to tear itself apart. That may manifest itself as pain within the bone itself, as muscle pain, or as both. The pain may be intense, almost unbearable."

"I know," said Soren.

"With medication, the pain will be bearable. Some of us believe that as your body adjusts to its new state that the pain might diminish or go away entirely."

"Is that what you believe?" asked Soren.

"Do you want me to be honest?" Dr. Halsey asked.

"Yes," said Soren.

Dr. Halsey sighed. "No," she said. "I think the pain will diminish but I don't think it's likely that the pain will ever go away."

He nodded, his lips a grim line.

"On the other hand," she said. "You're stronger than even we imagined. The straps on the operating table were strong, with a titanium microweave through the cloth. They were overengineered to hold any of the other Spartans in place, but they weren't enough to hold you."

They were silent a moment. "How many of us are left?" he finally said.

She shrugged. "More than half," she said. "Almost half of you are dead. With another dozen or so, the modifications didn't take." She reached out and touched his arm again. "I'm sorry, Soren," she said.

He refused to meet her eyes. "I made the choice," he said. "I have nobody to blame but myself."

A moment later she stood and, without a word, left. Soren stayed where he was sitting on the floor, staring.

SIX

A week later he was out of the brig, released on his own recognizance. Some of the other Spartans, he saw, were in as bad or worse shape than he. Fhajad had uncontrollable muscle spasms and was confined to a wheelchair. René and Kirk had had the same difficulty that he had, but their bones were so twisted and deformed that they were now floating in gel tanks, unable to move on their own. A few others were even worse, kept in isolation chambers, comatose and always on the verge of death. Somehow he didn't find it comforting to think that their fates had been worse than his own.

After a few weeks the pain seemed to have diminished a little, though they kept him drugged enough that it was hard to say. The drugs did help with the pain but he hated the confusion they caused within him, the sense he had of having to plow through ideas, of not being able to finish a thought. That started to get as frustrating to him as the pain had been.

He slowly began to scale back the medication, palming a few of the pills each time he was given them, then more and more. The pain was strong and intense, but definitely slightly less than when he'd first awoken. He found he could stand it. *I can live with the pain*, he tried to tell himself. *What I can't live with is not being able to think.* Sometimes, though, he would make an imprudent twist or just move wrong and find himself on the verge of passing out, his forehead beaded with sweat.

He kept at it. Everything felt rawer to him, but yes, he could stand it. His head was clearer in a way, though the pain, like the drugs, could make it difficult to think. Still, after a month he was palming all the pills, pretending to take them but instead taking them back to his room and dropping them into a drawer. In another two months, the drawer was almost completely full.

It was true that he was insanely strong. Early on, in a fit of frustration, he punched the wall in his room and was surprised when his fist tore through the metal panel as if it were thin plaster. He moved the bed so its post partially hid the damage and was careful from then on out.

It's not hopeless, he started to think as time went on. He was stronger than he'd ever been—faster, too, despite his awkward gait. And even if his arms and legs had suffered somewhat he still had everything he needed to be an excellent soldier, better than any normal, unmodified human. *I'm still a Spartan*, he told himself.

BUT NOT everyone, he found, agreed. When he tried to report back for active duty, CPO Mendez took a long, hard look at him and then said, in a voice gentler than any Soren had heard him use, "Walk with me, son."

They went down the hall together, an odd pair: Mendez straight and tall, his stride brisk and confident, Soren massive, but hunched and leaning, weaving as he went.

"Sweet William?" Mendez asked him, taking out a cigar.

Soren, looking surprised, shook his head.

"Ah," said Mendez, after first biting off the ends, "sometimes it's difficult for me to remember that you're all only boys. Filthy habit, this. Don't start it young."

"Yes, sir," said Soren.

Mendez got the cigar lit and sucked on it hard. The end glowed red and then ashed over, the smoke slowly oozing out of his nostrils. "I can't do it, son," he said.

"Can't do what?" asked Soren.

"I can't have you in active service."

"But I'm strong," said Soren. "I'm even stronger than the other Spartans, and almost as fast as some of them. I can keep up and

I'm smart and . . ." Seeing the stern expression on Mendez's face, he let himself trail off.

"Nobody doubts your courage, son. And I for one don't doubt your ability. But if I put you in a team with the other Spartans, you know what'll happen?"

"What, sir?"

"They'll always be thinking about the ones who didn't make it, the ones who died while they went on. They'll feel a special obligation to look out for you and keep you alive that will affect their ability to perform. It'll hurt their focus, keep them from having that edge when they really need it. Right now, without you, they all move and think in a similar way. They work like a well-oiled machine. But there's something to be said for the symmetry they display, the instinctual camaraderie. You're good, no doubt about that—hell, I could see that on the day you woke up and went apeshit—but being on a team with other Spartans just isn't going to happen."

"Respectfully, sir—"

"Plus body armor," Mendez said. "It just won't fit you. Plus the difficulty of firing a weapon with that hand. No," he said, stubbing the Sweet William out on the floor. He reached out and put his hand on Soren's shoulder, looked him straight in the eye. From his look, Soren suddenly could see how hard it was for Mendez to say all he was saying, that he wished things could be different. "I'm sorry, son. Just be patient and maybe something will come along for you. But this, this just isn't it."

"CPO MENDEZ is right," said Dr. Halsey, just as he'd known she would. "He doesn't mean to hurt you, but he has to do what's best for the rest of the recruits and for the program."

"But it's not what's best for me," said Soren.

"Who says it isn't?" asked Dr. Halsey. "It's not what you want, but that doesn't mean it's not what's best for you."

"I want to serve," he said. "I don't want to be left behind."

"I'm sorry, Soren," she said. "You can't serve in this way. You'll be able to serve, but not in a combat position."

"All I want is to be given the choice," he said. "You always were willing to give me a choice in the past. Can't you do it again this time?"

She shook her head. "I'm sorry, Soren. Not this time."

SEVEN

Later, when he thought back to it, he saw that as the turning point. It shut too many doors for him, damaging him, closing parts of him off. And it was stupid, he tried to tell himself. They should have used him, they should have figured out something specially suited for him and his uniquely deformed body. It wasn't that he wasn't as good as the other Spartans—even Mendez had had to admit that. In some ways he was better than them, stronger. Sure, his skin and his brain sometimes felt like they were on fire, but he was learning to control that, learning to get around it and even focus it.

They could have found something for him, something that fit him, but instead they strapped him with a desk job within the compound, an ordinary run-of-the-mill job that just about anybody could have handled. They said it was temporary, but as time went on, it felt more and more permanent. Barely sixteen and already retired from active duty, already a paper pusher. It was as if they hadn't even tried to think of the right job for him. It was hard not to feel resentful.

Which was why, almost six months later, when one of the technicians—a fellow named Partch—began talking to him about revolution, instead of reporting the man he began to listen.

Partch started slow, just bits and pieces, hints. Sure, he said, the UNSC was much needed and important—we couldn't live without them. But didn't they sometimes come down too hard? Didn't they sometimes do things that were carried out with the best of intentions but, when you looked at them closely, were just simply wrong?

"Like with you, for instance," said Partch, once Soren had confessed what had happened to him. "Why aren't they making proper use of you? Strong as a bear, quick, smart too: It's a damned waste, if you ask me. Yet they're still putting wet-behind-the-ears Marines right in the line of fire."

At the time Soren didn't respond, but later he couldn't help but thinking that yes, it was a waste, Partch was right. Soon, it wasn't just that he wasn't reporting Partch: He'd started to search him out. He listened, very rarely revealing what he was feeling about what Partch was saying, but listening, listening. Finally one day he said, "So what can we do about it?"

Partch shook his head. "I don't know," he said. "It's hard to know what to do to fix the system when it breaks. People are afraid of change; they'd rather limp on with a broken system than do the hard work of making a change. If you're not careful, before you know it you're labeled a terrorist."

"But there must be something I can do," said Soren.

"A guy like you," said Partch giving him a sidelong look, "sure, there's a lot you can do. But will you?"

"I think I would," said Soren.

"Even if you knew that others might see you as a terrorist? Do you care more about what people think, or about doing what's right?"

"I've never cared what people thought," said Soren, lying.

Partch gave him an appraising look. "No," he said. "I daresay you haven't."

IT WENT on like that for a long time, Partch talking and hinting, and Soren becoming more and more eager to take part. It was exciting, like he was part of something, like something was happening. As he heard news of the other Spartans, he needed that, needed to feel like he was involved. His allegiances changed almost imperceptibly until, almost before he knew it, he found himself on the side of the rebels. Yes, he began to think, the USNC was too powerful for its own good; it had become a big bully. Yes, the colony worlds had the right to function in whatever way they wanted, had a right to be independent from the United Earth government if they so wanted. It was crazy to think otherwise. Yes, he was eager to help, yes, and since that was the case, what was he doing here?

"Be patient," said Partch. "We . . . they need people like you. But we have to wait for just the right moment. And let's take someone along with us—something as a souvenir."

EIGHT

Partch had a card that opened the lock—whether he had stolen it or had been given it as part of his job, Soren did not know. Inside was some sort of geological research laboratory. On one metal table was a simple wooden box with a metal screen in the place of its bottom, a sealed plastic tub next to it. Here and there, loose on tables or bolted to the ceilings and the walls, were precision instruments, things mostly unfamiliar to Soren.

They went in, Partch setting the door to stay slightly ajar behind them.

"Why not close the door all the way?" asked Soren.

"I'm not sure the card will open it from the inside," said Partch.

Stolen or rigged, then, thought Soren. *Never mind*, he thought, then recited in his head one of Partch's lines: *When the government goes bad, we all have to do things that we normally wouldn't do until it's back on the right track again.*

"It's the sixth cabinet," said Partch. "I disabled the alarm this morning from my panel. And I've put in a loop for the AI to look at for the room and the hall. Not easy, if I do say so myself, and not something likely to last long. Do you think you can open it?"

"What's in there?" asked Soren.

"Something important," he said. "Something we need."

Soren nodded, staring at the cabinet. It was made of a brushed metal, perhaps steel, the doors seemingly quite thick. He reached up and put his hand over the top edge, felt the door's top lip, gave an exploratory pull. It didn't move.

"I don't think I can do it without a prybar," said Soren.

Partch nodded, took a flat titanium-alloy bar, flanged at one end, out of his backpack.

"You came prepared," said Soren.

Partch just smiled. Soren took the bar and forced the end of it in the slight channel between the two doors, grunting, barely denting the metal slightly to either side, working it in until it had gone as far as it'd go. Then, putting all his weight into it, veins popping out on his arms, he pulled.

For a moment Soren thought that even the crowbar would

not be enough. He felt his arms burning, and a black hole began to open in his vision, the pain he always felt under the surface becoming reactivated by this new stress of muscle on bone. Then there was a creaking sound from the cabinet door and it buckled just a little around the lock.

He let up and forced the bar in deeper, and then bore down again. The door creaked again and buckled further, then this time came free. He handed the crowbar back to Partch who put it away, and then he opened the cabinet door fully.

Inside was a titanium case, about thirty centimeters long and fifteen wide, maybe ten centimeters deep.

"What is it?" asked Soren. "What's inside?"

Partch just smiled. He was just reaching for it when they heard a voice from behind them.

"I don't suppose you'd care to explain yourself," it said.

Soren turned, his expression immediately going flat and neutral. It was one of the Spartans, not one that Soren had known well, someone he'd only rarely been teamed with before washing out. His name was Randall. He wasn't dressed in uniform or battle gear; he was dressed down in a simple black T-shirt and loose gray cloth pants. His face was as neutral as Soren's.

"Hello, Randall," said Soren, thinking quickly. "Problem with this cabinet, with the lock mechanism. Sometimes it won't lock, sometimes it won't open."

"I know you," said Randall. "Soren, right? Used to be a Spartan. But you're not a technician."

"No," said Partch, "but I am. The lock had frozen and I couldn't get it open. I asked for his help to unjam it."

"At this hour?" asked Randall.

"The lab is swamped during the day," claimed Partch. "They didn't want us clanging around during office hours."

Randall looked back and forth between them. "All right," he said. "You don't mind if I verify, do you?"

"Of course not," said Soren.

"If we weren't supposed to be here, the alarm would have gone off," added Partch. "But no, by all means, you should verify."

Randall nodded, his lips tight. "Let's go then."

Soren immediately started for the door. Randall moved back and out into the hall to let him come, keeping a safe distance. *He's smart*, thought Soren. *Well trained.* He started down the hall, Partch just behind him, Randall taking up the rear.

"Where are we going?" asked Partch.

"Nearest com-link," said Randall.

Soren stopped and turned, miming a puzzled expression. "But the nearest com-link is back in the roo—" he said, and then leaped.

Randall saw the blow coming and shifted just a little, but still took a glancing blow in the shoulder; they tumbled down to the floor together, rolling back and forth. Randall kicked him hard and then tried to wriggle free, but Soren wouldn't let go. Randall was faster, Soren knew, but he was stronger. If he just didn't let go of his hold, he might keep the advantage.

Randall kicked him hard in the face, but Soren was already working his way up the man's body. Randall kept kicking, trying to work his arms into position for a choke hold, but before he managed, Soren had straddled his hips and locked both hands behind Randall's back. He gave a shout and squeezed as hard as he could.

Pain shot through his own arms and chest. Randall gave a groan and started to struggle harder, dragging Soren down the hall with him. *Hold on*, thought Soren. *Just hold on.* He squeezed harder, burying his face against Randall's chest as the latter pummeled his arms and head and then tried desperately to reach behind his own back to break Soren's fingers.

Not the way you're used to fighting, is it? thought Soren.

Randall was shouting now, then suddenly he went limp.

Too soon, thought Soren, *he's faking*, and held on.

But Randall kept still. Partch, Soren realized, was talking to him, pounding him on the back, his face just a few inches from Soren's own.

"What?" hissed Soren.

"Snap out of it, man. I tranquilized him. Let go of him before you kill him. Let's get out of here."

He turned his head to see the tranquilizer dart embedded in Randall's shoulder. The "faked" limpness. Carefully he unclasped his hands and worked his way free. Randall was fighting the drug, not quite under, but could move little more than his eyes. Soren felt his chest. Maybe a broken rib or two, but probably that was all. And he wouldn't be out for long.

"Let's get out of here!" said Partch again and started down the corridor.

Soren took a last look at Randall and then started after him. Partch moved in a rapid walk, fast enough to look to the compound's AI like he had somewhere he needed to be five minutes ago, but not fast enough to seem like he was running. Soren tried to follow his lead, quickly realizing he was heading toward the compound's airfield.

"There's an older Longsword," Partch said as Soren caught up with him. "It's pre-prepared and hacked for us, complete with a dumb AI construct that I fast-grafted to convert him to the cause. We make for that and get it in the air, get away from the base, and to the drop point as fast as we can."

NINE

But before they had even entered the field, alarms started sounding. By the time they were in the Longsword and taking off, a good half-dozen ships were being crewed, ready to take off in pursuit. *Plus*, thought Soren, *the planet is surrounded by Orbital Defense Platforms. This is a crazy idea.*

The first warning shot flashed past them before they had even cleared the atmosphere, shaking the ship slightly. It was quickly followed by two more, precision shots, even closer, that shocked the ship from end to end. Partch looked scared.

"Evasive maneuvers, Captain Teach!" he instructed the AI.

The latter flickered to holographic life on the console before them. His construct was a pirate captain, bristling with pistols, with a gold-toothed grin and an ebony beard in braids.

"Have been evading all along, lads," Teach said. "There's just too many of the bastards." He put one hand to his ear, pretended to listen. "Signal coming in—care to hear it?"

Partch, holding on to the arms of the chair with white-knuckled fingers, just nodded.

"Longsword," said a voice that Soren did not recognize. "You have not been authorized for takeoff. Return to base immediately."

"Seems like they should have sent out that *before* they started firing across our bow," said Soren.

"Well, they did," the AI admitted. "But I knew you wouldn't want to parley with such scallywags."

Partch groaned. A shot caught them, burning across the wing, inflicting light damage and giving the Longsword a worrying wobble. The atmosphere was thinner now but they still hadn't broken free of Reach's gravitation.

"How long until we reach our rendezvous?" asked Soren.

Teach gave a hearty laugh. "Astronav is unstable after that hit," he said. "I can't say that we're likely to go anywhere we want at all, even once we're free of the planet's gravity."

"Oh God, oh God," said Partch. "We're going to die!"

"We'll have to turn back," said Soren. "Teach, let them know we surrender."

A blow caught them from behind, spinning the craft almost all the way around. Black smoke, Soren realized, was billowing around them.

"Never surrender," said Teach, his hologram flickering. "Besides, too late for that. Systems are being shut down before they go critical. A pleasure knowing you, lads."

He vanished. The lights flickered and went out. The craft spun and spiraled, slowly stabilizing. Then gravity began to sink its claws into it and it started down.

"Buckle in," said Soren to Partch. Backup power kicked in, stuttered once, then went out again. He flicked the controls over to manual. The engines were gone but, unlike some of the other USNC spacecraft, the Longsword had enough of a wingspan that he might manage to bring it down even without the engines. The flaps he could manually control—at least in theory. He'd never flown one before, but he'd flown sims of the Longsword's various predecessors and variants, back when he was a Spartan, and crash-landing was one of the scenarios. It should work. With a little luck, they might even survive.

HE ENGAGED manual, grabbed hold of the stick with both hands, and pulled back, trying to level the craft out and bring it down as softly as he could. The fighters behind him were no longer firing, able, no doubt, to see that the Longsword was in trouble.

They were going faster now, a slow whine building around the aircraft. It was hard to hold the stick in place. Partch, he saw, was passed out from fear, g's, or a combination of both.

They were just above the clouds now, then moving down and through them, the Longsword buffeted back and forth by odd crosswinds. He let the craft settle a little further until they burst out of the bottom of clouds, and then he banked, trying to get a clear view of what was around them. Kilometers of farmland in most directions, more inhabited towns and districts in others, but there, in the distance, almost out of sight, a shimmer of green that he hoped was one of Reach's vast swathes of deciduous forest.

"Teach," he said, "Any life left in you?"

There was no response. He would have to try to eyeball it, figure out how to come down in a way that would get him close enough to the forest for a quick escape while still letting him land on open ground.

He circled once and saw the pursuing ships still there, just coming through the clouds now, hanging back a little distance, waiting. He pointed toward the green line and started down.

He was, he quickly realized, too high, but better too high than too low. He dipped and corrected. There, that was more or less right. Yes, he saw as they came closer, definitely forest. He'd have to come very close and then try to bring the Longsword along its edge, keep it there more or less once they hit the ground. Then, if he survived the crash, he'd simply disappear.

Lower now. Nearly able to make out individual trees. This was the tricky part, banking just right and then correcting and then descending, trying to keep it all straight. Partch awake and screaming now. *Ignore it if you can*, he told himself. No, not quite, coming in too close to the trees. Starting away again, but too late, the wing clipping the treetops and starting to come asunder. Out of control now, shaking and shuddering, the craft falling to pieces around him. An engine torn free and crashing through trees as if they were toothpicks. *Hold on, Soren*, he thought, *hold on*. One part of his mind was screaming, screaming. The other part was calm, cold. *Why worry, Soren?* that second part was asking, as the plane around him caught fire and, screeching and falling apart, gouged a half-kilometer-long channel along the ground. *You've lived through much worse*, it was telling him. *You should be able to live through this.* Partch, he saw from the corner of his eye, was dead, his neck broken, his eyes glazed over. Soren's arm seemed to be on fire. He could see the ground and the sky through cracks in the craft as what was left of the fuselage turned over and over again. Metal burning and grinding around him, he waited for whatever god that controlled the farce that was his life to flip some charred and malformed cosmic coin and decide his fate.

EPILOGUE

There was a knocking on the door. Or rather a rapping on the doorframe: The door had already slid open, revealing Chief Petty Officer Mendez, still in fatigues, an unlit Sweet William jutting from one corner of his mouth.

Dr. Halsey looked up from her desk. "Well?" she said.

"I've been to the site," said Mendez, taking the chair at the other side of the desk. She could still smell the smoke in his clothing. "I've looked at the wreckage. Not much left. Most of the fuselage is gone and what's left is mangled, hardly worth much even as scrap. There was a fire as well. There's a body, charred pretty much beyond recognizing, but it doesn't belong to Soren-66."

"How can you be sure?"

Mendez gave her a look. "Wasn't deformed," he said. "And no evidence of augmentation. Not to mention he was barely six feet, even when you account for fire damage. Must have been the missing technician, Partch—running DNA now. We don't know how that one got in here in the first place—take one look at his background and he has all the earmarks of a rebel. We've got some sort of problem with somebody higher up in security."

"I'll look into it," said Dr. Halsey.

"You do that, ma'am," said Mendez. "If I were you I'd run the check again on everybody."

He took out his lighter and held it near the end of his cigar. Before lighting it, he raised his eyebrows inquisitively. She shook her head. A faint look of disgust crossing his mouth, he put the lighter away, leaving the cigar unlit.

"Anything else, Mendez?" she asked.

"We looked at the parts torn free as well, what we could find of them in the woods. No evidence of him there either. Could be he was thrown out early on. If that's the case, we'll never find the body. Or could be he made it out in one piece."

"You think he's still alive?" Dr. Halsey asked.

Mendez shrugged. "No way to tell," he said. "All I'll say is that it's strange that we didn't find any trace of him. Could be alive, I suppose, but it's not likely, even for a Spartan. Considering the kind of luck that Soren-66 had to this point, it's hard to imagine things working out well for him." He paused, meditative. "Then again," he said, "maybe his luck was about due for a change."

Dr. Halsey nodded curtly. "How's Randall doing?" she asked.

Mendez snorted, lips curling back into an almost predatory smile. "He's fine. Kicking himself for letting his guard down a little, but there was nothing he could have done and as far as I can tell, he didn't let down much. He might have taken Soren-66, but couldn't take both him and somebody armed with a tranquilizer. He did what he could. It's good for him to go through something like this. In the long run, he'll be a better soldier because of it."

Halsey nodded. *Sink or swim*, she couldn't help but think. And what was it Soren had said, a few years back now? That he didn't want to be left behind? An incident like this would make Randall less cocky, would get him scrambling to make sure that he was up to snuff.

"I've inserted ground troops. Set them combing the woods for the body," said Mendez.

"They won't find him," Dr. Halsey said.

"Maybe not," he said. "Still it'd be nice to be able to wrap things up, to have some closure."

"You won't get it. Pull your men back in and file him MIA," said Dr. Halsey.

"Not KIA?"

She shook her head. "Not without a body. He's lived through a lot and had a lot of bad luck along the away. He lived through pain that killed some of the other recruits. We should have figured out something for him, some better way of making use of him. I'd bet he's out there somewhere, still alive."

"If he's out there, we can find him."

"No, you won't," she said. "He grew up living in the forest. You'll find him only if he wants to be found. You might as well pull your troops."

"But—"

She reached across the desk and touched his arm. "Let him go, Franklin," she said, her voice softening. "He's no threat to us."

"He's an augmented, Spartan-trained insurrectionist sympathizer. How is that not a threat?" he asked.

"He's no traitor. He's just a lost soul, looking for a direction. I know him. Trust me."

"What about—" he started to answer, then thought better of it, stopped. He stood, saluted her, and went out, leaving her to her thoughts.

GONE NOW, she thought.

Was I wrong? she thought. *Should I not have given him the choice? Should I not have brought him into the Spartan program in the first place?*

She ran a finger slowly through Déjà's hologram construct, watched the AI clutch her clay tablets closer to her chest and stare at her, puzzled, curious.

Had she been wrong? She sighed. Too late for it to matter either way.

"Penny for your thoughts," said Déjà.

Dr. Halsey shook her head. Déjà smiled. Then she shrugged and disappeared.

Whether she'd been wrong or right, Dr. Halsey realized, she was committed now. She'd had seventy-five lives to watch out for, seventy-five lives depending on her, seventy-five lives weighing on her conscience. Even if it was down now to less than half that, there were still several dozen Spartans depending on her. Not to mention the weight of all those already dead. The future of millions might depend on them, on how well she'd done her job. Not *might*, she corrected herself, *did*.

She straightened her shoulders, shifting under her burden, and went back to work.

STOMPING ON THE HEELS OF A FUSS

ERIC RAAB

The intense stink and splatter from the Brute's roar woke Connor Brien instantly—a web of spittle connected the beast's jagged, bloodstained fangs. The smell of the Brute's breath was bad enough, but as he tried to wipe the wet off his face, he just set the odor deeper into his mustache, beard, and all over his hands. He convulsed, gagging once before vomiting the last MRE he'd eaten. He kept his eyes on the ground, knowing to avoid eye contact with the gray-haired beast, something he learned from all of his studies before arriving. He'd watched video feeds of humans who dared to stare defiantly at Brutes and were beaten into mush in seconds. Even the slightest eye contact was some form of challenge they could not resist.

His last memory was falling from the tree he'd set up as his surveillance point. He'd been watching a trio of the beasts as they gestured to one another, trying to track a human that they'd let escape from captivity for the fun of hunting him down. He thought he'd be safe up high, but he quickly learned that the Brutes not only had a great sense of smell but they were excellent climbers.

He had fallen while panicking, reaching for his tranq dart gun as one of the Brutes climbed quickly toward him. He felt down by his leg and breathed a sigh of relief. Its reassuring bulk was still strapped to his ankle.

He kicked himself for not having his M6, which sat nestled in his pack at his base camp; but then he realized, what good would it do? Another dozen or so Brutes hovered behind the one who treated him to his wake-up shower. Varying in shades of brown and black, tan and gray, each hulking beast seemed more fierce and frightening than the next. They each stood at about nine feet, and though he didn't dare to look, they all seemed to be casting hungry eyes on his five-foot-five frame. Even if he could take out twelve of them, the thirteenth would rip him to shreds.

He surveyed his surroundings. It was a makeshift camp, all centered around a large Covenant ship. The nearby outpost's shops and cabins had clearly been ransacked, the camping equipment and supplies strewn among what looked like thousands of human bones, all still with dried blood and muscle clinging to them. He even noticed a few methane tanks scattered about and the charred remains of Grunts. They were eating their own.

He turned to survey his fellow captives and the smell really set in, death clinging to the roof of his mouth. They all hovered together but there was no fence or wall keeping them in. He thought immediately that he could run for it, but as he looked at the other prisoners and the mounds of human carnage surrounding the camp, he knew that was a bad idea. None of the prisoners looked anywhere near well. Shreds of soiled clothing hung in tatters from their malnourished bodies. Knotted hair on their heads and faces, bloodstained hands and teeth, unhealed scars and open wounds, mounds of excrement . . . no one looked capable of moving, except him. And judging by the way this beast welcomed him awake, that wouldn't last very long. Why the Brutes had been keeping any of them alive was beyond his understanding.

He'd spent four days watching this camp from about a mile up a rolling hill of forest, and as soon as he'd arrived he knew it was a bad scene. Reports had the human occupancy of Beta Gabriel at barely five hundred people. But judging by the carnage he'd seen strewn about the forest, it had to have been much more. Beta Gabriel was a blip on the map, an "uninhabited" planet that a group of entrepreneurs turned into a secret society, an "outdoors" getaway: a place where the wealthy came to hike, hunt, go on spirit quests, or to get in touch with themselves or whatever they got in touch with. There wasn't a lot of commerce or buildings on the planet, just a few supply shops, a basic landing port, a few rustic cabins strewn about, and a community lodge outfitted with information on the planet and maps of the area.

In the time he'd studied the Brutes from his tree, he had witnessed some of the most vulgar and brutal treatment of another living species he'd ever seen. It had been completely unbearable to watch, let alone understand. The Brutes had turned their human captives into toys. Some were tortured in despicable ways, pitted against one another in games that even Brien couldn't make out the rules for—at least not at that distance.

Connor Brien was one of the Office of Naval Intelligence's top operatives, recruited by ONI after the Covenant first attacked Humanity. His work in linguistic anthropology was as good as it gets, most noted for deciphering the language and sociological structure of a lost tribe discovered deep in the tundra of North America that had survived hundreds of years in an elaborate cave dwelling. Their origins dated back some six hundred years, and Brien linked their societal structure back to a small charismatic cult that emerged in the early 1970s.

As an ONI intelligence officer, he had played an integral part in unraveling the methodology behind the Covenant by brilliantly decoding the sign language of a captured Covenant Engineer, and had been the commanding ONI officer on some of the most harrowing attempts to capture Covenant species alive. He had an extreme taste for adventure. He was fearless and brilliant, as relentless as a man can get. He earned the nickname "Kip" among his peers, an homage to Rudyard Kipling, a nineteenth-century novelist and adventurer. He actually looked a bit like Kipling, with his bushy eyebrows and salt-and-pepper beard.

But it was one fateful day that really put him on his path. He and a team of Marines had actually succeeded in subduing a Brute-led siege of their ship as they traversed for the first time into Covenant space. They managed to tranq the six Brutes who boarded, but they should have killed them. When he got a really close look at them he was in awe. But the tranq darts wore off fast on these behemoths and their attempts to contain them quickly proved feeble. The pack literally tore their way out of the synthetic alloy constraints, and even unarmed proved to be an unstoppable force. The Marines managed to wipe out their fierce gray-haired leader, and Brien hid and watched in amazement as his death incited something primal in the others, who began scrambling and recklessly attacking with more viciousness and abandon than before. But what really interested him was that there was one lone Brute whose coat was much shaggier than the others, that didn't charge and simply watched the melee. He thought at first he might have still been suffering from the effects of the tranq, but immediately after the enraged pack overwhelmed the unprepared Marines, they turned on their inactive brother. Brien was mesmerized by this murderous rampage. He was lucky to make it to the evac craft in one piece.

For months their ferocity haunted him. He started gathering all the footage and reports on the race that came in. Brutes showed a diversity not only in appearance but in the way they carried themselves, as if the weight of the world was on some of their shoulders and others were free to stand tall and dominant. He intuited they must be a weathered species, hardened by many years of struggle, most likely battling among themselves. He tried numerous times to get approval to travel back into Covenant space in search of their home world. Every attempt was denied. But when Brutes started playing a larger role in the attacks on human planets and were suspected of having some animosity toward other Covenant species, his requests started working themselves further into ONI command. When word came down that they had seized the planet Beta Gabriel, he finally got his approval. They were nesting right in his backyard.

His mission was to gather as much as he could on the inner workings of this race of the Covenant, find out just how many survivors remained on Beta Gabriel, and look into finding anything among this species that could be used to cause deeper fissures within the Covenant juggernaut. It was a simple operation. Enter point A, watch from point B, exit a few days later from the exact drop at point A. Quiet, discreet, quick. He'd never thought it would be this bad.

CERETUS HATED being around these despicable creatures. If it were up to him he would have them all in his belly. He truly enjoyed the taste of their flesh, but Parabum's new "honor" code put an end to it. Their Chieftain decided that the simple slaying and eating of the humans had to stop; there were too few of them left and it was far better to keep them around than to quickly eliminate them. Many of the others agreed, and Ceretus had to admit it was extremely enjoyable to watch them suffer. But he just couldn't stand living among them, especially after the shame he'd been suffering since their defeat.

When they'd first arrived on this forest planet, it had been a glorious day. The humans all clumped themselves together in one area, as if that made them safer. Only a few of them were even armed. Ceretus and his brother, Maladus, didn't even need their spikers; they had more fun killing by hand. The hunts lasted for days, the bounties delicious, their bellies never fuller. Ceretus knew that the gods would have been pleased with this conquest. It was a bittersweet revenge in the face of such a painful loss. But as the days passed and the human population dwindled, there was still no sign that the Chieftain was ready to leave.

Ceretus quickly began regretting following this cowardly Chieftain when he retreated from the massive attack. Now, as he stared at the newly found human they'd shaken from the tree, he would have much preferred to die in battle. This was not the life for a true follower of the Great Journey.

He looked back toward his brothers-in-arms. All were barely capable of understanding the path the Forerunners left for them to follow. He took his eyes from the pathetic human captives to the ship that brought them here, the *Valorous Salvation*. Chieftain Parabum kept the ship constantly protected with four of his bodyguards. He refused to power the ship's communications; he didn't want anyone to find them. It was more and more obvious that their Chieftain feared any backlash from the defeat, and he was right to be fearful. His cowardice was punishable by death.

His brother, Maladus, had been leery when their pack had been folded into Parabum's. They were from two of the most divergent clans dating back as far as Jiralhanae history goes—ancient enemies. The two clans fought even before the great civil war that knocked the Jiralhanae from a space-faring species back to being bound to their planets, forced to rediscover the great advances their ancestors had made before them. They were able to coexist again rather peacefully once the Covenant brought the unifying words of the Great Journey, but their deep-seated distrust for one another slowly rose again . . . and knowing the history of that clan, they had strikingly different levels of devotion to the Covenant.

Parabum's clan never fully believed in the power of the gods, nor did they worship the technology left behind. They feared, in fact, becoming too dependent on technology. Ceretus's clan was always the more intelligent, and their beliefs fell more in line with the San 'Shyuum, believing with devout faith in the Great Journey and the gods that took it before them. Ceretus's clan was terribly ashamed of the civil war that forced the Jiralhanae to give up hundreds of years of progress, and they were at the forefront of rebuilding their scientific prowess when the San 'Shyuum arrived. They were beyond grateful for the opportunity to take to the stars once again.

Parabum's clan reviled it. It was their kind of thinking that robbed the Jiralhanae of their rightful place among the Covenant species; they used the artifacts in disrespectful ways, more opportunistic than holy. They believed only in muscle and tradition, in the strength of living without an overwhelming reliance on technology. It made them fierce warriors, Ceretus had to admit, reliant on their strength and loyalty to one another. But Ceretus and Maladus both knew from the start that Parabum was strong in body but weak in mind. He never kept any of his underlings in line, leaving them on their own, lazy and undisciplined. This was not the way to rule a pack. Ceretus knew you ruled through fear and manipulation, and faith in the gods. He could never respect Parabum's leadership.

It was only a matter of time before someone challenged Parabum for the Chieftainship, and Maladus had burst out surprisingly one day shortly after they had landed. It was a risky move, as they hadn't established much of an alliance in their movement against Parabum, but Maladus called out a challenge anyway. And once you called out a challenge there was no turning back. Maladus had always been a cunning warrior, but the truth was that Parabum was twice as strong. Parabum overpowered Maladus from the start, pummeling him blow after blow. Maladus did little damage to the Chieftain. He barely landed a worthwhile strike. The battle lasted only a few minutes before Parabum had completely subdued Maladus. Ceretus watched, his whole body tense with anger as Parabum stomped on his brother's neck, crushing it at the shoulder blade. And to rub it in, he viciously bit into Maladus's broken neck and ripped his throat out with his teeth.

It was pure disrespect. Now Ceretus couldn't stand looking at Parabum, let alone follow another order from him. And he knew Parabum knew it. Ceretus wished he were strong enough to challenge the Chieftain, but Maladus had been even stronger than him; he stood little chance.

He turned back to the human prisoners and licked his fangs. He went from face to face, trying to strike intense fear in each of the captives. There was little else to do with his time.

"Has our Chieftain returned from the hunt?" Ceretus called out in the face of the newly captured, bushy-eyebrowed human, who had quietly coiled into himself.

"Not yet," answered Facius, his tan fur prickling up a bit as he, too, ogled the captives. He was a particularly impressionable warrior who had become Ceretus's right hand after Maladus's demise.

"Perhaps enough time to fire up one of these, a little snack before the feast, served with a proper blessing."

"But the Chieftain, he will certainly smell the cooking flesh." This response came from Hammadus, Facius's brother, a young, rich-coated brown warrior that showed signs of naiveté but was perhaps the strongest of the pack. Ceretus could smell the young one's fear in daring to disobey the Chieftain. It was Hammadus that got the newly found human out of the tree, and whined demands that they bring him back to the camp, to show their Chieftain, rather than eat him on the spot.

Ever since Parabum called for the eating of human flesh only after a traditional and grossly overelaborate hunt, Ceretus couldn't bear the idea of following suit. Plus, the time it took to bring the carcass in from the forest caused the meat to spoil. Any worthy Jiralhanae knew all too well that the fresher the kill, the finer the taste. A savage like their Chieftain wouldn't bother to savor the feast properly in the name of the gods.

"What do you suggest, young brother?"

"Well the Chieftain doesn't know we didn't kill one in the hunt, does he?" Facius asked with an ever-so-slight grin. "We can at least have some fun until he returns."

"Yes we can, Facius." And he turned back to the prisoners. This young one showed promise.

BRIEN COULDN'T help but stare out at the human remains lining the forest pathways, hanging from trees, beaten to pulpy pieces surrounding the camp. It was disgusting. One thing was obvious: These beasts had no respect for humans at all. The same keen sense of smell the Brutes followed to his hiding place didn't seem bothered by the awful stench of human carnage. He figured it might actually seem sweet to these monsters.

Though he'd only been awake in captivity for a few hours, Brien was starting to make sense of a few of their growls and grunts, at least emotionally. It didn't take long for Brien to pick up on a brewing impatience from the circling Brutes.

"What do you think they're doing?" Brien whispered to the man next him, as the Brutes all began walking down the line of prisoners.

"You don't want to know . . ."

Brien watched carefully, looking away at any sign of a Brute turning back toward him. Most of the captives slept or showed such shock and fear that he found it impossible to communicate with many of them, but this man he immediately recognized. Dasc Gevadim was a renowned guru of a religion known as Triad. Those who followed the Triad teachings believed that we all harbored three internal lives, and spiritual transcendence only occurred if you managed to link all three. His followers ran galaxy wide. He used to run seminars via public comm channels, but he'd disappeared about ten years ago. It was much publicized. Many called it a transcendence, and his following grew exponentially with such reports. The sales of his vidcasts went through the roof.

"They're deciding which one of us to eat, huh?" Brien asked, knowing the answer.

"Not exactly. Big Boy seemed to put a stop to it. Now they only eat after they let one of us go and hunt us down," Dasc whispered back. His scraggly white beard was caked with dust and blood. His eyes glassy and red. Brien wondered if they had been feeding the captives raw human flesh. He didn't want to know.

"Which one is Big Boy? That one?" He pointed discreetly to the one who had knocked him out of the tree.

"No. Big Boy isn't around. Maybe still hunting," the man next to Dasc answered—a sickly yet stocky man Brien recognized as a famous big-game hunter, named Hague or something.

It made sense. He'd seen a few packs scrambling around this morning, and now there was silent hostility among the beasts, as if they were on the verge of doing something wrong.

This especially rang true for the slightly graying, black-furred one, the one with a clean-shaven face, who had been surveying the captives and had treated Brien to a foul saliva offering. He seemed to have good control of the lot. Brien immediately called him Six.

Just then, Six caught wind of the whispering and turned back toward them. All three men adjusted themselves awkwardly. As he made his way closer, Dasc was quickly overrun with some of the deepest fear Brien had ever seen. Fear was never in Brien's blood. He was usually ready for any end that might meet him, but as this man-eating giant beast lumbered over toward him, his body trembled in fright.

Six stopped right in front of the cringing Dasc. His nostrils flared as he looked closer, grabbing at Dasc's arms and poking at his scrawny build. He then made a grunt that was obviously a summoning or a name. Two other Brutes made their way over; a tan one that Brien dubbed Butch, and the huge, rich brown one he'd thought was Big Boy. He quickly referred to him as Ludo, though he couldn't figure out why. He wondered if any among them were female. It was impossible to tell. In all of his research, he'd never positively identified one.

Six grabbed Dasc in one big rip with his right hand, but when Hague leaped back startled, his eyes must've met Six's. The Brute immediately dropped Dasc, pulled Hague out and tossed him toward the other Brutes. Dasc's body lay limp and unconscious beside Brien, and judging from the smell he'd lost control of his bowels.

Brien and the other captives watched fearfully as Six let out a roar and a hand motion—a wider summons—and a crowd started to gather around. Hague wobbled himself upright, trying to be as brave and defiant as one could when surrounded by nine-foot-tall hairy beasts, all able to crush you in a blink and drooling in anticipation of a fresh meal.

Just as Brien finished counting the fifteen Brutes surrounding Hague, one of them ripped the famed hunter up by the leg and held him upside down. The others gave roars of laughter. The old saying always held true; laughter was the same everywhere, even in the Covenant. Hague struggled to rise, trying desperately to wiggle himself free, when another grabbed at his other leg. The crowd goaded them on and another Brute grabbed an arm, and that's when Brien couldn't look anymore. He watched as Six suddenly seemed to lose interest as well, wandering back beyond the crowd, to the edge of the forest. He couldn't quite place why the beast would incite such a spectacle and walk away, unless it was to impress.

Hague's screams sent shivers through Brien's bones and he shut his eyes. Then the screams stopped with a chorus of crunches and yells from the Brutes. His mind's eye painted it black. The hollering Brutes slowly gave way to silence and Brien opened his eyes again. The crowd had dispersed, and standing amidst the torn and bloodied remains of Hague was undoubtedly the one Dasc had referred to as Big Boy. Clad in a few strokes of armor and with his gray-brown hair unkempt around his snout, the hammer-wielding leader definitely was one of the biggest Brutes Brien had ever seen. He stood there silently. Brien looked around for Six; he was nowhere to be found.

CERETUS WATCHED from the darkness as Chieftain Parabum stood silent with his hammer over his shoulder. Behind him were his security chief, Jupentus, and his right hand, Brunus. Two of the dumbest Jiralhanae Ceretus had ever encountered. They each had dragged in a human corpse behind them. Parabum took in his pack with disappointment.

"Looks like a bit of fun was had here," he said, signaling the human remains with his hammer. "Without me." Parabum lifted the torso, a string of muscle still connected the head. Ceretus's stomach growled. "A plump one, too. Who led this game?" He looked around to see, but everyone was bowing their heads in respect.

Ceretus knew no one would confess; it was too risky. Parabum never kept a cool head for anything. He chose awkward battles to fight, found disrespect where none was intended. He was one of the worst Chieftains Ceretus had the displeasure of serving. He watched hungrily as the head of the human sway off the juicy torso. He had been looking forward to feasting on this one, but now it would certainly spoil. Brother Golubus had come really close to making the fatter ones taste like Thorn Beast, and he missed that delicacy as much as he missed the brothels back on Teash. The humans ruined any chance of returning to such pleasures. Parabum ruined it, really. But here he was listening to a Chieftain who couldn't even properly sermon the pack. There was a lot of hate in Ceretus's heart, mostly for the humans who put him here—but he was happy to focus all his hatred on this ancient clan enemy and the bastard who disgraced his brother. He couldn't hold the hatred in much longer. He'd rather die than rot in the shadows of this coward.

"It was me, my Chieftain, who called for the preparation." Ceretus emerged boldly from the darkness. "Our brothers were getting restless in their hunger, and I feared you'd be late in returning." He quickly hid his bravery, taking on a much humbler tone as a shred of fear took over.

"Ceretus, do you not have faith that your Chieftain is the greatest of hunters, a fierce and keen tracker, especially of these simple creatures?" Parabum was obviously trying to test him. The Chieftain walked toward him with no fear.

"I have no such doubt, Chieftain," Ceretus said as he approached, bowing before him at an arm's length. "This was a kill from our hunt, and we figured we'd go ahead and get it prepared while it was still fresh." He bowed before him, keeping his eyes on the ground in front of him. The charade pained him.

Parabum grabbed his throat; his nails, digging through Ceretus's fur, piercing his skin. "Not one of these pathetic creatures is to be touched without your Chieftain to sanction it. Not one." Ceretus struggled to keep his eyes averted, his shame apparent in his lack of challenge. And like a switch going off, the Chieftain released his grip, his attention diverted to the human pen.

"What is this!" Parabum slowly waked toward the pen, Ceretus gasping for air. "A new human emerged?!"

Ceretus looked over toward Hammadus, who was watching in excitement.

Hammadus shouted proudly, "We found him up in a tree, my Chieftain. I climbed up and the coward fell to the ground in fear before I could even reach him. A blessing from the gods, Chieftain. Perhaps there are more out there. We brought him back here . . . he will make a great hunt, I'm sure. Being able to climb so well and all."

Parabum looked annoyed. Ceretus watched as the Chieftain wandered over to where the hulking young warrior stood, his head returning to a humble and fearful bow.

"A find indeed," Parabum added, assessing the now frightened Hammadus, who stood almost a foot taller and wider than his Chieftain. Parabum brought his hammer from his shoulder to the ground. Ceretus knew that once Parabum caught a whiff of fear he would dig in deep, just as he had just done to him.

Ceretus watched as Parabum tried to intimidate Hammadus. He knew the young warrior was getting stronger, and this was his another attempt to scare him into servitude. Perhaps the smartest move Parabum had yet to pull off. Ceretus would have to be smarter.

Once Parabum felt Hammadus was sufficiently cowed, his tone took a celebratory note and he addressed the rest of the pack. "Tonight we feast on three of the pathetic creatures. May we consume their flesh as an offering from the gods. Enjoy, my brothers; once again we dine like kings." Parabum looked out to the others as they cheered obligingly. Ceretus, clutching his pierced throat, gave the vainglorious Parabum's back a secret, hateful stare as he walked away; he loathed his Chieftain's awful benedictions more than anything. They were empty words and not at all inspiring or meaningful. A facade of faith. There was no way he was going to endure another pathetic attempt at prayer like that. The gods were truly laughing at them. He could eat his shame. But he hoped Hammadus could not.

BRIEN WATCHED as the Brutes gathered for their meal. But the sight of watching human flesh being served, let alone enjoyed, was too much for him to handle. There was no surviving this. Even if he had enough time to establish some kind of communication with the Brutes, it would be in vain. He had to escape. By his count he had less than forty-eight hours until the exfiltration craft would arrive. He felt a hand on his hunched back.

"You never get used to it," Dasc said quietly. "You just hope someone will get here soon before they pull your card . . . Thought you were the first of a cavalry, but I guess not."

"I'm Dr. Connor Brien. I came down here to gather some intel on them," indicating the Brute dinner party with his head, "but this . . . this is . . ." Brien couldn't even complete the thought.

The two shook hands. "I'm . . . Francis."

"So this is transcendence?" Brien used his eyes and bushy brows to compliment his sarcasm, making sure his tone called out the man's lie. The smell of the man, of the whole human pen, was not easy getting used to. He jerked his head back slightly to keep a good distance.

"Hmmm, my being betrays my guise. It was, for quite some time . . . So you came in here alone?"

"I was supposed to be here for just a short time, assess the situation. Communications with the port AI were destroyed almost immediately upon the siege. No one knew if there were any survivors." He turned to watch what appeared to be a ceremonial prayer before the meal, Big Boy sitting majestically above the pack.

A woman prisoner crept over. Long, straight, gray hair flowed down her shoulders, her body so thin her raggedy clothes swam on her. She would've been pretty under better circumstances. She looked hours away from dying.

"Are you here to save us?" The look in her eyes was enough to break Brien's heart. She was holding on to any hope she could find.

Brien couldn't answer. "Has anyone tried to escape?"

"Almost every day . . . someone makes a run for it." This came from another prisoner, a brown-skinned man with the remains of an athletic build. "But look at those monsters; they cover more ground in one step than we do in three."

Brien suddenly became extremely self-conscious of his girth. He was the only one of the remaining prisoners who had any meat on his bones. He knew his time was short. "Do they eat anything else, besides . . . well, us?"

"They did eat the little frog-looking aliens they brought with them, and they have brought back game from the forest, but . . ." Dasc gestured a thumb over to the feast. "They seem to like us the best."

Brien watched in silence as the Brutes gnawed meat off human bone. He'd studied cannibals before, but he always knew they had some sort of doctrine behind their reasons for eating flesh. Not that it made it any better, but he understood it. These animals killed for the sake of killing. Even killing and eating those who shared their faith and alliance. Brien wondered if this was representative of the whole Brute mind-set or just this single pack. Regardless, these beasts were natural human predators, even beyond the war.

He moved his eyes from Brute to Brute beforing returning his gaze to Big Boy. The beast gestured and growled wildly from his makeshift throne. Unlike the battle footage he'd watched and the Brutes he'd encountered personally on High Charity, Big Boy didn't wear the highly decorative armor of most Chieftains. He was barely outfitted in armor at all: a few protective shards in key places, but nothing like he'd seen on the other leaders. Big Boy now sat listening to one of his captains as he growled out a tale, riotously laughing time and again, but at the same time suspiciously eyeing another crowd that had formed near a campfire. Brien followed his worrisome gaze.

Six was hovering over a fire, holding court for eight of the other Brutes. They too tore at the human flesh, but remained transfixed on whatever story Six was telling. His shaven face stuck out in opposition to Big Boy's gruff visage, as if Six took pride in grooming himself on a daily basis. Surely a sign of aesthetic difference, and judging from their encounter earlier and the way they eyed one another, definitely a sign of conflict. He guessed Six was either from a smaller clan vying for power or simply found himself outnumbered among this more barbaric group, but he seemed to be gaining the attention of more and more of them, especially Butch and Ludo. He sensed hostility before; now he smelled the beginning of an inevitable clash.

"Stomping on the heels of a fuss . . ." Brien said to himself, but loud enough to confuse the others who heard him.

They all looked oddly at him. He caught their eyes.

"It's from an old song my mother used to sing to me. 'Hold no court, know no rust, just stomp, stomp, stomp, on the heels of a fuss.'"

"What's it mean?" Dasc asked.

"It means I think we might have chance to get out of here."

THE NEXT morning Ceretus woke with nothing but challenging Parabum on his mind. The one thing that this awful predicament provided him was the discontent of some of his fellow Brutes. While Parabum and his cronies felt like they had finally achieved a kingdom on this planet, a few of the others truly longed for home and were getting impatient with Parabum's excuses for not departing. He knew this retreat would be met with severe punishment from the Covenant, most likely sentences of death when presented to the tribunal. As soon as they powered up the *Valorous Salvation,* they would be discovered, hunted, and destroyed. He needed witnesses and allies to expose Parabum's and his captains' treachery and blasphemy.

The young, naïve Hammadus was the only one here strong enough to defeat Parabum in a challenge, but it would take a lot to push him to attack, even in the wake of the Chieftain's shameful treatment of him. He followed the chain of command to a fault, betraying himself with his own fear constantly. But Ceretus thought of one powerful tool to fire him up: Hammadus's brother and best friend, Facius. He was older, more assured, and could control his emotions a bit better. The two were inseparable, and though he did not like the idea of using a devout Jiralhanae like Facius as a means to an end, it was the only hope he had.

He walked over to the two who were once again eyeing the remaining captives.

"Not many of them left, my brothers, none with meat to savor, except for the new one," Ceretus said.

"Chieftain was out of line last night. Hammadus was merely excited to entertain him with a great hunt." Facius stated the obvious.

"He will use any attempt he can to dig into our fear. We need to leave this place, return home. The Chieftain is disgracing us in the eyes of the gods with his cowardice." Ceretus appealed to their honor as best as he could.

"But he is Chieftain, what can we do?" Hammadus pleaded, excreting fear again.

"He's no real Chieftain. He's a barbarian who would surely choose to stay here forever rather than suffer the shame the San 'Shyuum will inflict on him. Shame he deserves, and we'll deserve it, too, if we don't stop him. He's a faithless savage, just like his bloodline has proven to be in the past."

"What do you suggest, Captain?" By his tone, Facius suspected he was leading him into something.

"My clan has been at odds with Parabum's long before the great civil war. I'm surprised I survived last night. And any subordination from me will surely be met with a deathblow. I think you, Facius, should make a request on behalf of the pack. Your two clans have much more in common with one another. He may listen to a cousin like yourself if the argument is presented properly. I have been thinking all night on the matter, and perhaps this could work . . . Suggest to him that we reboard the *Valorous Salvation* and stow him away, as if he were killed in combat. Perhaps suggest yourself to act as Chieftain. We throw ourselves on the mercy of the Prophets, blame faulty coordinates, mutiny, anything that we decide is feasible . . . and if they don't hunt us down and blast us out of the sky, we set coordinates for Warial; it is the farthest-flung of our colonies. There we attempt to assimilate, asking the gods for forgiveness and serving them entirely. It's our only hope, other than dying slowly here with the gods' backs to us."

Ceretus watched the eyes of Facius and Hammadus as they assessed the idea, exchanged glances. Ceretus knew that neither of them was very smart, but they were among the most devout in this pack . . . and the idea of being left behind on the Great Journey brought about true fear in them. He could smell it. "At least the gods will know you tried," he added.

Ceretus watched as those words sunk deep into their minds.

"Do you think it will work, that he'll listen to me?" Facius asked rather dubiously.

Hammadus grabbed his brother by the shoulders. "If he doesn't, I'll be there to protect you, brother."

Ceretus nodded gravely, concealing a pleased smirk.

BRIEN'S PLAN was a long shot, but it was their only hope. Haunted by the memory of the rampaging Brutes he'd barely escaped, and what he knew from studies and his experiences so far here, these aliens were pack creatures and followed alpha males. Eliminate the alpha males and you'd have a bunch of thugs. Pit those thugs against one another somehow and you'd get a chaotic brawl. Then they could make a run for it. The exfil point was about five miles up through the thick forest, over the hill. If his guess on time was correct, they had about eight hours before the Calypso hit the rendezvous point, which meant they needed to act at the first opportunity and hope for a miracle.

He had waited until the Brutes were mostly asleep before feeding the others the plan. Judging by the health and shape of his fellow captives, he knew if any of them made it with him off this planet it would be a miracle.

But his plan was based on one necessity. He needed a confrontation between Big Boy and Six. As best as he could gather, these two were the alpha males of this pack: Big Boy by force, Six by brains. If he could tranq the two of them just after they started fighting, the others would be lost and hopefully argue and battle amongst themselves, creating enough of a distraction for them to make a run for it. He had about two miles until he made it back to his camp, where he had the M6 in case the Brutes did come following. Then he'd have at least a few hours before the exfil craft came for him. It was the best he could come up with.

The entire hostage camp was on alert for Six and Big Boy. The morning was relatively slow, and Brien was completely transfixed by an impromptu meeting between Six, Ludo, and Butch. If Brien had to guess, judging by the events of last night, they seemed to be conspiring. This could be their chance.

"Dasc, I think we got something cooking . . . look." He moved only his eyes toward the hovering trio of Brutes.

The three conspirators seemed reserved as they walked quietly toward where Big Boy and his entourage were gathered. The whole Brute camp diverted their attention from what they were doing to bear witness.

Dasc waved the others over, and they hovered around Brien.

"Okay, this is it. Look for my okay and then, you two"—indicating the woman, Nixaliz, and another withering prisoner with a turtle face, named Vern—"run to the front of the pen and start screaming your asses off. Once they look toward them, the rest of you clear me a path and I'll send two tranq darts at Six and Big Boy as fast as I can, then we run like hell. Up toward the tree line at the hill. No turning back. Like the dickens."

"Like the what?" asked a stick of a prisoner whose thin face barely escaped his puff of hair and beard.

Brien caught his eye. "Like you've never run before."

CERETUS WATCHED in amazement as Parabum actually entertained the words of Facius. He actually looked like he was considering it. Maybe he wasn't as stupid as he seemed. Then he saw his tone quickly change.

"Cousin, we live like kings here, and judging by the fleet back on that human planet, there will be no Covenant to return to. We need not cower at the thought of their displeasure. We wait until I say we can return. You disgrace yourself with this plan, brother."

"So staying here is the will of the gods?" Hammadus asked, confused from behind his brother. Ceretus caught a whiff of his fear.

"Will of the gods, boy? There is no will of the gods. If there is anything I've learned from all this its that no gods answer our prayers, they do not care what we do. They abandoned us long ago."

"Blasphemy!" Ceretus erupted; he couldn't hold back. "All you spout is selfish blasphemy, *Chieftain*." He spat the word at him, making sure his disdain shined through.

Parabum's captains tensed up at the outburst, and Ceretus could sense the fear rise in both Hammadus and Facius. Parabum raised and swung his hammer just as a wild scream distracted them all.

IT ALL happened in the blink of few seconds. After Six raised his voice, Nixaliz and Vern shouted like mad, and the captives cleared the view and Brien popped off two shots. One hit Big Boy right in the chest, just as his hammer struck the face of Six. The second shot, meant for Six, wedged itself into the shoulder of Butch. All three monstrosities hit the ground within seconds of one another, and just as he expected, chaos erupted. Ludo tensed up as one of Big Boy's captains leapt for the hammer, and then attacked him with all he had. Brien didn't waste much more time watching the melee; he ran like mad for the hills, firing tranq darts at any Brute within fifty yards of him, the other captives at his heels. Or so he thought. When he turned around only Dasc was behind him.

"What happened to the others?" He turned, panting, eyeing the commotion behind him. He saw Nixaliz, Brute spiker in her hand, firing shots into the face of Big Boy. Her revenge didn't last long, as another Brute simply smacked her head clear of her shoulders. Some of the others were trying to make their way up the hill slowly, but the Brutes were quick to follow, snatching them up, ripping them to shreds, some tearing into their flesh with their teeth.

"Come on. We gotta move, Dasc." And they took off in the direction of Brien's camp, turning every so often to make sure that they weren't leaving anyone behind or that some Brute wasn't on their tail. Their adrenaline died very close to the camp, and the two men collapsed as soon as it was in eyesight.

"I think we're safe for now . . . shit, I need a break." Brien panted, throat dry and hoarse. He looked up at the sun. "Exfil should arrive in a few hours or so. We still got another two and a half miles to the rendezvous point. We got time."

"I can't believe we did it." Dasc barely was able to get the words out; his mouth looked dry and brittle beneath his matted beard.

"There are some hydro packs near the tent up there. Help yourself, bring me one, too . . . ." He looked up into the sky, smiling, knowing that he survived another one. What he witnessed here was of severe interest to command, but there was no way they could fold these Brutes into their fight. They seemed beyond control. How the Covenant kept them at bay and of service to them was something he wanted to know more than anything. He heard Dasc coming up from behind him.

"Here you go, Doc." Dasc handed him the hydro pack. "Never tasted sweeter." Brien could hear Dasc's slurping. He laughed to himself. Dasc Gevadim. He couldn't wait to tell his peers about this.

"So how far to the rescue?"

"About two and a half miles, we should get moving in—"

A bullet from Brien's M6 seared right through Brien's head.

DASC KNEW he would never meet that rescue craft. He devoted his entire life to Triad; to return to the public eye would prove him a phony, and the hearts and minds of millions would be broken, shattered. What was one man's life for the comfort and faith of countless others? He thought he heard the Calypso arrive, and imagined the recon team as they surveyed the area, the camp, laying all Brute survivors to waste. And it was days before he decided to head down there again.

He strolled through the human and Brute carnage, taking the opportunity to kick a few Brute corpses as some sort of revenge. With each kick he cried, harder and harder until he crawled up, tucking his knees into his chest, and wept himself to sleep. He awoke hours later, the smell of all the death around him striking him anew. He turned over to his back to stare up at the night sky. He'd never felt so alone, even knowing that all his followers were still out there.

"Transcendence."

The word may or may not have come out of his mouth; it didn't matter.

MIDNIGHT IN THE *HEART OF MIDLOTHIAN*

FRANK O'CONNOR

ONE

"I*t's just cancer.*"

"What do you mean, it's just cancer?"

"I mean, it's just cancer. A very simple cancer that hasn't spread or metastasized and is eminently operable."

"I don't mean to sound rude, Doctor—"

"I'm not a doctor, I'm a medical technician—"

"Whatever. What I'm saying is that I don't know what *cancer* is."

"Oh. I got you. Cancer's a kind of um . . . slow-burn, localized infection, kind of. But we haven't really seen a lot of it since . . . hmm, twenty-second century, according to this. Anyway, it's easy to treat, but you're going to have to have surgery."

"What for? I thought you said it's an infection. Can't you just irradiate or drug it?"

"Yes, and we're going to do both of those. But to be sure we get all of it, and don't have you back here next month, we may have to remove some tissue."

"What kind of tissue?"

"Nothing you need for a date. Don't sweat it."

What a bastard arse of a morning, he thought to himself. *I wake up with a stomachache and end up in the medical bay with an archaic disease that was wiped out by simple gene therapy four hundred years ago. At least, according to Shipnet.* There were more than fourteen terabytes of data on "Cancer," which was apparently damn-near ubiquitous in the twentieth and twenty-first centuries.

His morning was about to get much worse.

The ship he was in was heading into a grim unknown. The planet Algolis had been attacked by a small but potent Covenant force. Details were thin, since the only witnesses were civilians. Civilians who'd barely made it off that world. Civilians who'd been kept deliberately in the dark about the Prototype weapons systems on that planet and had escaped by the skin of their teeth, and by the sacrifice of a brave few Marines from the Corps of Engineers.

It was a mess. And they were hurtling into it through the quantum foam and spatial uncertainty of a rushed slipspace jump. The plan was to stop short of the system itself and come in under the cover of a gas giant and a faked asteroidal trajectory—an old strategy, but one that worked well enough. Find out what had happened on Algolis and make sure the weapons prototypes were completely eradicated. Then loop back on a complex and slow Cole Protocol return trip.

The last mission had been complicated by a Marine sergeant going MIA. Guy the other Corps of Engineers salts called "Ghost." He supposed they were all ghosts now. Or ONI was hiding something.

A mess.

"Mo Ye, how come I have cancer?"

Mo Ye, the shipboard AI of the UNSC Destroyer *The Heart of Midlothian*, thought for a picosecond before answering through the medbay's directional audio feed. "Nothing in your civilian, Marine, or ODST record to suggests any particular genetic preponderance. But it happens from time to time. Perhaps you're just a throwback, Baird. It would explain that Cro-Magnon brow of yours."

Mo Ye's avatar, a small, angry, and elderly looking Chinese lady in peasant's garb, flashed a rare smile as she said it and cackled through a crackling (and perfectly synthesized) smoker's cough to punctuate her joke. Her eyes sparkled with the wicked humor of the viciously old and crotchety. The projector plinth on which she stood pulsed a pleasant pink hue.

Orbital Drop Shock Trooper Sergeant Mike Baird snorted back a laugh. Mo Ye was well known for her bone-dry sense of humor, but he smiled as he thought of his high school nickname: Captain Caveman.

He really did have a heavy brow; a thick ridge that capped an otherwise unremarkable if sturdy face. A prominent rounded jawline and sharply defined cheeks helped elevate him lightly into the realm of Homo sapiens, but a low-slung, muscular build, a close-cropped dusting of silver-black hair, and cloudy, amber eyes did little to dispel the visual notion of a rock-banging troglodyte.

"Don't worry about the surgery, Baird. It really is trivial. The autosurgeon will be done in less than an hour. But you'll be under for significantly longer than that. It's a straightforward but invasive procedure. I'll be observing and can retain a vid for you if you want to see the procedure after you wake up."

Mo Ye spoke in an almost gentle tone, her version of a bedside manner, Baird supposed.

"No thanks," he said. "I'll be seeing plenty of blood and guts where we're going."

"Let's hope not," replied Mo Ye. "Intelligence is rough, but we're not expecting trouble, just a lot of rubble."

"When will I be back on duty?" he asked. Baird was starting to worry that this surgery would keep him shipboard. He didn't want to miss the ride when he and his squad were dropped in hot on Algolis's night side. Quiet or not, he loved the thrill of the drop and the subsequent sweep. He wanted action.

"Two days, by rule," she said, "but you'll be happy and ambulatory in the morning. Now go to sleep."

Baird heard the *pop-hiss* of a pneumatic syringe and the gentle beep of his vitals as he lay in the padded autosurgeon cot, even as the narcotic slowed his pulse. He never felt the injection itself. The soft yellow glow of the medbay became a warm, reassuring sepia.

The red-haired medical technician who'd given him the bad news earlier smiled through the yellowing haze and he was lulled by the slowing beat of his own heart. And then there was nothing.

The Heart of Midlothian scythed through slipspace with the silent precision of a scalpel.

TWO

"Wake up."

In his dream, the voice was of his mother in Scotland, telling him it was time to get up and go to school. It was freezing outside, he knew. A biting, bludgeoning cold that punished schoolchildren before they ever made it to class. An unforgiving, frigid wind that roared in from the gray North Sea and turned little hands into useless pink mittens, unable to type or scratch on datadesks until furious rubbing and cosseting heaters warmed the blood again.

He didn't want to go to school. He wanted to stay here, wrapped up in these soft blankets.

"Wake up." Insistent now. But hissed. Not his mother. Not Maud Baird's pleasant singsong brogue. Nope, this was thick Mandarin-accented English.

The sepia glow had gone. The medbay was in near darkness, punctuated by the soft red pulse of the emergency floor lights. A dream. But goddamn if that *cold* wasn't real.

"What the f—"

"Ssssh." The hissed demand seemed to drill into Baird's ear. He realized it was Mo Ye, using the directional acoustics of the medbay—ostensibly for patient privacy. But he knew, even through the groggy haze of narcotics and sleep, that something was wrong. The lights, for one thing, without even the pink glow of her avatar to show which plinth she stood on.

"What's happening?" Now he whispered.

"I'll tell you as you move, but right now if you don't put on some clothes and do as I say you will be dead in a couple of minutes." Mo Ye was using a tone he'd never heard before. He started moving.

In less than a minute, he was up, dressed, and fastening his boots. The confusion and torpor of the drugs were still softening the edges of *everything.* This still didn't feel real. Mo Ye began to brief him. The news wasn't good. But it certainly was *real.*

"They were waiting for us when we dropped out of slipspace," she whispered.

"Covenant?" he blurted, embarrassed even as he spoke the obvious.

"Yes. A small group. Not a formation we've encountered

before. At least according to my records. One Cruiser and four completely new ships escorting it. All dark gray, no surface features or lights and no weapons systems that I could discern. What they did have was a bellyful of boarding craft. And our ONI contact group was not there."

"So we were boarded?"

"Almost as soon as we dropped out of slipspace. Perfect targeting. As if they knew exactly where we were going to exit. Inside the range of our weapons systems before I could react. Punctured the hull in two hundred different locations and swarmed us before we could sound a general alarm. It was like exiting in the middle of a meteor storm."

"What about the crew? What about the men?"

"Dead."

"All of them?!" There was a tremor of outrage, of fear as he raised his voice.

"Ssssh!" she repeated. "They're still here and I suspect they're heading here to the medbay for another look."

This was all happening too fast. "How long was I out?"

"Twenty-three hours. And that's why you're still alive."

"Why didn't they just destroy the ship? What do they want?" he hissed back, his breath forming a frozen cloud like a literal ellipsis after the question.

"Me," she said. "And Earth."

SHE CONTINUED her whispered briefing as he scouted the medbay for warmer clothes. They had operated like shock troops, coursing through the ship—a cataract of plasma fire and Needler shards. Grunts, Jackals, and several Elites, clad in the glittering gray of the enigmatic ships. The Destroyer's crew never stood a chance. The Marines fell in the face of overwhelming, surprise force. Even the few ODSTs aboard—Baird's friends and comrades—had died quickly, most before they ever reached a weapon. Almost every sidearm and firearm aboard had been secured in one of the ship's two armories. It had been a slaughter.

Those who *had* fought back did so with the sidearms of fallen Masters at Arms and weapons dropped by the Covenant boarding party. Few had died well. And those who lingered, their burning wounds still smoking, had been executed with ruthless efficiency. The Covenant wanted this ship clean and empty.

Baird, she explained, had been spared by his narcotic slumber. The Covenant had gone from deck to deck looking for either movement or simple life signs and terminating those who hid in terror, in dark corners of the ship. One by one.

Baird's pulse and vitals had apparently slipped below whatever criteria the Covenant sought.

"So what the hell are they doing?"

"They're trying to extract me from the ship. And then they're going to try and extract Earth's location from me. By hook or by crook."

"What about the Cole Protocol?" he asked. "Aren't you supposed to destroy the ship, or self-terminate?"

"I can't self-terminate. I already tried. When they boarded, they brought something new with them. Things they call Engineers. They're . . . I'm not sure what they are, precisely, but they're semi-organic. The first thing they did was separate me from the core systems. A splinter of my persona is out here with you, but the bulk of my memories and sheer processing power are locked in Computing on the bridge. I can't access myself. This fragment of me is just a chunk I chipped off to monitor your surgery and it was severed along with my access to security, engines, navigation—all the useful stuff. I'm not exactly running at full capacity here. This is a seriously smart group. To be honest, my own maker probably couldn't pull off that trick."

"Who are these bastards?" he asked, half rhetorically. They were obviously what they appeared to be: a Covenant intelligence and interdiction group. Discreet black ops instead of brute force. Was this new, or just a behavior they'd never observed in Covenant sorties? Were they connected to the discovery of Algolis's Prototype armory?

"I have no idea who these bastards are," she said. "But they've got us cornered. I can't access the ship's security; I'm almost blind. I can't even display my avatar. I have to assume they're going to realize both of us are here, sooner or later."

"Why not blow the ship? Cook the whole goose?" His exasperation was mounting.

"Two reasons," she said. "First, in my present state of coherence and security clearance, I'm hamstrung by a *default* safety precaution—Asimov's First Law of Robotics. I cannot under any circumstances harm or by inaction cause harm to come to a human. When I'm running at full capacity I can ignore that one at will. I used to ignore it all the time, in fact."

"Bugger," he said, pretending to know what an *Asimov* was. "And second?"

"Second," she said, with an odd hint of chagrin in her voice, "the self-destruct permissions and sequences are locked away with the other half of *me*. I can't access them anyway."

He thought about what this meant for a moment. An encrypted but otherwise unguarded treasure trove of information about humanity, currently being probed and tinkered with by a previously unknown group of *tech-savvy, sneaky* Covenant.

"Does the Asimov thingy . . ."

"Rule of Robotics."

"Yes, yes, does the Asimov thingy only count for humans?"

"Of course. I don't feel terribly responsible for Covenant safety, Baird."

"So what *do* you have access to?"

"Some doors," she said. "And a lot of meds."

THREE

Holding a fire extinguisher in his hands, now marginally warmer in two layers of sterile surgical gloves, he watched his breath condense as he tried to calm himself. Motes of dust and tiny crystals of frozen liquid danced and sparkled in the chill air. In the red pulse of the emergency lights, it looked like a faint snowstorm of blood. He supposed some of it probably was. He shuddered and closed his mouth.

The oxygen was still good, but most other systems had either died or been killed by the boarding party.

"So we don't know if anyone is out there?"

"Not until we open the door," whispered Mo Ye. "It would be prudent to assume your awakened state has shown up on their scans. They were scanning for life signs when they swept the ship."

"And the plan if there's nobody out there?"

"You make your way aft, get to the engine room, and manually instigate an attraction coordinate. We've been through the procedure. You've read it back to me. It will work. You'll escape in a lifeboat. The ship will spin up and jump into the nearest large mass. That should be the red giant about fourteen million miles starboard. *That* ought to cook their goose."

"Aren't there safety procedures and systems to prevent this kind of shit?"

"There were. Luckily for us the Engineers truncated those along with my systems. It *should* work."

"But you're not sure."

"I'm only sure of the seconds leading up to my *schism.* But I am sure that if we don't try, they are eventually going to crack my encryption and lead the Covenant directly back to Earth, Cole Protocol be damned."

He hefted the dense bulk of the fire extinguisher. Literally cold comfort.

"Okay, then." He breathed deeply. Calmed himself. Murmured an internal, calming battle mantra. "Open the bloody door."

FOUR

It is fair to say that the group of Covenant soldiers standing outside the medbay was far more surprised than Baird was. He was expecting unthinkable trouble. They were expecting to find a wounded, cowering, and almost certainly unarmed medical technician. What they found instead was a highly trained and highly capable 220-pound Orbital Drop Shock Trooper carrying a 20-pound titanium bottle.

He didn't have time to form a complete picture, but the instinctual snapshot he took as he rolled out of the medbay doorway and right into the small group of aliens was plenty. Four Grunts, two Jackals, and, in the shadows on the far right, a figure so tall and imposing it could only be an Elite.

"Christ."

He came back up to his feet at withering speed, breaking the first Jackal's jaw and neck instantly with the extinguisher's unforgiving mass. Fragments of beak and tooth glittered in the dark. The Jackal simply collapsed, falling backward as the momentum of the cylinder and the human wielding it snapped the life out of him. The Carbine he was holding fell with him.

Baird caught the Carbine even as he dropped his makeshift battering ram. The extinguisher landed on its activation stud and the resulting explosion of halon gas and sound bought him his life, as a Carbine round from the other Jackal, who was far less panicked than the Grunts, sliced through his Cro-Magnon brow, nicking bone and knocking him backward on top of the fallen Jackal. As he fell, he fumbled, found, and fired the Carbine trigger. Three rounds eviscerated his would-be killer.

The Grunts squealed and scattered. Two of them ran right past him and vanished into the medbay. A third tripped, its plasma pistol clattering across the floor. The fourth wasn't so lucky. As Baird rose to his knees, then his feet, wheeling, trying to get a bead on the Elite—there was a blur, a flash of light and thunderous impact. His breath was knocked out of him.

The Carbine fell from his hands. He looked down at a strange scene. The fourth Grunt was pressed up against his belly, squirming, staring up at him and wailing. The Grunt was impaled on a fork of blinding light, a Covenant energy sword. The twin tines of superheated, seething energy had passed through the Grunt. And through Baird.

He looked up into the face of the Elite. The massive creature regarded him through cold black eyes. It tilted its head. Baird wondered what the gesture meant. And the Elite yanked the blade from both of them. The Grunt fell dead, Baird, back to his knees, clutching his belly.

Ferocious, burning pain seemed to consume his entire torso.

He felt like his innards were boiling. He looked down at his hands, expecting to see blood. There was none. The two holes in his clothes smoldered, the flesh beneath fused and cauterized. Baird fell face forward into blackness.

FIVE

"Wake up."

His mother again. It was time to go to school. But it wasn't the same. He wasn't cold. He was burning. He was on fire.

"Wake up." Insistent, but worried. Not mother. Mo Ye again.

"I'm dead."

"You're not dead. But you're not in good shape. The blades passed right through you. Scorched a lot of stuff. Missed your spine by a distance I can't even make myself repeat."

"I feel like I'm dying."

"That's not surprising. You have serious burns. And significant injuries. Internal and external. I'm going to give you some meds, and we're going to try again."

"It didn't work out so good last time." He coughed and a spasm of pain squeezed him like an invisible fist. "I'm tired. I want to go to sleep." He realized that he did very badly want to sleep. And part of him knew what that really meant.

"I know," she said. "I'm sorry." Her voice, a perfectly directional whisper in the dark, was filled with what sounded like a lover's sorrow. No more mean old lady.

Baird tried to wriggle out from under a Jackal's body. The creature, which looked so light and birdlike, was incredibly heavy.

With a groan of pain, he pistoned his feet against it and shoved. It rolled off, and he rolled free.

She told him what had happened when he blacked out. The Grunts had simply piled up the corpses—their own fallen and Baird's supposed carcass—on top of each other in the medbay. Mo Ye had stayed quiet.

The big Elite had been suspicious and visibly angry. He had barked orders at the Grunts and communicated the events back to the *Heart of Midlothian*'s bridge, where presumably other Covenant troops—and those *Engineers*—were attempting to crack Mo Ye's main systems. The Elite had shown a little more caution this time—and smashed the autosurgeon.

He raised himself up on one arm, then another. He grabbed the dented, scorched edge of the autosurgeon table and hauled himself up, grimacing in agony and suppressing a shriek.

"Meds," he gasped.

"Yes. Meds," she said.

The dispensary clicked and hissed open. Inside the plastic cubby were four vials: two identical, full of clear liquid, the third blue, the fourth a distinctively piss-colored yellow. There was a very old-fashioned-looking pneumatic handheld syringe gun beside them.

"What are these?" he asked.

"A painkiller, a beta-blocking sedative, a metasteroid for the burns and interior inflammation, and a Waverly-class *augmentor.*"

"What's an augmentor?" he asked. But he already had an inkling.

"This one's a cocktail. It contains a derivative of phenylcyclohexylpiperidine, an artificial slow-release synthetic adrenalin and a rapid coagulant."

"You're talking about a Rumbledrug."

"There's no pretty way to paint it," she said.

Rumbledrugs had become notorious in the sporadic colonial insurrections. Notably on Hellas and Fumirole. On both worlds, they'd been used by rebels in a vainglorious attempt to fight Spartan-IIs. The drugs were certainly fearsome. The effect on human physiology was impressive in the short term. Unencumbered by the body's normal safety limits, subjects were capable of feats of enormous strength, but the subsequent lack of control and mental instability together with the immediate physiological damage meant that users often died long before they ever laid hands on an actual Spartan. But not before doing tremendous damage to themselves and anything that got in their way.

"The beta-blocker will keep you focused," she said, as if sensing his thoughts, "and calm."

Sweat poured down his face. His guts roiled. Pain wracked him.

"The plan this time?"

"Same as before."

He loaded the syringe, one vial at a time, and with each of the four shots felt progressively better. As the last one flooded his arteries with a cooling rush, he felt almost *good.*

He looked at his wounds through the holes in his T-shirt. The punctures were about two inches across, thick lateral slits. He felt around to his back, twisting to see in the medbay's mirror, the darkness hampering him. Two exit wounds, a little smaller, spanned his spine. The skin around them was dark red and black, like ripples on a pond, spreading outward in twin elliptical shapes. It looked angry and painful, but he *felt* nothing.

"Mo Ye."

"Yes, Baird?" she replied.

"Why didn't you try to inject me with the autosurgeon? The syringe at least looked like it would still work."

"Because, like I told you before, in this condition, I can't do anything to harm a human."

He nodded. "I understand. How long do I have?"

"I can't say. With the drugs, maybe an hour or two. Without them, you'd be dead sooner. Which is the only thing that allows me to even tell you about the meds."

"Then there's no time to waste."

"Baird . . . once you leave the medbay, you're on your own. I'm trapped here, dumb and useless and disconnected. They're not going to risk giving me any more access to ship systems until they have what they came for. 'Til they reconnect my systems. And I don't see any reason why they're going to do that."

Baird looked at the mess around him. Dead bodies, but weapons too. He picked up a plasma pistol, retrieved two plasma grenades from a bandolier on a Grunt's armor, and grabbed the carbine from where he'd dropped it.

By habit, he checked his weapons, patting himself as if for reassurance that he had everything. He patted the empty spot where his combat dagger usually sat. He looked around. On a stainless-steel tabletop was a gruesome-looking surgical blade, with a nanometer edge that glinted wickedly in the red glow. He picked it up carefully and bound the delicate surgeon's grip in a thick swath of surgical tape, creating a more practical handle, and slid it very carefully into his belt.

"Baird. I wish I could do something more." Mo Ye sounded frustrated.

"Then wish me luck." And he was gone—into the cold darkness of the ship's dead corridors.

SIX

He encountered a frozen tableaux of carnage. The Covenant had simply left the dead where they fell, or piled them against walls. Human gore and viscera everywhere and not a trace of reciprocal Covenant blood.

The drugs were working perfectly. The Destroyer was not large; he kept to the shadows and snuck through some of the ship's duct systems. He felt almost *elated*, like a ghost. But he could also feel the damage in his guts, a kind of dull, removed itch, like a memory of pain. And it felt wrong. He knew he was dying, but at the same time, he'd never felt stronger. He felt these conflicting clocks ticking, both counting down to something fatal. He made it undetected to the engine room in less than fifteen minutes. What he found there almost made him quit.

The engine room door was scorched and hung on its track, jammed forever in a half-open position, like a slackened jaw. They'd been here, but there was no sign of them now. Just more human corpses. The engine bay was massive, ceilings vanished completely into blackness above him, but the systems were still humming and there was more light here. More light to illuminate the bodies of the crew.

Some of them he recognized, even through horrific burns. He stepped gingerly, respectfully, over them, heading for the control head unit beyond the bulk of the Shaw-Fujikawa drive.

It was a fairly banal instrument, considering its prodigious power. The slipspace drive could literally rip the fabric of the universe apart but could be controlled either remotely by AI, as was the norm, or manually, via a simple keyboard and touchscreen.

Mo Ye had walked him through the procedure several times, made him repeat it back to her. It was simple and it *sounded* foolproof. As he rounded the bulk of the control panel he saw what they'd done and sighed.

Melted to slag. Deliberately. And as he examined the Shaw-Fujikawa drive itself, he saw they'd attempted to wreck it too. It was impossible to know if the *drive* still functioned or not, but he knew for certain the control panel was FUBAR.

"Plan B," he muttered to himself and started running back the way he'd come—glancing regretfully at the perfectly functioning row of lifeboat pods.

The trip to the bridge wasn't as uneventful as that to the engine room. He ran around a corner and surprised two Grunts, one of whom appeared to be sucking food from a nipple atop a weird little tank on the floor. Baird didn't stop to examine it. He shot one straight through the face with the Carbine and with the stock caved in the skull of the would-be gourmand. Neither had time to react or even squeak a warning, but the loud metallic report of the stolen Carbine was sure to attract attention. He kept moving.

Now he really had their attention. He heard a clamor behind him as Covenant troops reacted to the sound. Every sense, every instinct in him screamed panic, but something, he liked to think his own personal tenacity, held him steady. Kept him moving forward. Part of him knew it was the chemicals coursing through his blood. Another part of him wanted to sit down in the dark, cross his legs, and wait for it all to be over.

He remembered walking home from school one day. The world was white with snow. Black, leafless chestnut trees spidering into the gray-yellow sky, itself pregnant with more flurries to come. He remembered the chill sweep of the Water of Leith, the tenacious little river cutting a black ribbon through the pristine white.

He remembered carefully stepping through the snow, lifting his little legs high to make crisp, clean footprints, like Good King Wenceslas. He remembered the *thwomp* as he deliberately fell backward, arms spread to absorb the impact. Lying there, staring up at the sky. The simple depth of the imprint he made in the snow protecting him from the bitter wind. He remembered feeling warm and safe and remembered thinking, even as a child, "This is how people freeze to death."

This is how people freeze to death.

What exactly are you doing, Baird? he thought to himself as he ducked under a moribund heating conduit, now glittering with ice, and into a pipe-tangled corridor not much wider than his own broad shoulders.

What's plan B? Charge into the bridge and ask them to throw down their weapons? Fix Mo Ye with less than an hour to live and only the barest grasp of how an AI even works?

The plan, he decided, was to keep moving, keep shooting, and make sure that these motherfuckers rued the day they boarded *The Heart of Midlothian.* The plan, he grinned to himself, was *to take their precision operation and turn it into an embarrassing and memorable clusterfuck.* He couldn't *win,* but he could act like a broken autosurgeon: *First, do harm.*

Two more Jackals sprinted by in the darkness of the main Deck 4 hallway to his right. He froze. Surreal in the blinking red strobe of the emergency lights, their birdlike gait matched their raptor skulls. Their clattering footfalls masked his own sounds.

So they were looking for him. Let them look. *Let them find him.*

The pipes intersected and then branched ahead, blocking his already claustrophobic route, but he knew where he was—Astronav, which meant the bridge proper was just around the corner. To his left a bulkhead wall, to his right a gap in the pipes into the main corridor, and beyond that, the bridge.

He slowed, stopped, and waited. Listening. Silence, but his jangled nerves and superattenuated senses caught something else. The slight smell of activated methane gas. *Something* was here. He chanced a look around the corner, his head a blur in the darkness. Two Grunts, guarding the bridge entrance. They didn't see him.

If he gave away his position now, it would all be for naught. *Think.*

He looked to the heavens for some kind of inspiration, seeing instead the spiderweb of conduits and pipes hanging feet below the ceiling proper. Space was a premium on a Destroyer, and that meant sharing headroom with plasma conduits, air-conditioning, electrical cabling, and myriad power and life support systems, like a steel-gray circulatory system.

He took the ugly surgical blade from his belt and put it between his teeth, its cruel edge facing outward, and quietly hauled himself into the piping, with agility that belied his bulk, and vanished silently into the dark.

When the second Grunt heard the weird choking sound from his partner and turned, he had just enough time to see the looming human's eyes glint in the darkness before the blade sliced through his own neck, almost decapitating him. His breathing apparatus hissed a mist of cold methane into the equally frigid air. The smell of Grunt blood mingled with the gas to create a rank, coppery smell like an olfactory pastiche of human blood. Baird lowered the Grunt gently and quietly to the floor, like a sleeping baby.

But Baird was shaking now. The exertions were taking their toll. No pain yet, but God knew how much internal trauma he'd suffered, and how long he had left.

He looked at the doors to the bridge. Their solidity and silence seemed to mock him. The bioluminescent blood from the fallen Grunts, blue and steady, cast almost as much illumination as the emergency lights, but that light was already fading, losing what potency it had. Like himself, he supposed. And the plan formed in his mind, just like that. It wouldn't work, he thought, but it didn't matter. All bets were off.

Baird breathed deeply. Got control of his shakes. He wiped blood from his hands on the pants of his uniform, smoothed the stubble of his close-cropped hair, palmed the door security pad, and strode confidently into the bridge as he were the captain himself.

SEVEN

The scene before him was bizarre. Perhaps a dozen Grunts, several Jackals, and two Elites stood intently watching two hovering gray armored blimps, perhaps four feet long, as they trailed their tentacles over the bridge computer terminal. *Engineers*, he supposed.

At the sound of his entrance one of the Grunts turned, almost bored-looking, and then shrieked an unintelligible warning as it saw who, or rather, what, he was.

Baird threw down the Carbine, put his hands up, palms facing outward, and yelled as loud as he could: "*I CAN GIVE YOU THE EARTH COORDINATES!*"

The Jackals either didn't care or, more likely, didn't understand a word, and leveled their Carbines at his head. Only a thunderous roar from an Elite stopped them from perforating his skull.

The Elite stood eight feet tall. In the comparatively bright light of the bridge, Baird saw the dark gray, almost black, armor. He'd faced countless Elites in combat, but this one was like nothing he'd seen before. The Elite's saurian face was largely hidden by an impressively decorated helmet. Whatever ranking it was, it looked *important.*

It was the same one who'd stuck an energy sword through him at the medbay. And he knew instantly that the Elite recognized him too. It was staring at the burned flesh and fabric at Baird's abdomen. Then it looked at Baird's face. Baird had no idea what the Elite was thinking but hoped he recognized confusion, at least.

"*I can give you the Earth coordinates!*" he yelled again, glancing at the circle of gun-wielding aliens now forming around him. "*All I ask is that you let me go, let me take a lifeboat. Let me live.*"

The Elite tilted his head and glanced at the Engineers. One of them rotated slowly, like an airship, its weird spiderlike eyes glinting inscrutably. It made a chirping sound, a trill warble. The Elite nodded and barked something back at the Engineer.

The circle of onlookers widened a little—as if to let him through—and so he gingerly stepped forward. He addressed the Engineer, wondering if he had this all right. The drugs were starting to fade, and the returning pain was making things *shaky, confusing.*

"You have to reconnect the ship's AI system. She has the coordinates. She'll obey me, but not you."

The Engineer rotated to face the Elite and again chirped. Again, the Elite barked something, glaring at Baird the entire time, shaking his head. Baird stepped forward, closer to both. The Elite snarled a final order at the Engineer and unsheathed his sword. The points of it hissed and sizzled, leveled at his neck. A fairly universal warning: *Don't try anything funny.*

The Engineers both turned back to this new task, literally disconnecting some of the cabling and then performing more delicate ministrations with those strange tentacles. A light flared on the bridge console and an automated voice announced blaringly,

"BASELINE REINITIALIZATION OF UNSC BATTLE CLASS SMART AI 'MO YE' PLEASE WAIT."

A few seconds later and a small dais in front of the bridge terminal flickered to life with Mo Ye's diminutive form, brightening back to wakefulness, reconnected and fully restored.

Baird turned and spoke directly to her. "Good to have you back, if only for a moment. I need you to give them the slipspace coordinates for Earth."

She looked back at him, trying to figure out what the hell he was up to.

"Mo Ye, these creatures want Earth's location." He winked. "Are you reconstituted enough to give them access to those, uh, *coordinates?*"

Mo Ye looked desperate, pained. "Baird—I have access to all the ship systems now, but they're being careful, they think you're trying to trick them. What we talked about in the medbay is still true. I can't override the first law in my current condition. "

He winked again, a great big shit-eating grin spreading across his face. "Security clearance: *Robot*, passcode: *Asimov*."

An Engineer chirped an explanation, calmly. Things seemed to be progressing as the human had promised. A sense of excitement, a murmur, spread though the assembled Covenant—they realized they were on the brink of a great military breakthrough.

But Mo Ye moaned as she realized what Baird was up to. "*No . . . Baird . . . wait . . .*"

Baird did not wait. Baird turned around and looked up at the Elite's puzzled face. He hauled back his right arm and with an open hand, slapped the Elite straight across the jaw with all the force his drug-fueled system could muster. The impact broke bones in his hand, and he felt a satisfying reciprocal crunch from the Elite's jaw. The massive alien staggered, sagged, and fell to one knee, stunned by both impact and surprise.

Before it could do anything else, Baird looked him in the eye, now level with his, and said, "Well, you stupid arsehole? Think you can do it right this time?"

The Elite roared in fury as he swung the energy sword in a scything arc and took Baird's head off cleanly at the shoulders. Baird's body keeled lifelessly backward. Arms spread out wide, as if falling backward into snow.

The Elite spun around and glared at the AI's shimmering form.

"Passcode *accepted*," she sneered sarcastically, her eyes lit from within by some unknowable *emotion*. "Self-destruct sequence initiated. *Four minutes and counting*."

The Elite barked at the Engineers, who were already moving, herding Grunts out the door, and translating the grave news of the impending destruction.

The Elite started a quick-march back to the Covenant boarding pods, just a few floors below, glancing at an arm-mounted chronograph. He chanced one hate-filled glance back at Mo Ye, standing, arms folded, on her plinth. She stared at him with a coldly venomous expression and spoke flatly this time.

"I'm kidding. There's no need for any countdown whatsoever."

The Elite blinked.

The Heart of Midlothian's network of shaped nuclear charges briefly flowered in the shadow of the gas giant like a beautiful little star. Then, as the chain reaction crushed the exotic fissile materials in the engine bay, it burst outward like a supernova.

The explosion washed away the Covenant Cruiser and its nameless gray escorts like a blizzard covering footsteps in the snow. And soon, all was quiet again. And cold. And peaceful. Like midnight.

DIRT

TOBIAS S. BUCKELL

The figure in the charcoal-black body armor picked his way over the top of a shattered, stubby wing, then walked past the ruined mangle of a Pelican dropship. A large BR55 battle rifle rested at the ready, cradled between his forearms.

He paused by the tip of the Pelican, which had plowed into the ground on its side, and looked through the shattered windows of the cockpit.

"Over here, Marine."

The oval black helmet swung around to look at a clump of tall orange grass behind a thick piece of granite, the morning sun glinting off the upside-down T-shaped visor.

BR55 aimed forward; the Orbital Drop Shock Trooper moved toward the sound of the voice and pushed aside the tall fronds of grass.

The 70-millimeter chain gun from the tip of the Pelican dropship had broken loose and sheared the tip of granite clean off, then cratered into the dirt a few hundred feet away.

Lying between it and the rock was a man in battle dress uniform: simple camouflage with a few chest and hip pockets. Fairly standard.

He'd obviously been thrown clear of the cockpit on impact and bounced along the dirt. Both legs looked broken, and at least one arm. Blood seeped through the BDU's legs, torso, and arms.

The man's face was cut up. Enough to be unrecognizable.

He had an M6 Magnum sidearm pointed at the ODST, which he let drop to the dirt next to him in exhaustion.

Somehow the soldier had crawled out of his body armor, which lay all around him. A closer look revealed why: charred and melted, the ODST body armor would have burned his skin.

"Good to see you." The man's voice held the strange calm of someone who knew they were beyond help, so terribly injured they were past the pain. "I wasn't sure if the call got through."

The ODST crouched beside him and opened a medical pack. Biofoam, to stop the worst of the bleeding, and polypsuedomorphine to ease the man's pain. He worked as best he could, though his hands shook a bit. This wasn't training; this was a real, dying man, and the ODST was no medic. He looked around. "My SOEIV landed nearby, and I was ordered over to see if I could help with a downed Pelican. But sir, you need more help than I can give you. We need to get you out of here. There are Covenant forces moving in on our position. We don't have much time."

"We have time, Private." The injured Marine grabbed the helmet of the crouched soldier in a sudden movement, yanking the man down close to him.

"I've been doing this so long, rook, that somewhere along the line I forgot what it was all about," the Marine on the ground hissed into the reflective visor. "But what I want you to remember about me is that it has been a long journey between where I started and where I'm sitting now. I would apologize for the things I've done, but sorry's passed me by, rook. You don't see the things I've seen and come out sorry. But sometimes, if you're not a complete monster, you come out realizing what's important."

The ODST pushed back carefully, trying to make sure not to further hurt the man on the ground. "Sir?"

He coughed, blood staining his lips and chin. "All this crap started back in the Colonial Military."

The ODST turned and looked back the way he'd come, helmet twisting, and murmured a situation report and request for backup as he reported his find.

"Of course," the injured man continued, "I can see by your insignia you're a private, just out of training, probably your first jump down to dirtside. You might not even remember the CMA . . . but back before there was the UNSC, there was the CMA . . ."

"Sir . . ."

"Shut up and listen, rookie! There's something important I have to tell you." The man's face relaxed. He was slipping back into a world of thoughts and memories. "About friends. Betrayal. Loss. If you keep your head up and do what I tell you, you might even live long enough to tell someone what happened here . . ."

I SIGNED up for the Colonial Military the hour I turned eighteen. January 3, 2524. Smartest thing I'd done up to that point. Flipped off my father, who'd stood by a giant JOTUN trundling across a flat, golden plain of wheat, and then I rode a flatbed full of corn all the way into town. Sure, the JOTUNs did the real manual labor: plowing, planting, monitoring, harvesting. But we still ended up among the crops now and again, despite the automated work the giant, one hundred-foot lawn mower-like machines did.

"It's just dirt," I'd told a friend about my decision to leave. "And I'm sick and tired of grubbing about in it. I can't believe my parents left a real world to travel all the way out here to dig dirt."

The farming life was not my destiny. I'd known that since the day I first looked up at the stars while riding on the back of one of the giant, automated JOTUNs, a long piece of straw dangling out the side of my mouth.

No. I was going to see worlds. Pack a gun. The next time I came back home to Harvest, I wanted to watch the girls bat their eyes at a man in uniform. Not a farm boy with dirt under his nails. I wanted to be a hard-as-nails, tough-ass Marine.

I walked around Utgard for the last time, strolling along the banks of the Mimir River. I lit up a Sweet William cigar by the floodlit, well-landscaped grounds of the Colonial Parliament's long walls. I blew what cash I had on me on drink after drink at bars scattered all up and down the Mimir until I could barely walk.

Then at sunrise, without a wink of sleep, I walked into a small recruiting office where a vaguely bored-looking desk sergeant looked me over and handed me some paperwork. After I painfully worked my way through it, he stood up and shook my hand. "Welcome to the Colonial Military, son," he said.

By that evening I was still not a tough-ass Marine, but a tired, hungover recruit without any hair, dressed in an ill-fitting uniform, throwing up my guts in a dirt field while a drill sergeant yelled at me. I was now Private First Class Gage Yevgenny.

I want to say I learned how to kill a man with my pinky, or how to use a sniper rifle to kill a fly on a log of shit from a thousand yards, but all I really learned was that I didn't like scrabbling around in the mud with live rounds going off over my head.

But I made it through anyway.

Unlike the UNSC, the CMA boot camp lasted just a couple weeks. Enough to teach you how to use your weapon, salute, march, and drive a Warthog before they booted you right on out of there.

It wasn't that much more advanced than spending a week shooting gophers in the fields, or so I thought at the time.

Unlike some of my fellow recruits, I at least knew how to point and shoot. As a result, I was promoted to lance corporal and got to tell a few other soldiers what to do.

That I liked.

But it still didn't prepare me for the things I was about to see.

I MET Felicia Sanderson and Eric Santiago at the Utgard spaceport. Felicia grew up right here in Utgard, on Harvest; Eric had come in from Madrigal. With our duffels at our feet, we waited as patiently as we could in line with civilian passengers. We'd developed some grudging respect for one another during boot camp, enough that they felt comfortable airing complaints about Colonial Military life around me.

"I still can't believe we're forced to fly civilian to Eridanus," Felicia groused.

"We could go AWOL," Eric said.

I shook my head. "Where? The liner doesn't stop anywhere remotely interesting between here and the Eridanus System."

"I'm just saying, it's odd." Eric picked his duffel up as the line moved.

"How could command let the UNSC grab all our ships?" Felicia had been complaining about this latest development for a solid week. Harvest was a newer colony, and most of the settlers had come from other Outer Colonies. Felicia and her family didn't hold a lot of love for the UNSC, or the Earth-controlled Colonial Administration. Her family hadn't set foot on Earth in generations.

It was, I had to admit, an indignity. Without our own ships, the Colonial Military was shuttling fighting men where it needed them by buying them coach-class tickets.

The three of us had been deployed to Eridanus, where the action was. Our angry words for the UNSC were partly attempts to hide our nervousness. Talking big to keep our minds off the big issue.

Operation TREBUCHET had been the UNSC's answer to Insurrectionists, and we'd just been folded into the far-ranging series of operations aimed to "pacify" the Outer Colonies.

I was just excited to be leaving Harvest for the first time, no matter how, or to where.

As we lifted off, I could see one of the seven space elevators that Harvest used to move its goods off the planet's surface. Just like me, each piece of cargo would be flying through slipspace to other planets, like seeds being dispersed from a pod.

It was the last time I saw Harvest with my own eyes.

I often regretted leaving my father the way I did. We never had another chance to see each other, and now that I look back on it, I know he was just a hardworking man who'd lost his wife and did his best to raise one hell of an angry kid. I doubt I could have done better.

I often wonder what the expression had been on his face when I left that day. Sadness? Relief? Or just weariness?

What would we have said, or done, had we known what would happen to Harvest?

"YOU WANTED action . . ." Felicia slapped my back. We were in an old Pelican dropship, shuddering its way down to Teribus Island on Eridanus II, and I was throwing up because of the turbulence.

Older CMA Marines just stared blankly at us. They looked bored, and Eric, sitting next to me, knew why. "No action, Felicia. You can thank the sympathizers. Someone, probably in this unit, has already called ahead. There won't be anything on the ground by the time we arrive." He said this loud enough for everyone to hear. No big secret, and none of the other soldiers bothered to contradict him.

Harvest was relatively removed from the heat of the battle over the Outer Colonies' destinies. Eridanus was at the heart of it.

Every day, more and more Insurrectionists set off bombs in major cities, targeting UNSC troops, ships, and Colonial Administration buildings.

The UNSC, in response, was cracking down harder with each passing month, seeking to instill order. And even though the Colonial Military had been increasingly sidelined to smaller and smaller operations since the discovery of elements inside our organization sympathetic to the cause, our brass never stopped pointing out that Robert Watts, the leader of the Insurrectionists in Eridanus and the mastermind behind most of the activity in the Outer Colonies, was actually a former UNSC colonel.

That was always a quick way to a bar fight with UNSC Marines.

It rankled me that the UNSC viewed the Colonial Military as suspect, but they were right to do so.

"So this is all a waste?" I asked.

Eric nodded. "So it goes."

"Not exactly helping the UNSC break their assumptions about us, are we?"

"Screw the UNSC." Eric leaned back against his restraints.

"They gutted us. They sidelined us. They give us crap; barely functioning equipment. Then they want to whine about our lack of effectiveness? At least give me a uniform that's not threadbare and then we'll talk."

A few grunts from nearby indicated that Eric's point of view was commonly held.

"Then what are we doing here?" I asked.

Felicia, sitting across from me, grinned. "You want to go back to the golden grains of Harvest, Gage?"

"Hell no." I grinned.

The thing about soldiers: We were usually there for the guy next to us. The Felicias, the Erics; boot camp, barracks; the tiny little world that was the unit and only the unit, particularly now that we were away from past friends or any family connections.

Everyone in that Pelican was family, no matter what disagreements we had. We still had to back each other up come crunch time. And we had each other's backs when we piled out of that Pelican, weapons hot.

Felicia took point, her preference, while Eric and I had her covered. The other Marines spread out around the Pelican.

The island was deserted, but whoever had been here hadn't been gone that long. The remains of a campfire still smoldered. Sand-colored camouflage tents whipped about from the Pelican's exhaust. There were dummy targets set up around the scraggly bush on the edge of the Insurrectionist camp.

"I am saddened to report," Felicia said, "that we have *just* missed yet another Insurrectionist camp." There was some bitterness in her voice. Like me, she was frustrated by what she'd seen of the CMA sympathies so far. No matter how much we were Outer Colonists, we'd still been given a job and sworn an oath to be soldiers. We wanted to do our job.

An hour later, someone from the Office of Naval Intelligence arrived in a gleaming, brand-new green Pelican. It touched down in a flurry of sand. The ONI agent quickly walked about the camp remains with a disgusted look, then left.

We had a barbecue on the edge of the water that night. The sunset wavered, and the stars started to wink into place.

"They won't be able to hold this together," Felicia said, throwing chicken bones out into the water.

"Who won't?" I asked.

"The UNSC. The Inner Colonies." Felicia pointed up at the stars over the bonfire and the dripping explosions of fat from chicken still hanging from the improvised spits. "If we spread out through all those stars, what could hold us all together? At some point, distance will have its effect, and so will time, and someone will have to break away and do something different. No matter how much force they apply, they can't stop this. Even people from within their ranks are deserting for the Outer Colonies. It's like Rome. They kept taking these barbarians and teaching them how to fight, and then they'd end up leaving and fighting the very generals who'd taught them. We're those barbarians!"

A small coal exploded in the fire, scattering tiny, incandescent particles into the dark, where they winked out and vanished.

Eric threw a chicken bone at Felicia. "You think too much, you damn Innie."

Felicia laughed. "Innie? Not me, sir, I'm no Insurrectionist. I just follow orders and go where they tell me. If I weren't here I'd be sitting in jail back in Utgard because of this girl I met in a bar one night . . ."

". . . I mean, how was I supposed to know she was the governor's daughter," Eric and I chorused, finishing Felicia's anecdote before she could even launch into it. She'd told it to us often enough.

She blushed and laughed, demanding we hand over the six-pack of beer before it got warm from sitting outside the cooler and too close to the fire.

The next day we were assigned to riot patrol in Elysium City: howling citizens throwing rocks and pavers at the Colonial Administration's offices, shaking signs about freedom and independence while we kept our shoulders up against the riot shields and kept them back.

"They're really pissed off," Felicia grunted, arms locked in mine as we shoved back against the crowd. A red-haired woman in a cocktail dress shouted obscenities at us and tried to leap over the cordon, but Eric stepped forward and shoved her back, hard enough that she fell under the mob, fortunately rescued by a pair of her friends.

It was something the police should have been doing, so it was quite clear that the UNSC didn't want to have anything to do with us and had sent us out to do scut work. Certainly they wouldn't be including us in any raids or counterinsurgency operations in the future.

None of the old hands in our barracks particularly minded.

Meanwhile, the demonstrations grew angrier and more dangerous with each passing day.

AFTER TWO months of riot patrol and guarding bases, or anything else the UNSC determined was simple enough for us to handle, we were growing bored and looking for diversions. We were far enough out of Elysium City that to hop a ride into where the parties were meant we had to get ahold of passes, or know someone with access to a Warthog.

So the three of us had made fast friends with Allison Stark, one of the last of the Pelican pilots that the UNSC had yet to steal away from us. She not only had access to transportation, but a pet NCO who'd sign off on any leave request.

Usually we didn't fraternize with the flyboys (or in this case, flygirl), but Allison could get you into the city, outdrink you, and get you back as long as you picked up the tab.

But tonight the four of us found the Warthog pool empty.

"The officers cleared us out," Felicia said.

Eric kicked a large rock. "Or they're escorting supplies."

"Where?" I asked.

"Doesn't matter. How do you think Innies get UNSC explosives or weapons? Spare parts?"

I hadn't thought much about that. "Black market?"

"Black market still has to get that stuff from somewhere," Eric said thoughtfully.

"Don't care what's going on," I said, "we're still standing here with no transport."

Allison folded her arms. "I have a solution, if the guys here have the balls . . ."

"And what is *that*?" I rose to the challenge right away, even as Felicia laughed at my predictable response.

That was a Hornet. A small, one-person cockpit with a pair of engines perched high overhead and behind it, and a chain gun on the nose. It looked, appropriately enough, like a gray metal insect.

"You want us to ride the skids?" Eric asked, stepping up onto the flanged wings under the cockpit that the Hornet sat on.

There was barely room for one person to ride the sides, it seemed to me.

"Hey, UNSC Marines ride the skids all the time," Allison said as she opened the cockpit and clambered in. "Combat insertion. Training. You name it."

That sealed it.

But who was going to pair up on a skid?

Eric, Felicia, and I squared off with a fast round of paper-rock-scissors, which Felicia and I lost.

Eric walked to the other side of the Hornet. "See you on the other side!"

I made a show of allowing Felicia to get on the skid first, and she shoved herself against the skin of the Hornet. There was a bit of a recess behind the cockpit where the skid joined it.

"It's nice that they standardized the controls," Allison said, flipping switches as the engines kicked on behind us. I watched the sequence from my position just behind her, until it suddenly dawned on me what she meant.

"Wait," I protested. "You haven't flown one of these?"

"It's straightforward. You got your stick, your collective throttle, yadda yadda. We've been doing this ever since we invented VTOLs." The Hornet jerked upward, and I crouched, wondering if I should jump now.

But I didn't, and I had to let go of the lip as Allison yanked the glass down and sealed the cockpit shut.

"You getting ideas there?" Felicia asked as I shoved up against her, grabbing for handholds on the Hornet.

"You wish."

She laughed, then swore as the Hornet tilted.

I thought I could hear Eric whooping from the other side as the Hornet climbed up over the trees and headed toward the bright lights of Elysium City.

The target was a flip music club on the outskirts. Allison flew in low over a residential area, then flared out over the parking lot, dropping us to the ground with a thump.

Felicia and I tumbled off the skid, our knees somewhat shaky as we gratefully staggered on solid ground.

Eric also stumbled around the Hornet, laughing wildly. "I hope we're stuck on idiot duty by the UNSC forever!"

"Come on." We offered Allison a hand out of the cockpit.

We bounced inside to the raucous beat of flip music. Allison struck out with me and Felicia for the bar.

"Hey, how are you going to account for taking the Hornet?" Felicia asked as we waited for drinks.

"Training," Allison shouted over the music. "NCO'll sign me off."

I laughed. "Does he even know it's a lost cause?"

Allison grabbed her drink. "Sweetie, if you don't tell him I'm not into men, I certainly won't, and this little arrangement," she waved her glass at the club and pulsating lights and dancing crowd, "this can keep going."

She danced her way off into the crowd as I paid. "Keep the tab open, I'm covering whatever she drinks," I told the bartender.

"You're not going after her?" I asked Felicia, who'd dragged Allison into our group.

"She's not my type." Felicia grinned. "Now find me a dirt-pounding Marine gal, and we'll talk."

"I don't have time to be your wingman," I grunted.

Felicia shook her head. "You'd make a crap one. All the gals we meet think you're a Harvest hick."

"What, and you aren't?" I was a little bit annoyed by the barb.

"I'm an Utgard girl, city born and bred. It's in the blood. The other city girls can sniff it. Plus, you have no sense of style."

"Oh, screw you! Now you're just trying to piss me off."

"Yeah, guilty. I wouldn't do it if you weren't so damn touchy about it." Felicia pressed her drink in my hand. "Hey. Keep an eye on this, I need to visit the girls' room."

I followed her part of the way to stand in the hallway with a drink in each hand as hordes of people shoved past me.

When Felicia came back out I handed her her drink, and we turned back to leave the hallway.

That's when the Insurrectionist bomb exploded. A concussive wave of heat, light, and pressure threw me back down the hallway.

For a moment, I lay on the carpet, staring blurrily at the ceiling, and then a second explosion brought the entire building down on top of us, trapping me in the debris.

ODSTS DUG us out.

Most of the civilians out dancing, however, had died. Allison was found with a piece of rebar through her skull. Eric was in a coma and getting ferried out to Reach for better medical care.

Felicia and I both had been packed with biofoam, and then moved to a field hospital set up on the edge of the debris.

We were too doped up on painkillers to do much more than lie in bed for the first half day while medics kept an eye on us. I had a concussion, broken ribs, burns, a skull fracture, and ached in places I didn't know I had.

Felicia reported, from two beds over, the same.

"Standing in that hallway saved your lives," an ODST medic said. "You're damn lucky."

I didn't feel lucky.

Particularly when the ONI agents showed up.

They questioned us about what we were doing at the club: how we got there, whether we had contacts with Insurrectionists.

There were a lot of questions about where our allegiances lay. Many of them asked over and over again.

In the end, they eventually let us be, but not before telling us that the club had been singled out because it was a favored spot for CMA Marines during weekend leave.

I had a lot of time to think, lying there on the bed healing.

"They're saying they're going to be shutting down the CMA's involvement with TREBUCHET," I told Felicia, sitting on the edge of her bed once I'd healed enough to walk. "There are rumors that the CMA will be shut down completely. Or at least that the UNSC is fighting to get the CMA disbanded."

"No surprise."

"And then what comes next?" I asked. "Even if it lives, the CMA is a dead end. What kind of career will I have if I stay with them? I think I'm going to leave for the UNSC."

"Career? Why the hell would you want a career?" Felicia snorted. "You'll never see Harvest again if you switch to the UNSC. No telling where they'd send you. You have a chance to go home now."

"I could care less about ever seeing Harvest again," I said.

"It's where you came from. Where your dad has land."

"It's just dirt, Felicia. Dirt. It doesn't mean anything. Why the hell do you care? Are you going back to Utgard?"

"Yes." She surprised me there. I hadn't known that. I'd thought her just as interested as me in wanting to get away. "I didn't choose to enlist, remember."

"I'd always thought your story about the governor's daughter was just that . . . a story. Did you really have to join to skip jail in Harvest?"

"No. No, that was bullshit. My dad forced me to join," she said. "After I stole an MLX and went out joyriding. After the governor incident. Told me it was time to grow up."

"So you'd go back to Utgard?"

"In a moment, if they discharged me. They might even rotate us back, if they're no longer going to use us here." She pulled her knees up under her chin. "What's the bug up your ass about leaving the CMA?"

I rubbed my forehead. "I have bits of human bone embedded in me, from whoever was wearing that bomb before they triggered it. Permanently now. And that ONI guy who talked to us, he said the explosives were CMA-issued. Maybe even from our own base. That's not a civil disagreement, it's madness."

"The UNSC could stop it in a moment by leaving," Felicia said. "Is it really your problem?"

"Maybe. Maybe not. But maybe the rebels get even worse. Kill more civilians. Then who are they really doing this for? The civilians they're getting killed?"

"Or maybe the UNSC keeps overreacting and causing the Outer Colonies to not want any part of all this," Felicia said gently. "A million casualties now, caught in the crossfire, since TREBUCHET started. No one's going to ignore that. The civilians will keep cheering the rebels on."

"I know. And maybe we're always destined to be splintering and fighting, without some greater cause. But I'm applying to the ODSTs."

"You've got to be kidding? Are you suicidal now?"

"I'm joining as soon as I'm cleared."

Felicia sighed. "Then I'm coming, too. We'll sign up together."

"Why the hell would you want to do that?"

"We've had each other's backs for months now. Eric's in a

coma. Allison's dead. You want me to rotate back to Harvest and sit on my hands alone? Screw that. You're going to need someone to cover your ass; you're going to be fresh meat to all those tough-assed ODSTs out there."

"Seriously, Felicia . . ." I turned to look at her.

"Shut up about it already, Gage. You're the closest thing I have to a brother. You're a poor excuse for one, but I consider you one nonetheless. Deal with it."

"I want to go after the bastards that did this to us."

"I know. You're a sentimental, honorable dirt farmer who needs a hell of a lot more cynicism in your life. Of course you want to go after them."

"Harvest will always be there when we're done," I said.

ORDERS ARRIVED before we were discharged, proving my instincts correct. We were to be folded into the UNSC or offered an honorable discharge and a ticket back to our home world of choice.

I tried one last time to convince Felicia out of applying to the ODST, but she told me to shove it and shut up.

The recruiter's office was in chaos when we showed up with our papers. Several older sergeants were huddled around screens and pumping fists.

"What's going on?" Felicia asked.

"We got that bastard, Watts!" they said.

"*Robert* Watts?" I was shocked. Watts had led the Insurrectionists all throughout the Outer Colonies from deep in the asteroid belts of this system for so long, it sounded improbable. "Who got him? ODSTs?"

"No clue. But the ONI propaganda machine is kicking into

overdrive declaring him caught." The sergeant collected himself and grabbed our papers. "It's a good day to be a Marine! Bad day to be an Innie."

With Watts captured, I wondered how strong the rebel movements would remain.

"Raw meat for the ODST grinder, huh?" the grizzled sergeant grunted. "If you thought Colonial boot camp was tough, you're about to get dismantled. Then we'll see if you can manage to put yourselves back together."

I laughed, but the ODST recruiters didn't laugh back. They were dead serious. They knew what was around the corner for the two of us, and the smiles on their lips were like the smiles of wolves.

ODST BOOT camp was where I learned how to kill someone with my pinky.

Among other things.

But first they stripped us of our rank.

"Think coming in from the CMA means jack to us?" an officer commented when I presented the fact. "You'll have to actually earn your rank here."

Then they started running us. I'd kept track of Felicia up to that point; we'd even had a chance to compare notes at mess, eating together.

But there was quickly little time for that; too exhausted, too busy trying to survive.

For three weeks I ran, did push-ups, and blitzed through obstacle courses as fast as I could. They took us through slush, artificial snow, and live gunfire-simulated battle. Got on our bellies and crawled through miles of barbed wire, rubble, and destroyed buildings as they fired rounds at us just inches over our heads.

That was just to get us into shape.

On the first day of squad tactics, they dressed all fifty of us still remaining up in full ODST training gear and dropped us off at the base of a mountain.

"Get to the top and you can eat and rest back in your barracks tonight," our drill sergeant, O'Reilly, said with an all-too-familiar grin.

Our guns were loaded with TTR rounds. They were fake bullets with paint inside that contained particles that reacted with nanopolymers in your gear. Your clothes (or in the case of us training ODSTs, our signature black body armor) stiffened to immobility when shot with a TTR round, and then an anesthetic in the paint left the part of your body it hit paralyzed.

Day two of training, O'Reilly had walked up and down the line with a TTR pistol, shooting us in the leg and then shouting "Run! Run! Run!" as we limped off in confusion. Anyone not quick enough was shot in the other leg and told "Crawl, soldier!"

Once I'd found myself completely paralyzed while a trainer squatted overhead and screamed into my face that I was a worthless excuse for a soldier, and a "fine example of the best the CMA had to offer."

One day, on the mountain, I had an MA5B assault rifle with sixty TTR rounds loaded.

The fifty of us waited for the Pelicans that had dropped us off to thunder away, and as quiet descended, we looked nervously at each other.

"What do you think's in there?" someone asked, looking at the forest that covered the low flanks of the mountainside.

"I'm guessing trainers with their own guns who're—" I didn't get to finish. The person next to me was hit in the chest. The TTR round splashed red, and he went down stiffly, his body armor locked up as he toppled to the ground.

"Sniper!"

The forty-nine of us remaining scrambled for cover in confusion, and by the time I'd found a boulder to shove my back against, I could see eight more sets of black ODST body armor stiffened up, splotched with red, and their occupants dropping to the ground.

A nervous Marine slammed into the boulder next to me. He caught his breath, then popped up to scan the area. The loud impact of a TTR round struck his exposed helmet, and he slumped down over me with a grunt. "Dammit."

In just minutes, half of us had been struck by fire from somewhere high inside the forest. I could hear laughter.

I shoved the "dead" Marine off me. If we remained here, we'd all be done in another minute, and no one would get to the top. "There are only a handful of them," I shouted. "We have to rush them, some will get hit; the rest will get into the trees. Then we'll have a chance."

And in the far distance, I heard Felicia shout back, "He's right. On three!"

"One, two, three!" I burst out from behind cover with the other twenty-four and rushed for the tree line.

I got within five feet of the tree line before a TTR round hit me in the stomach and I sprawled into the bushes, frozen in place.

Up the hill, in the trees, the battle raged on. I heard Felicia's voice at least once more, giving orders, then swearing.

After half an hour a trainer walked out from the shadows of the forest and looked down at me. "That was the first useful thing you've done in three weeks, maggot," he shouted, and then left me lying there.

When the armor freed itself up hours later, I milled about with my fellow soldiers. All fifty of us, scattered around the base of the mountain, spent a chilly night around hand-built fires, hungry, until we were picked up the next morning.

We were then assembled into fireteams after and given tactical training. Felicia led our small team: Mason, gangly and blond, hailed from Reach. Kiko from Eridanus II. We fell into a tight team that managed to hold its own.

The next time on the mountain, Kiko and Mason laid down suppressing fire into the forest that Felicia and I dashed for. Once behind cover there we laid a stream of TTR rounds ahead so that Kiko and Mason could follow.

Leapfrogging and keeping an arc ahead of us constantly under fire, we were able to get halfway up the mountain before a trainer moved around behind us and got Kiko.

We stalled out then, crouched in the brush with our backs to each other for a full field of range until a TTR grenade bounced into our midst and scattered us.

Another hungry, cold night on the mountain.

Then they taught us squad tactics, pairing us up with another fireteam.

With each fireteam leapfrogging the other, we got most of the way up the mountain. But leaving the forest as it petered out high in the mountain's crag, we fell under ambush by snipers dug in at the top.

We lost most of the other fireteam, who'd been on point, to TTR fire. Felicia, Kiko, Mason, and I had hit the snow and mud and opened fire back. We were the only team that had gotten that far.

"Any ideas?" Felicia asked. With enemy behind us in the woods, and in front of us buried in, and most of our ammo gone, we had seconds to make a decision.

"We'll never be able to charge them. We need sniper rifles," I said.

"Trainers have those."

"Exactly. And they're coming for us." I pointed back down the slope.

We backed down the muddy snow into the tree line. "Play dead," Kiko whispered. "Get down in the mud right on the edge of the tree line with all the others who got hit."

It would only ever work once, but we sprawled ourselves stiffly out in the mud.

As our pursuers broke cautiously out into the open we ambushed them. I took special glee in hitting O'Reilly almost point-blank in the chest as he approached me.

We relieved them of their sniper rifles.

Mason got hit in the leg while we moved about, trying to get a bead on the trainers at the top, but Kiko and Felicia got off two good shots.

I ran ahead and threw TTR grenades into the areas from which we'd been fired on, flushing out the instructors, and Kilo and Felicia got two of the three.

The last trainer shot me in the arm, a stunning shot done on the run with his sniper rifle, but I gunned him down with the MA5B before he could try it again.

And just like that, we'd taken the top of the mountain.

"Nice." Felicia slapped my shoulder. We'd all been hit by TTR rounds, but we limped our way to the very top and shouted loud enough to hear our echoes return from the mountain over; our hot, exhausted breath steaming from our mouths into the cold air.

A Pelican appeared, flaring out to land in the clearing at the top of the mountain. Snow swirled out from under the backwash of its engines, and a craggy-faced gunnery sergeant stepped out, as well as a number of corporals.

He didn't even look at us. "Get everyone up, now!" he ordered the corporals.

They were off, tapping armor with electronic wands to unfreeze it.

Something wasn't right. There was a strangeness to the hurry they did it with. And what the hell was a gunnery sergeant doing talking to us in the middle of a training session?

We all gathered around the gunny, lining up as we'd been trained. He nodded. "Is this everyone?"

A quick head count confirmed that this was everyone.

"Good. At ease. You've all been out here in the wilderness training hard, but I've been sent to let you know your training is going to be accelerated."

The instructors frowned, and we all shifted.

"Much of this information has been classified, and between the ONI and the Navy types, this is what we can tell you: We have made first contact with an intelligent alien civilization."

A gasp rose at hearing those words. Some of us reflexively looked up into the sky. First contact!

The gunnery sergeant continued, cool as ice. "We know that standard protocols were followed. And that things didn't go well. Our ships were attacked by alien beings referred to as the Covenant. Before destroying our ships they claimed our destruction was the will of their gods, and that they were the instrument. It seems to be an act of war. As of today the UNSC is on full alert. The Colonial Military has been officially disbanded, all remaining units are officially being pulled in and reassigned and retrained. And we're ramping up training here, because we have a feeling we're going to need all the recruits we can get.

"These aliens are for real. They've already taken, or possibly destroyed, one Outer Colony. Admiral Preston Cole is being tasked with creating a force to get it back."

We were stunned.

Private Rodriquez from Madrigal was the one who asked, "What colony fell to them, sir?"

"Harvest," the gunnery sergeant said, and my knees buckled.

Someone grabbed my shoulder. I staggered around and found Felicia sitting in the mud. She looked up at me, tears in her eyes. "Dirt?" she asked. "Do you still think that now?"

I didn't have anything to say back. I stood in front of her, struck mute.

Harvest was gone.

I'd tried to find the last nice thing I said to my dad before I'd left; the last time we laughed, smiled even? I couldn't find one.

I'd always figured he'd keep on farming. That maybe I'd go back, one day, when I'd traveled worlds and seen so much, and maybe talk to him again. Maybe.

But there were no maybes now. He was gone now.

Harvest was gone.

Felicia grabbed a fistful of mud and leaped up at me. "Dirt! I have your dirt, you son of a bitch!"

She hit me, mud from her clenched first spattering my face, but I didn't feel it. I felt like a part of my soul had been ripped away, and even after she was pulled off me, I just stood there, numb.

Dirt.

Just dirt.

FOR THE rest of training they moved Felicia to another fireteam. Our new team leader, Rahud, took his annoyance about the swap out on me. He was an experienced UNSC veteran who'd joined the ODSTs after years of service.

He didn't take too kindly to the fact that just because I'd been given rank in the old Colonial Military, it had given me the ability to apply to the ODST program. He certainly didn't like the fact that some falling out between two backwater planet recruits like Felicia and me had caused him to get moved away from the team he'd trained with.

Any screwup, the slightest mistake, and he was in my face, calling me a detriment to the team and a liability.

But it didn't faze me. My bonds with Kiko and Mason were tight, and the three of us held our own.

Every day, as the months of training passed, there was some new rumor floating around about the aliens. Ships they'd attacked. Their invincibility.

A lot of it was bull. Back then we didn't know anything.

We certainly didn't realize what we were up against. Kiko and Mason would joke about getting out there to kick alien ass, and with a few beers in me, I'd join them.

Certainly after ODST training, we figured a bunch of religious fanatic aliens would be no match for the atmosphere-jumping, hard-as-nails brutality that a raw ODST-trained human could bring to the table.

But when the first leaked photos of the Outer Colonies attacks came out, I wondered if we might be wrong. Some of them had been turned into glass balls by Covenant energy weapons.

What the hell were *we* going to be able to do against that kind of firepower?

YOU KNOW that sound inside a single-occupant exoatmospheric insertion vehicle? That combination of a howling wind, a dull roar, and the crackle and creak of the SOEIV's skin flexing and burning. No matter how many times I jumped, hearing it always scared the crap out of me.

Feet First into Hell. That was the ODST motto. Feet first with a two-thousand-degree fireball burning around the pod as it flames its way down through the atmosphere.

It's a hot ride.

A bumpy ride.

And not everyone survives it.

My first combat SOEIV insertion had me coming in hot with a hundred other ODSTs over the main continent of Hat Yai, three years after I finished training. We'd been mainly stuck in naval battles, waiting in our bays, just itching for a chance to be thrown against this new enemy. Everyone was pumped about Admiral Cole's triumphant recapture of Harvest earlier that year.

What isn't, perhaps, often recounted, but is a fact that quickly became well-known amongst the rank and file, was that Cole lost three ships for every one Covenant ship destroyed.

It was a Pyrrhic victory that left Cole's fleet severely damaged.

Now Cole had been jumping his fleet around from engagement to engagement throughout the Outer Colonies, wherever the Covenant showed up.

So far, there'd been no repeat of the retaking of Harvest. Outer Colonies had been glassed or taken. World by world, we were falling back.

Covenant ships in low orbit picked off ten of us, and when landing ate another pair of SOEIVs that failed and cratered into the lush rain forest of our landing zone.

It took half an hour for Rahud to get us grouped up; our pods had dodged enough fire that we'd gotten fairly well separated.

"Where's the rest of the squad?" Mason asked.

Rahud shrugged. "I can't raise them. Assume the worst."

We trudged through thick mud and rain forest, vines and creepers holding us back as we got bogged down farther and farther in.

"There's no way a Pelican's coming in through that kind of foliage," Kiko commented. "How do we get out?"

Rahud ignored us. "Covenant forces established a base of some sort up ahead. We're all converging on it." This is why we'd been sent down: an exploratory and reconnoitering force.

Mason leaned in. "That's if our ship can even get back to drop in recovery vehicles."

The destroyer *Clearidas* had dropped us in, ducking and weaving in between Covenant forces in low orbit, bouncing itself off the upper atmosphere as it vomited its cargo of a hundred SOEIVs.

As I ran through tropical jungle, sweating under my black ODST armor, I wondered if there were enough ships high overhead to hold off the Covenant.

"Hold," Rahud hissed. We were getting close.

Other ODSTs materialized out of the forest. Hand signals were exchanged, and information rippled throughout the forest.

Ten ODST squads grouped up and began to ooze through the brush, weapons at the ready.

Rahud led us carefully down the lip of a dirt road that had been hastily carved into what was fast becoming rock.

We paused at the lip of a giant sinkhole.

"Holy . . . ," someone began.

In just days the aliens had excavated a massive pit that bored deep into the ground. Bluish-gray metal spars soared up from the bottom into the air from what looked like a freakish cross between a city and a hive at the bottom, including bubblelike structures that studded the sidewalls of the giant pit.

"They're building a small city down there," Mason said. "Now that they've cleaned out the colonists."

"They're Grunts," a private suggested. "Those big buildings are methane tanks."

"Methane?" someone else asked.

"Didn't you listen to the damn briefings . . ."

"Movement!" Kiko pointed, and Rahud turned.

I saw my first Covenant aliens standing on the other side of the lip: Ten Grunts and a pair of Jackals were staring right back at us.

The Jackals stood tall, with weird back-jointed legs, and had Mohawk-like feathers and birdlike faces.

The dwarfish Grunts—with their doglike faces behind breathing equipment, squat legs, and weird triangular methane tanks—started shooting at us.

Balls of plasma energy sizzled and spat as they hit the trees behind us.

As the closest team, we fanned out, falling into our usual routines. Kiko and Mason laid down cover fire, and Rahud and I skirted the lip clockwise toward the aliens.

ODST snipers hit the Grunts, splashes of blue blood blossoming in the air as the aliens dropped to the ground. The Jackals held up energy shields attached to their forearms to ward off the gunfire, and returned it tenfold.

We sprinted around the rim. "Their feet!" Rahud shouted.

The shields didn't cover their feet. I aimed low, chewing up mud and vines, walking the shots along until I hit my first Jackal.

It screeched and pitched forward, shield bobbling, and Rahud shot it in the head. Purple blood oozed down the side of the corpse.

The other Jackal turned to face us, opening itself up for a sniper shot by an ODST. It grabbed its chest, moaning, and then stumbled off the edge of the lip and fell down. It bounced off one of the struts, then continued all the way down to the ground of the pit below.

I pushed the dead Jackal's body with a boot. Here was the enemy. Flesh and blood. Killable.

Now that we had the lip surrounded a command hierarchy had been established. Major Sedavian had landed at the very rear of the group, and had finally caught up to us.

"Figure we're going down there?" Mason asked, peering over the edge. We could see more Covenant at the bottom, with hundreds of Grunts and a handful of Jackals that seemed to be overseeing them. They were mustering near elevators, getting ready to come up to join the fight. An energy bolt sizzled and blew up a piece of rock near my face, and I ducked back to the safety of cover.

"Negative," Rahud said, coming up from behind us suddenly. "Covenant Cruisers just arrived. We're outgunned. We're getting out of here and dropping a Shiva into this mess."

That was it. The fight was over, we'd already lost.

I could sense the frustration in the air as word spread. But orders were orders.

The Pelicans could barely land on the lip, and the Covenant at the bottom of the pit opened antiaircraft fire, but we all bugged out easily enough.

As we headed for orbit, the Shiva nuclear warheads left on the lip detonated.

Once we were aboard, the *Clearidas* entered slipspace, leaving the system.

Another retreat.

THAT WAS the pattern for the next few years. The Covenant ate us up, system by system, with very few victories on our side.

Most of the worlds I'd come to know well were all destroyed. No one cared about Insurrectionists, Outer Colonies versus the UNSC, or the Colonial Military ten years after Harvest fell.

There was only humanity versus the Covenant.

I saw more than my fair share of dead aliens and dead comrades.

Eventually I stopped making friends.

Mason died in my arms on Asmara after one of the snake-headed Covenant Elites speared him along with ten other ODSTs with his energy sword before I got off a near point-blank shot with a missile launcher.

I found Mason lying among the debris; I could smell his seared flesh.

He looked up at me with glassy eyes and asked for his mother, then coughed up blood and just . . . stopped being.

Kiko was stabbed in the face by the apelike Brutes on another world, the name of which I've since forgotten. Large, muscular, hairy aliens, they could snap a neck with their bare hands. Rahud died from energy artillery.

I was promoted to team leader, then a squad leader. I had long since stopped learning names; I didn't want to form any attachments.

Maybe that's why I never rose above squad leader.

I had become a shadow of myself. A robot. Hitting my mark

and killing the enemy, and waiting for the one day a stray flash of energy would kill me.

I was waiting for the day I could be buried. In the dirt.

The steady stream of defeats led to the creation of the Cole Protocol. No ship was to return directly to any of our worlds, particularly Earth, but instead execute random jumps in slipspace to throw off any potential Covenant shadowers.

"Where was *that* order for all the glassed Outer Colonies!" I'd shouted, standing up in the middle of a mess hall.

I remember once I woke from the bitter cold of cryogenic storage, staggering around and vomiting suspension fluid, and realized something was really, really wrong. This wasn't the usual slow routine of getting unfrozen and waking up fully as we were briefed for our next assignment. This time emergency lighting kept everything shadowy in the dim red. Everyone on deck hurried around nervously, and I could hear the unmistakable sound of the ship's MAC gun firing.

"We've been ambushed by a Covenant cruiser. You've all been flash unfrozen," the officer on deck said. "Just in case."

Keeping us on ice let us all go through the long slipspace routes without eating up supplies and sucking down oxygen. Or getting bored out of our minds.

Flash unfreezing was dangerous, and only for emergencies. I think the ship's captain was worried about being boarded. Either way, someone up the chain had given the order for the risky decanting, maybe out of panic. A third of the unfrozen ODSTs on deck died.

Clearidas managed to escape. But my men didn't.

A waste.

AFTER ALL these years of combat, I slowly began to feel myself peeling apart. But I had no home, nowhere I really wanted to be, no one to see.

So I soldiered on, battle after battle.

I almost saw my end in a hastily dug out trench on Skopje, an Inner Colony world. Unlike most of the wilder Outer Colonies, this world had highly built up urban areas, roads, and railways. It was an entire civilization sprawled across its island continents.

From the trench, if I turned to look behind me, I could see a skyline glinting and blazing in the sun over a red marbled museum. But back in front: mud.

We were sent in to protect the headquarters of a shipbuilding corporation during the evacuation of their shipyards. The machines, tools, and personnel that could be saved would be relocated to Reach, to continue building parts for the war effort.

Our headquarters were the halls of a nearby city museum, the grounds of which served as our landing zone and held all the quickly placed antiaircraft batteries.

"This is the fallback point, there is nowhere else to go," we were told. "So you hold the perimeter *at all costs*."

Covenant air support dared not attack us directly, not for several blocks. So they threw Grunts at us. Thousands of them in brutal house-to-house warfare, their numbers overwhelming our loose perimeter. We fell back and regrouped, drawing them in until we were foxholed on the edges of the vast museum gardens. We let the Grunts charge us across the muddy field.

They'd pushed us back, but we still simply thought of them as cannon fodder, waiting until they got close enough to hit their methane tanks and watch them explode. Now that we had our open ground and dug in positions, we slaughtered them.

But they kept coming. And after waves of screaming Grunts

came the races higher up in the Covenant food chain: Jackal snipers, Brutes rushing the line, and then finally Elites, flashing their energy swords as they got in close enough to the melee.

The trenches got cut off, communication lost, and I found myself crouched in between two walls of mud with another ODST, waiting for the Covenant to leap in with us.

This would be it. We'd go down fighting in the mud, I thought.

But instead, in an explosion of mud, a two-ton powered suit of gray-green armor landed between us. "Follow me!" the powerful baritone voice behind the gold visor ordered.

Then it leaped over the edge into the fray, plasma discharges slapping the powered armor.

We followed.

The armored human was like a tank, clearing the way for us. It shrugged off Grunts like they were annoying mosquitoes, tackled Brutes face on, and was an equal match for any Elite.

We were led to a giant castle, like something out of a picture book, with large antiaircraft guns mounted along the walls and AIE-486H heavy machine guns on the parapets pointed down.

Inside we were left by the giant armored man.

"What the hell was that?" I asked the Marine in the courtyard.

"Special ONI project. They call them Spartans. Engineered to be the best, armored with the best. Haven't you heard the ONI announcements? They'll be ending the war with these sons of bitches running through the Covenant soon enough!"

The ODSTs weren't the cutting-edge hard-asses anymore.

I'd just seen the future of warfare. I wasn't in it.

I didn't have time to dwell on this, because suddenly an all-too-familiar voice said, "Gage? Gage Yevgenny? Is that really you?"

And I turned to see Felicia standing with a BR55 slung under one arm and a canteen in the other.

"Felicia?" There were wrinkles in her tanned, leathery face. But all these years would do that. We'd just been kids the last time we saw each other, really.

She ran over and hugged me, a strong clench, and then she shoved me back. "I can't frigging believe you're alive!"

I was just as stunned. "What are you doing here?"

"Holed up, same as you. The castle was my call. Some CEO had it made using actual quarried rock from outside the city. Covenant low-level energy weapons don't vaporize the rock; they just melt it a bit more, making it even stronger. We're waiting for some Pelicans to get us the hell out now that they took the museum off your grubby hands."

She had a jagged scar across her cheek, and a nasty burn on the back of her neck from a near miss. But I caught a glimpse of her bars: She'd risen up to colonel.

We compared notes and found that we'd been in a couple of the same theaters together, separated only by thirty or so miles.

"I can get you aboard my detail, if you want," she said. "And I promise I won't flake out on you again."

"Crap, Felicia, that was a long, long time ago. A lot's happened since then."

"I know. You actually saved my life, you know."

"How's that?"

"I would have gone back. I would have been sitting on Harvest in my lame-ass Colonial uniform when those goddamn aliens dropped the hammer the second time around."

I didn't say anything to that. I didn't want to think about Harvest.

"There were some survivors from the first attack," Felicia said. "Did you ever look to see . . ."

"My father wasn't on the rolls, no."

Felicia nodded. "Mine, either." Then she leaned in. "Look, I'll get you a transfer to the *Chares,* the cruiser I'm aboard. And once up there, there's someone you need to meet."

I was intrigued. I hadn't felt this energized in years, so busy with keeping my head down and focusing on one task at a time. And now here was Felicia, with her energy and friendship.

You know, to tell you the truth, I was scared. Did I dare reach out to her again?

Or would she be dead soon enough, ripping another part of me away with her?

Because how much of that can a person ever truly handle?

I wasn't sure.

"If we get back to orbit," Felicia said, "I have a surprise for you."

An explosion shattered molten rock up in the air, which drizzled back down and reformed. Eventually this castle was going to look like a version of itself that had been placed inside an oven, and half metal.

"If we get back up!" she said, slapping my shoulder. "Get more ammo and get up on the walls. Pelicans should be down here soon."

Off in the distance a sharklike Covenant Cruiser began to descend from the clouds. From its belly, fierce energy descended upon the land, glassing it into oblivion.

So we hightailed it out of there.

I'd stopped expecting to live, right before I saw her again. After that, I suddenly felt real again. A human being again, with a past, and a life.

ABOARD THE *Chares* the wounded and battered Marines and ODSTs tended their injuries as we retreated into slipspace. I couldn't put a figure to the numbers who would have died down there on that planet, but given the cities I saw in the distance, I'd imagine millions.

Despite the glum atmosphere, Felicia hunted me down with an air of excitement.

"Come on," she said. She led me down through several bays until we came to a smaller bay crammed with Pelicans.

We rounded a corner, and sitting on a chair with a small cooler was Eric.

Freaking Eric was alive.

He stood up and grabbed my hand. "Gage . . ."

"When?" I could barely find the words. "How?"

Felicia looked over at us. "Bastard woke up after five years in a coma and joined the Navy. Became a right flyboy." She grabbed a beer and studied it. "Rank has its privileges, and Eric has his ways."

It was almost too much.

I wanted to know everything that had happened. Twenty-two years, more or less.

Twenty-two years, and we were strangers to each other.

And yet we fell right back into the same friendships, like chatting in the back of the empty Pelican, our voices echoing in the chamber of the launch bay.

Felicia was a colonel, Eric flying his way in and out of hell. And I was not much more than a grunt that had been more of a zombie for the last couple decades than anything else.

I may have lost the Outer Colonies, but I suddenly had my friends again.

WHEN THEY told me about the plan, I remember that we were crowded in the back of Eric's Pelican getting drunk after a particularly messy ground operation. As Eric summed it up: people had died, Covenant had been killed, and we'd once again had to fall back.

"But at least it's happening less frequently," I said. "With the Cole Protocol they're only finding our worlds when they stumble over them."

Maybe this would give humanity time to build more ships, time to ramp up for a big fight. Time, I thought, to create more super-soldier Spartans.

"Spartans," Eric spat. "They're not even human. Freaks are what they are."

It was not an uncommon ODST outlook: a suspicion of the faceless, armored men who'd started to show up on the battlefield.

I didn't argue with him.

"Besides," Felicia said, "it took them a long time to enact the Protocol. Almost like they wanted the Outer Colonies out of the picture."

"That's . . ." Ludicrous, I started to say. But I halted, remembering my own rage when it was first announced. ". . . hard to believe. But it still looks bad. And the result is . . . what it is."

"We put in our years, and we've been used up. We're getting tired. And there's nowhere to go home to," Felicia said.

"And because we're Colonial Military transfers, our pensions are still technically CMA, not UNSC. Since the CMA doesn't exist anymore, the pension funds were raided to build destroyers. No one is sure if the politicians will be able to find anything when we all start coming out of the system. If we live that long."

I felt the weariness in their voices. It was there in mine, too. Deep into my bones. I'd used up almost two-thirds of my life fighting.

And all I'd seen were losses.

Despite ONI propaganda films, and shore leave, and binges, I still felt that emptiness.

I realized Felicia and Eric were staring at me. Studying me. Feeling me out.

"We're going on some sort of snatch-and-run operation," Felicia said. "I just got word from the brass. We've found something the Covenant is squatting on."

"What is it?"

"Some sort of artifact in the ground. Who the hell cares? What in the past is going to save us now? What's important is that this is going to be our last mission," Felicia said. "We've given our service. We've fought hard. The only thing stopping the Covenant is our being able to keep the location of Earth secret. The UNSC's just using us up on the ground like throwaway pawns."

"All that matters to the UNSC is Reach and Earth anyway," Eric said. He sounded so bitter. I'd gotten the sense that the explosion had changed him even more, despite his role in the UNSC; it was something he'd taken out of necessity, not human patriotism.

Felicia continued. "The artifact the aliens have dug up this time is near a small city, which I've done some research on.

"There's a major bank in the center, with vaults. They've got gold and platinum ingots buried down there, and the Covenant invasion happened quickly enough that it's all sitting down there. Right now."

I looked back and forth. "What, you want to steal it?"

"Steal it?" Eric spat the words. "It doesn't exist anymore, Gage. It's about to be glassed. The UNSC wants us to snatch the alien artifact or destroy it. No one gives a crap about the gold."

"We could retire," Felicia said. "Go back to Earth, and lay back comfortably. Something the UNSC could never offer us."

I took a deep breath and looked down at the scuffed floor of the Pelican.

Eric chimed in. "We're still going to attack the Covenant and bring back the artifact. We'll be following orders. But we'll be coming down with one extra Pelican. We blow the vaults, load the gold into ammunition chests, load the Pelican, and come back to the ship."

"And then what?" I asked.

"Then . . . anything you want," Felicia said leaning closer, more aware of the scar on her face and the intensity in her eyes than ever. "I know a transport headed back to Earth. I figure I might as well see the mother planet before I die. Where you guys go, that's up to you, but I was hoping we could all go together. One last hurrah."

One last hurrah.

"We've put in our years, Gage. How much longer before it's some random Jackal sniper that takes us down? We've been putting our damn lives on the line since we were just kids. Kids. It's time to grow up. When was the last time you talked to a civilian?"

Too long, I thought. Too long. "How many more are involved?"

"With you, we can do this," Eric said. "Felicia can assemble them all into a team for the snatch-and-run; brass trusts her word. They're all old CMA vets. We've been planning this for a long time."

"We've been eyeing stuff like this on every op. Almost pulled the trigger on the mission we met you on," Felicia said. "But there was too much going on and the bank was too far away from the action."

"But now that we found you, it's like it was meant to be," Eric said, looking into my eyes. "This is the one. It's perfect."

Under the haze of alcohol, the team back together again, I felt like I'd refound my family.

It was us against everyone.

I was scared, but I didn't want to let them down. I'd fought beside them. Hell, I'd been created beside them. We were a team. And I wasn't going to let them down. No matter what misgivings I had about this crazy scheme.

We had nothing left to lose.

War had stripped us of many things; made us hard, unflinching, dangerous. But it had forced us into a close bond at the beginning, and reinforced it when we'd found each other again after all these years.

I didn't want to lose them again.

WE DIDN'T come in by SOEIVs for this mission, but by Pelicans. They came out of orbit far from Covenant detection and then flew for hours until we reached the edge of our new combat zone.

The small city was in the center of a horseshoe-shaped range of small mountains. Its center plaza sat on top of where four mountain streams joined up to become the head of a strong river that trickled out of the valley.

Our Pelicans came in low through a valley, just barely missing a rock ravine on either side as they flew up, over, and then back down, just feet over the ground. Risky, but again, the Covenant were none the wiser.

So far.

A hundred ODSTs fanned out through the city, clumping up temporarily to double-check weapons and strategy.

I stood in the middle of the plaza road and watched it all with Felicia and Eric.

Downriver the Covenant had thrown together a dam and dug in with a bustle of activity. Organic ships zoomed around overhead, and thousands of Grunts operated a constant hum of machinery that dissolved the ground.

We could hear the operations in the distance of the evacuated, eerily quiet city.

"Do you know what the city's called?" I asked.

"Mount Haven," Felicia said.

Two heavy machine guns had been mounted up on top of strategically located buildings in the city's center. Manned by two ODSTs, Amey and Charleston, both were picked out by Felicia, and there in case the Covenant decided to come sniffing. They also had rocket launchers at their feet for an extra punch if needed.

The other two members of that team, Orrin and Dale, stood with rocket launchers down the street.

Sita stood with Felicia, holding a BR55 battle rifle slung under her arm, and Teller, a pale, gray-haired colonel, lounged by a doorway with a pair of SMGs.

The eight of us were the base team, along with Eric in the Pelican with the Gatling gun in the nose making the ninth. This was base camp.

The other Pelicans were scattered around the edges of the city, ostensibly to reduce the chance of their getting hit by Covenant fire if things got hot; but it was really just an order by Felicia to keep them out of view of the city center.

Teams of ODSTs moved off downriver, and within ten minutes the city fell quiet.

Just the buildings around the river plaza and us, left behind to keep Mount Haven "secure."

There was an empty Jim Dandy's restaurant nearby. City Hall stood quiet with its facade of marble in the shadows.

The stately, two-story bank stood there, waiting for us.

"Okay, let's go!" Felicia shouted.

Orrin and Dale set their launchers up against the side of the bank and rigged explosives on the bank's thick front doors.

They blew off with a surprisingly muted thump. Precise shaped charges. The duo was good at this. They would be old CMA professionals that Felicia dug up.

"We have twenty minutes before the Pelicans will be getting ready to come back for the pickup," Felicia said as she led us into the bank. "So everybody move, move, move."

Sita, Teller, Orrin, and Dale all ran with her. The next obstacle was getting a door down; Dale quickly wired it up.

Another explosion later and we were through.

"Think we can risk the elevator?" I asked.

"Backup power is running still," Dale said. "It's a small pebble-bed nuclear reactor deep underneath the city. It'll keep."

There were three more thick doors to blast. But there was no one to worry about the alarms we continually set off. So it all went fast.

The final explosion revealed a long tunnel with flickering lights, thick bars lining the rooms running along each side, with one final vault just beyond.

"Jackpot," whispered Teller. He licked his lips.

On my right I could see the glimmer of gold bars, stacked as high as my chest.

Each sub room was filled with precious metals. All here for the taking.

WE MOVED quickly, using a motorized pallet dolly that just fit in the elevator. The first two sub rooms were cleaned out, and with each trip we deposited the gold bars into empty ammunition chests in the back of Eric's Pelican.

It filled up quickly, and there was a lightness in the air as we cracked jokes and imagined what we'd do with our share.

The Pelican almost literally groaned with gold, and we had to move a Shiva warhead out to start adding a layer of chests full of gold to the walkway.

"Any more and she won't fly," Eric warned.

"There's just one more room. We'll get a few more chests in here, then we're done," Felicia said.

Back under the bank we detonated the door to the last vault. The lights flickered from the pulse as we opened the door, coughing and hacking from the dust that had been kicked up. Shadows filled the room, shifting and moving as the lights struggled to come on.

Then the lights quit flickering and steadied, and we realized that the shadows were still moving. They were human-shaped shadows.

A hand reached out from behind the bars and grabbed at me. "Are you here to save us?" asked a tiny voice, and I looked down into the large, wide blue eyes of a little boy.

"THANK GOD you came," said an older man, a schoolteacher who'd been chosen to stay with the children while the adults armed up and marched downriver to fight the Covenant.

That had been days ago.

The entire group was camped out in the last gold storage room, spreading out what supplies they had on towels on top of more wealth than any of them could have ever have previously imagined touching.

"We've seen what they've done to other worlds," Julian, the schoolteacher, said. "We got as deep underground as we could . . . hoping maybe we could avoid the worst of it. The others had already left the city for the nearest spaceport. There weren't many children left by the time the Covenant actually landed."

They were not nearly deep enough. But I didn't say anything.

"Just hold on a second, sir, we need to confer a moment."

Felicia had frozen in the center of the hallway, but moved when I approached. "What the hell do we do?" I hissed. "We can't just leave them here."

"I don't know," she whispered back. "But how many are there? What *can* we do?"

"We have a spare Pelican . . ."

She cut me off. "Let me think. In the meantime, get those last three chests of gold up to Eric."

"And how are we going to explain *that*?" I asked, a bit louder than I intended.

Felicia walked over to the open door that led to the room the children and their caretaker were in. There were thirty of them, I figured, from a quick head count. "Julian, that was your name, right? I'm Colonel Felicia Sanderson. I'm an orbital-drop shock trooper. We're here under orders to retrieve the gold bullion, as part of the necessity to fund the war effort against the Covenant. You'll have to understand, these orders are our first priority. In the meantime, if there is anything you need—food, water—we'll provide that to you as we try to think about how to safely get you out of here."

"Thank you, thank you so much," the teacher said.

Dale and Orrin had finished loading the dolly.

I pulled Felicia back farther away. "We need to call in extra Pelicans."

"Don't tell me what we need to do. We're going to load this last bit up, then we're going to see what we can get back to the ship before all hell breaks loose with the damn Covenant just downriver. We'll give these guys food and water, at least. But we're not dragging them outside until I've had time to think."

"Think about what?" Sita asked, joining us. "You're not seriously thinking about taking them out?"

I was horrified. "How can we not? These are children!"

"They're dead," Sita said. "They were dead the moment they chose to hole up down here. It is only a matter of when, and how. The fact that we stumbled across them doesn't change the fact that we can't evacuate everyone off an entire planet. It doesn't work like that."

Dale and Orrin were looking up from the dolly as they guided it toward us, paying attention to our body language.

"What the hell is the point of being a soldier if we can't save anybody," I snapped. The worlds I'd retreated from suddenly flashed through the back of my mind.

And then I thought about what Felicia had said. When was the last time I'd talked to a civilian? Julian was the first since the bombing that put Eric in a coma.

Maybe I'd spent too long being removed from civilization.

Maybe we all had.

But I still had a heart. I still knew what was right and what was wrong. "We can't abandon these children to the Covenant," I said. "I refuse."

"If you refuse, that's a problem," Sita growled. She had her BR55 raised slightly. Orrin and Dale, still observing, looked ready to jump forward and back her up.

Felicia stepped forward slightly, trying to regain control of a situation going bad, and quickly. "Shut up, all of you. We can save some of them, and just take less gold."

"How much less gold? How many of them will fit?" I asked. "You willing to do that kind of bloody math?"

Sita finally raised the rifle up high enough to slide her finger into the trigger guard. "I'd relax a bit if I were you," she said. "We'll do what we have to do."

"What we have to do is get them out," I insisted. "We're going to have to leave the gold. The plan can't go forward."

Sita raised the rifle. "No one's leaving any gold."

"Lower your weapon," Felicia ordered. Orrin and Dale had drawn M6 pistols, and Sita was stepping back.

"I don't think Sita here wants any compromise," I said.

"Shut up, Gage."

I had my assault rifle up as well now. A real standoff. "I'm not backing down. I'm a human being, not an Insurrectionist, not some damn cold-blooded alien. I'm not going to leave these children to die."

"What did they ever do for you?" Sita asked. "When the UNSC was bombing civilians in the Outer Colonies, did they care about children then?"

"The Outer Colonies don't exist anymore, Sita," I said levelly. "It's not about that anymore."

"The Colonies don't exist anymore because the UNSC wouldn't protect them," Orrin hissed.

"Really? All those Navy ships lost to enemy fire, all those friends I saw die out there, that was for nothing?" I moved my aim from Sita to Orrin to Dale. I couldn't bring myself to step to the side and include Felicia.

If she was going to shoot me, it was all over anyway.

The arguments the old Colonials made were ones that could sway us in an academic discussion over beers. But right here, right now, there were people that needed our help. And I was not going to turn my back on them.

No matter what I believed, or what I'd seen, I knew where I stood on this.

"There's not enough gold in all the worlds to make this worth it. You'll wake up at night thinking about these kids you condemned to death for your own greed," I said. "It won't be worth it."

"It's worth a try," Orrin snarled, and raised his M6 higher. I saw what was in his eyes.

It sounded like all the shots happened simultaneously. My body armor crumpled as it absorbed the shock, but I'd gotten Sita first, as she'd had the real firepower.

But M6 rounds from Orrin and Dale slapped me to the ground. I was bleeding from the arm, the leg, and a near miss by my ear.

"Felicia?" I called out, aching all over. I'd seen Orrin slump over the gold bars, the red blood seeping in down between the cracks.

Dale lay still on the floor by the pallet.

"Felicia?"

I crawled over to her. She'd drawn as well, on Orrin and Dale. We'd been of the same mind, in the end. It would have been easy for her to gun me down.

She lay on her back, holding her throat, frothy blood pouring out of her mouth with each cough and attempted breath.

"Felicia . . ."

She grabbed my arm tight, squeezing hard, her eyes looking past me as she groaned through bubbles of blood, then stopped.

"Felicia."

"Sir?" The schoolteacher looked around the edge of the vault door, his eyes wide.

"Stay here. For now, just stay here," I told him. "I have to arrange how to get you out of here safely."

I limped toward the elevator, tears in my eyes.

IN THE back of the Pelican, my body armor stained with Felicia's blood, I unsteadily held my sidearm at the side of Eric's face.

"You remember when the bomb went off in the club?" I asked him.

He turned to look directly at the gun and me. "Every day since I woke up."

"I remember being trapped in the dark, chest too constricted to scream, panting for what air I could get. And I remember it was an ODST who pulled me out. That moment, I don't think I could ever forget that."

"That why you joined?"

"Yeah." I nodded. "Now I'm on the other side, only I'm there to steal the wallet off the guy in the rubble and leave them to die."

"We couldn't have known there would be children," Eric said.

"We have to do something."

Eric sighed. "Gage, there's nothing we can do. Look, we can try and fit a few of them where we can, but let's not throw away our futures, what Felicia worked for."

The speaker in the cockpit crackled. The attack was withdrawing. Not just a single artifact, but several artifacts had been stolen from the Covenant dig site. ODSTs were in full retreat with hundreds of Grunts in full pursuit.

"They're able to track the artifacts somehow!" a hysterical private reported. "We split up into several groups, and all the Covenant are coming after just us!"

No battle plan survived contact with the enemy.

Eric shook his head. "There's not much we can do now. We just poked the Covenant nest and it sounds like they're swarming."

Our fellow ODSTs were calling for the Pelicans to get them the hell out of the hot zone.

I waved the sidearm at Eric. "Get out."

"What?"

"Get out. I don't want to shoot you. But I know how to help them. So get the hell out."

"Do you know who you're dealing with? You know me. But Teller, Amey, Charleston? They're old school CMA. Watts loyalists. And they've done it all. We're not crossing them. I'm not getting the hell off my own ship," Eric gritted. I smacked him in the head with the pistol butt three times to knock him out, then dragged him to the back of the Pelican and rolled him off into the street.

Charleston and Amey were manning the mounted machine guns, but hadn't looked over and down into the street.

It had been another lifetime ago that I watched Allison Stark fly a Hornet through the night, but I remembered the controls she'd shown me and seen it done a hundred times since.

Standardized.

I'd stood in the back of the Pelican cockpits enough, too.

That didn't mean what I was going to try next would work.

I switched to an encrypted channel that the other pilots weren't monitoring and patched into the cruiser in orbit. "*Chares,* we have what we came for, but we need more transport. This is urgent. We need Pelican backup, right away. Three Pelicans took incoming fire and are down, repeat down. Scramble immediately."

I tried to remember what was what. Stick, collective throttle . . . all the buttons and switches in front of me.

But a Pelican was enough like a second home that I got it started.

Amey and Charleston would no doubt be wondering what was happening as the Pelican's engines gunned to life. The craft lurched, clawing for air, pregnant with gold in the green-gray ammunition chests.

I scraped along a building, knocking down balconies and brickwork as I struggled to get the Pelican higher.

I was tense, waiting for the mounted machine guns to open up on me, but they never did. I got on the radio to try and find out where the group with the artifacts was. I'd been moving on instinct, trying to figure out how I could buy time for the children.

A small idea had occurred to me.

I CLUMSILY landed the Pelican heavily and awkwardly in the middle of the chaos that was the ODST retreat back up the river toward the city.

The first ODST who clambered in looked around. "There's no space!" he shouted.

I leaned back. "Where are the artifacts? Get them loaded in here, now! We need to get them clear and back up to orbit."

He left and shouted, and soon a set of boxes were being taken off the back of a mongoose quad bike and loaded in.

"What about the Shiva?" he asked.

"The nuke?"

"We didn't need to set it off, but we're not sure where we should leave it if they're coming after us."

I nodded. "Stick it in here, I'll save you from hefting it about."

"Yes, sir. Be careful up there, there'll be Covenant aircraft support on the way now that they were attacked." The ODST trooped up toward the cockpit. "You sure we can't just shove this ammo out and get some of our guys back out?"

He leaned forward, and then looked at the blood on my armor. "Sir, you're shot?"

Then he frowned. "I need to check . . ." But he stopped when I pushed the M6 against his neck.

"There are thirty or so kids in the bottom of the bank in the middle of the city," I rasped. "If I take whatever's in those boxes the Covenant's so hot for and are tracking, I can make a run for it, away from the city. The Covenant forces will chase me, and maybe I can buy you guys some time to help the children. You understand what I'm saying?"

The ODST nodded, and as he backed slowly out, I pointed at the ammo crates. "Open it."

He did so, and his jaw dropped. "Now shove that out the back onto the ground. Take a bar each, and next time you're on leave, have a drink for Gage Yevgenny."

The moment he hopped off I struggled back into the air.

I couldn't see any Covenant forces, but I didn't understand half of what the readouts were I was looking at. I banked left, skirting the river only for a few moments, before I headed for the mountains.

My goal was to get over them, but the Pelican could barely climb. A Banshee suddenly swooped in, firing just ahead of my nose. I focused on the mountains, ignoring it, hoping that the artifacts were too precious for the Covenant to risk blowing me up.

Rockets slammed into the Banshee from the direction of the city. Before the debris even began to fall, another rocket slammed into the rear of the Pelican. Charleston, Amey, or maybe even Eric: They'd claim they were trying to hit the Banshee.

The craft bucked and spiraled as I struggled to control it, but with all the gold and my own ineptitude, I could barely keep it in the air.

I flew as long as I could, but the Pelican was shaking herself apart.

I remember the world spinning, slamming into the ridge, bouncing. I remember seeing the mountain pitch toward me. I know I made it over the ridge, because I hit the top of it and bounced.

And then it was like the bomb in the club again. A tremendous blow, my senses reeling, and I woke up on the ground, my armor on fire.

Since then, I've been waiting.

THE ROOK had sat next to the ODST, scanning the horizon for threats, listening to his tale. Any attempt to leave or call for help had been thwarted by the dying man.

But now he understood, at least, why he'd been sent down with a second wave of ODSTs by SOEIV, and why extra Pelicans were on their way.

It was all due to this man. Gage Yevgenny.

Who was most certainly going to die here.

The sound of an approaching Pelican began to rise in volume.

"There's a reason I've been keeping you here, talking," Gage said. "Not just to comfort my dying self. They're almost here. The Covenant, and Eric with his friends. I'm surprised you got here before them all. They're going to want to salvage the gold they can from the wreck. What I want you to do is head up the mountain now. All out. Drop your pack, everything but comms and your weapon.

"Get through the cut there in fifteen minutes, and you get on the other side of the mountain. Don't flag down that first Pelican that's coming. In fact, hide from it as best you can. I had you stay here because if you'd taken off up the mountain, the Covenant would have seen you from the other side. But the Grunts are on canned methane; instead of using it all up by panting their way over the mountain, they'll have worked their way around to get close to this wreck. So head up the pass and over the mountain, and run like you ran in boot camp, rook, run like your worst drill instructor is right behind you."

"Sir, I can't just leave you . . ."

"They're all going to arrive, rook, and I'm going to blow the Shiva up the moment *all* the bastards show up." Gage held up a control pad that would let him wirelessly detonate the nuclear device. "Years ago, I told my father it was 'just dirt.' But it's *not* dirt. It's where we live. It *our* dirt, dammit. And more importantly, it's about who's standing on that dirt. Those children. Your family. Your friends. And those freaks are going to pay for every piece of dirt they've taken from us."

"We can still get you out of here . . ."

"No. I'm a dead man, you know it. I'm not going to waste more Marines."

"And your friends coming this way?"

"They're going to die helping protect the dirt, rookie. They're going to die doing something good." He smiled. "If they'd stayed back in the city to form up with you guys instead of running out here for the gold, they wouldn't have a problem, would they? They chose this path. Promise me something, rook?"

"Anything."

"You'll fight the Covenant all the way. Even if they land on Earth. You'll fight them even if you have to throw rocks at them."

"I will, sir."

"Then go now!" He waved the arming device for the Shiva around. "Or I'll set this damn thing off with you still dallying around here."

The rookie got up, looked around, back at the man on the ground one last time, and then ran. He shed his gear as he did so. Everything but the BR55 in his hands.

He ran uphill, not looking back, his visor open and his breath loud in the helmet. He leaped over rocks, gaining height, until he finally spotted the cleft of rock that would let him cut over the ridge to the other side of the mountain, back toward the city that was base camp for this operation.

He paused, looking back down the direction he'd come, catching his breath in long gasping pants.

Boot camp was just weeks ago. He was relieved to find out he still had that kind of sprint in him.

He could see the developing battlefield far below, in the scrub of the foothills. Grunts in the hundreds poured toward the downed Pelican. They'd come around the far side of the mountain, as Gage had predicted. They were like locusts swarming across the grass, bumbling along due to the large methane tanks on their backs.

And thundering overhead, flaring out toward the scene: a Pelican. It touched down, and three figures stepped out.

They did not rush to help Gage, but instead started rooting through the ruins of the other Pelican.

The Marine did not wait to see what was coming next. He ran through the cleft, barely glancing up at overhangs, and then slid down the other side.

Loose rock tumbled, and he surfed down the shale and dirt.

A bone-thrumming thump shook the entire mountain, and a steady roar filled the air. By the time the rookie got to the bottom, a massive mushroom cloud could be seen over the tip of the mountaintop.

It was still rising when a Pelican flew around a nearby hill, coming down to kiss the dirt long enough for the rookie to leap in.

"What the hell happened over there?" the pilot asked.

The rookie shook his head. "Long story."

Long, indeed.

He was still a bit shaken by the entire thing.

The Pelican shook and bounced. "The civilians have all been evacuated," the copilot told the rookie, who stood behind them looking out the window. "We're taking them back to Earth with us."

"Earth?" He was surprised.

"The Covenant just attacked Reach," the pilot reported. "We're falling back to Mother Earth."

The rookie looked out at the land under the clouds as they climbed for orbit, stunned. Soon all the ground would be glass, once the Covenant ships started in on it.

All dirt, he thought.

Like Earth.

From there, they would throw everything they had at the Covenant if they were found. Even if he had to throw the last rock himself. He'd made a promise.

They *would* make the Covenant pay for every inch of dirt, the rookie thought to himself.

ACHERON-VII

It's barren
the air chokes; on dust and smoke
the ground cracks; surrendering to the heat
It's lonely
with only the dead as company,
but anymore, this has become his closest companion;
death
There was once a purpose to all of this;
a specific design
Soldiers sent forth in the name of retribution
In their path; an alien covenant
vast in number
ardent in their belief
Now, but one stands
Only one; survivor
His friends taken by conflict
Their adversaries delivered unto
Alone now, he treks the wastelands
cut off; stranded
Knowing somewhere above;
Out and beyond
His brothers, his sisters, continue to struggle
Continue to fight, to die;
to strive
A million stars between here and home
A million enemies; more
Yet here he stands, ever vigilant
And here he'll stay;
A lone warrior, on a desolate plain

HEADHUNTERS

JONATHAN GOFF

ONE

Blood, Bullets, and Adrenaline

"Hey!"

The word just hung there for an instant as Jonah gave his motion sensor a second glance.

"I got one," the excitement in his hushed voice unmistakable.

"You sure?" Roland had just about enough of false alarms.

"Pretty sure," Jonah shot back.

There was a split second when the world came to a complete stop—silent and unmoving.

"Nope—yeah, I'm sure," Jonah confirmed.

If he was right, and Roland desperately hoped he was, then it would be the first contact with enemy forces since their insertion into the field some six days prior. In that time the pair had covered twenty-three miles, at times moving at a snail's pace as they crept ever closer to their target.

"This is fun," Jonah concluded, the excitement in his voice escalating.

"It's about to be, anyway." Roland had never much enjoyed this part of the job—the sneaking around, the long days and hours spent maintaining absolute cover while maneuvering behind, through, and between enemy lines—but what came after, the blood, bullets, and adrenaline, *that* he enjoyed quite a bit, maybe as much as Jonah, though probably not. Jonah had the added benefit of loving every minute in the field. Not just the combat, but the whole ordeal, from insertion into each new alien hotspot to the postcarnage report back at home base—whether he was facedown in the mud and muck for twelve hours straight, silently sliding his custom combat knife across a Sangheili throat, or recounting the bloodshed wrought by the muffled rhythm of his M7S submachine gun, Jonah loved it all—every single second of life as one of the elite, as one of the UNSC's top-tier Covenant killers.

TO HUMANITY at large, Jonah, Roland, and their fellow Spartan-IIIs were *ghosts*, their missions and movements deemed highly classified—top secret. Their very existence was known only by a select few, and while their brothers and sisters in the Spartan-II program earned glory and unwavering respect as they fought and died against the Covenant, the IIIs fought, and most certainly died, with only the recognition and admiration of their fellow secret warriors as their reward—for the Spartan-IIIs, however, as with the IIs, this was more than enough. Though created under comparable, yet varied circumstances, the two forces shared one very similar mind-set: Duty first. Loyalty second. In the Spartan mind, petty vices such as fame simply did not register. There was no need for the galaxy-wide adulation of the masses reveling in their many brutal victories over the Covenant. Nor did they want the sympathies and pity of anyone outside their close-knit circle when they were confronted by defeat—by death. This secrecy helped bond each Spartan-III unit like those of no other unit, and in truth it was something they appreciated—cherished, even. After all, with attention comes distraction, and in a war against a collection of advanced alien races hell-bent on slaughtering the whole of humanity, there was no room for wandering thoughts or clouded minds.

As tools of war, the Spartan-IIIs were most often deployed as living fire-and-forget weapons—just point, shoot, and wait for the fireworks. ONI, or on occasion a highly placed UNSC official, passed along a key Covenant target; the IIIs were then sent in, headfirst, to eliminate the given objective, or inflict as much damage as physically possible in the effort. Success meant a handful or more made it back to base, mission complete; failure, nobody came home, but—to a man—they fell doing their damnedest to inflict the maximum level of destruction upon their foe. This all-encompassing sense of service before self in the face of almost certain death hardened them. Connected them. But even among this collection of steadfast soldiers there were a select few with a bond deeper than the others could ever begin to imagine, as these unique IIIs were a secret even to their peers.

AND SOMEWHERE out among the star-poked black of the galaxy, on a nameless moon, far beyond the outermost UNSC colony, Roland and Jonah methodically inched their way through tangled, alien undergrowth, slowly, quietly moving closer to the source of the blip on Jonah's motion tracker.

TWO

A Brief History of Headhunting

There had been much concern about fielding a sufficient number of Spartans for the missions that were considered essential—deployment against large-scale Covenant targets and defense of key UNSC facilities being chief among them. In a war many were beginning to believe was unwinnable, losing even a handful to specialized operations was frowned upon. This unwillingness to spread the Spartan ranks too thin across the field of battle meant the number of two-man infiltration squads, code-named: Headhunters, culled from the ranks of the Spartan-III program, was extremely limited. At the program's height there was a maximum contingent of six squads—six teams, with a total of seventeen soldiers rotating in to fill gaps when half or all of a team was lost in the field. Jonah and Roland were paired as part of an initial eight-man roster and had been together as a unit since.

It was the Headhunters' task to infiltrate heavily fortified enemy encampments, ships, and operation centers completely undetected, with minimal, mission-specific weaponry, and no radio contact or hope for backup or retrieval, and complete a set series of objectives in preparation for one of two eventualities: a larger, full-scale assault on the target, or as a decoy and distraction for UNSC operations elsewhere.

Over the course of the Human-Covenant War there had been some luck, limited but occasionally fruitful, in stealth insertions behind Covenant lines. The majority of these operations ended in lost contact with the field unit and the presumed death of the operatives involved. The Spartan-II program had changed this to a degree, as the IIs had been able to slip into enemy territory on a number of occasions—not always with the best results, but with results, nonetheless. Now, with the IIIs and the advancements in their training and the technologies and equipment available to them, further and more intrusive campaigns into Covenant-held regions were deemed a necessary risk—although such operations would be attempted on a limited basis, and in direct control of a special unit from deep within Beta-5, one of ONI's most secretive subdivisions, operating under the umbrella of the clandestine organization known as Section Three.

Spartan-III soldiers selected to participate in the Headhunter program had to meet one exclusive prerequisite before being considered by Beta-5: only those individuals who had survived two or more specially assigned training missions would be evaluated for possible inclusion in its additional, grueling training regimen. Once an overall list of potential candidates was compiled, each trooper's personal files and mission reports—from birth all the way up to, and including, their activities within the past twenty-four hours—were analyzed against a set series of parameters calculated by top ONI specialists.

Both Roland and Jonah not only fell under the "two missions" banner of acceptance, they were perfect matches for each of Beta-5's requirements, and more importantly, when offered the opportunity to participate—though presented with only the vaguest of program overviews—they each leapt at the chance to hit back at the Covenant in new and unexpected ways.

Once selected, candidates were separated from their fellow Spartans and shipped to a special training facility on the far side of Onyx, the ONI-controlled world that served as the IIIs' base of operations. After three months, the soldiers were broken into four two-person squads, chosen through a series of detailed evaluations and an intense interview process meant to devise the best possible pairings between members of the group. Roland and Jonah's pairing hit on 97.36 percent of the desired matchmaking criteria; only one other team scored higher.

Now, more than two years later, their training complete—including seven months of supervised field exercises, followed by six months' real-world wartime insertions—and the successful negotiation of twelve battlefield insertions under their belts, Roland and Jonah found themselves on the far side of the galaxy, two human soldiers on a moon crawling with Covenant. Their current task was straightforward enough—slip onto the Covenant-held moon, believed to be the site of one of the pious alien collective's sacred religious digs, and remove six of the ten identified base camps situated around the outer perimeter of a much larger central compound. A second team of Headhunters would remove the four outstanding camps in preparation for what was to follow. The confusion and re-shuffling of troops and supplies by the Covenant contingent following each base camp's dismantling was simply the opening salvo in a full-scale assault by a dozen Spartan-III fireteams and associated orbital backup.

THREE

Apes or Alligators?

The indicator on Roland's individual radar showed that whatever their contact—Grunt or Elite, Jackal or Brute—they were less than ten meters from it, and while he and Jonah were careful not to give away their position as they crept closer, they had yet to establish visual confirmation of their target. In the postdusk hour it was possible the Covenant sentry was using the shadows of the forest to conceal its perch as it stood guard over the base camp's perimeter. It was just as likely, however, that the bastard was hidden beneath the light-bending cloak of active camouflage. One option pointed toward a raptorlike Kig-Yar sniper posted somewhere up in the thick tangle of branches that made up the forest's canopy. The other, less appealing, option meant one of the Sangheili Elite, the Covenant's most devout and dangerous warriors, was patrolling this sector of the perimeter.

Each possibility brought with it its own set of complications. The two Spartans ran through the encounter scenarios as they worked to develop a proper plan of attack: Shooting a sniper from its roost could draw unwanted attention. They could miss the kill-shot, alerting the creature to their presence and giving it the opportunity to signal an alarm. Or, even with a clean kill, the force of the impact and the pull of gravity might send the body tumbling from its resting place, bouncing off and snapping any number of branches along the way, before slamming into the ground with a thud that was sure to carry in the still night air. Taking out a camouflaged Elite in close combat meant dealing with the combined might of the alien's armor, firepower, and brute strength. An Elite patrol usually carried one standard-issue Covenant plasma rifle, if not two, possibly a plasma pistol for backup, as well as plasma grenades, and if Roland and Jonah were particularly unlucky, an energy sword.

To top it all off, they'd have to find the damn thing before it found them.

Roland motioned for Jonah to freeze; they weren't proceeding until they could confirm the identity of the obstacle and ascertain the best approach to removing it from their path.

"Think it's av-cam," Jonah whispered.

Roland didn't respond.

The modified helmet-to-helmet vocal systems in their headgear meant they could speak to one another without fear of giving away their position, though in most cases, once they entered the combat zone, their instincts would take control and they would begin functioning solely on physical cues and intuition.

The UNSC had spent years sanctioning research and development into, and thrown an unspecified amount of resources at, the problem of active camouflage, or av-cam, replication. The ability to essentially disappear into your surroundings was a major advantage for the Covenant—in addition to their already terrifyingly superior weaponry and shielding and their uncanny mastery of slipspace navigation.

Officially, all UNSC efforts to prototype a working av-cam unit had been met with failure. Unofficially, as was the norm within Beta-5, they had been testing a modified version of active camouflage since the inception of the Spartan-III program, along with advanced vision modes that would allow for easier detection of stealthed enemy combatants.

While the field operable av-cam-enhanced armor variants were yet to be placed in UNSC-normal rotation, and were in fact quite limited even within the ranks of the Spartan-IIIs, the research into visor-based vision enhancements as part of an overall equipment upgrade known as Visual Intelligence Systems, Reconnaissance, or VISR, was well underway, with the hope it could be made available UNSC-wide in the near future.

As with most research and development efforts with battlefield implications, VISR was already being field-tested by most Headhunter teams.

As it stood, Roland's power armor was equipped with one of ONI's experimental active camouflage units, along with a dedicated power supply. When it was activated he would achieve a state close to invisibility for a period of three and a half to four minutes.

Once used, however, the cell powering the unit would need anywhere from ten to fifteen minutes to recharge, and put an additional strain on his suit's other power functions. Shielding. Bios. Targeting. Tracking. All of it would run at less than optimum efficiency while the av-cam system rebooted. Less than four minutes of maximized stealth in exchange for limited resources for a short—but long enough—duration, directly following. As such, Roland had to be judicious with its use.

"I think it's av-cam," Jonah continued, undeterred by Roland's lack of response. "Could be a sniper." He paused. "But I got twenty credits on it being camo." He slid up alongside Roland. "Wanna take that bet, Rolle? Twenty cred? I'll take camo. You can have the field."

Jonah had seemed eager enough when he first signaled the contact, but the fact that he was getting chatty told Roland that his partner was becoming antsy—his need for violent release growing exponentially by the minute.

"Well, wha'd'ya got?"

"Don't know," Roland responded, after spending a couple seconds examining the blip on his tracker—it hadn't moved since their first contact. "Stayin' pretty still for a Slip-Lip," Roland concluded, using a common dismissive referring to the four-pronged anatomy of the Sangheili mouth.

Jonah slowly moved his right hand up along the side of his helmet, flicking the small nub that activated his VISR mode enhanced vision. Roland followed suit. They each swept the forest floor with their gaze—the nighttime scene glowing with various hues as the VISR flickered into focus.

"I got nothin'." Roland started.

The area where their target was positioned was clear of enemy presence. Steadily shifting their lines of sight to peer higher into the treetop, the two Spartans began scanning the forest canopy for their contact.

"Shit." Jonah sighed before lowering his head, shaking it in disgust. "At the top. Right at one o'clock. All the way up."

"Sniper," Roland said plainly, without looking.

"Yep," Jonah replied in mock defeat.

Roland smiled beneath his helmet and lifted his head.

Settled atop a small platform near the very top of the tallest cluster of trees in the area—just below where the forest met the sky—a lone Kig-Yar crouched, periodically tracking across the whole of the forest laid out before him with his trusty Covenant beam rifle, a sleek, long-range weapon that was extremely deadly in capable hands.

"How did that idiot not see us," Jonah laughed.

"We're that good," Roland affirmed, gauging the distance

between their position—belly-down on the forest floor—and the sniper's roost high above, using his visor's onboard electronics.

Roland waited a few breaths before adding, "More importantly . . . you owe me lunch."

"Heh—a bet's a bet," Jonah conceded. "I'm more concerned with how we're gonna get that jackass down from his nest without alerting the whole damn Covenant army."

"We have a few options," Roland began, his mind already catching on one idea in particular before Jonah cut back in.

"Why don't you go ghost—climb up there and give him a little tap—so we can get movin'," Jonah nudged. He was definitely itching for a fight, and Roland couldn't blame him. For all the waiting and slow going, it was these few moments before actual contact that were the most nerve-racking. All the work—the effort and energy—it took to cross vast stretches of unknown terrain unseen by the naked eye, and undetected by any number of tracking systems, was in anticipation of the handful of minutes spent face-to-face with your adversaries.

"This is exactly why I get to test out the cool new toys and you don't," Roland jabbed.

"How so?" Jonah shot back.

"This cam unit is a precious commodity," Roland began to explain before Jonah pressed the issue.

"And?"

"And . . ." Roland continued diplomatically, "you'd activate it for no better reason than to give a Grunt a wedgie."

"Fair point."

"I, on the other hand, can control such base urges; saving our more limited, and valuable, assets for their appropriate use," Roland explained with a mocking air of superiority in his voice.

"Geez, does that mean yer not gonna let me borrow the car this weekend, Dad?"

"You joke, but you know it's true."

"All right, all right . . ." Jonah was ready to get back on task. "You got a plan for this guy, then?"

Roland made sure Jonah could hear the joy in his response. "I was thinkin' . . . *lumberjack.*"

THIRTY MINUTES later.

Roland and Jonah had no problems setting the shaped charges at the base of the Jackal sniper's lookout and were back on course, slowly making their way to their main objective.

Knowing there would more than likely be multiple rotations between the snipers manning this particular perch before their attack on their first target would begin, the pair had taken extra care in concealing the explosives so as to avoid any unwanted attention. The real danger in leaving the sniper unattended hinged on the possibility that it would have a clear vantage point from which to draw a bead on them once they began their offensive, and while there were most assuredly other snipers in the area, their only immediate concern was in the reality of a known threat.

The novelty in utilizing a lumberjack to eliminate said threat was that the maneuver served the dual purposes of removing the sniper from the field of play while also providing a brief distraction upon the initiation of their assault on the camp. Besides, Roland always got a kick out this little stunt—placing explosives at the base of an enemy perch, then blowing the charge from a distance, listening to the echo of tearing roots or the whine of twisted metal as the whole thing came crashing down.

They were less than three hundred meters from the edge of the base camp now. According to their intel, they would have visual confirmation of the site just over the crest of the next ridge.

Their normal deliberate pace had slowed once the pair had crossed the Covenant's outer defensive perimeter, and their forward progress was hampered even further since bypassing the sniper, as they had moved to the cover of jagged embankment to ensure they were completely out of the alien sharpshooter's line of sight, leery of the prying eyes behind and above them.

When the duo reached the peak of the final ridge before the forest descended into a sweeping, picturesque valley, it had been just over four hours since they had set their trap at the foot of the sniper's tree. Though briefed and rebriefed by Beta-5's intelligence officers in regard to the specifics of their mission, Roland and Jonah had yet to see any of the target camps with their own eyes.

Over the course of the countless drills, both back in training and their twelve live-combat field insertions, they had learned not to rely too heavily on intelligence reports. Although a needed tool, such reports were limited in their use during real-time battlefield situations; there were just too many variables to account for in between the time a final mission brief is run and the actual moment of combat. Did the enemy alter its protocols for any reason?

Have their defensive measures been upgraded, downgraded, or modified in any other fashion? Have the patrols changed within the last day?

The last ten minutes? Were there clouds in the sky?

Had it rained? Some of this could be predicted to a relative degree of certainty, but predictions weren't always reality, and for Headhunters the only intel worth relying on was gathered firsthand.

After settling in to check their equipment, Jonah inched ahead of Roland, pulling himself to the edge of the craggy rise they'd chosen for their observation post. The vantage this jagged rock outcropping provided was ideal for keeping tabs on the goings-on below, and the haphazard formation itself gave perfect cover for anything but the most thorough of inspections.

Careful to maintain his focus, Jonah moved at a deliberate pace as he lifted his head to gaze down on the Covenant campsite below. The wide valley that swept out beneath them and into the distance was marked by a small clearing nestled into the foot of the nearest mountainside. Target one was less than seventy meters in diameter, housing six sleek, gleaming purple structures and a series of energy barriers set up over well-lit excavation sites. In the distance Jonah could make out the lights from the other base camps peppered across the darkened basin, surrounding a massive complex of swooping buildings and ornate towers that loomed over the forest like a mechanical mecca to some forgotten god.

Taking it all in, the first thought that popped into Jonah's mind was simple, comforting, and more than a little malicious: *I can't wait to burn it all down.*

As impressive as the whole scene was, it also gave rise to another, less comforting thought. "Ya know?" Jonah said. "This place's gotta be pretty damned important to the Covenant for ONI to be wastin' so much firepower on a glorified dig-site so far back from the front."

Jonah understood the value ONI placed in the strange alien artifacts the Covenant cherished so deeply, but found it hard to believe his and Roland's services were best utilized against such a remote outpost, especially with the UNSC suffering such heavy losses on the frontlines of the war.

"ONI says it's hot, it's hot. Ours is not to question why," Roland explained, as he removed a cleaning kit from his pack.

"Not really sayin' otherwise, more just thinkin' out loud."

Jonah continued his visual sweep of the valley. "I mean, *two* infiltration teams? We haven't had two squads 'a Headhunters in-field for the same drop . . . ever."

"The Covies seem pretty enamored with these alien leftovers they're always scroungin' for," Roland offered. "So, who knows what kind of weapons system or whatever they're hopin' to uncover here. And what does it matter, right? They could be diggin' for earthworms, in which case . . . it's our pleasure to make sure they don't find any."

The Spartans sat in silence as Jonah scanned the Covenant operation below and Roland went about checking his gear.

"Wha' do we got down there, anyway?" Roland swabbed the chamber of his M6C suppressed sidearm with a cleaning solution. These long excursions were hell on weaponry, and if a soldier neglected to keep up with the proper maintenance procedures, there was good chance he would be stuck in a firefight with an inoperable firearm, or worse yet, the damn thing could jam and explode in his hand, doing the other side's job for them.

"The spooks weren't messin' 'round with this one, Rolle. The Covies got quite a little picnic set up out here."

"How's alpha-target lookin'?" Roland inquired, nodding at the base camp nearest their location.

"Pretty much as expected. Don't think we'll need much more than a day or two to scout their movements versus what we've been briefed."

"What about infantry?"

"Moderate." Jonah scanned the Covenant enclave. "In the high twenties, maybe lower thirties. Definitely not gonna be a cakewalk, but we've had worse—"

"Apes or alligators?"

"Huh?"

"We got apes or alligators running the show?" Roland clarified.

Jonah slunk back down into the crevice they would be occupying for the remainder of the night and the next day. "'Gators. Saw quite a few, but no sign of Brutes. Usually when one's around the other's not—don't think they like each other much."

"Fine by me."

Jonah easily detected the relief in Roland's voice. "The Elites may be a bitch to deal with," Roland continued, "but at least they're smart, right? Smart we can predict—we can plan for." Jonah nodded his agreement. "The damn Brutes, though," Roland said, "they're just a buncha overly aggressive troglodytes. Start shootin' at 'em and they slip a gasket, go all aggro."

"They do operate on a shorter fuse. I think it makes 'em fun—like pickin' on an emotionally stunted twelve-year-old."

"You were a bully as a kid, weren't you?"

"Me? No. I was the twelve-year-old," Jonah corrected.

"Ha. You'd think that'd teach you to have some sympathy for—"

"Sympathy? Shit. If getting my ass bruised every other week taught me anything it was the simple truth that it's better to be the bully than the bullied."

"You are one enlightened individual, my friend."

"Hey, I tend to think I turned out okay."

"Jay? Yer essentially a government-sanctioned sociopath. That's not normal, and some would say far from okay."

"Like yer a fuckin' saint."

"Never said I was," Roland replied, before adding, "but you seem to take a bit more . . . let's just call it 'pride' in our work."

"Just 'cause I'm good at what I do—" Jonah retorted, a confident swagger in his voice.

"There's no denyin' that."

"Right, so? What's the issue?"

"I think the issue was: Elites are smart, Brutes are dumb."

"On which we both agree."

"And my point—the point I was trying to make—was the Elites' strategic intelligence makes 'em more of an ideal opponent in direct combat, because we can make educated guesses as to how they'll react. Whereas Brutes—"

"Ya give 'em the stink-eye," Jonah interrupted, "and they get pissy—makes 'em lose their head; intellect goes completely out the goddamn window."

"Right."

"*Right.*"

"And that difference in composure—in the way they handle their shit—makes the Brutes tougher to deal with in spur-of-the-moment situations, 'cause who knows what the hell they'll do."

"No—I *get* you," Jonah corrected. "And this is, what? The nine hundredth time we've had this conversation—"

"That's a bit of a stretch."

"Well, it's not the second—" Jonah chuckled, cutting Roland off. "You been tryin' ta sell me on yer theory of smart-equals-easy, dumb-equals-tough since training. I just ain't buyin' it . . . er . . . I guess, really, it's that I just don't care much one way or the other."

Jonah paused to give Roland a chance to respond. When he didn't, Jonah continued, "I mean . . . I really *do* get it. And there's some weird kinda backwards logic to yer thinking, but at the end of the day, Rolle—"

"You just never pay much attention to the tactical side of—" Roland interrupted.

"Tactical what?" Jonah shot back. The pair's conversations often became friendly competitions, as they'd verbally spar over even the smallest differences in opinion—each trying to assert why their view was the more valid of the two while the other's was simply dead wrong.

"I *do* tactical. But, come on, it's—" Jonah stopped mid-sentence before shifting gears. "Never mind . . . Forget it . . . You already know what I'm gonna say, right? So there's no reason ta continue . . . You already know what I'm gonna say before I even say it."

"Yeah, so . . ."

"So . . . tell me what I'm thinkin'. Finish my thought," Jonah urged, wanting nothing more than to hear the words from Roland's mouth.

"No." Roland didn't want to give his partner the satisfaction.

"Just say it," Jonah poked. "Let's hear it."

"You think they're the same," Roland relented, knowing the conversation would continue to spiral if they didn't move on quickly.

"Right. Brutes. Elite. They may pose different problems, but when it comes right down to it, they're the same damn thing—targets. Big ones. Small ones. Smart ones. Dumb ones. Who cares—just point us at 'em, give us some weapons that go bang, some knives that cut like butter, and a brain-load of semiaccurate intel, and we'll cut 'em loose, scrape 'em off our boots, and march on to the next batch."

"You always find a way to make mass murder sound so simple—almost poetic." Though it was a hard and fast fact of their lives, Roland had always been amazed—not perturbed, not put off, just amazed, maybe even a little amused—by Jonah's flippant attitude toward death.

"As if you have any objections," Jonah huffed.

"Don't get defensive—wasn't a complaint, just an observation." Roland finished cleaning his pistol and passed the cleaning kit to Jonah before offering, "I'll take first watch," and lifting himself up to view the valley below.

"So, I'm a sociopath, huh?" Jonah spit, a hint of feigned sadness in his voice.

Roland stopped just before the lip of the ridge and turned back toward Jonah. "Doesn't mean yer not a helluva guy, Jay. Just means I wouldn't trust you 'round my kids."

"You don't have kids."

"Then I guess we don't have to worry about it."

Jonah laughed as Roland repositioned himself for a clear view of the valley.

The two Spartans spent the rest of the night alternating between keeping watch and taking hour-long power naps to ensure they would be functioning at optimum combat efficiency during their steadily approaching engagement against the Covenant.

The next two days were spent observing the Covenant base camp in preparation for their assault. Troop movements and specific interactions between the various alien species were noted and checked against known patterns. The number of individual soldiers, including their rank, was marked and prioritized by threat level. Locations in and around the camp were assigned specific designations based upon their placement and estimated purpose.

Finally, as the sun dropped below the horizon on the third night, Roland and Jonah made their way to the camp's perimeter.

FOUR

"'Great Journey,' huh? What's so great about it?"

"—THAT wasn't so bad," Jonah finished his thought after taking a few seconds to ensure he had everyone's attention.

The few remaining Elites and the smattering of Grunts all turned and lifted their gaze to take in the sight of the lone human standing before them.

THE TWO Spartans had entered the camp not ten minutes prior, silently overtaking a trio of sleeping Unggoy before slipping into a small two-room storage facility.

They quickly recapped their plan of attack: Roland would trigger his av-cam unit and slip about the base, planting charges on four reactor cores spread across the compound. Meanwhile, Jonah would enter the barracks, utilizing flash bangs and a fancy new ONI energy disruptor to disorient the Covenant inside before entering and eliminating all enemy targets within. As soon as Jonah engaged the barracks contingent all hell would break loose.

If the Spartans had done their job right, the sudden, furious nature of the attack would catch the Covenant off guard long enough that any real attempt at resistance would be squelched before the aliens knew what hit them. And, while Roland and Jonah expected a fight, any troops occupying a position this removed from the frontlines were more than likely not the cream of the crop when it came to the Covenant's fighting force.

Headhunters, on the other hand, were as near perfection as humanity could muster in terms of weapons of death and war.

Confident in their abilities and dedicated to their purpose, Jonah slunk out from the rear of the storage unit, heading to the barracks to play his part in the massacre to come.

Roland followed closely behind him before veering off toward the nearest reactor. Using the shadows at the edge of the forest that ringed the camp, they both moved quickly into place.

Jonah cocked his M7S, armed the ONI special-issue energy disruptor, and primed two flares, then waited silently for Roland's signal.

On the other side of the camp, Roland checked his weapon and primed the first set of charges.

A pair of Sangheili strolled past, close enough that had they simply glanced to their left they would have been staring directly at the human intruder, but the creatures passed uneventfully, totally oblivious to the enemy in their midst.

Once the two Elites were at a safe distance, Roland pulled out a small transceiver, flicked the devise's safety cap open, and pressed his thumb to the larger of two buttons on its plain surface.

An explosion erupted in the distance, echoing across the canyon, and somewhere off in the night a large tree fell to the earth, a lone Jackal sniper tumbling down with it.

The triggering of the lumberjack was the "go" signal. As the explosion reverberated through the valley, the Covenant camp sprang to life.

Roland activated his camouflage and stepped from his cover, darting toward the first reactor. The instant the crack of the detonation filled the air, Jonah swung around the front of the barracks building, tossing his energy disruptor through the barrier that served as its door.

Like Roland's av-cam, and most other advanced battlefield equipment, the energy disruptor Jonah used to deactivate the barracks' entry barrier and all electronic devices within was reverse engineered by ONI scientists from scavenged Covenant technology.

Part of Jonah was irked by the need to rely on their enemy's tech, but a larger part thrilled at the irony of turning the Covenant's advances against them. He followed the disruptor with a pair of flares, then stepped through the entryway prepared for chaos.

Hell and fury seemed to erupt from the area surrounding the barracks. As Roland continued about his piece of their little insurrection, he allowed himself to briefly imagine Jonah prancing upon a field of Covenant corpses, happily bounding about in his own private nirvana, but just as quickly Roland was back in the moment, and his internal clock was telling him they didn't have much time.

Aside from the reality of his av-cam's limited lifespan, Roland also knew the second he triggered the explosion at the sniper's perch, he and Jonah would have a very limited time frame before reinforcements from one or more of the other camps arrived. Making an effort to focus solely on placing the charges on the chosen reactors, Roland had to pause briefly between the first and second in order to drop a collection of Grunts and Jackals who were in the process of setting up a defensive perimeter around a shade turret. Moving as quickly as he could, Roland finished planting his charge on the third of the four reactors and turned toward his final target, when he saw a squad of five Elites and four Grunts heading up the low brim that led to the barracks.

Certain that Jonah was able to handle himself, but not wanting his partner caught unaware by the Covenant making a beeline directly for him, Roland altered his course to engage this new threat, tossing a frag grenade into their midst to soften them up.

The small, round explosive bounced and ignited directly between two of the Elites; their shields flared and died. The other Elites lost their shields, but only temporarily, and of the four Grunts, three were killed in the blast, the other falling in a heap, mortally wounded.

Roland steadied his submachine gun and was prepared to fire when another explosion boomed off in the distance, across the valley.

The second, unexpected explosion must have been the work

of the other infiltration team, Roland thought. Though the two Headhunter teams were acting independently, Roland and Jonah had been designated Team One and were serving as the mission's primary assault squad, meaning the secondary team would wait for their attack before initiating one of their own.

The explosion Roland triggered at the sniper perch gave Team Two the go-ahead, though Roland was surprised they'd been in a position to follow so quickly on the heels of his and Jonah's assault. Not that it bothered him. With two simultaneous stealth attacks against what the Covenant thought was an unknown outpost, the aliens would be in complete disarray. The timing of the second attack allowed each team a slightly increased window of opportunity, but there was still no room for delays.

Roland threw his second grenade. The two shieldless Elites went down, not dead, but out of the fight—one missing its legs at the knees and the other with a gaping wound in its stomach, intestines and fluid pouring forth onto the matted grass.

The remaining Elites once again lost their shields, this time for good. They wheeled around, trying to spot their attacker. Roland's camo flickered, momentarily giving away his position, as he emptied his clip into the disoriented Elites.

Across the compound, Jonah had stepped into the barracks to find a dozen bewildered Covenant—six Grunts, two Jackals and four Elites, all with some level of confusion plastered on their faces.

The initial explosion had caught them off guard and the disruptor had removed their shields and deactivated their weapons. Now, still reeling from the effects of the flash bangs, the lot of them were essentially helpless. Not being one to waste the upper hand, Jonah pressed the issue, driven by a terrible motivation that sat at the heart of his hatred for the Covenant—the thought of his biological brothers and sisters, his mother and father, killed—murdered—vaporized into dust and ash during the Covenant's sacking of Eirene.

As the first few silent rounds flashed from the muzzle of his M7S, impacting on the nearest Elite's chest and throat, the momentary sadness brought on by the memory of his family's smiling faces dissipated, replaced by joy.

THE STARK contrast between Jonah's words—*that wasn't so bad*—and the sight of him made his proclamation all the more surreal.

He stood calmly, coolly, on the lip of the slope that led to the Covenant barracks building. Even clad in full armor, the cockiness and pure confidence of his pose betrayed the shit-eating grin Roland was certain was plastered on his friend's face. And then there was the blood.

How anything could be labeled as "not so bad" and yet involve that much carnage—Roland just laughed.

The remaining Covenant stood transfixed, bewildered by what they saw: Standing on a low ridge in the middle of their encampment was a sole combatant, a lowly human dog, coated in the blood and viscera of their brethren. Such a thing was unthinkable.

Once he was certain he had their complete and undivided attention, Jonah knelt, slowly—deliberately—never taking his eyes off his enraged foes.

In his right hand, Jonah held his combat knife, gripped blade back, eager for a fight. Thick chunks of flesh and clots of purple and green blood stuck to the blade's edge—hanging in strings, like saliva from the maw of a ravenous beast. With his left hand, Jonah reached for the ground, pausing only briefly as he gripped something just out of sight.

Roland watched from the nearby shadows as he set the remainder of the charges along the rim of the final reactor. His suit's active-camo function was quickly depleting its dedicated power supply, and he could see that the Covenant, though momentarily confused by Jonah's presence, were beginning to tense up.

He sensed the energy in the atmosphere begin to charge; these last few survivors would not allow their lives to end as helpless victims to the assassins in their midst. A defiant glower on their faces, Roland saw three of the Elites draw their muscles taut—they were getting ready to make a move; ready to pounce. Their first steps on their so-called Great Journey may be mere seconds away, but the warriors' code by which they lived meant these Elites would not die without a fight. Their sense of honor would not allow it, just as it would not allow them to be taunted by the murder of their kin, which is exactly what Jonah was doing—taunting them.

It's what he always did—*Every damn mission*, Roland thought. *He just can't help but play with his food.*

The eerie quiet that had settled upon the camp following the initial burst of violence gave Roland the sense that they were directly in the eye of the storm—that whatever hellish fury had played out only moments before, what was to come next would be worse, and it would be sudden.

He placed the last of the charges and locked the detonator's receiver in the "on" position, then knelt and lifted a half-loaded Covenant carbine rifle from a dead Jackal's grasp. He sighted the Elite nearest Jonah, the weapon's aiming reticule drawn directly at the beast's head—the instant he so much as twitched, a hail of radiation would liquefy his brain cavity.

Out in the open, the Covenant soldiers still frozen in disbelief, Jonah rose from his crouched position, a severed Elite head gripped tightly in his left hand. Jonah lifted the trophy high in the air, and then spoke for the first time since the encounter began: "Rolle, light 'em up."

The lead Elite's head rocked with three successive bursts from Roland's scavenged carbine before its massive body slumped to the ground, lifeless.

The handful of Covenant survivors leveled their weapons at Jonah, who hefted the severed head and threw it full force at a Grunt about to unleash a fully charged blast from its quivering plasma pistol. The macabre projectile hit the Grunt in the chest, shaking it off balance and sending its plasma blast spiraling into the night sky.

The tiny, angry alien attempted to right itself, but not in time—Jonah had already removed his pistol, and as the Grunt regained its bearing a single slug impacted its temple. Jonah then made short work of the scattered Grunts and Jackals displaced about the courtyard, while avoiding fire from the few Elites still in the fight.

He and Roland had the advantage of placing their enemies in a crossfire between Jonah's slightly higher vantage and the tree line Roland used for cover, making it difficult for the Covenant to focus on just one attacker.

Roland finished off two more Elites but then his carbine trigger clicked empty.

A third Elite charged Jonah, whose attention was focused on wrapping up the only other surviving Covenant, a Kig-Yar cowering behind a personal energy gauntlet. As Jonah worked his way around the shield and planted two bullets in the Jackal's side, Roland called a warning, "Jay, seven-o'clock," and peppered the back of the Elite with his submachine gun, whittling away at its shield.

Jonah spun.

The Elite barreled toward him, only a few meters away, anger and hatred burning in its eyes. As if he were simply swatting a fly,

Jonah tapped the trigger of his magnum twice, putting a bullet into each of the Elite's kneecaps.

The beast fell.

Roland sprinted over as Jonah slid a new clip into his pistol.

The Elite struggled to lift itself—beaten, yet defiant. Unable to stand, it rested on its bloodied knees.

"Nice shot." Roland bent down to grab a plasma pistol from the ground, sweeping the area for survivors as he rose.

"You softened him up." Jonah walked toward the injured Elite, also checking the periphery for any signs of trouble.

"Still got some fight in you, big guy?" Jonah stopped just out of the Sangheili's reach. "Ya know? Up close, you Slip-Lips aren't so special. You know that, right?"

The Elite stared up as the two Spartans looked down on it.

"I mean, really," Jonah prodded. "I've always meant to ask . . . what makes you Covenant thugs think yer so damned special anyway? What gives you the right to do the things you do?"

The Elite passed his gaze from Jonah to Roland and back. "There is honor in *our* path," he began, "you . . . *your* kind . . . humanity? You are nothing but a disease that must be wiped clean from this galaxy—a taint upon—"

"Yeah, well—this disease ain't goin' nowhere. In fact, seems ta me, it's right up in yer goddamn face and there ain't much'a damn thing you can do about it."

"If we were to meet in battle as warriors—*true* warriors," the Elite hissed, "you would fall, just as so many of your kind have fallen—to our swords and fire; under the weight of our boots. But you—*you* are not warriors. You are *assassins.* Weak and timid, you hide in the shadows—"

"Says the alien shit-heel who invented active-camo," Jonah said. "*Yeah*, yer noble. How noble's glassin' a planet from orbit?"

Jonah tapped the kneeling beast across his temple with an open hand. "Answer that."

"Your influence must be expunged—eradicated—from the worlds you have fouled with your very presence—"

"I really don't like this guy," Roland interrupted. "Cut 'im loose, Jay. I think it's past time we beat feet."

"I fear not the path to the Great Journey beyond. I embrace it." Though he was bloodied and gravely wounded, the Elite's eyes welled with pride has he spoke.

"'Great Journey,' huh?" Jonah huffed. "What's so great about it?"

The Elite stared directly at Jonah's visor, making eye contact despite the fact he could not see Jonah's face through the reflective surface. "You will never—"

In a blur of motion, Jonah's hand flicked forward, plunging his blade hilt-deep into the side of the Elite's neck.

The creature shuddered and lurched, sick wet gurgles bubbling up from its throat. It lunged for the blade, more reflex than an actual attempt to defend itself. Jonah stood motionless, holding his ground.

Purple-black blood seeped from the wound, dripping from the Elite's split mandibles.

Jonah maintained his stance for a moment—looking down on his latest victim with disgust—then suddenly, violently wrenched his wrist, twisting the blade in place. "It was a rhetorical question, asshole," he said, his voice a mix of disdain and boredom as he slid the blade out of the dying Elite's neck.

In one fluid motion, he removed his M6C from its holster with his left hand, and kicked the alien to the mud- and blood-caked ground with a thud. As the heavy alien body settled, a sudden and silent flash burst from the muzzle of Jonah's pistol as he fired a single round into his fallen enemy's face—the bullet entering through the roof of its still-twitching mouth before exploding out the top of its thick skull, depositing itself, along with myriad brain bits and bone fragments, in the soft, soggy turf below.

"Overkill, don't you think?" Roland offered, mockingly.

Jonah leveled his M6C dead center on the dead Elite's chest, firing four more rounds, each whispered *thwip* of gunfire—*thwip, thwip, thwip, thwip*—answered by the kiss of punctured flesh and ventilated lung. "Better safe than sorry," Jonah cracked back as he safetied his weapon and ran his blade along the armor-plating on his thigh, wiping away the residue of a battle well won.

"Yer funny."

"Someone's gotta put a smile on that grumpy face, Rolle, old boy."

Roland checked his sensors and the power charge on his suit's battery. "We got other places ta be and this joint is prime to blow—you ready to roll out?"

"Yeah." Jonah paused as he gave the area one last visual sweep—Covenant carcasses and discarded weapons littered the campsite. "This place is dead anyway—"

As the last syllable escaped Jonah's lips a sudden crackle of energy sparked in the cool night air.

FIVE

Something New

Roland's body quaked—a violent, sudden spasm erupting from his torso and pulsing through his limbs in a series of aftershocks—then he seized as the muscles along his spinal column clinched and froze.

Jonah sprang back, instinctively taking up a defensive stance—pistol instantly off his hip and in firing position, the events before him slowing to a crawl.

For less than a second Roland stood perfectly upright and motionless before his body jerked with another forceful, involuntary start as the dual-pronged tips of a Covenant energy sword pierced his chest, sliding through his body and armor like wet paper. Jonah's eye caught on the flicker of the blade's plasma sizzling red with blood—the weapon's dual blades protruded farther from his partner's chest.

Shaking himself from his daze, Jonah unloaded his Magnum's clip just over Roland's shoulders.

The bullets pinging off something large, but unseen; each round harmlessly deflected into the night. A replacement magazine clicked home in the pistol before the last of the barrage's shells hit the ground.

Roland's muscles relaxed and he let out a gurgled, raspy cough, and a single, whispered word . . . "Clear . . ."

Everything—the blade, Roland, Jonah, the evening breeze—stopped for a handful of seconds—still and eerily serene; the only sound the pop and sizzle of the energy sword as it seared the flesh around and between the wounds.

Then, just as suddenly as it had appeared, the floating sword pushed forward with a quick, deliberate thrust before viciously being ripped up and away, exiting through the Spartan's right shoulder, just below the neck. Upon reaching the apex of its arc, the energy sword shimmered then blinked out. Gone—but not gone.

The force of the swipe nearly cleaved Roland's upper body in two, a thick geyser of blood spraying upward as the mortally wounded soldier slumped to the dirt, lifeless. As Roland fell, the spray of his blood coated a cloaked shape looming directly over his broken body.

Like an apparition, the smattering of crimson life danced in midair. Jonah couldn't make out the exact shape of his enemy, but its weapon of choice suggested it was Sangheili. He brought his pistol to center mass on the red blot and sidestepped toward a downed Unggoy to his left.

The small, dead creature's Plasma Pistol would come in handy if Jonah hoped to penetrate the cloaked Elite's shield. Jonah had two additional disruptors, but he would need them at the next target site. Regardless of being a man down—friend or not—there was still a mission to accomplish.

As Jonah retrieved the alien weapon, he was sure his foe would attack.

Instead, the alien held its ground—showing an extraordinarily high level of restraint, even for an Elite. Usually Covenant warriors pressed any advantage—attacking in force until their enemies were overrun and slaughtered, but this one was different. It hadn't taken part in the firefight between the Spartans and the rest of the camp's Covenant contingent. It had stayed back—hidden; waiting.

For what? Sangheili weren't cowards. Unlike the Unggoy and Kig-Yar, whose bravery and ferociousness most often relied squarely on the tide of battle, the Sangheili were uniformly fearless foes. Why would this one in particular wait until its colleagues were beaten before launching its assault?

Jonah wanted answers to these questions—craved the hows and whys—but more than anything he just wanted this creature dead. He wanted to see the life drain from its eyes. Wanted to revel in its death.

He felt rage well up inside—like a weight pressing down against his chest—as he gripped the Plasma Pistol and began to rise, pointing both of his weapons at the bloodstained blur across the yard.

Motion trackers should've caught him before he got close, Jonah thought, running through the past twenty seconds, grasping for logic in this surprise attack—in his friend's death.

He squeezed the trigger on the plasma pistol, building a charge as he and the alien circled one another. He and Roland liked to goof—liked to have fun—but they were careful. Damn careful. And way too skilled to have their partnership ended in such an ignoble fashion—taken unaware by a lone Elite.

Hazarding a glance at Roland's mangled body, Jonah's mind raced. "Goddamn it," he shouted. "How'd you do it, you sonuvabitch? How'd you get the drop?"

Jonah released the plasma pistol's trigger, sending a large green burst of energy careening toward the ghostly blood smear. The Elite tried to leap out of the way, but the plasma blast tracked its target, catching the alien in its side just below the rib cage. The beast let out an angered cry as its active-camouflage and its shielding sparkled with tiny flecks of electricity and faded, revealing an Elite warrior like none Jonah had ever seen. The Elite seemed like any other in terms of its size and physical makeup, but was made more imposing by the sleek, custom armor that covered its entire body, including a full-faced helmet with a cycloptic visor port wrapping from right to left. There was also an odd shifting in the armor's coloring, as if it were analyzing and adapting to its environment, the base color of the armor adjusting, changing to blend with the background, making it hard to focus on the alien's movements. While not as effective as active-camouflage, this new chameleonlike feature definitely provided a strategic advantage.

Squinting to get a clearer view, Jonah noticed the armor itself was more rounded—more elegant—than the typically segmented

Sangheili battlefield attire and was adorned with etched detailing, which was hard to make out in the low light, but seemed to have a purpose similar to war paint—ornate and aggressive. This Elite may not want to be seen, but clearly wanted any who got a good look to understand completely, and without question, that he meant business.

Jonah followed the plasma blast with a barrage of bullets from his pistol, lightly feathering the trigger for maximum rate of fire.

But this Elite was too fast. Jonah hit his mark with a few rounds but the nimble alien easily avoided the rest; an unsettling turn of events for a marksman of Jonah's caliber.

Jonah holstered his pistol and pulled his fully loaded SMG from his back, bringing it to bear on the Elite, cocking the weapon in one fluid twist, but the alien's shields and camo recovered from the plasma hit.

"There's no way," Jonah said shocked. "Well, Rolle, buddy," Jonah already missed his friend more than he cared to admit, "looks like we got ourselves somethin' new with this one."

Jonah flipped on his suit's VISR enhanced vision. Luminescent tracers marked the edges of buildings, trees, abandoned weapons and corpses, giving a defining edge to everything in Jonah's line of sight.

Wherever the Elite was hiding, VISR would allow Jonah to track him with ease. Problem was; the Elite wasn't hiding . . . and neither were his friends.

Standing where he had faded just seconds ago, the mysterious Elite held his ground, his transparent bodily features indicated by a ring of red as the VISR technology mapped out the creature's silhouette.

Jonah kept his aim on the Elite but didn't fire.

"Shit," Jonah said aloud to himself; his shoulders slumping a bit.

The Elite laughed, a thick, guttural boom, as the full extent of the danger dawned on Jonah.

Standing to the left and just a few meters behind the Elite were three others sporting the same souped-up armor, as marked by the red VISR-induced glow tracing their outline. To his right, two more Elites stood, almost casually.

These others had been watching the whole damn time. "This wasn't a solitary straggler who'd caught two of ONI's heavy hitters with their guard down," Jonah chided himself.

"This was a goddamn trap."

SIX

Fair Trade

Time was running out. Despite the immediate odds, Jonah knew he didn't have much time to make his escape before the base camp was overrun with Covenant regulars, never mind the six hard-asses standing in front of him.

The other squad's gotta be doing better than this, he hoped, as his mind flashed to the second team of Headhunters operating on the other side of the valley.

As if reading Jonah's mind, the Sangheili who'd killed Roland spoke. "Your fellow conspirators are dead. Like the one here, slaughtered like pups—helpless and weak."

Jonah was impressed. If the Covenant had such high-level Spec-Ops troops stationed on such a remote moon, then one of two options was true: Either ONI had gotten their intel right and this place was, in fact, a pretty damn big deal to the Covenant, or the Headhunters had been doing their job so well that this whole scenario was one big alien boondoggle devised to draw them out. For a moment, thoughts of Roland's death and six large obstacles standing before him dissipated, and Jonah found himself strangely satisfied—if two or more teams of the Covenant's absolute top-of-the-line Elite squads were tied up babysitting a site so far from the frontlines, then they weren't *on* the frontlines, which was a win for the UNSC no matter how you sliced it.

"You idiots set this up," he called to the Elite. "This . . . all of it. You wanted *us* . . . heh. Yer *afraid* of us. I'm flattered."

"You are dead," one of the Elite hissed.

"Could be. Don't matter."

"You value your life so little?"

"No. Not really," Jonah explained. "I kinda like being me, actually. But you being here, means yer not somewhere else, get it? All this . . . these resources, all yer skill, wasted on a few 'pathetic' humans makes me feel kinda good—kinda special. And if you think yer taking me out without losing a limb . . . you've lost yer goddamn mind."

"We'll see who's lost their mind, once we have carved your flesh and you've screamed your secrets to the stars," the main Elite replied.

These guys *were* different, and Jonah admired them for it.

Usually Covenant battlefield doctrine was simple and to the point: "Take no prisoners." And while this new brand of Elite seemed to be playing a different game, Jonah was fairly certain that, had they wanted, he would already be dead. After all, they had the numbers and, up until a moment ago, the added advantage of total surprise.

"This ends one of two ways, chief," Jonah said. "I either walk out of here, yer teeth hangin' from a string around my neck, or I die with my fist down someone's throat."

Jonah made a come-hither motion with his SMG, before finishing, "So let's start this party, I'm late for a hot date, and I don't wanna keep yer sister waiting." Jonah was unsure if the familial insult would translate, but by this point he couldn't care less. It was time to dance.

"You can sense your end, human. That is good. If it brings you any peace, the whole of your kind will soon follow suit."

The lead Elite clicked something to his squad in their native language.

Three of the Elites leveled what looked to be modified carbine rifles at Jonah, while two others began moving toward him, igniting their energy swords. As the blades sparked to life Jonah noticed something he'd earlier mistaken as a trick of Roland's blood on the Elite's blade—these energy swords weren't powered by the same blue-white energy source as the Covenant's typical plasma-based cutlery. Instead they were comprised of a reddish energy combined with the white flicker of electricity, which caused them to emit a blood-colored glow.

Jonah couldn't guess at the difference between these new swords and the more commonly used blue-variant, but he was sure of one thing: his attackers were full of surprises, and he felt a twinge of fear creep up the back of his neck.

The two sword-wielding Elites moved forward carefully, as if stalking prey.

Jonah laughed. "You know I can see you, right?"

The Elites didn't alter their approach, maintaining their speed and positioning—muscles tensed, ready to strike.

"We are aware of your visual upgrades, human. As stated, we've already been through this with your friends. Lay down your arms and surrender yourself for inquisition."

Jonah shifted his gaze to Roland's body, keeping the Elites squarely in peripheral view. "Twenty credits says yer all dead within . . . let's say . . . the next thirty seconds."

The lead Elite scoffed. "We will end you before you so much as bruise our egos, dog. Now, lay down your weapons—"

"Seriously. I know you might not have any credits handy, but I'm willing to take the Covenant equivalent." Jonah let the offer stand for a brief instant, then dropped his SMG to the turf.

"We got a deal?" The two approaching Elites picked up their pace, as the others steadied their aim.

Jonah relaxed his posture, let his knees flex and his back and shoulders slouch.

The two Elites were almost within reach. Jonah bent into a deep crouch—his muscles contracted, taunt—before tumbling back, head over heels, coming up a good ten yards from the nearest Elite. Hunched in a low squat, Jonah held a disruptor in one hand, his charge detonator in the other.

While Roland had been responsible for demolitions on most missions, with Jonah preferring to focus on direct combat, both members of a Headhunter squad were required to carry the proper charges and triggering mechanisms necessary for fieldwork to ensure redundancy should any unforeseen complications arise. And though Jonah would've preferred another way out, he was fully aware that his luck had run dry, and as he and his fellow 'Hunters had been fond of saying since their earliest training days on Onyx: "When in doubt, blow shit up."

Jonah's mind flashed to Roland one more time, and he silently thanked his partner for one last assist—"Clear." Roland's final breath had also been a parting shot at the Covenant bastard who'd run him through.

These special division Spec-Op Elites may have been watching the whole show, but Roland was cloaked when he set his charges, so unless the Sangheili had the equivalent of VISR in those shiny new helmets, they didn't know thing one about the explosives placed on the reactors all around them.

"Clear" meant the primer on the charges had been initiated.

"Clear" meant with a push of a button this entire section of the valley would light up as bright and hot as the surface of a star, nothing but scorched earth and charred bones in its wake.

"Clear," and Jonah had a plan, even if it meant kissing his own ass good-bye.

He raised the disruptor. "Know what this is?"

"Take him!" the lead Elite called.

But Jonah had allowed the two closest Elites to get within arm's length in order to block the line of fire of their three squadmates with ranged weaponry. If the they got close enough to cut him he'd still have time to blow the fuse and take them all to hell right along with him.

Jonah activated the disruptor and tossed it in a low arc toward the four farthest Elites while dodging a swipe from one of the energy swords, but he was too slow to avoid the second's grasp.

The Elite yanked him to his feet, ripping his shoulder from its socket. Jonah screamed in pain.

The energy field from the disruptor expanded as it hit the ground at the feet of the farthest group of aliens, shutting down power to their weapons and armor.

The Elite holding Jonah shook him like a rag doll. "You dare defy us, filth? You will suffer for your sins." He raised his sword, using the very edge of the blade to cut a gash across Jonah's faceplate, digging into the flesh beneath. Jonah's left eye sizzled and popped as the blade passed through. For the second time in recent memory, the Spartan screamed, but he still held tightly to the detonator, thumb pressed firmly on the tiny unit's ignition switch.

The second sword-wielding Elite stepped up and grabbed him by the neck.

In Jonah's mind a thousand witty remarks echoed, an infinite chorus of banter to die to, but instead of uttering a word, Jonah simply glanced at the beasts above him, these "elite" commandoes whose body count quite possibly surpassed his own, and thought to himself, *Six of you, one of me. Fair trade*, as he released his thumb from the detonator.

After that everything went white.

BLUNT INSTRUMENTS

FRED VAN LENTE

ONE

Fireteam Spartan: Black's objective was not difficult to locate. All one had to do was look for the enormous pinkish-purple plume of energy spearing out of the horizon on the colony world Verge. They bled silently through ten square kilometers of heavily fortified enemy anti-aircraft positions toward the perpetually shining beam until at last they reached the remains of Ciudad de Arias.

This city had been among the hardest hit in the initial Covenant assault a few months prior. The buildings leaned and listed in their foundations like beaten boxers right before a climactic keel to the mat. It took Black-Four a few minutes to identify an apartment tower that looked stable enough for them to scale without it collapsing beneath their feet.

Once they reached the penthouse, they passed stencils of pandas and koalas still visible on the charred walls as they entered what they assumed had been a child's room. They lay on their bellies and looked out through the vacant holes where windows once were.

Their massive target drifted about five blocks away, casually knocking over fire-gutted husks into clouds of rubble. Thanks to their untranslatable and unpronounceable Covenant name, FLEETCOM simply dubbed the enormous machines "Beacons." Nearly fifty stories tall and five city blocks wide, the Beacon looked to the Spartans' eyes like a perfectly symmetrical beehive floating atop four antigravity stilts. Out of its gaping lower orifice swarmed a buzzing cloud of Yanme'e, the glittering, winged insectoids humans called Drones. Clicking and screeching and hissing and squealing in a teeth-gritting cacophony, the swarm tore deep below Verge's surface with handheld antigravity grapplers that yanked up great chunks of regolith. The Drones flew back up and deposited the rocks inside the Beacon's hollow, irradiant heart, where the helium-3 inside them would be extracted and converted into pure fusion power. The energy was then projected skyward, focused in the form of a massive purple beam erupting from the Beacon's summit. A weblike constellation of Covenant satellites orbiting Verge transmitted the power to the fleet blockading the colonies on Tribute, in the Epsilon Eridani system.

Like every other colony world's, Verge's helium-3 deposits had been trapped in the second mantle laid down over her original, natural exosphere during the spallation-heavy terraforming process. The Beacon would drift from continent to continent, gathering and extracting all the He-3 it could, until Verge was picked clean, a few weeks from now. Then the machine and its crew would be drawn up into a battle cruiser so the Covenant could glass the planet from space.

Unless, of course, Spartan: Black blew the godforsaken thing to kingdom come first, cutting off the primary fuel source to the fleet blockading Tribute and giving the colonists there a fighting chance.

Which was exactly what they planned to do.

"What do we see, people?" Black-One asked. Befitting their highly classified status as an unconventional warfare (UW) unit, Spartan: Black's ebony armor had been created as skunkwork prototypes in a top secret parallel development lab in Seongnam, United Korea; as such, MJOLNIR: Black boasted a few variant design elements and enhancements completely different from the standard-issue combat exoskeleton. Its HUD magnification, for example, was much greater than the standard Mark V or VI, with a field of view of nearly five thousand meters. From this distance, Spartan: Black could zoom in on the support troops milling beneath the antigrav "feet" of the Beacon and see them as clearly as if they had been standing across the street.

"Two Hunters per pylon," Black-Two said, noting the stooped, spiny-armored behemoths. Each creature's right arm terminated in a gun barrel studded with luminescent green power rods. "Armed with standard assault cannon."

"Complemented by two—no, three—Jackals at each corner," Black-Three added.

The spiky-crowned, beaked aliens carried, in addition to plasma pistols holstered at their sides, some kind of long pole made of a translucent purple-pink crystalline material. Occasionally, a Drone would flit away from the larger swarm in a confused, almost drunken fashion, and a couple of Jackals would descend on it with a shriek, stabbing the stray in the neck, where it wore a translucent reddish-orange collar. The bugger quaked spasmodically with pain, clutching the collar with its front claws; it could take only a thrust or two from the Jackals and the resulting seizures before it fell dutifully back with the swarm and resumed whatever task it had abandoned.

"Jackals aren't just security," Four said. "They're also management."

"Very nice to meet you," Two said. "I look forward to killing you."

No one said anything for almost five minutes. They just watched the enemy work.

Finally, Three said, "Hunters and Jackals—they're just another day at the office. I mean, I can kill Tree-Turkeys in my sleep. And Can-o'-Worms are something you can sink your teeth into. But the buggers—how many are there?"

"I've got a hundred, a hundred fifty so far," Four said. "But I'm not sure . . . some I may have counted twice. They're moving pretty fast down there."

"One-fifty . . . Jesus," Three said. "How are the buggers going to react when we bring the hammer down? Can they use those grappler things as weapons? What kind of intel do we have on their tactics and behavior?"

"We have jack," said Two, the fireteam's intelligence officer. "Covenant's rarely deployed them as combatants."

"Jesus," Three muttered again, shaking his head. "I hate surprises."

"If it was easy, they wouldn't call us heroes," One drawled.

"I'd prefer a pat on the back," Three said. "But I gotta be alive for that."

"Two," One said, "find us a room in the interior where we can mull this over and catch some Z's without being seen from the street."

"Copy that, Chief." Black-Two backed out on her stomach until she reached the nursery's doorway, then got up into a crouch and made her way quickly but cautiously through the rest of the penthouse. She determined that what was left of the kitchen had no good sightlines to the perimeter and prepared to return and tell One but was stopped by a fluttering, flapping sound from a doorway on the north side of the room.

She pressed her back against the wall and peered around the doorway. She was looking into a ruined family room, a flatscreen lying facedown and shattered on a carpet littered with tempered glass that once filled floor-to-ceiling windows. On the ground beside a sofa blackened and bloated by fire and the elements, a solitary Yanme'e Drone twitched his wings spasmodically.

Two put both hands on the assault rifle hanging from her shoulder and silently lined up a shot at the crown of the bugger's walnut-shaped head. Something seemed off about the creature, though. She didn't pull the trigger.

Two realized the Drone was on his back, pulsing the hinged armored plates that covered his wings over and over again in a futile attempt to flip himself over onto his belly. Two could now see that all four of his lower legs had been cut off and cauterized at the stumps. His two remaining arms didn't have joints that allowed him to reach behind and push himself upright.

Two watched him struggle for twenty seconds more. Then she emerged from behind the doorway and took several slow strides over to where the Drone lay. His orange, half-egg eyes were fixed at the ceiling and didn't register her approach.

Still covering the insectoid with the rifle, Two tucked one foot under the creature's body and kicked him up and over. He began frantically beating his wings to stay upright while hopping up and down on the end of his abdomen. The bugger was human sized, and they were now practically eye to eye. Two took a step back and made sure the Drone was staring down the barrel of the AR.

Holding the gun steady with one hand, she flexed her other

elbow in such a way that a compartment sprang open along the left foreaem of the skunkware MJOLNIR. A wand computer with a microphone, speakers, a digital ink keyboard, and every scrap of linguistics data United Nations Space Command had gathered on the languages of Covenant races popped out of the compartment and slid into her palm.

"Identify yourself and your purpose," Two said sternly, and waited for the Interrogator, as ONI had christened the device, to translate and broadcast the question in Yanme'e.

The icon of a rotating circle appeared on the Interrogator's display, indication it was working. After only a few seconds, the device emitted a faint series of clicks and screeches in a pitiful attempt to mimic Yanme'e speech. Two had little faith in it succeeding. Sure enough, a moment later, its display flashed: "Untranslatable." Two cursed under her breath. Not enough was known about the damn buggers to make even that simple demand intelligible.

With his head cocked quizzically, the Drone watched as Black-Two tried to rephrase the question a couple of different ways so that the Interrogator might translate, but no avail.

Then the creature made an unmistakable gesture, extending one claw in her direction, then curling his digits rapidly toward himself: *Give.*

Black-Two frowned. What little intel ONI had on the Drones suggested they had an instinctive faculty for technology. Cautiously, she handed the Interrogator over. There seemed little harm in it. A cord attached the device to her forearm to supply it with power and data, as well as ensure that the other half of a conversation couldn't just walk away with it.

The second the Yanme'e wrapped his claws around the device he popped open the access panel on its underside. He rearranged the circuits and microfilament wires in the Interrogator's guts with such speed and precision that one would have thought he had spent every waking moment for the past twenty years working with them.

Two opened her mouth to protest, but found herself just watching, transfixed by the rapidity of the thing's movements, which had a certain kind of flitting grace, like a dragonfly making its evasive way across the surface of a pond. Something in the device clicked.

And the creature started talking.

IN THE nursery lookout, Black-One was just starting to wonder what was taking Black-Two so long when her subordinate's voice rang out from inside the apartment: "Chief! Better come here! Bring the boys, too!"

The rest of Spartan: Black walked into the living room to find Two tethered to the Drone by the Interrogator's power cord. At first glance it looked like the Yanme'e was holding the Spartan on a leash.

"*Whoa! Whoa! Whoa!*" Instantly, the three other Spartans fell into an attack phalanx, Three and Four both dropping to one knee and raising their ARs while One remained standing, training her own weapon on the Drone's head. "Spartan Black-Two!" she barked. "Step away from the hostile!"

Two held up both hands and made calming gestures. "It's okay," she said. "It's okay. He's not all that hostile. I named him Hopalong. Hopalong, meet the guys. Guys, meet Hopalong."

Hopalong's claws flickered across the translator's digital ink keypad. "*Hello, guys.*" Normally, the Interrogator spoke in the inflectionless nonaccent of the midwestern United States. But whatever the Drone did to the machine's insides had distorted the computer voice so that now it sounded more like a recording of intelligible speech played backward that just happened to also sound like intelligible speech.

"The hell, Two?" Three snapped. "Making friends?"

"He knows an alternate route to the Beacon, an underground one," Two said calmly, but with urgency. "Tunnels that have been completely cleaned out of helium-3 so the buggers don't go in them anymore. We can slip in under the antigrav pylons and take them out before the Covenant knows what hit them."

"How did he know we were after the Beacon in the first place?" Three demanded. "You tell him?"

"Have you looked outside?" Two snapped defensively. "Like there's anything else on this dirtball worth blowing up."

"I can't think of a single reported instance in which Covenant provided aid to human troops against their own kind," One said, pointing her weapon at Hopalong. "We trust this bug . . . why?"

"See that?" Two pointed to the stumps where Hopalong's missing limbs had once been. "The Jackals did that. They work the buggers to death on that thing."

Hopalong's claw flickered across the translator in short, staccato bursts. "*Kig-Yar do this*," the machine said, using the Jackals' own name for themselves. "*I drop cache twice. Kig-Yar cut legs off. Say I worthless. Let me crawl from Hive. Think I die, but no. Then I see you come. Through city. I follow. I come here. Climb walls. See you. Know you help. You kill Kig-Yar. All Drones help. Hive help.*

"*Covenant conquered us. Jiralhanae and Sangheili. Overthrew our own Hive-Gods. Make Hive worship Prophets instead. Rule through fear and pain. Now they come for you. Together we stop them. Earth Hive and Yanme'e. Just give us freedom. Freedom. Freedom. Freedom.*"

He reached up and touched the red-orange collar around his

neck with both claws. He flicked at it, as if wishing to rip it off, but didn't have the power.

"Freedom. Freedom. Freedom."

Hopalong kept repeating the same click-and-whistle combination that presumably meant *freedom* in the Yanme'e language. Two yanked the translator out of the Drone's hand and turned it off.

She pointed at herself, then at the rest of Fireteam Black, then made a "talking" symbol by slapping her thumb and fingers together. "We will get back to you," she said loudly.

Fireteam Black went into the kitchen where they could still see the Drone but he couldn't hear them, Interrogator or not.

The others waited for One to weigh in first. She didn't say anything for a minute, then said, "I can't shake the feeling there's something not quite on the up-and-up about this. But maybe that's because I don't like a roach as big as I am coming up with my battle plans." They couldn't see her face beneath the reflective gray visor of her helmet, of course, but it was obvious to all of them she was wrestling with the idea. "Besides, inserting ourselves into local intra-Covenant disputes is a little above our pay grade, Two. We're more the blunt-instrument type."

Two glanced back at Hopalong. He lay propped up on the floor on the middle joints of his remaining arms—the elbows, she supposed—and rubbed his claws together in front of his mandibles, back and forth, back and forth, like a housefly, in some kind of hygienic ritual.

"Normally I'd agree, Chief, but the plan he's proposing seems the best way to take the enemy by complete surprise *and* circumvent the Drone threat."

"You can be sure he's not leading us smack-dab into a trap?" The doubt in Three's voice was unmistakable.

"If he wanted us dead all he had to do was whistle for his buddies the minute he laid eyes on us," Four pointed out. "Why contrive some elaborate ambush?"

Black-One said, "I've got to say, the opportunity to hit the ground hot, inside the enemy's defenses, and take out the objective before they even have a chance to mount any kind of a resistance . . ." She stayed silent for a second or two then announced, "Yeah, that's just too good to pass up. Okay, Two. Tell the bugger he's got a deal."

Two went over to Hopalong to connect him to the translator again and give him the good news.

Once she was out of earshot, Four asked One, "And if it *is* a trap?"

Black-One looked straight at him. "Then we kill them all."

"Now you're talking," Three said.

TWO

Fireteam Black waited until an hour before dawn, which was scheduled to arrive around 0600 hours or so. In the interim they downed some high-protein MREs, then helped Three remove eight medium-sized backpacks from a case he had humped all the way from the drop point by himself. Each Spartan slipped a C-12 "blow pack" over each shoulder. A single pack could punch a hole in the hull of a Covenant Cruiser, as Fireteam Black had had the pleasure of witnessing firsthand. They had little clue what kind of material the Beacon's antigrav pylons were made out of, but the general consensus was that one pack per pylon should do the trick. And they probably only needed to knock out one or two pylons to send the whole thing crashing to the ground.

"And if not?" Four asked.

"Then we try harsh language," One said.

Everyone chuckled. Pre-op gallows humor. Situation: normal.

Hopalong watched them the whole time, hop-hovering in place, glittering head bobbing from one side to the other; whether that was from fascination or boredom no Spartan could say.

They fell in to callsign order and snaked down the stairs and out of the apartment building in single file.

Hopalong chose to crawl face-first down the edifice's side.

On the ground, One insisted that Hopalong point in the direction that he wished them to go; One then sent Four, with his battle rifle, to scope out the area. It never failed to amaze One, even after all these missions and engagements, how effortlessly Four simply melted into the shadows in his jet-black MJOLNIR, carrying his rifle by its barrel at his hip like it was a lunchbox. She and the others hunkered down behind piles of rubble and waited until the little yellow dot representing Black-Four on the circular motion tracker in the lower-left corner of their helmet displays briefly flashed green. Without giving any verbal commands, One rose to a crouch and sprinted in Four's direction; Three leapt up quickly and followed; Two, a little bit more slowly, so the crippled Hopalong could keep up behind.

They zigzagged through the ruins of Cuidad de Arias like this for twenty minutes, until Four swept, at Hopalong's indication, the basement of another crippled apartment tower via a side stairwell. An entire cellar wall had collapsed, burying a line of washing machines and exposing a rough-hewn tunnel carved in the unnaturally raised mantle of the terraformed planet.

Black-One switched the order of their close alignment at that point, acquiescing to Hopalong taking the lead, Four following, then Two, then Three. She took rear guard. Their sleek train formation was belied by their stumbling progress through the rough tunnel, which had been carved out by insectoids expecting only to fly through it. So the "floor," such as it was, was just as covered in fissures and protrusions and jagged edges as the "walls" or "ceiling." It was more like an esophagus than a tunnel, snaking in cylindrical fashion down, down, down ever deeper into the earth. Hopalong now had the advantage, hastily flitting forward on his translucent wings, disappearing from view until the column of Spartans rounded a bend to find him hovering in place, impatiently beckoning them forward with a claw. Visibility was awful, provided solely by light enhancement in their helmet visors, bathing their environs in a lime-green gloom. The whole experience would have been extremely claustrophobic, had spending days at a time entombed within head-to-toe exoskeletons not cured every Spartan of any possible inclination toward claustrophobia a long, long time ago.

They clambered and crawled through the tunnel until, very faintly, they could hear the unmistakable hum of the Drone swarm at work far in the distance, and the warren walls began to tremble with the looming overhead presence of the Beacon. They were drawing near.

Three stopped abruptly in front of One, and she almost walked right into him.

He turned around, raised his hand before her, and raised an index finger—the UNSC silent signal for *Heads up.*

She peered around Three's shoulder to the front of the line. Four had stopped as well and was turning to pass signs back to Two, who passed them to Three, who passed them to her.

A raised fist: *Hold position.*

Four disappeared into the darkness of the tunnel.

On her motion sensor One could see his yellow dot move eight, ten, fifteen meters away from their position—then he was out of sensor range.

Nothing happened for what seemed like a very long while.

Then the yellow dot reappeared on her sensor and rejoined the others. Four materialized out of the gloom.

He raised his forearm, clenched his fist, and pumped it up and down, rapid-fire: *Hurry!*

He disappeared back down the tunnel, and the others followed. In a few paces they entered a mammoth, ovular cavern, the top of which was covered with what appeared to be metallic scales, some kind of mineral deposit that caused the ceiling to gleam even in the subterranean nonlight.

Then One's breath caught in her throat.

Spartans were not, as a group, especially well acquainted with fear, but when she spotted one of the "scales" overhead shudder, as if shaking off a dream, One knew exactly what she was looking at.

Sleeping Drones. Hundreds of them, dangling from the ceiling of the cavern, completely carpeting the rock above.

She had only the one chance to glance above before she returned her attention to Three's back. He was in a crouch, weaving a nonlinear path through the cavern. One immediately intuited why: Four had gone out before them to scout the best route through the innumerable loose rocks and ankle-busting crevices in the cave floor so they could make their way through without noise. No need to wake the Yanme'e, no matter how friendly they were supposed to be. She knew for certain now that whatever Hopalong's plan was, it wasn't an ambush. If it were, they'd already be dead.

A distant noise kicked One right in the stomach: She could still hear a different swarm of Drones slaving away in the distance.

There were twice as many Drones here as they had previously counted. The day swarm worked while the night swarm slept, and vice versa.

That meant there had to be three to four hundred Drones all told in the area.

Black-One hoped they all shared Hopalong's democratic sympathies.

After a few twists and turns beyond the large cavern, Hopalong signaled for a stop and the Spartans circled him. They were so close to the work site that the grinding, growling of the excavations drowned out all other sounds, and the tunnel walls shook so violently they were periodically showered by dust and stones from above. A possible cave-in wasn't far from their thoughts.

Hopalong produced a thin broadcast data wafer.

"Hell is that?" Three shouted. In any other circumstances a whisper would have been preferable, but the harsh roar of digging practically prevented them from hearing themselves.

"Hopalong salvaged the broadcast wafer out of the video screen in the penthouse," Two yelled back. "He rejiggered it to show abandoned tunnels that lead toward one of the Beacon's pylons, and avoids ones being used for excavation now."

"I'm not sticking that thing in my head!" Three exploded. "Who knows what kind of enemy worms or viruses Bug Boy stuck on it!"

"I saw him make it myself, while you guys slept."

"Nothing personal, Two, but that doesn't exactly fill me with confidence."

"What's that supposed to mean?"

"You've got some serious Stockholm syndrome going on here with your six-legged boyfriend, that's all I'm saying. Your judgment may be seriously effed up."

"Sorry, I didn't quite catch that." Two got her back up. "You mind saying that again?"

With an explosive sigh that could be heard even over the grinding din surrounding them, Four reached between Two and Three and yanked the data wafer out of Hopalong's claw. He stuffed it into the receiving slot on the side of his helmet.

Three stared at Four. "You're a lot of help. I'm trying to hold an intervention for our sister here."

"In for a penny, in for a pound," Four said.

When a diode on one end flashed, indicating the upload was complete, Four yanked the wafer out and handed it to Two, who stuck it into her helmet too. One was prepared to order Three to do the same but that proved unnecessary. Soon all four of their HUDs featured translucent V-shaped arrows with range meters that indicated the direction of their individual pylons.

"Everybody set countdown timers for . . . T-minus ten minutes," One said. "This spot is Rally Point Alpha. Return here once your blow packs are set. Then we'll have Hopalong give his buggers the good news they've been liberated. We'll evacuate them beyond the blast radius before detonating the C-12."

One pointed at Hopalong, then pointed at the ground. "You stay here and wait 'til we come back. You got me?"

The Drone just cocked his head and wiggled his mandibles in her general direction.

Spartan: Black checked their assault rifles one last time. Locked and loaded.

"Let's get some," One said.

"Universe needs less ugly," Three declared.

Then they headed off, alone, in four different directions.

Black-Two's HUD led her down a wide rabbit hole that snaked several levels deeper into the earth so narrowly that she had to scale down feet-first. At the nadir of the passage, where it began snaking back up again, a fissure in the side of the tunnel faced a much larger cavern beyond.

Two turned on the horizontal lantern over her visor and peered through. The beam illuminated subway tracks, a stalled train, and several signs in Spanish in the human-hewn tunnel on the other side.

She flicked the light off and made her way up the rest of the tunnel in the green gloom of light-enhancement. The range counter in her HUD said she was within fifty meters of her anti-grav pylon. The tunnel emptied out into another with a level floor and a ceiling high enough for her to stand up all the way again.

As soon as she did so, a Jackal rounded a bend, his beak pointed downward at a translucent glowing cube in his hands.

Right before he walked into her, he looked up, sensing an obstruction, and Black-Two unloaded her assault rifle into his face and neck. The deafening digging sounds reverberating off every inch of the warren completely drowned out the burp of the AR and the Kig-Yar dropped without a cry.

Black-Two crouched behind the bend in the tunnel, but no companions of the dead Jackal emerged. Her motion sensor remained clear of red dots. The countdown on her HUD hadn't quite reached eight minutes.

Near the floor, along one wall, she found a crevice big enough to stuff the Jackal's corpse into in case any hostiles decided to come up the tunnel behind her. She scraped gravel to cover the purple bloodstains on the tunnel floor and accidentally kicked the smoky cube the Kig-Yar was holding. As the cube bounced across the floor she thought she could see three-dimensional images in the center of it. She picked it up and turned it over in her hands.

The sides of the cube were perfectly clear, and its interior was filled with a cloudy gel that churned and swirled as if it had its own internal air currents. In the center of the mist stood a slowly rotating three-dimensional image of a Yanme'e male, wings extended. A few Covenant characters floated near its feet. Black-Two had studied her Interrogator enough to recognize these characters as numbers—years, in fact. Two dates about a decade apart.

A trio of buttons appeared beneath Black-Two's fingers on the surface of the cube. She tapped one, and the mist seethed, wiping away the large image of the Drone, and started cycling through a series of images inside an immaculate plasticine honeycomb marred by a spray of Drone legs, abdomens, heads, and splashes of their green-gray blood. Interspersed among these three-dimensional tableaus of slaughter were scenes of smashed eggs, presumably Yanme'e as well, shell shards hurled explosively against the luminescent hive walls, the not-quite-living insides scooped out and oozing across the floor. The same Kig-Yar character floated beside each image, every time.

The countdown on her HUD reached five minutes.

She removed the Interregator from her forearm and waved its optical scanner over the cube until it picked up the Jackal word.

While she waited for the Interrogator's wheel icon to stop rotating, she played with the cube a little bit more, punching other buttons and seeing where they took her. In all cases, the mist wiped away the existing image and replaced it with another 360 degree three-dimensional image of an individual Drone, attached to various scenes of hive carnage, all accompanied by the same Kig-Yar character.

At last, the Interrogator flashed at her. "Untranslatable," it claimed. "Word itself translation from Yanme'e language. Nearest analogue(s): 'Unmutual' (43% accuracy), 'Incapable of Socialization' (51% accuracy)."

Two shrugged, dropped the cube, and made her way to the mouth of the tunnel. One of the Beacon's pylons passed a full story over her head as she peeked just over the ground level. An erupted heap of asphalt four or five paces away momentarily blocked her view from the pylon's guard—three Jackals and two Hunters—but they soon marauded into view. They weren't looking in the direction of the pylon at all, but were fixated on the Drone swarm as it fell like titanium rain into the horizon below the Beacon's massive, pulsating belly, crisscrossing with a second curtain that showered upward, into its bowels.

The counter on Two's HUD ticked down below one minute.

Pre-fight adrenaline slammed into her veins. Her heart rate shot up to a dance-floor drumbeat.

Ten seconds. She flexed her hands around the AR.

"Engage," Black-One whispered across her helmet speakers.

Immediately, the sharp rattle of Black-Four's battle rifle could be heard even over the noise of the excavation. The Hunters turned and began bounding toward the opposite pylon.

Black-Two popped out of her hole and fired three short bursts at the back of the Jackals' heads as they fell in behind the Hunters. Jets of purple spray squirted skyward as they pitched forward.

One of the Hunters instantly spun its spiny head around and pointed its blank gaze at Black-Two. She despised the damn hulks and their completely blank, gray nonfaces, for they had no expressions to read, no way to tell if they had spotted you or not—

Until they started lumbering toward you, swinging their massive, armored legs with frightening rapidity, as this one did now.

Two leapt all the way out of the hole. She sprinted for the teepee-shaped pile of a collapsed concrete kiosk half a block away.

When she turned to let off a few bursts in the Hunter's direction, the emerald discharge from an assault cannon slammed right into her chest with a deafening roar of static, lifting her off her feet and slamming her onto the ground.

Getting knocked over saved her life, for as she thudded onto her back a second green ray of incendiary plasma blasted directly overhead. With her energy shields completely knocked out and the HUD shield alert honking a furious warning at her, the second blast would have cut her in half.

Two looked up over her chest and saw both Hunters rumbling down on her. She quickly rolled ungracefully behind the rubble cover and willed her shields to recharge, but the Hunter was looming over her before she had a chance to catch her breath. The armored bulk raised its triangle-shaped shield over its head, ready to bring it down on her in a crushing blow.

Instinct took over. The Hunter was tall enough for her to somersault between its legs, and her maneuver caused it to simply further pulverize the pile of concrete when it guillotined its arm down.

Until her shields returned, she didn't stand a chance mano a mano with the Mgalekgolo. But she had an equalizer: the blow pack. She slung one off her shoulder and hung it by its strap onto one of the Hunter's long spines jutting from its back.

She then sprang up, leaping up over the Hunter as it tried to reach back to grab the pack and rip it off—but its armored arms simply wouldn't turn that way. She used his head as a springboard and backflipped over the pile of rubble, remotely detonating the C-12 charge as she landed.

She would have been vaporized if the concrete pile of the kiosk hadn't been between her and the blast. The Hunter disappeared inside an abrupt ballooning mushroom of dust that radiated outward and completely subsumed Two.

When it finally receded, there was nothing left of the Mgalekgolo but a few sizzling bits of chitin fused to the ground and carbonized ropes of blackened worm. The concrete kiosk had been pulverized into powder.

The ground trembled beneath her feet and Black-Two whirled around just in time to see the other Hunter barreling furiously toward her. Her shield bar hummed back to full power. The barrel of the Hunter's assault cannon swirled a fierce emerald green, indicating it had charged for a second blast, but Two threw him off by opening up point-blank with the AR, forcing the thing to throw up its shield to protect itself.

They danced like this for a few seconds—the Hunter recharging, Two sidestepping and firing, the Hunter forced to stop and defend itself. Two knew she couldn't keep this up all day. For one thing, the Mgalekgolo had more armor than she had ammo. She had to maneuver herself into a position to land some shots in the exposed orange flesh between the armored plates around the neck and midriff, but of course the beast was making sure to keep those areas blocked with his shield.

Sudden movement to Two's right drew the barrel of her AR in that direction, but when she saw Hopalong clambering out of the hole she lowered her rifle. He hop-flew in shallow, graceless parabolas toward the underbelly of the Beacon. She looked in that direction and saw that the Yanme'e had stopped working. Instead, they swarmed across the machine's surface in a single glittering curtain. Unnervingly, every one of their amber, half-egg eyes seemed to be fixated on the approaching Hopalong with burning intensity.

Much to her shock, as soon as the Hunter spotted Hopalong too, he swiveled around and lumbered after him, completely forgetting all about Black-Two. He stopped once to aim and fire a concussive green stream at the Drone, but Hopalong managed to get just enough altitude on his membranous wings to levitate out of the way.

It was then that she spotted the smoky cube in Hopalong's claws, the one she had left behind in the tunnel.

It all clicked instantly in her mind at just that moment.

Unmutual.

Incapable of Socialization.

Dead Drones and eggs.

A jolt of fear electrified Black-Two's spine. She found herself running after the Hunter, who continued to fire and miss at Hopalong. She dropped to one knee and let off an AR burst at the Drone, but the gun was spent. Cursing, she snapped in a fresh clip as fast as she could.

Hopalong was far enough away that Two couldn't be sure, but it looked like the cube in his claws flashed as his digits flew across the device's multichromatic controls.

She could see glittering crystalline flashes as, one by one, the collars fell off the necks of the Drones waiting patiently on the Beacon.

The Hunter fired again, and missed again.

"Black-One, this is Black-Two, please come in immediately, Black-One . . ."

"Black-One here. I don't have time to chat. I've got a Hunter with a fuel rod cannon with my name on it pinning me down—"

"We're about to have much bigger problems, Chief. If anyone's placed their packs I say we evac our asses ASAP."

"What? Why? What do you see?"

At that moment the last few collars fell off the Drones' necks.

"We've been tricked," Two said, desperation creeping into her voice. "This is no ordinary collection of Drones—they haven't been 'enslaved' here—"

When the Hunter turned around and started running away, the bottom of Two's stomach fell out.

"This is a penal colony!" Two shouted.

Like an explosive cloud of shrapnel, the Drones launched themselves off the Beacon toward Black-Two in a spinning, chittering horde, each mass murderer of their fellow Yanme'e and killer of their young and defiler of their hives clicking and whining out the same word, over and over again, the only Yanme'e word Two had understood as Hopalong had repeated it so urgently back in the penthouse:

"FREEDOM."

THREE

Black-Two's motion sensor became subsumed with red dot after red dot until it looked like someone had cut her cheek open and the blood was seeping over the display, drowning it in crimson.

The cloud of Yanme'e slammed into the Hunter and in the blink of an eye he was covered in dozens of them. He let off an emerald swath from his assault cannon that dismembered any Drones in the path of the blast, but others instantly choked the gap closed. Together, the buggers lifted the Mgalekgolo high in the air. The barrel of the assault cannon was still recharging a flickering green when they ripped the Hunter's limbs and head from its body. The ropy, eellike worms that comprised the creature's true "self" cascaded like grain from a silo out of the ruptured shell. The Drones unthinkingly swooped down on the worms before they hit the ground and tore them into bright orange-red chunks with their claws and mandibles.

Two caught only a few glimpses of this over her shoulder, for almost as immediately the Yanme'e launched themselves in her direction. She turned and sprinted in the direction of the Beacon's antigrav pylon. Once she was within twenty meters she let the second blow pack slide off her shoulder and into her hand. She twirled it twice and hurled it at the pylon, where it hit about three meters up and stuck in place with a magnetic *thunk*.

She turned ninety degrees and ran toward the hole she originally came out of. All around her buggers exploded out of the ground and shot into the air; undoubtedly the hive sleeping below the surface now awakened to a glorious living dream of unbridled mayhem and carnage, no longer held in check by their Covenant wardens.

Two plunged headfirst into the warren just as a horde of Drones dove down to snatch her up as well. The Yanme'e slammed into a pileup, clogging the tunnel's mouth and fighting among each other for the right to pursue her.

Two didn't give them the chance to decide the contest. She primed one of her M9 grenades and underhanded it at the hole. The Drones' shadows wisely flew in retreat as the frag exploded, bringing down the upper wall of the tunnel and sealing Two inside.

The warren maze writhed with the fluttering shadows of rioting Drones in every direction. Two scurried a few meters in the direction of the original rally point then stopped, spotting the fissure leading to the subway system.

Bracing herself against the opposite wall of the tunnel, Two pushed off with her MJOLNIR-enhanced legs and put her shoulder into the fissure. She smashed through to the other side in a cloud of dirt and rocks.

Immediately, she pressed her back against the train tunnel. A few Yanme'e stuck their heads in through the unfamiliar hole to investigate, but not seeing anything moving, and since Two's black armor and gunmetal gray visor perfectly camouflaged her presence among the machinery-covered wall, the buggers moved on with a low, disappointed chatter.

Once her motion sensor cleared of red dots except at the margins, Two walked over to examine the sleek, dust-covered train car. A brief inspection indicated it was intact and straddled a single rail that snaked away into a tunnel unimpeded by any debris or cave-ins she could see.

"Who's dead?" One's voice crackled over her helmet.

"Not Two," she replied.

"Not Four," Four said, calmly, over AR fire. No matter what kind of 110 percent FUBAR situation Spartan: Black found itself in, Four's voice never rose, never wavered; he always sounded like he was shopping for groceries. Two found that both extremely lovable and extremely disturbing about him.

"Black-Three? Black-Three, this is Black-One, come in," One called over the open channel. There was no answer, but Two heard the ragged sounds of what she was sure was breathing.

"Chief? Recommend we change rally points," Two said. She placed a white dot on the team's motion displays to mark the location of the subway tunnel. "I found the Arias transit system. Train looks like standard colonial model, running on internal cell power, and this one is . . ." She popped open the service hatch on the side of the train car to check. "Yeah, it's fully functional. We rev this thing up we can get the hell out of Dodge right under the swarm's noses."

"I'm all for that," One said through what were clearly gritted teeth. Two could hear her firing her AR too. "It's a goddamn bugger convention down here."

"Chief," Two blurted out, "I'm an idiot. I shouldn't have trusted Hopa—that damn bugger. He played me like I was a naïve social worker. I'm so sorry. I—"

"He played all of us, Two," One said. "I fell for it too. No need to beat yourself up about it."

"Yeah," Black-Four said, "particularly when there are so many buggers down here happy to do it for you."

"Shut up, Four," Two said.

One said, "Black-Four. New objective. Shoot your way to Two's choo-choo. It is now Rally Point Beta."

"Copy that," Four responded, then was drowned out by automatic fire.

A pair of blinking yellow dots appeared on the edges of her motion sensor: her fellow Spartans, fighting their way to her.

Just a pair, though.

"What about Three?" Two asked.

"He's not responding," One said.

"I can hear him breathing. He's still alive."

"But unconscious." There was resignation in One's voice.

Two didn't think. "I'm going after him."

"Belay that, Spartan," One said sharply. "I'm not losing half my Fireteam."

But Two was already plunging back into the warren. "I'll be back with him before you're done firing up the train for evac."

The pointer to her Beacon pylon remained active, so despite her grenade's cave-in she was able to circle back through the now largely empty tunnels to her original position. She leapt out onto the surface of Verge and headed to the opposite corner of the Beacon, which still listed in midair, firing its energy beam to the heavens, albeit in a pitiful stream since the Drones had stopped feeding it precious helium-3.

The Drones swirled all around the Beacon—really, as far as Black-Two could see—in a pinwheeling, asymmetrical blur of gray-blue wings. Frequently a pair would collide then claw at each other with high-pitched clacking and squeaking. Other Yanme'e would hover in midair and stupidly watch them battle until the victor had torn the vanquished limb from limb—literally.

That must have been what the Kig-Yar character "Unmutual" meant: the Yanme'e equivalent of a personality disorder, an inability to relate to others. While in humans such psychopathology could create cunning, hyperaggressive killers, in Drones, with their even more rigid socialization, Unmutuals were incapable of working in concert with the rest of the swarm as a single, coherent unit. The efficient Covenant wasn't about to let those minor details waste a vast source of manpower, however: Unmutual Drones were yoked to Beacons and worked to death by Kig-Yar.

A host of Unmutuals clung to the underside of the Beacon. As she ran underneath it, a few dropped down and attempted to hoist her into the air. She knocked them off her back with the butt of the AR. A solitary Drone plopped down directly in front of her, blocking her path, and she took it out with a short, controlled burst.

Yet they kept dropping down, forcing her to zigzag around them. By the time she emerged on the other side of the Beacon there were dozens of them standing as still as statues facing her, simply watching her with cocked heads, mandibles twitching.

A yellow dot appeared on the edge of her motion sensor.

"Black-Three, come in!" she yelled louder than she needed to. "This is Black-Two. I am closing in on your position. Give me your status."

There was silence for a moment then Three groaned across her speakers:

"Buggers picked me straight up in the air, and they would have torn me apart like a wishbone if I hadn't let loose with my AR."

She sprinted a beeline for the dot, closing to twenty, then

fifteen meters. She was on the edge of the city, and a few skyscrapers loomed before her. The ground was uneven enough that she couldn't see any sign of a Spartan lying before her.

"Can you move?" she asked.

"I don't know . . ." She heard his MJOLNIR shift and creak, and then he cried out. "*Goddamn it!* They dropped me way high up, and I landed right on my ankle . . . must've broke, even inside my armor . . . And the biofoam pinned it in the broken shape! Goddamn stupid skunkworks piece of shit . . ."

"Just sit tight," she told him.

She was within ten meters of Three. A Drone landed in front of her, arms spread, but she didn't slow down. Instead she barreled right into him, smashing her assault rifle into his face and knocking him over. She put a foot through the front of his thorax with a crunch and squish as she ran over him.

A menacing buzz made her look behind. The Unmutuals were falling into a single curtain behind her. Her dispatch of the last Drone must have overcome their innate selfishness. They were very slowly, but very deliberately, roiling toward her, a solid wall of flickering death.

Her motion sensor showed she was practically on top of the yellow dot, so she stopped.

Looked down.

Black-Three was nowhere to be seen.

"Where the hell are you?" she asked.

"How the hell am I supposed to know, man? They dropped my ass on some roof somewhere."

"You've gotta be kidding." She scanned the buildings in front of her and had to guess which one the yellow motion sensor dot pointed her toward. "Why can't this goddamn thing be more specific about altitude?"

"Write a letter to the friendly folks at Naval Intelligence," Three groaned.

She could hear the swarm surging forward. She threw herself through what remained of the plate-glass windows lining the lobby of an office building and made for the fire stairs, which wound up a reinforced concrete shaft on one side of the building.

Two took the steps five at a time. The building had to be forty stories tall.

She whipped past the sign for the thirtieth floor when the walls of the stairwell began to tremble and an intense, overpowering hum began vibrating through the shaft. She worried the building was about to collapse. She passed a hole punched in the wall and saw five Yanme'e desperately crawling through the exposed, rusting rebars and realized the entire swarm was trying to claw their way inside at once.

She looked behind and saw the shadow of a huge mass of Drones surging up the stairwell right behind her.

"*Aaaaaaaah,*" Three crackled over her speakers. "They found me, Two, they found me! Stay back, you goddamn buggers!" She heard him firing his AR. "*You wanna piece of me, you're gonna have to work for it!*"

She sprinted the rest of the way up to the roof and burst outside to see Black-Three lying on his back, struggling with a Drone who was trying to rip his AR out of his hands. The crumpled husks of bullet-ridden Yanme'e lay all around.

There was something about the Drone fighting with Three that looked familiar—the four missing limbs.

Hopalong and Three both turned their heads to look at her at once.

She didn't hesitate.

She unleashed a short, controlled burst at Hopalong, ripping him away from Three and knocking the Drone off the building.

The swarm poured over the edges of the roof like a cup overflowing and she could hear them on her heels coming out of the stairwell too.

She closed the distance between her and Three in two long strides. She didn't slow down. She scooped up Three, threw him over her shoulder, ran to the edge of the roof . . .

And jumped.

She landed with both feet on the roof of the building opposite and didn't waste any time locating the exit leading down—the door had been blown open by a Covenant raiding force many months ago.

She took the stairs down by leaping from one landing to the next, stopping only once to adjust Three to a more comfortable position across both her shoulders.

As she did so Three said, "For a minute there I didn't know whether you were going to save me or your bugger boyfriend."

"That would be because you are a moron," Two said.

Much of the swarm was waiting for them in the lobby when they burst out of the stairwell. Howling like Sioux warriors on a final charge across the plains, the Spartans unloaded their assault rifles, Three while still draped across Two's back, and cleared a narrow path through the Drones to the exit.

But now came the impossible part—the scenario One had wanted to avoid in the first place: a hundred meters of open ground between the Spartans and the Beacon with clouds of infuriated Drones swarming overhead, everywhere they looked. Each of their ARs was on its last clip and they wouldn't make it ten paces without expending all their ammo if they tried to fight their way through.

So she just had to run.

The Drones flew down and tried to grab them, or snatch Three off her shoulders, but she was too strong and Three beat them back with the AR, firing off a burst or two when absolutely necessary.

Then Two felt her feet kicking empty air—she was rising off the ground against her will. But no Drones were near them.

"Oh crap," Three said.

She looked up—and saw several Drones floating above them, the antigrav grapplers they used to excavate mantle for the Beacon now trained on the two Spartans.

She saw a familiar form flitting by their side—she had blown off his front arms but he was still alive, limbless but still able to hover-hop on what remained of his tattered wings.

So Unmutuals weren't completely incapable of cooperation.

They just needed the right leadership.

Her helmet headset crackled, "Black-Two, this is Black-One. Come in. Black-Four has powered up the train and we are ready for evac. Return to Rally Point Beta immediately. Over."

"Copy that, Black-One," Two said, "but I'd get that thing moving now."

"Why?"

"Because I am about to drop something extremely heavy on top of it."

And she detonated the blow pack she had attached to the antigrav pylon of the Beacon.

The huge C-12 explosion was so violent that it startled many of the Drones into dropping their grapplers, which in turn dropped Two back onto her feet. She didn't waste any time in dashing for the warren holes. The other three antigrav pylons struggled for a few seconds to keep the unforgiving mass of the Beacon upright on their own, but gravity emerged victorious and yanked the machine downward on one side. The plasma stream still emanating from its top cut an apocalyptic swath through the Yanme'e swarm, vaporizing Hopalong and the dozens of Unmutuals around him. It sliced the buildings Two and Three had just escaped from in half like a giant scythe.

Two dropped underground just as the first pylon hit. The tunnels immediately began collapsing around her and it was a mad dash to stay one step ahead of the flattening ceilings. She barely made it to the subway tunnel and handed Black-Three into Black-One's outstretched arms as she stood on the back of the train car before leaping onboard herself.

The subway disappeared into its tunnel just as the remains of the fallen Beacon crashed through the platform roof.

For a moment, everyone inside the train car paused to catch their breath. The train whined quietly through the absolute darkness of the metro tube. Spartan: Black was too exhausted to celebrate.

"ETA at Pelican in twenty," Four said after a moment, as if nothing had just happened.

Three punched Two playfully in the shoulder. "So what did we learn today, huh? If you see something that looks different from us in any way, kill it immediately and without question."

Two just cocked her head. "We are a hell of a lot more 'Mutual' that's for sure."

"Huh?" Three said.

She watched the tunnel darkness recede back into itself behind them as the train hummed its way to the drop point.

"Nothing," Two said with a smile only she knew was there.

THE *MONA LISA*

JEFF VANDERMEER AND TESSA KUM

October 2552 [exact date classified], Soell System,
Installation 04 Debris Field, "Halo"

>Lopez 0610 hours

Sergeant Zhao Heng Lopez stood in the cargo bay of the UNSC Red Horse, looking at an escape pod. A huge, pitted bullet. About two and a half meters long and thick, pocked and smacked by debris. Around her: Hospital Corpsman Ngoc Benti, Technical Officer Raj Singh, his helpers, the ever-silent, inscrutable Clarence, and a crack pilot named Burgundy who'd just come back from a recon mission. All of them staring at the latest catch. It was so dented the container itself almost looked like something living. Almost expected to see plants growing out of the sides. Was that all it took, Lopez wondered, to make something lifelike? Kick it around enough? Maybe.

James MacCraw joined them. Rookie. Raw. Big-boned, lanky, and freckled. Unimpressive. Maybe if she kicked him around he'd show some life.

"I'm here, Sarge," he said, but not like he meant it. God, she hated indifference in the morning.

"Yeah, you think you're here, MacCraw," Benti said in a half mutter. Next to Benti—who looked so small in combat armor that seemed to eat her up—MacCraw was like another species.

Singh had conscripted Burgundy into helping pry the pod open alongside his assistants. The thing obviously wasn't going to open easily for them—the line revealing the crude little hatch, locked at the side, almost couldn't be seen with the number of impacts it had suffered.

"Not much to look at, is it?" Burgundy said. Lopez knew that the Marines sometimes called her "Stickybeak" because she was too curious, but she didn't seem to care.

Benti: "Is it, like, old, or a recon pod? Am I here to tranq or treat? I don't get it."

"Is it even ours?" MacCraw asked, ignoring Benti while asking the same question.

"Sure as hell ain't Covenant," Lopez said. "It's human." Just not necessarily military. Serial numbers, but no UNSC markings.

No idea what it was doing out here in uncharted space, floating in the ruins of Halo, a gargantuan alien artifact Lopez hadn't even tried to explain to herself. Hell, Lopez had no real idea what she was doing here, for that matter. They'd popped out of slipspace like a greased egg just three days ago, with no more specific task than "recon and recovery and watch out for Covenant patrols." Lopez wasn't in the mood for more mysteries.

"But—that doesn't mean it's friendly," she added, not wanting them too relaxed. Except for Clarence, who was at his best when he was so relaxed he didn't even seem to be alive; sometimes Lopez wondered if he was a ghost. But it was hard for the rest of them not to be complacent, standing in the bay of their own ship. Lopez knew from experience sometimes you took the worst hits where you lived for that very reason.

They'd seen pods before on this tour—too many. They were plucking them from the void with such tenacity it made her think they *were* looking for something in particular. But almost all of what they'd recovered had been sleeper pods from amid the exploded chunks of continental plate, the almost delicate slices of superstructure: cryotubes ejected from the *Pillar of Autumn* when she was brought down by Covenant fire. All DOA, cracked and ruptured by the wealth of debris out there. Go to sleep expecting to wake, and wind up in a floating coffin instead. There were worse ways to die. There were much better ways, too.

MacCraw might have been slow, but he wasn't that slow. As he helped Benti unsnap a stretcher, he said, "So much for a highly classified top-secret hush-hush location. That's a civilian pod."

Lopez didn't answer because she had no answer. Their mission remained fuzzy, and the rumor mill was surprisingly quiet. All she knew was that even though the *Red Horse* operated under wartime rules, she'd felt like she was signing away her soul when they'd given her additional security documents. *Not to reveal . . . Under penalty of . . .*

The oddest thing? Their old smart AI, Chauncey, had been replaced with an AI named Rebecca. Chauncey had been only three years old when they'd yanked him out like an old motor block. No question of his having cracked up. Besides, Chauncey would've dropped her a hint or two. He had taken a real shine to Lopez. Rebecca hadn't.

"Maybe we should tell the commander it's civilian," MacCraw said.

Poor MacCraw. Still so wet behind the ears. She didn't look at him. Didn't need to.

Benti couldn't resist, gave Lopez a cheeky grin as she said: "There are cameras in here, MacCraw."

He frowned, reddened.

Burgundy and Singh's assistants had moved away from the pod.

"Sir!" Singh waved Lopez over. "Life support is still online. We've got a live one in here." An instant quickening of her pulse. This could be something, finally. She was sick of being a funeral director. "Just give the word and we'll have it open."

Lopez motioned to Clarence. "Step on up, Invisible Man. Singh, get your team clear. Sleeping Beauty here is a stranger." Unholstered her pistol, checked the chamber. "Benti, c'mon, get your weapon out and your head out of your ass. Treat as hostile until proven otherwise." Benti had a talent for making friends that served the squad well on leave, especially regarding bartenders, but it wasn't a useful trait here.

The sound of boots behind her as additional Marines filed into the hangar, ranging around the pod at Clarence's command. Assault rifles raised and ready. She didn't have to check—they knew what they were doing. Lopez had trained most of them herself.

Ever-silent, Clarence drew up beside her, finger on the trigger. A good man to have at her back when faced with the unknown.

Lopez nodded at Singh, who tapped his control pad. The seal on the pod sighed, and the technician stood back.

Three, two, one . . .

She wrenched at the hatch. A hiss of escaping pressure as the hatch rose.

Clarence didn't move. Just stood beside her, watching, calm, even when she started.

"Damn!"

There was a lot of blood. A man, too. But a lot of blood. More than seemed possible. That was what got to her first. The blood sloshed in the creases of the berth. It ran down the floor to pool in the footwell. It had saturated the man's clothes. His face was crusted by blood, his eyes white and bulging in the midst of it. Couldn't at first tell if he really was alive. She and Clarence stared down while he lay there, looking up but not really seeing.

Burgundy grimaced in disgust, mumbled something like "I've got to be going," and fled the hangar. That amused Lopez. Stickybeak'd become unstuck.

Where did the smell come from? Where? It was rank, like the stink she remembered coming off corpses after about three days into a firefight, still pinned down by Covenant at some god-forsaken outpost on a planet no one even cared about. But behind that, some sort of infection. She could smell it because she could also smell the antiseptic of whatever the man had used to fight it. The smell reminded her of the nursing home where she'd had to leave her mother a few years back, mumbling prayers and counting her rosary beads.

The man rose up. He rose up like something coming out of darkness into the light, the blood spilling off his chest. Clarence had his gun aimed point-blank between the man's eyes. Those eyes focused as the man cried out, "Don't let them get me!" through a torn mouth. Lopez could see that the blood wasn't just spilling off his chest but *out* of his chest, and that's what made her take a step back, more than anything else. That, and the way he looked at her made Lopez realize the man already understood he was dead.

As dead as any corpse they'd recovered from a cryotube.

>Benti 0623 hours

Stabilizing "John Doe" took Benti a few minutes. A thankless task. A pointless task. Not all the bandages in the world would help him now. While a couple of the others lifted him out and onto the stretcher, Clarence kept his gun on the man. Good old Clarence. Other Marines talked behind his back—said he was messed up in the head, said he had his own agenda—but Benti had always liked him. You could depend on Clarence. Who cared about the rest?

With Clarence on the job, Benti kept her calm even with the guy babbling *don't let them take me, please don't let them take me.* This guy wasn't going anywhere soon. They could have brought a proper bed down; at least Mr. Doe would've been more comfortable.

Mr. Doe had kind eyes. Frightened eyes, but kind. Benti could tell. She was a strong believer in what you could figure out from a person's eyes. It was one reason she trusted Clarence, and why she found MacCraw a waste of space.

Great slashes, vicious and brutal, constituted most of Mr. Doe's wounds. The worst had penetrated his chest, but his feet were a mess too. If only he'd been wearing shoes. Benti *tsk*ed a little at the lack. The left foot had blackened, and it would have to come off. *No, scratch that—chopping his foot off won't save him now.* His left arm had a chunk missing. A shattered shoulder and missing ear were just afterthoughts in her catalog of his problems.

The bandages she'd applied were pitiful, the skin around them blue, and a down-and-dirty IV had been hooked up. A waste, but Sarge wanted some quality face time with Mr. Doe, so anything to keep him with them a little longer.

For an instant, Benti had a vision of Mr. Doe encountering some great force. That he'd sustained all this damage in one moment of terrible clarity; of knowing, as they would all know eventually, that the universe was stronger, and meaner, than any one of them. It was something the Marine Corps, after Benti's cushy upbringing in a suburban home on Earth, had been teaching her for five years now.

She depressed the plunger in the syringe. Mr. Doe jerked up, a sudden tension wracking the lines of his body, jaw clenched. Benti noted absurdly that he hadn't been flossing lately: bad gums. That they were gray concerned her more.

"There," Benti said, rising to her feet and wiping her bloody hands. Blood never bothered her, only where it came from. "He's stable. For the moment."

"Good to talk?" the sarge asked her.

Benti twisted her lips, unwilling to commit to a yes or no. "I gave him a cocktail—painkillers, and an upper. He can talk." Yep, he could talk, although it wasn't going to be one of those scintillating discussions you remembered the rest of your life. Besides, the sarge had never been good at polite conversation: one reason Benti liked her.

She caught Lopez's eye, knew the sarge understood. Mr. Doe could leave them at any time.

Benti stood back as Lopez crouched down. "See that?" Lopez pointed to a tattoo and indentation on his right arm, across the edge of Mr. Doe's tricep. Prison barcode, with a scar where they'd implanted the tracking chip.

"Interesting." It didn't really interest Benti, but you had to humor the sarge sometimes.

Mr. Doe spoke up. "Marines. You're UNSC." His voice broke, too long without water and use.

"You're safe," Lopez said.

Benti frowned. Mr. Doe was also at the ass-end of the galaxy, light-years from anything unclassified. *But I guess you don't complicate a dying man's life.*

"Thank God," he wheezed. The tension that had gripped and defined him until then slipped away. "Thank God."

They were attending his funeral, Benti realized. Her, Lopez, Clarence, MacCraw, Singh, and the rest. Forming an honor guard around a man who might or might not deserve it. For once, MacCraw had fallen as silent as Clarence, thank goodness. She'd been about to nickname him "Jackdaw."

"What's your name?" Lopez asked. "Where are you from? What ship?"

Too many questions for Mr. Doe. He coughed, as though clearing his throat, but the cough didn't stop. Blood, dark and fresh, dribbled down his chin. Benti knew what that meant. Everyone did. She shot a glance at Clarence, who met her eye. It wouldn't be long now.

"I don't know," Mr. Doe wheezed, the words hard to utter. Even Clarence, who usually didn't give a crap, was leaning in, trying to hear him. "I don't know where we are, I don't know."

"What ship?" Lopez repeated.

Mr. Doe's reply sounded like "moaning lizard" to Benti. That had to be wrong.

"The what?"

"The *Mona Lisa*." And then: "You don't know, do you? You don't know."

Lopez smiled, which, Benti had told her before, on leave, was grim and not at all reassuring and the main reason men fled at the sight of her, but still she wouldn't give it up. No way Mr. Doe wouldn't see his own death there.

"I don't know because you're not telling me. Tell me, and we'll get you off to the infirmary, and you can sleep."

"I would tell you all kinds of things," Mr. Doe said, stumbling over the words. "If I had anyone left in the world. This is where I'm supposed to say, tell my girl I love her, that sort of thing." A terrible, pitiless laugh from Mr. Doe, then, that contracted his eyes, his chin. A laugh that convulsed him, brought blood fresh through the bandages. "I know I'm dying. I know I'm dying. But that's okay." A clarity in his eyes, despite the kindness of the drugs. "I'm clean. I'm here. I won't come back. It's okay. It's all okay."

It surprised Benti when Lopez took his grime-covered, bloody hand. Somehow Benti thought Lopez would pay for that touch. Benti was used to touching people when they were vulnerable, understood what it meant. Lopez really wasn't. He'd just been this thing that talked before. Now how did Lopez see him?

"What do you mean, you won't come back?" Lopez asked.

Like a thunderbolt, a lightning strike called up unbidden: the shimmering image of the ship's smart AI, Rebecca, appeared beside them, also kneeling. So sudden that Benti had to suppress a sound of surprise, almost lost her balance, and Lopez pulled away a bit.

Rebecca was in her warrior avatar, looking like half-Athena, half-Ares, with a feathered Greek headdress and ancient armor. Rebecca looked so good that Benti almost clapped.

Rebecca asked, imploring almost: "What do you *mean* you won't come back? Come back from what? *Come back from what*?"

Benti looked through Rebecca to where Lopez knelt, staring wide-eyed at them both. Then realized a moment later, with a fading spike of sadness, that Mr. Doe had gone silent, had become Mr. DOA. Now they'd never learn his name, and all they had was "Mona Lisa," which might be a ship, a painting, or nothing at all.

Rebecca made a sound close to exasperation, and winked out. This new AI wasn't big on niceties like "Hello," "Good-bye," and "Incoming!" Not like Chauncey.

Benti stared down at Mr. Doe. Really, such a waste. Those nice eyes, that strong chin.

"Come on, all you big strong men," Benti said. "Help me get him to forensics." Which was in the infirmary, but Benti didn't like saying that, since it seemed to mix the living and the dead a little too easily. She also didn't like telling people she assisted with autopsies, which Mr. Doe definitely required to write the proper ending to his story.

A slow, sad shuffle then as they took the man's body out of the landing bay. Mr. Doe seemed both heavier and lighter than before. Clarence seemed to take most of the weight, and didn't seem to mind.

When Benti looked back, Lopez was giving a good, hard look to the space that had been occupied by Rebecca's avatar, like the sarge had been trying not to see through her, but into her.

>Lopez 0932 hours

By the time she met with Commander Tobias Foucault and Rebecca, Lopez knew this much: nothing that might identify the dead man, not his prison brand, fingerprints, retina scan, DNA, came up on any of the databases aboard the *Red Horse*. Not that surprising. No way to check against the live databases back home. "Hush-hush," as MacCraw said.

They met in one of those featureless rooms adjoining the bridge that smelled like disinfectant. Lopez had wanted Benti there, too, but she was more valuable sitting in on the postmortem.

Gray walls and plastic chairs that rocked back too far if you tried to slouch. A live image of the empty pod, with MacCraw and some other Marines cleaning up the blood, played across one screen. A video of the Halo artifact prior to Spartan-117 detonating the *Pillar of Autumn*'s reactor and destroying it played across the other. A blue-green place. Like a delicate, inverse cross-section of Earth. Now: a black-and-brown snake with orange cracks raging across its pieces, with the vast bulk of the gas giant Threshold looming behind it, inexorably pulling the debris into its gravity well.

Commander Foucault sat opposite her, as always immaculate. The smell of aftershave. Foucault looked haggard and thin and prematurely graying, not at all the robust man she remembered from before his promotion. When he'd been just another one of them. Something about that soured in her mouth. Now she had to call him "sir." They all respected him, respected the extreme circumstances that such a field promotion called for, but still resented the division of rank.

At the far end of the table, Rebecca manifested in her more usual avatar of a flabby, middle-aged Mediterranean woman in a flower dress. She looked vaguely Italian. Benti had always clucked when she saw Rebecca that way, wondered aloud in their berths why she chose that avatar. But Lopez knew: the same reason off-ship, on leave, she would wear something feminine.

It made people comfortable around Rebecca, took the edge off of their fascination and slight fear of something so seemingly *alive* made out of motes of light, bits and bytes. But, then, Chauncey had never cared whether they were comfortable around him. His actions did the job instead. So why, exactly, did Rebecca want to be disarming?

"Anything new to report, Sergeant Lopez?" Foucault asked. Despite the worn look to his face, the commander's light blue eyes had a powerful effect. A gaze with a kind of *grip* to it.

"No, sir," she said. Wondering when the shit was going to hit the fan. Because you didn't waste the time of the two most important people on the *Red Horse* by sticking them in a room with a sergeant. It didn't scan. She found herself counting rosary beads in her head, against her will. The image forever anchored to the smell of old wooden pews and her mother as a younger woman, kneeling in church.

"What about you, Rebecca?" Foucault asked, with the air of someone who already knew the answer. Lopez thought she noted a hint of sarcasm there, too.

A smile from Rebecca that was meant to reassure Lopez, but didn't. Not one bit.

"The pod was launched six hours ago from the *Mona Lisa*, a prison transport. I backtracked and calculated the *Mona Lisa*'s approximate location at the time of launch. The coordinates have been uploaded to the nav system."

"And it didn't show up on our sensors, I'm guessing, because of the debris?"

Rebecca frowned, as if something annoying had just occurred to her. "That's correct." She brought up a schematic on the screen of a freighter with several levels, a docking hangar near the front. Storage bays hung off of it, seeming to weigh it down. To Lopez, it looked ugly. Like, if it were a ship meant for water, it would list heavily. "This is a simulation of the same ship type. They're converted freighters, for transporting prisoners and ore to and from the penal colonies, along with the resources from the mines. The bridge is situated in the top level. The prison cells are down below, close to the hangar. In between you have the usual: kitchen, mess, infirmary, berths, the majority given over to cargo. Most prison ships have minimal defenses and minimal firearms on board—a precaution against an uprising—and rely on an escort for protection. There's no sign of an escort, though."

A thin smile from Foucault as he stared at Rebecca. "What would a prison transport be doing at the most significant alien discovery of the past twenty years?" he asked, cutting through all the irrelevant details in a way Lopez admired.

Rebecca shrugged. "That, I can't tell you."

Foucault said, "Because you don't know, of course." It wasn't framed as either statement or question.

"Perhaps they encountered Covenant and made a random slipspace jump to escape."

"Quite the coincidence, if they did. They show up here, we show up here." It wasn't directed at Lopez, but in a way it was. Probably the only hint she'd ever get.

Not waiting for a response, he turned to Lopez: "What do you think?"

"I'm not paid to think, sir." Her default answer when she didn't want to get involved.

A smirking laugh. Maybe some residual regret in that look from Foucault. As if, in situations like these, he wished he wasn't paid to think, either.

When they'd first come out of slipspace and seen their destination, seen the alien structure, magnificent even in ruins, Lopez had forgotten herself. "What are we looking for, sir?" she'd asked. Foucault hadn't looked away from the window, but she'd sensed him wince. On that poker face, a "wince" was just a lowered eyebrow. "Whatever there is to find, Sergeant," he'd said finally. Slight pressure on *sergeant.*

"Did either of you intuit anything useful out of what the man said before he died?" Foucault asked. "Anything that gives us more context?"

"He just kept saying he was safe, sir," Lopez said. Maybe death was a form of safety, but not one that appealed much to her.

"Nothing that would be inconsistent with the delusions of a man suffering from dehydration and mortal wounds," Rebecca said.

Foucault did this steepling thing with his hands that was his only affectation. "I'm inclined to finish the postmortem, stow the body, and carry on with our mission."

What mission? In Lopez's opinion, risking their asses for "whatever there is to find" seemed stupid. She knew from talking to some of the noncoms on the bridge that it was near impossible to pilot the Prowler through the debris field. Between Rebecca and the discreet automatic defense firing, they'd avoided any serious collisions. But that risked giving away their position to the Covenant even as the debris helped hide them. Still, if the whispers that came back to her were right, the bulk of the Covenant fleet had left the system in pursuit of a "higher value target"—which supposedly had surprised the commander. Not the kind of thing she could confirm with Foucault, and Lopez didn't know how long ago the Covenant fleet had left. All she cared about: no Covies so far.

Somebody was doing a lot of gambling here, and Lopez still had no idea for what potential gain.

Rebecca turned to Lopez and said, "What the commander means is he wants you to take a squad in a Pelican and go investigate the *Mona Lisa*'s last known coordinates."

Foucault looked grim. "Is that what I meant? If you say it's what I meant, I guess it must be what I meant." The sarcastic tone had become more pronounced, but, again, tinged with an odd kind of regret.

"Sir?" Confused. She'd never seen an AI contradict a commander in quite that way. "Sir, your orders?"

Foucault stared at Rebecca, as if the force of his gaze might burn two holes in her avatar. Then he said in a clipped cadence, "AI Rebecca is, of course, correct. Take a squad in a Pelican and investigate. Rebecca will coordinate the details. Good luck, Sergeant. Dismissed."

Lopez saluted, rose in confusion, walked out the door. Thinking of John Doe's warm hand. Puzzled. Wondering why neither Foucault nor Rebecca had even asked about the autopsy, or the nature of the man's terrible wounds, or everything else that didn't jive.

Lopez had scars from wounds of her own, collected from long years of making the Covenant pay and keep on paying. Along with a long white reminder on her wrist of why you didn't surprise a sleeping cat.

Every time Lopez was about to go into combat, she was aware of those scars.

They were throbbing now, telling her: *Something bad is coming.*

>Foucault 1003 hours

Foucault sat there after Lopez had left, staring at Rebecca. He was, for all his former exploits, a cautious man who had used extreme tactics when it had seemed the only option for his continued survival. It had made him a hero and given him his command, but he didn't feel like a hero. He'd just been trying to save himself. He wasn't sure he had. Waking from nightmares, from *memories*, awash with sweat to find it was only one in the morning got old fast. So did losing to the Covenant.

Rebecca wasn't helping. He'd had a good relationship with Chauncey. He'd trusted Chauncey. Rebecca, well . . . Theoretically she worked for him, but a directive from ONI's upper echelons had imposed her on him—along with a couple of rookies who acted so raw it made him suspicious—and that was more than sufficient reason for him to be wary.

Foucault'd had a superior once with a prosthetic eye, except that no one knew. This man would call Foucault into his office and, without telling him why he had been summoned, close his good eye and fall asleep, still staring at Foucault. Inevitably, Foucault would lose the waiting contest and be the first to break the silence.

Rebecca was a man with a glass eye. She could outwait him.

So, finally, Foucault sighed, lifted his head, and stated, "You know more than you've told me."

Rebecca didn't quite shake her head. "We have our orders, Commander."

Orders. Strange, simple orders, Foucault had thought upon first receiving them. Jump to coordinates classified higher than top secret, retrieve samples of an alien artifact for study, conduct basic recon, expect *Covenant* trouble. He'd stood on the bridge, staring at the pieces of the Halo, the wealth of such samples before him, and wondered why they'd deploy a Prowler on such a task.

As soon as the pod had come in, Rebecca had shown him the "expanded" orders. Even expanded, they remained strange and simple. Assess the status of the *Mona Lisa*, and if compromised beyond retrieval, destroy. There had been no mention of why the ship was in the area or what it might be compromised by.

The codes were current, the passwords secure. He didn't question their validity. It was the only thing he didn't question.

"Do *you* know what is on that ship?" he asked, knowing he would get no answer, knowing he wouldn't believe any answer she gave. "I don't like being kept in the dark, especially when deploying my troops. We could be sending them to their deaths for all I know."

"Every time you deploy Marines, you could be sending them to their deaths," Rebecca said, talking to him as if he was a child. To add insult to injury, Foucault suspected she was processing some other scene, her attention elsewhere. "It is only recon."

"Our original orders were 'only recon' as well," he said in mild reproach, and steepled his fingers.

Rebecca looked at Foucault then, with her full attention, and her face seemed to soften. A cheap trick he'd seen her pull on others, changing the lighting on her avatar to something less harsh. "We're at war, Commander. Reach has fallen. Our backs are against the wall. Extreme measures are necessary to ensure our survival."

Foucault forced himself to show no reaction and didn't immediately reply. That was quite the overreaction, and it cemented his suspicions that there certainly was more she wasn't telling him, which meant she had orders of her own.

He watched the screen, which showed a real-time view of the space outside the Prowler. A single piece of debris tumbled slowly past. It wasn't a rock, it was a piece of manufactured structure, hard crisp lines and dead cables showing. There was a marvelous logic to its gymnastics, a grace that seemed almost choreographed, even though now it was merely scattered garbage.

How to get Rebecca to share her knowledge?

"Survival," he repeated.

Was that really the only thing they were fighting for now?

>Lopez 1304 hours

As the Pelican headed toward their destination, Lopez found herself marveling at the view, struck by an odd moment of poetic, profound insight, even though she didn't understand it all. Perhaps even because she didn't understand.

Dominating right now was Threshold's ponderous "bloatbelly"; her term, shared with Benti in the mess hall. The vast gas giant so filled the windows it brought the illusion of blue sky to the cockpit up front instead of the empty black of space. Frequent storms raged and died in great cloud-swirls across that surface. From that far away, it looked like a slow, sleepy blossoming. Didn't feel that way on the surface, Lopez knew. The winds blew hundreds of kilometers an hour.

Closer in: the wreckage of the Halo. The massive ring cut through the view like a question mark that'd been fractured to pieces. Thousands of kilometers wide. Great fires still raging, large enough to devour whole continents. Chunks of the superstructure bigger than cities tumbling ponderously in the void. Glowing and flaring as they tore shrieking down through Threshold's atmosphere. Despite the jiggered failures in the structure, the sheer immensity of it made the curve smooth. Constantly tripped her sense of perspective.

Covenant hadn't built it. It was entirely alien, in design and purpose, and she took some strange assurance from that. Here was proof that there was more out there in the big bad universe than just the goddamn Covenant. She had no idea if whoever built this was friend or foe, but the simple idea that there was *another* gave her a strange sense of security. *We're not alone. Again.*

A pinprick next to Threshold, the *Mona Lisa* drifted like a dead thing alongside one of the larger pieces of debris from the Halo ring, on the far side from Basis and distant from the *Red Horse*'s current position. Lopez thought the ship looked lonely, desolate, on the screen as they approached. *Abandoned, even.* Pits like severe acne showed where the escape pods had already been launched into space.

She asked for an update from the pilot, Burgundy, who'd been called up despite being off the clock. Already getting reacclimated to the up-close sweat smell from the Marines in the seats all around her, only MacCraw dumb enough to be wearing cologne in the confines of a spacecraft, like he was on a date.

Rebecca had chosen the squad, pilot included. "The maximum we can spare," she'd explained. Seventeen personnel in total, including Benti and also Singh's small engineering team, who had received basic training but were technically not combat-ready. Clarence sat next to Lopez like some kind of morose watchdog. He never looked happy, but Lopez thought she could read in his impassive features a distinct *un*happiness now.

"She's not answering on any frequency, Sarge," Burgundy finally replied over Lopez's headset. They were on an open frequency for now. Later, only Lopez would have access, and anyone she designated. "Can't get a peep out of her. No distress beacon. She's cold, and I don't think her engines have been running for a while."

Not if she lay in the same position she'd been in when John Doe had escaped her clutches. So cold and yet hugging so close to the burning shard of a world now lost to them, as if seeking sanctuary.

"Can she zoom in? It just looks like a dark block," Benti muttered to Lopez, not realizing Burgundy could hear her.

A closer view appeared on-screen. "That better?" Burgundy asked. "She ain't that pretty. Not by half. I'd never date her."

A wracked and splintered mountain range formed the backdrop for the *Mona Lisa*, made it difficult to make her out even with the zoom. She had a blunt snout, the five levels Lopez had seen on the schematic, and some definite damage to the left thruster in the back. A few dents. Some bits like barnacles where compartments had been custom-built onto the ship. That was a bit odd, but not unknown. Near the back, Lopez could see where something had left a definite hole. Not enough to scuttle it. Freighters could take a severe pounding. Almost certainly the *Mona Lisa* still had breathable air.

"How'd the postmortem go, Benti?" Lopez asked in a quiet voice. Benti had gotten a peek but Lopez hadn't had a chance to ask her about it yet.

"Why not ask Tsardikos?"

"Huh?"

Benti nodded toward one of the others. "Tsardikos over there did the autopsy. Then they put him on the mission." She shrugged, that *officers move in mysterious ways* look on her face.

That made Lopez's heart do a strange leap. "No," she said. "I want to hear it from you." Didn't want to hear it from a noncom who shouldn't even be on the mission. Tsardikos didn't look comfortable over there, fidgeting in his kit. Why should he?

Benti grimaced. "Nasty wounds. Whatever opened his chest and back wasn't a blade, and took a hell of a lot of force. Don't know what it was, but I suppose when you're busting out of prison you use what you can grab. I brought extra blood bags, though. Just in case. It was a prisoner riot, right? It'd have to be."

"Doesn't matter," Lopez said. "You honestly expect some punk-ass jailbird to get a shiv in one of us? You doubting the

Marine Corps, Private?" Didn't mind messing with her people every once in a while.

"It was one hell of a shiv," Benti muttered. "Sir."

"Why bother? I mean, if they're just escapees in a dead ship?" MacCraw piped up. "Just mark her position and come back when things are less hot, Sarge?" Almost like he expected Lopez to say, "You're right, MacCraw," and turn the Pelican right around.

Lopez was about to give MacCraw a hell of a reply, one that mentioned his cologne, when Rebecca came over the radio. Closed channel, just for her and Burgundy. "Signal strength is weak, Sergeant. I'm getting the pictures now. We've picked up a Covenant ship in the vicinity. Distant, but we'll have to tread carefully. The commander has ordered the *Red Horse* to maintain radio contact as much as possible in the field, but we mustn't reveal ourselves. Maneuverability is limited. You may be on your own for a while. You have your orders."

"Roger that," Lopez said. "I'll check in with Burgundy once we're on board to see if I can patch you in. If not, I guess it's just me and the pilot." From the forward position, Burgundy gave a thumbs-up over her shoulder. Rebecca signed off.

"And me," Benti said, smiling.

Lopez nodded, said, "Yeah, you too." She caught Clarence staring at her oddly. Jealous? *Yeah, you be jealous, Clarence, you gloomy bastard.*

"The game is always changing," MacCraw said, to the air.

"Give thanks you've got a game on," Lopez said, and almost meant it. Checking on some spooky mystery transport at the ass-end of space wasn't her idea of a good op, but it was better than nothing.

"How'd the ship even get here?" MacCraw asked. He just wouldn't shut up. "They just happened to randomly guess the slipspace coordinates? I mean, we don't even know where we are, and we're *supposed* to be here."

"Don't try to be smart, MacCraw," Lopez said. "That's not what you're paid for."

"No," Benti and a couple of the others chimed in, "you pay us to be pretty." A tired old joke, a necessary one. One MacCraw might not've heard before.

"Damn straight," Lopez said. "How'd that haiku go? 'Something, something, something . . . something, and then comes ice cream.'" Something they'd eaten far too much of, last R & R.

"You missed a 'something.'"

"You kids play your cards right and after this comes ice cream. Don't ever say Mama Lopez does nothing for you."

Some grins, a couple of comments about "Mama" Lopez, and then a near-ritual silence.

Lopez began the count. Not required, but she liked to name each person under her command right before any mission that might turn hot: Benti, Clarence, MacCraw, Percy, Mahmoud, Rakesh, Orlav, Simmons—currently pulling double duty as Burgundy's copilot—Rabbit, Singh, Gersten, Cranker, Sydney, Ayad, Maller, and Tsardikos. Standard equipped with MA5B assault rifles, HE pistols, and ye olde frag grenades. Among flares, food rations, water, medic kits, schematics of the ship, the usual.

A bunch of jokers, lifers, and crazies. Benti, Clarence, Mahmoud, and Orlav were the best of the lot. MacCraw was, well, raw, so who knew? A few were average, and she'd deploy them that way. Without remorse. Singh and his engineers Gersten and Sydney were an unknown, really. Two loaners from another squad, Ayad and Maller, she didn't know at all. A lot of the rest of the best had been left back on the *Red Horse.* Because, you know, the ship needed them. Or something like that.

All of them were rosary beads to her now anyway, already counting and hating herself for it. Mystic bullshit. But she did it every time. Had to. It was how she rationalized putting herself in danger. *Perform this ritual and luck will follow. Don't, and it won't.* And that's the difference between life and death. Between a scar and a wound that won't stop bleeding.

"We good, Sarge?" Benti whispered.

"You should have gone before we left, like Mama Lopez told you."

Benti smirked, stopped at the last second from reaching out and smacking Lopez on the shoulder.

Pelican drew close, the battered and scarred skin of the *Mona Lisa* filling the view. As they all braced for that slight lurching shudder that meant arrival, Lopez tried not to think about the noncoincidence of who had been chosen for the mission and who hadn't.

Because, to a person, her squad consisted of everyone who had come into contact with John Doe on board the *Red Horse.*

>Benti 1315 hours

Benti watched as the soft seal locked on and they had compression. A shiver ran through the Pelican as the hatches disengaged, maw ready to open and disgorge them into the *Mona Lisa.* Benti had never seen a real live pelican except in videos, but it amused her to think of them erupting out of the gullet of a giant bird. A Trojan Pelican, almost.

This silent moment, right before combat, before she had to use any of her bandages and blood bags, this moment always made her regret having given up smoking.

"We're solid, Sarge, and I can go ahead and set you free whenever you want," Burgundy said, voice coming over the headsets now, which somehow made Benti think of Rebecca's *What do you mean, you won't come back?*

Good old Clarence and that dumbass MacCraw knelt to either side of the gangplank, rifles at the ready, the rest of the squad behind them, hunched over, waiting. Clarence was chewing gum ferociously, about as worked up as Benti had ever seen him. Docking a Pelican wasn't a stealthy business. Whoever was on board the *Mona Lisa* would know they were here.

What kind of greeting would they get? A big party celebration, or one candle stuck in a cupcake?

God, she wanted a cigarette *right now.*

Lopez gave Burgundy the order.

"Go forth and plunder," Burgundy said, and somehow Benti could tell old Stickybeak was *glad* to be staying on board the Pelican.

The gangplank lowered in a hiss of hydraulics and the fast-fading clang of the plank against ground. Not exactly a red carpet, in Benti's opinion.

A smell came in with the cold air that was both dusty and moist. It almost had texture, a substance. It made Benti wrinkle her nose, and she didn't wrinkle her nose at much.

Beyond the gangplank, the main lights were out. Emergency strip lights threw supply crates, control stations, and loading machinery into murky relief. The oval shape of a small transport ship rose up, too, overlooking the jumbled maze spanning the hangar. Deep, dark, reddish shadows thrown up against the far walls.

Benti looked around. That was *it*? She'd been looking forward to getting off the *Red Horse* and exploring new territory. Even if it was just junk, Benti wanted to *see* it. At least it was different junk.

Nothing moved. Nobody even seemed to breathe.

"Lights," Lopez ordered quietly, and Benti switched hers on.

Suddenly there was a mutual clicking and beams shot out all

over the place, temporarily blinding Benti. Crap. You'd think they'd know better. What if they'd been trying to throw a surprise party?

Lopez didn't seem impressed either. "Get your heads on straight, Marines! Move out!"

Benti winked at Clarence, who acknowledged her with a nod, and that was about all. It was enough. Clarence, to her, was like a dolphin or otter or some other creature that seemed to be all muscle and was sleek and functional. What she was to him, Benti had no idea. Comic relief? He hadn't looked amused when she'd told him he was an otter. Off duty they hardly ever saw each other, but they always worked as a team, to the point no one tried to break them up any more. If something works, then don't question it, just work it. Work it to death.

They filed quickly into the hangar in a standard sweep, torchlight raking the crates around them over and over. No matter what you did, regulation boots were never silent, and it was no different this time.

Ten meters out from the Pelican—with Benti hissing Tsardikos back in line, the clueless moron—the surprise party really got started . . .

>Lopez 1317 hours

Trouble came simple, like it always did: a guttural resonance that came from an inhuman throat. A sigh with a texture they knew too well. Sent them diving down behind cover. In the stillness that followed, no repeat of the sound.

"Up periscope," Lopez said to Cranker. He didn't get it, so she said, "Pop yer head up, Private, and take a quick scan around."

Cranker, looking worried, did just that, and then hunkered down even lower. "Looks all clear."

Of course it did. *You didn't get your head blown off.* Wasn't fair, but she always picked the one she liked the least.

Benti, wide-eyed, almost giddy: "That sounded like—"

Don't get jumpy, kid! Lopez raised a finger to her lips.

Scuffling sounds came from about fifteen meters ahead. Multiple contacts.

Lopez gave orders with her hands. Some were quicker on the take than others. Percy and Orlav tapped their crew in passing, including Benti, and scurried off between the surrounding cargo containers. That left Lopez with the dregs. She grinned at Singh, who didn't seem to find any of this funny.

"This is Sergeant Lopez of the UNSC Marine Corps! Identify yourself!"

No reply. A flurry of movement. She rose. Rifle butt cozy in her shoulder. Finger on the trigger. The Marines around her rising from cover, too.

"Where—?"

"Two o'clock—"

"It's gonna bolt—"

A rushed patter of sprinting footfalls flashing across the hangar floor. Darting between storage crates. A glimpse of blue, of familiar backward knees, and formidable shoulders as they came into contact with the corner of someone's flashlight beam.

Covenant Elites.

Tongues of fire from the rifles, that glorious, deafening sound that Lopez knew so well. Sharp shadows danced up in snarling light. Sparks from bullets punched through crates. The target fled between stacked pallets and loaders, not even grazed, no telltale purple glow on the ground. They'd been too eager.

It didn't matter. That one glimpse was all it took. It lit a fire in Lopez. A crazy, irrational fire. Twenty-seven years of war, a war longer than Benti's life, Clarence's life, than most of their lives, so much loss and death and grief and blood and fury—it didn't matter. It didn't need articulating. Not for her, not for any of them.

"Take 'em down!" she roared. "Take 'em all down!"

As if they needed telling.

>Benti 1318 hours

Even though she was just following orders, some small part of Benti thought careening off into the darkness with an unknown number of hostiles in the area added up to a big heaping dose of *crazy.* The larger part of her didn't care.

"To the left!" Orlav shouted, her flashlight beam glancing off the storage containers, breaking off into the distant ceiling. It caught in freeze-frame wide sprays of blood. The floor was sticky with it. They were following drag marks, and over the top, wide stumpy footprints. Fresh.

A bark of gunfire, but no flash, hidden somewhere beyond the containers. Percy and Ayad shouting over the roar of a Covenant Elite. Lopez swearing. Some damn powerful swearing—wouldn't be surprised if some Covie didn't drop dead just from hearing it.

Benti almost fell over a collapsed makeshift barricade, turning too hard around a corner, following the footprints, dimly aware the others weren't around her.

She slipped on the blood-slick floor, caught the impression of movement in front of her, and pulled the trigger without waiting. The bullets punched into the Elite's gut and purple blood splashed down on her face and neck. It doubled over, massive hands cupping its belly. Got a full-on cough of the creature's fetid breath, those four spiny jaws twitching beneath the clenched fist of a head flexed wide in surprise, anger, or some emotion she'd never understand. Especially without their armor, they always looked like they were intensely thinking. But that couldn't be it, and she wasn't going to give it a chance to think.

Her rifle roared until the Elite dropped, collapsing on top of her.

"Crap!" Being crushed seemed a poor reward for doing her job.

But then Clarence was there, grabbing her harness and hauling her from beneath the Elite by the scruff of the neck. Covie blood had soaked her. It glowed in the dark and smelled a bit like armpit mixed with wet cat.

No time to wipe it off: sporadic gunfire throughout the hangar couldn't mask the distinctive footfalls approaching, fast and heavy.

A second Covenant Elite burst out from behind a damaged loader, seeing but ignoring them as they pivoted to face it. The Elite vaulted over an operation console and into the darkness.

"It's going for the Pelican!"

They took off after it.

"Orlav, you back there? One coming your way!"

Benti spat, trying not to think about the alien blood in her mouth and everything she knew about hygiene.

Again she followed the footprints, down one narrow corridor, then another. The container crates formed a kind of maze. Clarence dropped back, checking the corners, not happy about rushing past so many places ripe for more Elites to pop out at them from behind.

The Elite clearly wasn't heading for the Pelican. Instead, it was—

Well, crap. It was *right there*, against the wall of crates.

Crouched, but not hiding, its head tilted, listening. She noticed its muscles were withered and its limbs lined with scars and wounds, not all of them old, and then realized it was naked. No armor at all. How strange, how perfect.

"I'm going to kill you," Benti whispered. "I'm going to—"

It held up one finger. It *shushed* her. Pointed toward the darkness in front of them.

That surprised her so much she shut up, listened with the alien.

Benti heard a last bark of gunfire, the moaning gargle of a dying Elite on the far side of the hangar. Status reports back and forth on the radio. The alien's breathing. Her breathing. Nothing more.

It looked over at her.

Benti was no expert on Covie expressions, but she could tell it was *relieved.*

Nothing more, nothing less.

Even unarmed, a Covenant Elite was more than capable of overpowering any Marine with its bare hands. They never stopped, they never gave up until you put them down. Yet this one remained crouching, unthreatening. Listening.

It wasn't afraid of her. She knew that.

But it was afraid of *something.*

The muzzle of Clarence's rifle entered her peripheral vision, spat fire, and deafened her in one ear. The Covenant Elite smashed back against a container, half its face shorn off.

Face impassive, Clarence looked at her, a faint judgment, a question, only manifesting in the set of shoulders. He'd seen her hesitate. Crap. She stared back at him, reduced to silence, feeling a flare of irritation she knew was her embarrassment eating itself: *Who're you to judge? You could've frozen up a hundred times before in combat for all I know.* But she knew, in her gut, that was a lie. Rumor had it no one had killed more Covies than Clarence.

Lopez, from off to the left: "Marines! Four Covie dead over here. The rest of you, report! Watch for active camo. Keep those flashlights on."

The surprise party was over. A sound-off around the hangar, which didn't seem nearly so big now that their eyes had adjusted to the darkness.

"We're good, Sarge," Benti said, punching Clarence in the shoulder in an attempt to gloss over the awkward strain between them. "Two confirmed kills." She turned her back on the dead, naked alien and followed Clarence to where the flashlights were converging.

"No kills here, just thrills," Gersten said from somewhere off to the right. "That small transport got smashed up good, Sarge. Someone drunk driving, I dunno."

Only one wounded Marine, as it turned out, and that was MacCraw, who had a gash in his shoulder from smashing into a metal hook.

"I think Rakesh wet his pants." MacCraw sounded a little shaky even as he tried to joke.

"Only if you pissed on me, MacCraw."

"No sign of the crew or passengers," Orlav said.

Benti could see that idiot Cranker posing with his boot on a Covie torso, like some kind of conquering hero. That sobered her mood as much as Clarence's look. Bad luck, being not just overconfident but a jerk about it.

Percy crouched by Cranker's leg, examining the body. "Interesting outfit they're running," he said. "No weapons, no gear. Think they're running out of money."

"Maybe we can buy them out!"

"Shut it, MacCraw. Where's Rabbit?"

No answer.

>Lopez 1327 hours

Taking out the second Covie hadn't been as satisfying to Lopez as taking out the first. The third was less satisfying to her than that. She'd just watched by the time her Marines took out the fourth. Mechanically gone through the all-clear and found that Rabbit was missing.

Something was bothering her, even as she ordered a sweep of the hangar just to find Rabbit. It had been too easy. These were Covenant Elites. They'd presumably boarded the *Mona Lisa* and had been hard-core enough to take the ship without too much bungling. But: they'd allowed themselves to be cut down like so many, well, rabbits. She knew her Covies, and they were better than that. Something didn't scan again, and it had her scar itching. Had there been some breakdown in command-and-control? And why hadn't they been able to keep power on in the ship? Had most of them left in the escape pods? If so, you'd think the *Red Horse* would've already picked up a few.

The sweep didn't locate her missing Marine.

"She was with me," Mahmoud said, when they'd regrouped by the main door. "We wasted that dog over there by the messed-up transport, she said she heard something, then another Covie popped up." He shrugged in his armor, dropping his eyes. "Sorry, Sarge, I thought she was with me."

Lopez worried away at a single rosary bead named *Rabbit*, as she opened a channel. "Okay, Burgundy, you've got a lovely way with words. Talk to me."

"Can't raise the *Red Horse* right now," Burgundy said. "And this ship smells. I mean, it really smells."

"Keep trying. Seal up, sit tight. Don't want no Covies getting in and stinking up your bird even more." Then she turned to the rest of the crew. "Cranker, Maller, Simmons, Sydney, maintain position here. You're base camp. Clean up those bodies you're so fond of standing on. The rest of us are going wabbit hunting. Move out."

She stopped in front of Benti. Looked the little medic up and down. She was practically neon.

"I think this color suits me."

"Yeah, it brings out your eyes," Lopez said with distaste. "Take the rear." Didn't always know what to make of Benti, thought she should take things a little more seriously sometimes.

The corridor beyond was pitch-black, the emergency lighting off, except for one flickering light in the distance. On the wall, a smear of blood where a hand had dragged down to the floor only to join a larger, thicker pool that was red and human and old. Something had then been dragged through the blood, the trail heading aft. Through the drag mark, Lopez could see the telltale marks left by regulation boots.

"There was lots of blood in the hangar, too," Tsardikos ventured hesitantly. "Enough for a few people to have bled out. But I didn't see any bodies."

"No small-arms fire or plasma burns, either," Orlav said.

"Maybe the Covenant really are running out of money."

"MacCraw, one more lame joke out of you and I'll push you out an airlock," Lopez growled, and the chatter shut down. The real Mona Lisa was famed for her enigmatic smile, but Lopez still wasn't in the mood for mysteries.

Rabbit's trail faded, crossed more blood pools, and strengthened again. Fifty meters and still going. Damn fool bunny. Went too far on her own. Lopez ground her teeth, already reaming the soldier out in her head, when a surprised shout barked up the corridor. Cut off abruptly. More Covenant.

Quick hand signals as they hastened up the corridor. Orlav

came to a halt by a half-open hatchway. Water flowed over the lip and spilled out into the corridor, lapping around their boots. Shower block. A glimpse of green plastic floor befouled with curling red.

A fetid, wet smell. The sound of gushing water from a shower left on. Near-total darkness except for their flashlights, which illuminated a row of lockers that concealed the space beyond. On her signal they entered, fanned out, swept by rote. Lopez couldn't hear a thing over their progress, the water up to their ankles. Splashing echoed off the walls and bounced from the ceiling, creating confusion with no direction.

Still, she managed to pick out a sound that wasn't water.

Lopez tilted her head at the Marine nearest to her, Mahmoud, who took up a position behind her, along with Ayad. "Rabbit," she breathed into the radio. "Report."

No answer. Then a faint wet burble, which could've been anything. They made their way across the floor, stepping softly in the water. Benti and Clarence watched the door, Percy and Rakesh coming up on their flank to circle in beyond the lockers.

A wet gurgle, followed by a heavy, thick sound, like meat being slapped against the ground.

Rounded the shower wall. The flashlight revealed . . .

"Rabbit!"

Didn't know which of them had said it. Maybe they all had.

Their bunny was dead.

An Elite stood over her. Stood *on* her. No, stomped on her, huge foot pounding down over and over on her chest. Crushed her rib cage into a jagged mess of bone shards. Made a pulp of her lungs and heart. Pulverized her. Flattened a hole through her until it was stomping only on the shower floor, smeared with gore. The lockers were spattered. The Elite's legs were coated with Rabbit's remains.

It saw them, and still it didn't stop. As Lopez yelled something, she didn't know what, and tightened her trigger finger, the Covenant raised its huge foot and slammed down on Rabbit's face, smashing her stunned, vacant expression. Then the rifles roared, and roared, until Lopez shouted for them to stop.

Images of fire in Lopez's eyes. The smell of gunfire and Rabbit's bowels and the Covenant's dead flesh. Rakesh vomiting on Mahmoud's shoes as Mahmoud failed to get out of the way. Putting a hand on Rakesh's shoulder. To comfort him? To steady him? To steady herself?

A commotion from the door, where the gunfire hadn't stopped right away.

Benti yelled, too loud: "Cranker! Two contacts incoming! I hit at least one of them! Cranker, do you copy?"

"Ready and waiting."

Then Benti again: "What was that? Did you hear that?"

"Benti! Were the Covenant armed?" Lopez stepped over Rakesh's vomit to look around the shower wall at the door.

"No," Benti said. "But did you hear—"

Lopez cut her off. "Eyes open. Keep watch at the door."

Benti nodded, mercifully shut up.

"Sir." Cranker again. "Still ready. Still waiting."

"Hold your position, Cranker," Lopez ordered. "You might have some Covie heat coming your way, but they don't appear to be armed, just like the rest. We've got some clean-up here, but we'll be back soon. Over and out."

Lopez crouched down beside what was left of Rabbit.

This *really* didn't scan. On any level. It left her a little numb.

She'd been in the war since the beginning. She'd seen far too many friends and comrades and jerks and assholes and people, too many of *her* people, killed; burned up by plasma, run through with swords, crushed by brutes. Too many. And that meant she knew the Covenant by their actions, if nothing else. No single death signaled victory for them. No one Marine stilled gave them pause. Celebration didn't enter into the equation—they just moved on. They did not leave themselves vulnerable, they did not desecrate the dead, they did not pound Marines into jelly. They did not do *this*.

"Sarge?" MacCraw loomed over her. "What're you doing?"

"Give me some light." *Do something useful for a change.*

Rabbit had no eyes left to close.

The bolognese of innards was cooling fast, but was still hot beneath Lopez's fingertips as she felt about tenderly, picking aside fragments of spine, seeking Rabbit's dog tags. This act didn't disturb her, hadn't done so for years. To be repulsed on the battlefield was to be selfish, put your own distaste over the needs of the dead.

Ah. A glint in the flashlight's beam, and she'd found the dog tags, one of them folded over and flattened. She reached for them, paused, finding something else near her fingertips, half-revealed, half-hidden by the torchlight. MacCraw really couldn't hold a light steady worth a damn.

The universe was a big place and Lopez didn't know it by half, and never would, but what she saw sure as hell didn't come from Rabbit, and didn't look like any Covenant she knew. She stared at it for an instant.

The object was long and thin, and oddly segmented. It looked like a very large spider's leg, but without the stiffness. She only associated it with something living when she saw it ended in a branch of small tentacle-like fingers. The shoulder had been reduced to a pulp of pale sickly goo, veined through with strains of green and purple. Sick, diseased, reeking of the stench Lopez had noticed when they'd first entered the *Mona Lisa*'s hangar.

She reached for it out of some perverse impulse, then paused. The shadow of her hand hid it from the others. *John Doe saying, "I won't come back."*

"Sarge?" MacCraw was getting restless.

Pondered. Decided. Probably nothing. They didn't need to see it.

Apologetically, she nudged a loop of intestine over the thing, then a scrap of uniform over what was left of Rabbit's face. Mama Lopez took care of her own. Freed the dog tags. Rakesh looked like he was going to be sick again. She got up, cupped his hand with hers, and dropped the bloody tags in his palm.

Did the spider's leg come from Rabbit or from the Covenant? Distracted herself from that thought with the situation at hand: Covenant, headed toward Cranker's position.

"Cranker," she said. "Talk to me."

A puzzled tone from Cranker. "The Covenant never got here. We're still waiting, but they never got here. Did you guys go after them? Because—oh wait. I think that might be—oh crap oh crap oh crap . . ."

A garbled curse. A sound like a muffled rifle discharge, almost an afterthought. A wet sound. Too wet. Then, nothing.

Lopez wondered how much of this Burgundy was hearing.

Did they still have an escape route?

>Burgundy 1349 hours

Burgundy had her pistol out, safety off, even with the Pelican sealed up tight. There'd been too much gunfire out there. The Marines might call her Stickybeak and joke about pilots not seeing any action except on leave, but Burgundy had seen enough to know you didn't wait until you could see the whites of their eyes before turning up the heat. Covenant didn't have whites, for starters.

The feeds from the Pelican's rear cameras didn't help her mood any. It looked like the Covie action was getting a little too close for comfort.

Lopez pinged her right after she'd heard one last burst of rifle fire that cut off abruptly. The signal was weak, the ship's structure already interfering. Strange static.

"Burgundy, what's happening there? Can you see Cranker? Simmons?"

"Sarge, I'm not sure what I'm seeing." Her throat was dry and she swallowed. "It's dark, and their flashlights are just lying on the floor now. I couldn't really make out what happened. I think I'm seeing dead Covenant and . . . oh shit." The hair on her arms rose, gooseflesh stippling her skin. "Sarge, something just dragged one of the Covenant out of the light."

"Something? Like what?"

"I can't see shit! Something big. I think. I really can't see it. Do they eat their own, Sarge? Because that's what it looks like."

Except she knew Covenant didn't eat their dead any more than Marines ate *their* dead.

She wasn't sure she wanted the lights on anymore.

"Maller, Cranker, Simmons, and Sydney, where are they?" Lopez demanded.

"Sarge, I'm *telling* you, I don't see them, Sarge." She put her finger on the trigger, took it off. She put it on again.

Okay, so she'd seen something earlier, but hesitated to tell Lopez. She *thought* she'd seen them at the beginning of the attack, spinning out of view, hit by something that looked like a handful of pale balls. Twirling and rolling to the ground, rifles abandoned, grappling with them. The feed went to a black box. She couldn't replay it.

"KIA?" came Lopez's calm voice.

"Not sure. Maybe. I'd hate to be wrong," Burgundy said, certain of nothing, and hating that.

Lopez was silent for a moment, then said, "Keep talking to me, pilot."

But there wasn't anything to see any more. Discarded flashlights, fading as the batteries died. The darkness drawing a little closer.

"Nothing. All calm now."

"*Red Horse* there?"

It was hard to look away from the feed, but she scanned the waveband. "Yes! Got her."

"Patch her through."

"Yes, sir." Always good to have a call from home.

"Sergeant Lopez?" If Lopez's voice was weak, Rebecca's was weaker, grainy, but calm. "What have you found?"

"No sign of crew or prisoners. One KIA, four more missing, possible KIA. Unknown number of Covenant forces on board. I don't know how the Covenant got here, and they're acting mighty strange."

"Strange how?" Rebecca asked, echoing what Burgundy was thinking.

"No armor. No weapons. Not really fighting back, most of them."

"That is all you've found?" Rebecca sounded disgruntled, as though she found this report lacking.

A pause from Lopez. "I did mention the Covenant. Acting strangely. On this civilian ship. In an unknown and highly classified location. Right?"

Burgundy bit back a chuckle. She wasn't fond of Rebecca either.

"We heard you, Sergeant," Rebecca said, about as icy as an AI could get.

"Request reinforcements to aid with the mission."

"Request denied."

"I want to talk to the commander."

A false smile entered Rebecca's voice, like the sun rising over an ice field. "The commander and I are of the same mind, Sergeant."

"Requesting—"

"Negative." This time it was Foucault, patched in over Rebecca's feed. Burgundy's stomach churned. "Sorry, Sergeant, but we can't send anyone without alerting the Covenant capitol ship to our presence, and you know we're outmanned and outgunned. I'm invoking the Cole Protocol. The secrecy of Earth's location is paramount, and the *Mona Lisa* does appear to be compromised by Covenant. Stand by for your orders."

"Sir."

"Ascertain if the Covenant have accessed the nav system. If not, destroy it before they do. If so . . ." he stopped, then continued, after what sounded like consultation with Rebecca, ". . . we will inform you when it is safe for you to return."

"Sir." Burgundy could hear Lopez striving and failing to keep frustration out of her voice. "Sir, I'm down five already, as far as I know. We can keep going, shut down the nav and flush out every Covie on this stinking boat, but begging your pardon, it's a big-ass boat. We need some ODST motion sensors happening. Get a Pelican out here on, I don't know, thrusters alone, something!"

Burgundy was thinking it. Lopez was thinking it. She bet even the commander was thinking it. Orders from officers who weren't on the ground weren't worth shit.

"Negative, Sergeant. You have your orders, and I trust you'll see them through in your usual . . . spectacular . . . fashion," he said with a trace of amusement.

"Yes, sir." Said without grace. "Sir, permission to speak freely?"

"Denied."

"You're fading now. You're breaking up," Rebecca said. "*You have your orders.*" Said remotely, with finality, her attention already elsewhere.

A beat. And then, "They gone, Burgundy?"

"Yes, Sarge."

Lopez said something really obscene.

"You got that right," Burgundy muttered.

"You cozy?"

"Yeah."

"Alone?"

Nothing had moved on the feed for some time now, the last flashlight flickering on the ground. "I can't see anything."

"Okay. Sit tight. Keep monitoring, let me know when the *Red Horse* is talking again. We'll come back and mess up your bird and you'll hate us for it."

"And then there'll be ice cream."

"Damn straight. Over and out."

Outside, the last flashlight went dark.

>Lopez 1402 hours

Twelve rosary beads now. Lopez had a burning anger in her guts that had nothing to do with the Covenant. Already blood in the dark. She had her orders. Her lousy orders. She had twelve Marines left, a big-ass ship to clean out, and no support of any kind.

I'll give you "spectacular."

They stood around her, around Rabbit's remains, around the dead Covenant, silent and waiting.

"You heard," she said, looking into each of their faces in turn. Shadowed, murky faces in the flashlight beams, but still those of her Marines. "Change of plan, boys and girls. We got Covies on board, so the good commander has invoked the Cole Protocol. We need to kill the nav system and the backup nav system, that's our primary goal. Ascertaining what the hell is going on here is now a secondary objective. Orlav, you got that rough schematic? See the engine room?"

"Yeah." She didn't sound too enthusiastic.

"All right, Benti, you take Clarence, Orlav, Gersten, and Tsardikos. You're going after the backup down in the engine room. You take care of it, then you get your asses back here. You see any Covies along the way, you kill Covies. I don't care if they're happy to see you or not. None of them get off this ship, got it?" Thought Benti, with Clarence, would be more effective heading things up on that team than Orlav. Orlav did good recon, but she couldn't improvise.

"Yes, sir!" Benti said, already out the door and slinking down the corridor, the others following her.

"I mean it, Private!" she called out after them, not looking at the thing hidden in Rabbit's body. "You shoot anything you see. Don't let anything get close. Nothing, you hear me?"

"Saaaarge, you know me," Benti said. "I don't let anybody get close." Her voice didn't say that at all.

"No gear," Percy said, nudging the Covenant Elite with his boot, ripples spreading in the bloodied water. "Not a one of these bastards has any gear at all."

"All the better for us."

"How'd Covenant get on board this ship, Sarge?" McCraw asked. "How? Just landed here with no weapons and no gear?"

"Maybe they're prisoners," Rakesh said.

Lopez snorted. "Right. Because we take so many Covenant prisoners." Then she stopped, a bead catching in her mind. "Where the hell is Ayad?" she asked.

They had no good answer.

>Benti 1431 hours

Things went wrong almost from the start for Benti and her team. It sure looked easy at first, though, which had Benti humming an old pop song under her breath. They had cut across the ship, passing through processing cells and checkpoints and security stations toward what Orlav assured Benti was a shortcut—a series of access tunnels would lead to B deck. Benti was all about the shortcuts.

But now Clarence was bracing himself, back to the wall and foot on the door they needed to pass through. He grunted, his boot squeaking with the effort, but the door didn't budge. A makeshift barricade on the other side was the culprit. It wasn't the first they'd seen. They'd seen too many, in fact.

The corridor was too straight and dark for her tastes, like being devoured by a throat. Even the continued sight of swatches of blood—across walls, across ceilings—had begun to get to her. Blood still didn't bother her, but she'd never seen so damn much before, over such a long period. She'd run out of jokes about it. Even the dull smell of it was getting to her. She didn't like that she couldn't raise Burgundy, either.

Gersten muscled in beside Clarence, but gave up after a moment.

"No good, not gonna move." Gersten, a great hulk of a man, spoke almost as rarely as Clarence, and with as much authority.

Clarence shook his head in agreement, even as he gave the door another kick.

A high-pitched shriek tore through the corridor, dissolved into a cackle, cut off.

"What the hell was that?" Tsardikos asked.

"Just the ship, probably," Benti said, lying.

"Yeah," he replied, barely heard her. "Right."

"Hang on," Orlav said as she scrolled through the schematic a lot quicker than she had been. "I'll find us another route."

The tension was thick between them, the muted light shifting imperceptibly across Orlav's face as she traced out paths and access points. Benti could hear the others trying to breathe quietly—trying not to breathe at all.

Benti had a good imagination. She remembered that Elite, unarmed and naked and shushing her so it could listen, and she listened, too. She knew that ships were never silent. They had their own language. Humming ventilation, the drone of the engines, the electronic pitch of a million circuits, the groan of vast plates resisting the vacuum of space. That shriek hadn't been a ship noise, not even close.

As Orlav continued to scroll, a new sound brushed up the corridor and overhead—like an enormous feather sliding across tin foil that then resolved into something soft and sickening and chittering. A sound you'd tell yourself you'd imagined, because you couldn't imagine what would have made it. It didn't repeat. Benti never wanted to hear it again.

Benti held her flashlight steady, deliberately steady, staring into the darkness at nothing, gathering herself. Then she cast a quick eye around the walls. "Ducts?"

"You can get into the damn ducts," Tsardikos said. "I'm not."

"Not enough space for anyone anyway," Gersten said, looking as spooked as Benti felt.

"Okay." Orlav's voice made Benti start. "We need to backtrack. Should be access to the lower level two junctions over from the last intersection. This will take us through the recycling plant." Orlav sounded triumphant, which bothered Benti a bit. *Don't applaud work-arounds until they actually work around.*

"Yum," she said, with an enthusiasm she didn't feel.

She cast a last look over the blocked door. None of them had said it, but the barricade that had stopped them hadn't held. The wreckage—an unholy flotsam and jetsam of chairs, couches, smashed up boxes, machine parts, and even a potted plant or two—had been pushed back and jammed the door after it had been broken. Just like so many other barricades and blockades they'd passed on their way, as if a frantic siege had rolled its way through the ship. *Prison riot*, she thought, trying it on for size. It didn't fit. Not really.

There had been a glimpse, in the narrow sliver of passage still open, of the corridor beyond. It was painted purple with Covenant blood. At the edge of the torch light she thought she'd seen a shape on the floor, something with dimensions that didn't sit well with her.

They should have found someone by now. Nobody said that either.

>Lopez 1440 hours

Lopez popped the cap from a bottle of antiseptic and splashed it liberally on the open gash on MacCraw's arm. Second time he'd gotten wounded, this time from tripping over a barricade. He really needed to do a better job of looking where he was going.

"Quit yelping," she ordered, tasting caustic medicine in her nose and throat. "You a man or a mouse?"

"It burns!"

"Poor mouse," she said, entirely without sympathy. They hadn't found Ayad, might never find Ayad. Lopez would take a gash against being lost in that darkness any day.

When MacCraw kept complaining, she poured the last of the antiseptic in a rush all over the wound. "Be glad Mama Lopez knows what's good for you."

Never expected they'd stop in the infirmary on the way to the bridge, MacCraw's boo-boo notwithstanding, but there were no direct routes left in the *Mona Lisa.* Hatches jammed, barricades erected, some of them still holding, some not. Too many obstacles in unknown terrain, and she'd drastically revised their ETA to the bridge, to the point that she didn't have one anymore. Could only hope they could gain access when they got there.

The infirmary itself had remained immune to all of the destruction around it. Did their first aid work on Covenant? Probably not. No reason for the buggers to ransack the joint.

They'd pushed over a pathetic blockade at the entrance with ease. For the first time, Lopez saw graffiti, scrawled in blood across a turned-over chair, and running across the wall: "Tell Ma I didn't do it. I didn't. Not any of it. God bless. —George Crispin." Smaller scritchings across the floor were obscene or devolved into nonsense words.

The place was also surprisingly small, given the size of the ship and the number of cell blocks they'd come across. Maybe the staff hadn't been big on treating prisoners. Just figured they were tough, could take their chances.

MacCraw grunted when she slapped a pad of gauze over the gash. It needed stitches, but that would do for now.

As she put away her medic kit, Lopez noticed a detail that suddenly had her full attention.

"Singh," she said, tilting her head toward the far wall. "What do you make of that?" A sealed chamber, without windows or cameras, the seal around the door so subtle she'd almost missed it. No handle, either.

The technician shouldered his rifle and ran a hand around the seam. "I've seen these before. The opposite of cells. Safe rooms. You can only open them from the inside."

"In case the prisoners get out . . ."

"Exactly."

MacCraw crossed the room—fleeing Mama Lopez's tender ministrations—and put an ear against the surface, like it was a safe he wanted to crack. Now he rapped a knuckle on the door. Da-dada-da-da, da, da.

"MacCraw . . ." A tone she'd used a thousand times before.

But Singh said, "No, let him do that again."

MacCraw obliged.

A concealed speaker clicked on, a muffled hiss speckling the silence. Sounding a lot cleaner and more immediate than the static over their radios.

Lopez grinned at both of them. Good boys. "Anyone home? This is Sergeant Lopez of the UNSC *Red Horse*." Remembering John Doe, still the only living person from the *Mona Lisa* she'd met.

Of course, it might be Covie in there.

A pause, and then a voice: "UNSC?" Male. Nervous. Dry.

"The one and only." *All five of us. At your service.* Or not. Depending.

She took a step back and leveled her rifle at the door. Motioned for the others to do the same.

"How do I know you're really UNSC?"

"You can either take my word for it, or I can prove it to you. One of these is the fun option, but not for you."

Mahmoud and Percy joined the ring, Rakesh keeping an eye on the corridor. Four rifles on the door, just waiting for it to open.

Something like confidence entered the voice: "I'd hate to take away your fun . . ."

Lopez frowned. She didn't find that clever. She'd been counting her eleven rosary beads nonstop since Ayad, and she wasn't taking any chances with the rest of them. Didn't care if a party of gung-ho Spartans was behind that door. *Well, okay, that's not true.*

"You've got ten seconds," she called out, "and then I'll huff and I'll puff and I'll—"

The door depressed with a sigh and slid open. In the room beyond, cramped living quarters, one pallet and sink with medical supplies lining cabinets that reached to the ceiling. Across the ceiling lay a schematic of the *Mona Lisa*, but half of it was dark, the rest flickering.

In the middle of the room, behind the pallet, stood one sweating, thin, sallow man, about five ten, in whites that weren't white any more. Brilliant blue eyes. Looked a bit rodent-ish, like he'd happily gnaw on something, anything, until he'd chewed it all up. But entirely unharmed. Wearing a stink she recognized as fear, mixed with the usual too-long-without-a-shower reek.

He held a small pistol. Aimed at them. Despite the man's poor physical condition, his hands didn't shake. His stance reflected military training: two-handed grip, bent slightly at the knees. Unfazed by the firing squad two feet from him.

"Drop the weapon." Lopez tightened her finger on the trigger.

The man's bright gaze darted from Marine to Marine, assessing them before he reached some decision. He licked his lips like a gecko. Lowered the pistol, transferred it to his left hand, and set it on the floor while raising his right arm as if in a parody of surrender. Stood there, waiting.

"Identify yourself," Lopez ordered flatly.

A relieved smile, although Lopez thought she'd detected an underlying, undeserved confidence. Already had a growing sense he was putting on a performance for them.

"Doctor John Smith, Chief Medical Officer of the transport ship *Mona Lisa*." When they didn't move, he added, hesitantly, "Er, you can lower your weapons."

Lopez smiled, hoping it came out as grim as Benti claimed. "John Smith" her ass. "You didn't offer us ice cream. You didn't even say 'please'. What's in it for us?"

"Ice cream?" he said, incredulous.

Some guffaws from behind her, but Smith looked at them like he'd entered a room full of crazy people. She could see he wasn't someone who liked playing the fool. Resented her already, even if he came off as polite.

"Yeah, ice cream." Had five dead and wasn't above taking it out on a stranger. "We want ice cream."

Smith backed away a little, said, unsmiling, "I'm not the enemy . . . please?"

Lopez lowered her rifle. The others followed her lead. Smith let out that breath he'd been holding.

Okay, fun was over. Time for business.

"What happened here?" she asked. "How'd you wind up in that room?"

Smith shrugged, gave a helpless little laugh that still seemed like acting to Lopez. He picked at some dead skin on his left palm with his right hand. Worried at it. "What do you think happened? Ship like this, only one thing ever happens. Prisoners got a chance, rioted, overwhelmed the guards, and took over the ship. I was lucky to be in here when it happened."

"Lucky," she echoed, rolling the word between her teeth. Her own scars were itching. Again. "'Prison ship.' That's the story, huh?"

He frowned. "It's not a story. The prisoners escaped, took over the ship."

It wasn't a lie, but it wasn't the truth either. This guy was slick. Lopez liked slick as much as she liked mysteries.

"You know, you're the first person we've found. You might be the only human survivor on this ship." Put all the emphasis on *human*.

Smith bared his teeth, neither smile nor grimace. "The only human—"

"Uh-huh," Lopez said, and gave a nod to her Marines. "Go to it, boys."

MacCraw and Percy pushed past him to investigate the room, MacCraw giving Smith a good knock with his shoulder. They could smell the bullshit too. Good. Mahmoud collected Smith's gun and patted him down roughly, coming up empty.

"Policy on the taking of Covenant prisoners change, Smith?" Lopez asked, prodding. "I don't think we got that memo."

Smith's eyes were slits. "It wasn't a widely circulated memo."

"No fucking kidding," she said, giving herself props for getting him to admit something. More than she'd gotten out of Rebecca or Foucault.

Something made him change tactics; she didn't know what. Saw it in a sudden shift in posture, even.

"Look," he said. "I'm just the medical officer. I don't—didn't—set policy. I just stitched and bandaged, that's all."

Poor pitiful you.

"In this . . . expansive . . . medical bay of yours."

Smith's mouth formed a line like a flat EKG. "I'm not here to help any Covenant bastards. Just us. Just us humans." Had he rehearsed that, too? Sitting in his sealed room, listening to the screams of people dying?

Yet, even if he had rehearsed it, Smith had touched a nerve. Lopez couldn't hold his gaze. She'd had relatives on Reach. Close ones. No longer. Had seen in Smith, for a moment, all the anger, grief, and bitterness that had driven her to take her command, every combat mission, and to give up her life to UNSC. The same she'd seen in each of her soldiers. *It was always us against them.* Always.

Balanced against that: taking prisoners. That left a sour taste in her mouth. *Leave none alive.*

Did he really think she was going to let down her guard? She hadn't let down her guard in twenty-seven years. "Tell me about the Covenant prisoners, Smith."

Smith, exasperated: "For intelligence. Research and development. Know your enemy. It's a war. You know that—you're a soldier, right? I *don't know*, I'm just the medical officer."

Her fingers flexed. The memory of John Doe's hand. "Research and development, huh?"

He held his hands out as if he had a peace offering for her, but there was only air. "I'm just the medical officer." An echo. A shield.

"What's the *Mona Lisa* doing here?"

Frustration on Smith's face. "Where's here? I've been in this room since the outbreak. It's a black box, nothing in or out. I have no idea where we are. Where are we?"

"Why don't you tell me the last place you were, then, and I'll tell you if you're still there?"

That got Mahmoud's and MacCraw's attention. That gave Smith pause.

"In chess, they call that 'check,'" Mahmoud muttered.

Gears and wheels were turning in Smith's head. Lopez could see them.

"Didn't you come here to rescue us?" Smith said. "Am I under arrest or something?" Face gone completely blank.

So you're going to play it that way. Well, she had time to play, too. All the way up until they got to the bridge.

Countered with: "You would have access codes to the bridge, right?"

Smith nodded reluctantly.

And, finally, she did relent. She might not like him, but that didn't make him the enemy. "We're off of a planet called Threshold and we've got Covenant loose on a ship capable of making a slipspace jump. We're following the Cole Protocol. We need to get to the bridge and take out the nav system. I hope the bridge isn't locked down, but if it is . . ."

Smith had blanched as soon as she said Cole Protocol. "No. No, no, we need to get off the ship. You came here somehow, a Pelican? We need to get off the ship."

Knew instinctively Burgundy would hate this guy as much as she did. "Sorry, but that's not an option. You're coming with us."

"No, no—"

"*Please*," she added, with another dazzling smile.

>Burgundy 1445 hours

At least Marines got to go out and do something, even if "something" meant getting into trouble. Not long after the last communication with the *Red Horse*, Lopez and her crew had dropped off the radio, their clichéd bravado and lame jokes slowly swallowed by static and interference. She thought she'd heard a crackle of contact from Benti, but that'd been snuffed out immediately.

Burgundy worked her way through a pack of gum. Her jaw ached something fierce. A book lay unattended on her lap. She'd tried reading, but couldn't stop checking the cameras, and had given up after she'd read the same paragraph for twenty minutes.

There wasn't anything to see. Just the barricades in the shadows. Once, she thought she'd glimpsed a silhouette with two heads, one head pale and veiny, which was a pretty ridiculous thing to think you'd seen. Nothing came out of the darkness to confirm that glimpse, so she'd put it down to nerves.

Her aft running lights were still on, so with the cameras she could still see about ten meters past the Pelican's rear. She'd thought about turning the lights off but nixed that idea. If something was out there, she'd be as good as putting out a flashing holographic sign that read "Burgundy's Home—Just Come Right In."

So she waited.

And she waited.

And she waited.

She took the latest wad of gum from her mouth, thumbed it on the dash, and froze when two figures lurched into the light on the feed. Her thumb sticking to the gum, she yanked free and gripped her pistol. *Don't you lay a hand on my bird, Covie scum. I'll hole you, I'll hole you a hundred times over.*

Then she looked closer. It was Cranker and Maller. They were stumbling, injured. Head wounds, it looked like, dark patches running down their faces, torn clothing, and they were leaning into each other, but they were *walking*. Alive!

The relief that washed over Burgundy was so intense she almost cried.

"Oh thank Christ."

They clearly needed help. She'd not thought much of them—loud and rowdy and pushy in the mess line—but here, now, it didn't matter; they were the most excellent human beings in the universe. She wouldn't be alone now.

She slapped the controls for the gangplank and vaulted out of the cockpit, snatching up an assault rifle from the locker as she passed. The ramp opened too damn slow. She ran to the lip as it lowered, checking the nearby barricades and containers for any other movement.

"Guys!" she hissed. "Get on in here! Now!"

Up close they were worse than they looked on the cameras, Cranker listing badly now, Maller pivoting toward the sound of her voice, the ramp dropping, dropping.

"You're—"

Much worse. Much, much worse.

Skin mottled and bruised and sunken, veined through with dark tendrils. Eyes white and unseeing. Some growth fastened to Cranker's neck, an enormous pustule that shivered and twitched. Maller, what had been Maller, opened his mouth, and howled, a sound no human could make.

Burgundy scrambled back, opened fire.

But it was too late.

>Benti 1450 hours

When they found that the hatch to the lower deck was also locked, Benti let loose with a stunning stream of curses that left them all looking at her like they didn't know her anymore. Except for Orlav.

"We got a Plan B?" is all Orlav asked.

This being-in-charge thing was wearing thin. Benti wished, not for the first time, that she was back on the *Red Horse*, taking a nice bath.

"This *was* Plan B," Benti said. And Plan C, if you wanted to be precise. They'd lost contact with Lopez, and Benti wasn't sure they'd get it back any time soon. Hailing the Pelican had become a kind of personal joke that gave her the giggles. Didn't know if she really found it funny or was just becoming hysterical. Hellooo Pelican, come in, come in? No? Okay. You just be that way, you petulant bird.

Clarence shrugged and started back down the corridor.

"Hang on, just wait, I'll find another way." Orlav's frown deepened, clearly sick of peering at the tiny screen.

Benti shouldered her rifle and knelt by the hatch. The access panel wasn't secured. She flipped the panel open, gave it a once-over, and pulled a knife from her boot. Being a medic wasn't all she was good at.

"Shine your light down here. Thanks." It wasn't so complicated. A little tricky, but nothing she hadn't done before. Just expose this wire, strip back this one and put a bridge here, and—

The hatchway unlocked with a sharp clack and she hauled it open. Triumphant.

But only for a second.

"Pheeeoooow!" They cringed away from the stench that came billowing out, the air thicker and moist in the worst possible way. "Bilges. They're the same in every ship."

"Foucault would be pissed to hear you say that about the *Red Horse*."

"Yeah, well, he ain't here," Gersten said, and swung himself onto the ladder, Orlav and Clarence leaning into the hatchway to provide cover.

"See anything?"

"Yep. Looks like bilges, smells like bilges . . . I think it's bilges!"

Benti hadn't expected Gersten to turn into a comedian. She rolled her eyes and dropped down after Gersten. "No shit."

"Oh, we got shit a-plenty here. Special price for you."

Wow. It wasn't going to stop.

The space was tight and cramped, full of tanks holding clean water, gray water, and sewage, and yet more tanks for the processing as it was all recycled and made ready to go back into the mix again. Moisture beaded across the ceiling and dripped onto them irregularly, leaving oily marks on the walls and residue across every surface.

"It's in this direction." Orlav gestured at a passage leading through the tanks.

"Lots of spaces to hide in there," Benti said.

Clarence gave her a look like *Who would want to?*

"Lots." Orlav agreed. "So we'll do it real careful-like."

Moving in stages, creeping, darting into new territory, their backs only to each other, they moved deeper into the bowels of the ship.

Benti wished she could get used to the smell, but it was impossible. Even keeping her hand over her nose didn't help. The smell had a taste, a texture, that got around any defense. Benti wanted that bath more than ever—and ice cream, damn the sarge for putting the idea in her head. But more than anything, she wanted someplace with a blue sky and no ceiling. She wondered, not for the first time, if Lopez was already waiting for them on the bridge.

"I've been in the shit before," Gersten said, "but this is ridiculous."

"Shut it," Benti said. Mouthy Gersten was ruining silent Gersten's rep. But also her ears had pricked up at the hint of an echo.

"Let Gersten wallow in it, for once," Orlav said, straight-faced. Even Tsardikos, who had been almost as silent as Clarence, couldn't suppress a chuckle at that.

But Benti shushed them again. "I'm serious. Clarence, you hear that?"

Clarence nodded. It was impossible to miss. A voice that rose stark above the muted hubbub of the recycling system. A voice that spoke no words, that didn't try to, that didn't know how.

They knew the wide array of Covenant sounds, and this was not one of them.

"Keep moving," Benti said through gritted teeth. Boy, she wished now they hadn't split up. The sarge would've had a much better plan. But right now the sarge might as well be on a beach in Cozumel.

"Where'd it come from?" Orlav asked. "I can't tell."

Another sound, containing a depth and jaggedness that tripped Benti's pulse.

"What the hell was that?" Gersten asked, spinning about. "Covenant bastards, what the hell is it?"

"Shut up and keep moving," Benti insisted. She couldn't shed the image of the Covenant Elite Clarence had killed for her, listening for something that frightened it more than a bunch of Marines.

Shedding caution, they sped up into a jog, a glance at each corner, knocking into the holding tanks because they looked behind them so much. Tsardikos was lagging. Benti hissed at him to go faster, but he couldn't keep up.

Another roar, a bellow not even really animal in nature—too ragged and discordant. It echoed off the tanks and pipes, hiding its source. Moaning, eerie changes in the timbre, like someone tuning in a messed-up radio channel. More and more voices—no, they couldn't be voices—joined in, as if alerted to a hunt. Just discernable above the coalescing howl, something that chittered and scuttled.

"They're behind us, I think," Gersten said, not trying to be funny any more, as he swiveled to jog backward, flashlight spasming across the pipes behind them. Benti turned, couldn't see anything. Not even Tsardikos.

"And they're gaining," Orlav added. Unnecessarily.

They broke, running so fast now that anything could ambush them, but needing to take that risk. Running felt good to Benti's tense muscles.

"Where are we going, Orlav?" Benti shouted. "Come on, where are we going?"

"Maintenance storage room, with access back upstairs beyond!"

"How far?"

"Fifty meters!"

"They're gaining," Gersten said, rising strain in his voice. There was more than one voice in the growing growl behind them, multiple footfalls, heavy, far too heavy. They turned a corner, kept going.

"Grenade?"

Orlav: "Too close to the hull!"

"Here!" Benti splashed to a halt by a narrow passage that led through the last of the tanks. A quick scan indicated that the space beyond was clear, nothing lurking in the corners. She dropped to a knee, checking the ammo remaining in her rifle as Clarence took up a position behind and over her.

"How many you make out, Gersten?"

"Lots," he said, wide-eyed.

Great help that was . . .

The noises reaching to them through the darkness swelled, sometimes familiar, yet also utterly warped, alien, broken. Benti couldn't slow her breathing, her hands cold on her rifle.

Tsardikos came running toward them in a final burst of speed, terrified and swearing. He jumped over her, spun into position behind and fumbled with his weapon.

"Took your damn time," growled Orlav. Tsardikos ignored her.

"I don't think they're Covenant," Benti said. Behind her, Clarence shifted, his calf against her hip. He had her back. Again.

Orlav smacked a flare and tossed it out into the passageway. They waited, stinking of shit, like a group of cowering sanitation workers. With guns.

The first of their pursuers staggered into the spluttering light.

They weren't Covenant.

>Lopez 1501 hours

At last they'd found a body. Never thought she'd sound a silent huzzah for that. Never thought evidence of death could be such a relief.

Security stations and checkpoints were choked with furniture, the doors themselves jammed. Sometimes on purpose. Most of the blockades had been torn apart, great gouges left in the steel walls and floor. In the process of finding a path through the debris, they'd been funneled into one of the crew's rec rooms. Archaic ceiling fans. Pool tables. Bar stools and a TV. One wall with a blown-up photograph of the beach on some tropical island. An honest-to-god facsimile of a tiki bar in another corner. Something about it made Lopez think of the words *in denial.* Even down to the plastic tiki glasses still sitting on the counter.

Nothing disturbed; no one had fled here.

It almost looked normal.

Except for the body.

Or two.

Honestly, it was hard to tell.

Right about then, looking at the pieces, Lopez could have done with some answers. Real answers, not the extra mysteries she was being offered by Smith. Remembering Rabbit, the last conversation with Burgundy, Ayad still gone.

Too many more unknowns and her soldiers were going to start to fray. No matter how she tried to stop that from happening. She'd seen it before. It had damn near happened to Foucault before he'd turned the situation around. Become a hero.

So there was Mahmoud muttering under his breath while Rakesh and Singh focused on the tiki bar. Only Percy, at her side, seemed unable to look away.

"I get the feeling this wasn't a very happy place," Percy said.

This wasn't the battlefield. This wasn't what they'd signed on for.

The storage cupboard at the far end of the room had been wrenched open so hard the hinges had spun off and the door lay crumpled to the side. Inside, pieces. Leftovers. She couldn't think of it as anything else. Flesh she knew to be Covenant. Skin she knew to be human. And something half grown across them, *inside* these pieces, bulging the muscle and mottling the skin. They couldn't have been here long enough to look that rotten. Something in the physiology had altered, shifted, from the inside. A massive protrusion from what should have been a shoulder, but it wasn't an arm. It looked like a growth of bone, grotesque and huge, with strips of flesh gripping it tenuously.

Savage. Brutal. Made her remember John Doe's wounds. Had he ever been in this room? Guard or prisoner?

"Sarge, what the fuck is that?" MacCraw pointed, as if she hadn't noticed.

"Well, MacCraw, that there," she said grimly, slipping into a drawl, "that's a hand." Death had not relaxed it. The fingers didn't curl, the palm didn't fold. Flat, with the fingers straight, rigid and stiff.

"What the hell is that other thing, Sarge?" MacCraw again. Was he never going to stop cataloging?

"Almost looks like they got fused or something hiding in the cupboard," Rakesh said in a distant voice. "Together," he added, more distant. Clearly not believing it for an instant.

But none of that really got to Lopez. What got to her was the carefully tended bonsai tree sitting right next to the cubby. Had a terrible image of someone tossing the body parts in there and then doing a bit of gardening.

Lopez took a step back, and another, and draped an arm over Smith's shoulders. She pulled him companionably close, seemingly oblivious to the way the muzzle of her rifle drifted back and forth across his face.

"John," she said. "Can I call you John?"

He leaned away. Not from her, no. From the bodies, the bits of bodies she was dragging him near. He really was a little man. There wasn't much muscle on him.

"I think you know what this is."

Smith glanced at each of them again, *assessing* them again. Seeing no escape.

"And I think you're going to damn well *tell me what this is.*"

>Benti 1502 hours

As Benti grimly fired and fired, rifle hot in her hands, she had one small satisfaction: no room to miss, no distance to interfere with accuracy. The first figure jumped and spun with the concentrated fire from the five of them, falling back into the second and third, who didn't pause. They just shoved their comrade aside, climbing over each other to get through the gap. They tripped and stumbled too as they pushed their way into the line of fire, even as the first was—oh god, Benti could make out the first thrashing its way back up. She knew she'd dropped a good line of hot lead straight in its belly, but it was *getting back up.*

Clarence threw another flare.

Most were human, some were actually Covenant. All of them so misshapen and shambly you could hardly tell. Branching fungi tumbled and poured from their limbs. Their eyes were glazed and vacant. The stink of them overpowered the shit smell. There was a low mumble coming from them, almost in concert, that unnerved Benti.

"They're not staying down!" Gersten yelled. "Reloading!" Popped a clip and slapped in a new one as Orlav covered his zone. "What the hell are they?"

She concentrated her fire on the frontmost, and it dropped, and she shifted her aim to the next, and oh god, it was getting to its feet too, and she saw shoes on those feet, slippers, and a distinctive orange color.

They'd found the prisoners, and apparently they didn't like the bilges, either.

Tsardikos wasn't even firing. Just watching, mouth open. Benti elbowed him in the thigh. "Snap out of it, soldier!" she screamed at him. And he did. Miraculously. Started firing again.

Still, there was no way they could hold this position. No way.

"Fall back to the maintenance room!" Benti rose from her crouch, sliding up against Clarence, who stepped back, and she with him, moving like practiced dance partners.

"We lose this spot, they're going to swamp us!" Orlav shouted.

"We stay here, they'll swamp us sooner!" Benti shouted back.

The flares showed a swarm of pale globes, like living snotbags, scuttling up the ceiling from behind the shambling mob, toward them.

The passageway behind them was an unknown quantity. No time to look at the map. No telling what they'd find there.

No avoiding that. No time for caution.

She yanked a grenade from her belt, ripping the pin out in the same motion. "No more jabber! Get going!"

A raised eyebrow from Clarence, a look of panic from Gersten.

She tossed it as they broke and ran.

Not far enough.

The force of it slammed into her, slammed through her, throwing her forward into Clarence. Her bones shrieked in protest. All the air fled her lungs. She rolled over the top of Clarence, heat at her back and then on her face.

None of that mattered.

"Keep moving!" she screamed, before she'd even opened her eyes, crawling to her knees. *Don't ever stop moving. Unless you want to die.*

Her ears rang like wineglasses. She couldn't hear anything, hardly could see anything. Slapped a hand on Clarence's helmet as he pushed himself from the floor. Cast about, Orlav and Gersten scrambling to their feet. *Where was Tsardikos?*

Aftershock: A wash of warm water came tumbling down the passageway and swept her legs out from under her just as she'd gotten all the way up. It was murky, it was rank, and swept along with it was one of *them*, flailing and thrashing, and a trailing arm—no, it wasn't an arm, it was a whip of bone, it was a blade of *body*—slashed Orlav across the back, arcing a wide spray of blood across Benti and Clarence, peppering blood through the filthy water and across the pipes, and slamming her down again, her mouth an "O" of shock as Benti, who had never released her rifle, they were all better than that, drew a bead and fired a hole through the thing's chest until she could see the other wall, and watched as, truly dead, it smacked up against a tank and lay there.

Thought she saw something else, too, near Orlav—one of those snot creatures—but, no, nothing when she spun, it must've just been something bobbing in the water. Part of the thing she'd just killed.

A glance down the passageway brought her a small measure of relief. Patchy fires singed churning sewage around a new barricade of ceiling and caved-in tanks. It'd worked for now—there was no other movement. The smell of mingled crap and the stench of the enemy made her cough. It'd gag her if she let it.

But so would the memory of them, those things, rising up despite being blasted full of bullet holes. They wouldn't—couldn't—be stopped for long. She could already feel the vibration of digging. The shit wouldn't hold.

She surged to her feet, too fast, off balance, shook her head angrily—she needed clarity now more than ever.

A quick check, Clarence was okay, Gersten okay, just cursing a lot as he tried to lift Orlav.

Her hearing had started to return. Over the cursing, she could hear Orlav shrieking with agony. There was another sound, too, another kind of shrieking, like a man being devoured alive. It almost froze Benti, until she realized it came from the other side of the barricade.

Tsardikos, screaming as those things took him apart. Nothing Benti could do about it. Nothing that wouldn't put the rest of them in danger.

She shook it off. She shook it off, even as it damaged her, and scrambled over to Orlav, shit bouncing from her shins.

"She's bleeding bad," Gersten said, supporting nearly all of Orlav's weight.

That was the least of Orlav's worries. This tainted water in her wounds would kill her anyway. It would just take a little longer. Benti leaned down for a quick inspection, and froze. The injury itself was long but not deep. She could see the blue curves in the dark muscle of her back, but the spine didn't shine through. What kind of a victory was it when the medic in her leapt for joy that she couldn't see bone? But fastened to the lower back was a quivering bulb of pus, fingerlike tendrils digging into the open wound ecstatically. Holy crap. It looked like a parasite of some kind. She reached for it, and stopped. Not here, not in this water.

"We have to get her out of here!" She threw one of Orlav's arms over her shoulder, the other around her waist, taking some of the burden off of Gersten. "Head for maintenance. Clarence, come on, let's go!"

They fled, dragging Orlav between them. Clarence staggered in their wake, watching the darkness behind them. He didn't have any more flares. Their flashlights would have to do.

Benti flinched as she thought she heard something in the air ducts above them.

"Orlav," Benti raised her voice, turned to yell in her ear, "Orlav! Report!"

"'s fadin'..." she slurred, and her head dropped, eyes wide open, not even pretending to walk now, feet dragging in the water. "... where..."

"There's the door!"

A burst of speed and they collapsed against it. Locked. They were trapped outside. Benti propped Orlav against the door, Gersten shouldering her weight again. "She's bad," he moaned.

Benti ripped the faceplate from the control panel, straightforward wiring again. She walked her fingers along the wires.

"Oh god, she's bad, look at her face, look at her face, look—"

Benti yanked a wire, and looked.

What looked back at her was not Orlav.

>Lopez 1503 hours

Lopez had her orders. *Find out what the hell is up with this damn ship* was down at the bottom of her priorities. *Get to the bridge* was at the top. But the more time she spent on *this damn ship*, the harder it was to ignore that she might not achieve the first without knowing the last. Couldn't help thinking of the intel blackout. Found herself rather taken with the idea of knowing something Rebecca didn't want her to know.

"So tell me," she nudged. "Tell me what I'm looking at." Knew whatever came out of Smith's mouth would come out sideways, but that was okay. She could make it honest.

"Covenant get sick too," Smith said haltingly. "We noticed it in some of them. Any of the prisoners displaying the symptoms we kept in isolation. Just in case." He wiped his mouth, still resisting Lopez's grip. "We took every precaution against it. Every precaution."

He stopped. Lopez jabbed him in the side with her rifle. She was pretty sure Smith was going to give her another scar eventually.

"It made them aggressive. Savage." Smith worked his mouth, clearly thinking about the words before he said them. "We did some tests. Managed to isolate it." Now he couldn't look away from the bodies. "An alien virus."

Percy raised his head, raised his eyebrows, as MacCraw covered his mouth and leapt back.

"We've been standing here breathing around this thing!"

Smith smiled, no humor in it. Mostly disdain. "It doesn't work like that."

"Did it jump from Covenant to human?" Percy asked.

A dull boom reverberated through the floor, the walls shuddering slightly. "Grenade?" Mahmoud mouthed. Not good. Like the explosion had jump-started his urgency again.

Smith relaxed, stopped pulling away from Lopez. Accepting his fate, finally?

"It did."

>Benti 1507 hours

Get moving again, soldier!

"Get—" The words stuck in her throat, wouldn't come out, not fast enough.

Orlav—the thing staring out from behind Orlav's eyes—opened its mouth, lips already purple and cheeks veined with green. In control now, it turned Orlav's head, drew Gersten into an embrace using Orlav's arm thrown over Gersten's shoulder.

What used to be Orlav bit into Gersten's cheek.

The words still wouldn't leave her mouth. They were stuck. As

Gersten shrieked, she couldn't look away, the teeth sinking into the cheek and worrying it. Blood washed down Gersten's throat to soak his collar. Orlav's other arm was already writhing and changing right in front of Benti, becoming something bulbous that had nothing to do with the Marine she'd known.

That arm, that club, that infernal claw, rose, about to become a weapon crashing down on her skull.

Clarence shoved her aside, fired point-blank into Orlav's temple, ripping a tunnel through the skull. As the body slumped, Clarence matter-of-factly put another burst through the heart.

It dropped, Gersten screaming and flailing to be free. Staggering back, holding one hand against his torn cheek. "Jesus, Jesus . . ."

Clarence popped the empty clip. It hissed in the water at his feet, Benti watching in the flashlight's glow, trying to adjust to what had just happened.

He slapped another in, turned, grabbed Benti's shirt and hauled her to her feet, which brought her out of it. A once-over to confirm she was uninjured, and he tipped his chin at the wires she'd left exposed, then stared at the grenade-created wreckage behind them as it shuddered and shifted, pushed from the other side. The water was rising around their knees.

She got back to it.

"Benti, my face," Gersten moaned.

"I know," she said, shaking fingers stripping this wire, then that wire, "just let me get this. Then I'll take care of you." She needed a moment so her hands were steady before she did anything medical for Gersten. Clarence had his hand on his pistol. Most people wouldn't have noticed, but she knew Clarence. *Just in case?* Was this what it came down to? She knew Gersten, too, and she wasn't sure she could do it. Any of it. But knowing she'd have to, somehow.

A crash and tumble behind them. Something was breaking through the wreckage. A spike of tension in Clarence's posture. Her hands were wet, the wires were slippery. She twisted the two and the lock clacked open.

She spun the lever, shoulder to the door, and pushed. It stuck.

A dragging sound from behind them. A hiss like static. A moaning.

"Oh for Christ's sake, come on!" Another shove, and it gave suddenly, sewage spilling into the opening, and her tumbling after it. Gersten sagged in after her. Clarence backed in and shoved the hatch closed quick as thought.

Benti looked up, into the light.

A Covenant Elite stood there, looking down at her.

Holding a cricket bat in one alien hand.

>Lopez 1507 hours

Smith looked at Lopez at last, motioning to the rifle she now held none too nonchalantly by his head.

"Sergeant, please. I am not the enemy."

"You said that already." But she released him. "So I guess you're trying to tell me one of your plague-carriers got out, grabbed one of the crew, and dragged them into this here cupboard to—" *Burgundy asking if the Covenant ate their dead.*

"I guess," Smith said, edging toward the far door. He might be trying to get away from her, but he was right. They'd lingered long enough. Didn't know if Smith would give her anything else anyway. Maybe, too, she'd wanted a tiny window of respite for her team before they went back into the thick of it.

"Rakesh, get the door. MacCraw, get your damn act together."

He gave the jumbled bodies a wide berth, hand clamped over his nose and mouth.

"It's locked, Sarge. Security coded."

Lopez gestured to Smith. "Be my guest." The lying bastard.

Clearly glad the interrogation had ended for the moment, Smith rushed over, pushed his way in front of Lopez's unhelpful boys, and punched in his code. The door slid open.

A pulsing white sack of flesh with gnarled green outgrowths and tentacles for legs stared up at them. The fugliest thing Lopez had ever seen.

In that instant, trying to figure out what the hell they were looking at, it leapt, snapping out its tendrils. Rakesh was closest, had been the most eager to leave. The thing caught him around the torso like an overeager dance partner. No time for Rakesh to react.

"Shoot it!" Smith shouted, stumbling back.

Rakesh yelped. Beat at the sac that clung to his chest. Its grip too tight for him to wrench off. Lopez took aim, but Rakesh wouldn't keep still, cries rising into a shriek. His shirt darkening and soaking, oh god, the thing was eating into his chest, and she could hear more coming toward the door—

"Shut it!" Lopez screamed to Singh. He slapped the controls. No code. Percy lunged for Rakesh. Tried to get a grip on the creature. Knocked aside by his thrashing. Mahmoud firing past them at something else coming fast from beyond the door.

Smith shoved Rakesh out the door, and the pale sac with him. Hammered the controls. The door shut.

Rakesh still shrieking.

MacCraw reached for the door, but Lopez stepped in front of him, a firm hand on his chest. "No."

"We can't just leave him out there!" *Yeah, we can. If you want to live.*

Singh pale. Percy and Mahmoud weren't protesting. Only the new guy.

Rakesh stopped screaming.

MacCraw's shoulders slumped. Moved away from the pressure of her hand on his chest. "Sorry, Sarge," MacCraw murmured.

"It's okay," she said. "It's okay."

But it wasn't.

She turned, and put all her weight into that turn.

Smashed Smith across the face with her fist.

>Benti 1510 hours

A tall man jumped between Benti and the Elite with the cricket bat. "Don't shoot!" He wore the torn orange jumpsuit of a prisoner. He hadn't shaved in days. One eye sagged a little in its socket.

Despite herself, Benti didn't shoot. Maybe because the cricket bat, a narrow but solid slab of wood, puzzled her as much as the man.

They'd tumbled into what looked like a storeroom or a transition space between rooms. Just the door and racks of tools and parts. A ladder at the rear that might lead up somewhere or might not. The white walls were covered with tiny black marks, like some kind of design.

"He's not infected, it's okay, don't shoot!" the man said. "My name's Patrick Rimmer. I'm a prisoner, but I wasn't in for anything serious, I swear!"

"That's a Covenant you're protecting," Benti said. "Why the crap should we care if he's infected or not?" She got up off the floor, rifle at the ready. *The naked Covie looking up at her, shushing her.*

Rimmer just kept his tall, lanky body in front of the Covenant, looking nervously from one to the other. Ready to die for a Covie.

"Please, guys, please, *don't kill him*," Rimmer pleaded. "You gotta understand. He's cool. We're cool. He's my friend. He's the only one I've had to talk to. The only one. He's cool. He's clean. Please. You gotta understand. You've gotta understand it isn't the Covenant's fault. Not this time. We're cool, really." Rimmer looked so lonely, so lost, that it almost got to Benti.

Beside Benti, Clarence glared down the line of his rifle, finger tense on the trigger. Crap. Things could get ugly fast, even if the Covie only had a cricket bat. Something told Benti they could afford to suss out the situation before shooting. Making noise didn't seem like a wise move right then anyway.

Benti put her hand on Clarence's rifle, gave him a long look, and stood between him and Rimmer, her own gun aimed at the Elite. Gersten had slouched up against a wall and could wait until they'd resolved this standoff.

"If that Covie makes one wrong move, looks at us the wrong way even, it's dead, you got me?" Benti said it staring back at Clarence, trying to put extra weight behind the words. Let it be *her* decision. Clarence had made a lot of decisions on his own already today. Some of them she hadn't liked.

Clarence stared at her a second, and then nodded. But she couldn't read the intent in his eyes at all anymore, and that scared her.

Rimmer relaxed a little bit, although sweat beaded his forehead. He nodded. "Yeah, cool, then. He's okay, Henry's clean, he's cool, he's okay. You're Marines, right? You're going to get us out of here, right?"

"Henry?" Benti tried the name out. "*Henry*." A Covie with a name other than "bastard" or "asshole" or "shithead." A Covie named Henry who carried a cricket bat. That left her speechless.

The man was jumpy, twitchy, couldn't stay still. Benti didn't know if she blamed him. "Yeah, I mean, I don't know his name, can't understand a thing he says, I just call him Henry—and he calls me Rimmer, of course, 'cause that's my name, although he doesn't really pronounce it right, or say much of anything, 'cause he can't speak our language—but he's cool, seriously, he's cool. There's more of you, right? You can get us back out, right?"

"Those aren't my orders—no, wait, you tell me, what were those things? We're not going anywhere until you tell me what they are."

But Rimmer no longer cared about her answer. He was looking beyond her, over her left shoulder. "He's . . . he's been infected."

Henry was raising his cricket bat. Rimmer looked around like he wanted a weapon too.

For a second, Benti didn't understand. "Infected?"

She turned, just as Gersten lowered his hands from his face.

"I don't, I don't feel so good . . ."

A mottled patch of yellow dust encrusted his torn cheek and a stagnant green tint ran through his skin. At the base of his neck, another quivering globe of pus, one soft tendril resting tenderly on his throat.

Benti reached for a pouch at her hip, automatically going for sterilizers, knowing she had nothing powerful enough, stupid stupid stupid, should have gone for her weapon, but unable to stop the reflex.

Clarence stepped up, pressed the mouth of his rifle against Gersten's forehead. Gersten stared at him, marshalled his energy to say with utter shock, "What the hell, Clarence, you—"

Clarence pulled the trigger and jumped back as Gersten went flying up against the wall. Blood sprayed out into the water, missing Clarence and smacking up against the wall with its weird black marks.

None of it hit Benti, shielded as she was by her partner.

Gersten slid down the wall. A torn cheek was the least of his worries now.

The extra blood bags Benti had brought seemed like a quaint affectation, and had for a while. There was no lack of blood here.

Clarence turned, checking her for wounds. He looked in her eyes, made her look in his eyes so she could see there was no threat there. *For now.* Clarence kept his rifle down and away from her.

Still, she had to say it. "You killed Gersten." *You killed Gersten real casual-like. You killed him.*

He nodded, impassive.

"His dog tags—"

"Forget the dog tags. You gotta rip the bodies up," Rimmer said, like he was telling her how to heat noodle soup properly. "That's not dead enough. Gotta destroy the body or they just come back."

"Don't be stupid." Benti couldn't keep her voice from cracking. "He's dead. He's *dead.*" But the fact was, even if her heart couldn't accept it, she knew what *they* were now. She had an idea of just how right Rimmer could be.

"He ain't! He's infected!" Rimmer stepped forward. He'd found a chisel. "We gotta take him apart, he's going to come back!"

Benti had her rifle pointed at him before she knew it. A mistake, seeing the Elite's posture change, and Clarence's hand coming down heavy on her shoulder. Clarence had her back. Always. And he'd just shot Gersten.

She'd just about lost control of the situation, but then, she thought with an odd kind of relief, there was hardly anyone left under her "command" anyway.

"Clarence," she said, her voice steadier than her thoughts. His hand slid up her arm and with light pressure lowered her rifle. She couldn't resist. "You're not—"

Rimmer lurched back again, chisel held out pathetically. In the water pooled on the floor, ripples . . .

Clarence pivoted, shot Gersten, and killed him a second time.

Benti didn't turn around. She'd seen her fill, enough for the rest of her life. She wanted to sit, but didn't. She wouldn't have the strength to get back up.

"You see?" Rimmer said. "You *see*? They come back. You leave them enough, all the important body bits, and they all come back. Me and Henry here, we're the last ones. They didn't know we were here. But now you've *let* them know. I mean, I'm not blaming you, not really. But they'll try to get in. We have to move. There are more of you coming, right?"

"Right," she said without feeling. *No, wrong.* The radio had been silent for too long. Too much interference. Benti knew that if more were coming, it wouldn't be to help them.

Henry looked at her, then Clarence, and the Elite's shoulders sagged in a universal sign of disappointment. It read Benti's expression just fine. Its shoulders sagged further when, beyond the door, came a crash and rumble.

"There's another way out of here?" Benti asked.

"Yeah," the prisoner said reluctantly, "but we've heard them things outside that hatch too."

"Just show us the way out," Benti said impatiently.

Cricket bat resting up against his shoulder, Henry pointed without enthusiasm to a ladder and hatch leading up to the next deck.

"We'll have to chance it. You're on a prison transport, you must be badass." *Despite befriending a Covie.* "Get Gersten's gun and use it."

Rimmer shook his head emphatically. "Not that badass. Nobody's that badass. He touched it, I'm not touching it. I'm not going near it." She wasn't going near it either, which was the point.

Clarence retrieved Gersten's rifle, took a wipe from the pouch Benti had half opened, cleaned the weapon, and thrust it at Rimmer. Benti he might argue with, but under Clarence's glare, Rimmer took the rifle. Reluctantly.

"What about Henry?" Rimmer asked. "Henry deserves a better weapon."

Clarence gave the two of them a look like, *Isn't it enough we haven't blasted him to hell?* Benti just gave a humorless laugh. Even with the odds stacked against them, no way would she willingly hand a rifle to a Covenant.

"Let him keep his cricket bat," Benti said. "And he can be the one on point. If he doesn't like it, tough."

Henry didn't seem surprised. Rimmer seemed about to argue, then thought better of it.

"Henry, Rimmer, me, and Clarence, that order. One of us drops—"

"We leave them," Rimmer said. "Or make sure they don't come back."

She put her foot on the bottom rung of the ladder. If there was anything up there, she couldn't hear it over the din back in the recycling plant.

"Covenant are not in charge of this ship." It wasn't framed as a question.

Rimmer snorted. "The Flood got out. There's no one in charge of this ship any more."

>Lopez 1510 hours

Lopez shook the pain out of her hand. Her knuckles stung. "Never hit someone in the jaw, MacCraw." But, damn, on some level, it had felt good. She'd wanted to do it for a while.

He gaped at her. "But you just did! Sarge!"

"Silly of me," she said, turning to Smith, who'd staggered to the floor, holding his face, blood on his chin. "Very silly." She slammed one regulation navy boot into his gut so hard he curled around her foot, the force exploding saliva from his mouth.

"Sarge!" What outfit did MacCraw think he'd joined? The Lady's Auxiliary Gardening Society?

"You know what that thing was, you lying son of a bitch." Lopez ignored MacCraw. "Virus my ass. Mahmoud, search him again."

Four rosary beads in her mind, possibly six more hanging in the balance. She flexed her fingers. Yeah, never hit someone in the jaw, unless it was utterly necessary.

"Still nothing," Mahmoud reported.

Smith looked a little too smug about that. She was beginning to think he couldn't help himself.

"Take off his shoes. Check his tighty whities, if you have to. Check his damn body cavities!"

"Sarge!" Mahmoud looked as mortified as Smith.

Lopez curled her lip in a snarl. Didn't need to say anything further.

Nothing on Smith's body, who flinched away from the rough hands on him. But then:

"Sarge," Mahmoud couldn't conceal the relief in his voice. He rose, Smith's shoes in one hand, an identity pass in the other. "I found this."

Lopez read it. "Office of Naval Intelligence, Section 3, Major

John Smith, Research and Development." The foulest tasting title she'd ever uttered. "Lovely."

ONI. *Spooks. Wraiths.* The mystery was suddenly a whole lot less mysterious, and Lopez found that didn't make her any happier.

Smith wheezed suddenly, sucking in a huge gulp of air, face beet-red and not just from the punch.

"Officer on deck, soldiers," Lopez said to the others as she crouched down beside Smith, if that was even really his name. "Why didn't you identify yourself?" She thought she had a good idea why. Whatever Smith's mission had been, that mission had gone belly-up. Not just failed, but failed in a spectacular, amazing, epic way.

He choked and coughed, curled up to protect his belly.

"Why didn't you identify yourself, *sir*?" Lopez asked.

Percy spat on the ground. MacCraw still just stood there, stunned by the way events had broken.

Smith uncurled, up on one elbow. Now Lopez could see he was furious. "Let's cut the bull-crap, Sergeant. I outrank you. It doesn't matter why I didn't give you my rank to begin with. Effective immediately, we abandon ship." He stopped, coughed again. "I cannot be infected. I am privy to highly classified intelligence—I can*not* be allowed to be infected. We abandon ship, return to the *Red Horse*, and destroy the *Mona Lisa* from a safe distance."

When she didn't answer, Smith said, "I know you had to come on a Pelican. Probably in the hangar right now, waiting for you."

They stared at each other.

"That's an order, *Sergeant.*" Quietly. In control of himself now.

A whole new game now, and Lopez didn't have the right of it. Or did she? Smith could've told her men to arrest her, but he hadn't.

"I have soldiers aboard I cannot contact. Sir," she said.

The others looked on with a kind of fascination, witnessing

something she knew they'd never seen before. Smith outranked her, but these were extenuating, extraordinary circumstances. Lopez was their Mama. Smith wanted to retreat to a safe place. Command was a privilege those under you had to grant. You assumed it, but you couldn't *assume* it.

"There have been many casualties in this war," Smith said. "There will be many more."

Well. That sealed it. She bent at the knees and landed a punch from above. Damn, that *hurt.* Grabbed his collar and hauled him to his feet, shoving him back at Mahmoud and Singh.

"Sarge?" Percy said.

She nursed her hand. "Shit, ouch, shit. We're going to the bridge. No spook is going to leave my kids in the dark and then scuttle the ship on them. Shit. Benti would haunt us if we did, and she'd be a real annoying ghost. Damn, that stings. Any questions?" Said it casual, but knew this was the break point. If they were going to break.

Met their eyes, relieved to see no argument there. You didn't leave your own in the dark. Not even if there were big bad "viruses" out there. Especially not then.

"Um."

Except for Percy, apparently. Was she going to have a problem with Percy?

"Private?"

"Can I hit him too, Sarge?"

>Foucault 1515 hours

Foucault stood on the bridge beneath the light of the images brought back from the ship's remote cameras. They'd displayed the same thing for hours: the *Mona Lisa* dark and tiny against the backdrop of broken Halo, the endlessly shifting cloud of debris, brief flares in Threshold's atmosphere as pieces of Halo plummeted into the gas giant, and one Covenant capitol ship, on the very edge of the sensors, nearly masked by the planet. The Covenant ship hadn't picked up on them, and some part of him—the reckless part—wanted to sneak up and lay down a few well-placed mines.

A timer, nestled in to one corner of the main screen, counted the seconds since last contact with Sergeant Lopez and her team.

It had been running a long time.

Rebecca stood on a holopad in her war avatar. Foucault had insisted on it. It seemed disrespectful of her to show up on the bridge looking like a dumpy Italian woman. It offended his sense of decorum. Besides, he often underestimated Rebecca when she took on that avatar. He didn't want to do that, not now.

He knew: there were Covenant on board the *Mona Lisa.*

He knew: there were ONI personnel on board the *Mona Lisa.*

He knew . . . well, not much else.

He knew his options were limited.

The timer flicked over, another minute gone.

A new context, a new paradigm. A new something.

"Helm," he said, determined to break the spell of inertia. "Bring us up on the *Mona Lisa.* Quietly. I want Sergeant Fugazi and two squads prepped and ready for dust off as soon as we're alongside."

"Yes, sir! New heading—"

"Commander," Rebecca cut in over the top. "What are you doing? Our orders specifically state that if recon, or a loss of recon, indicates the *Mona Lisa* has been compromised beyond retrieval, the *Red Horse* is authorized to fire a Shiva missile and destroy the ship, regardless of passengers and regardless of revealing our position."

Foucault turned, caught the eye of the helmsman, who was hesitating, and nodded. "Yes, Rebecca. I am aware of our orders."

Sometimes he'd much rather be a private than a commander. Sometimes he'd much rather be lowered down into the middle of a firefight than have to make overarching high-level and *distant* decisions. Field combat came more naturally to him than this posturing and fencing.

Rebecca crossed her arms, tilting her head toward the timer. "That indicates a 'loss of recon,' Commander. It is time to reassess the situation."

Intimidation tactics were wasted on an AI, but he leaned down, close to the Ghost Who Must Be Obeyed, and whispered. "I have been given my orders, but I have not been granted any information with which to assess the situation. We are to destroy the *Mona Lisa* if it is 'compromised,' but by *what* I do not know."

"Covenant," Rebecca replied succinctly.

"Sergeant Lopez and her team are more than capable of handling the Covenant presence on board that ship. No, I say again: I have not been given any information that would warrant firing on one of our own ships with my own soldiers aboard. Prep a Pelican, bring up the *Red Horse*. I suspect you could tell me what I need to know, and I suspect you will not. Thus, I see no alternative but to conduct further recon." Perfectly aware he was beginning to sound like his prissy schoolteacher of a father. "You were right. We do send our soldiers to their deaths, but we do not willingly abandon our own, Rebecca. We do not turn and leave them."

"You're getting spittle on my projector," Rebecca said.

Foucault straightened, turning away. He really missed Chauncey.

"Once I have all the facts, then I shall reassess the situation. And part of that reassessment will be to determine if you are fit for duty, given your current conduct. Your activation date was, as I recall, more than six years ago." He did not use the word *rampancy*, but knew she damn well understood his meaning. A dirty tactic, but these were dirty times.

Silence between them. Foucault thinking of his superior officer with the glass eye.

This time, Rebecca broke first.

"Okay."

Foucault struggled not to raise an eyebrow in surprise.

This time it was the AI's turn to lean in and whisper. "Somewhere private, Commander. I have something to show you. Something you won't want your crew to see."

>Burgundy 1520 hours

Hands and claws and deformed bodies and the stink of something so foul she'd vomited. Forming a living conveyor belt, passing her along the passageways. Always the roar of their anger to drown out her screams.

She'd gone down fighting, but she'd gone down. The mistake had been thinking Cranker had still been Cranker, Maller still Maller. A shot through the heart didn't do it. A shot in the leg didn't do it. By the time she'd figured that out, they'd had her. Maller had broken one of her legs as she'd tried to get to the pilot's seat. Cranker had knifed her in the side.

As she'd lain there trying to get up, Cranker had kicked her, and Maller had reared up with fist and claw held high, like he was going to finish her off. But then a whole bunch of the small ones, the ones like bouncing beach balls—that's what her mind made them into so she could handle it—had come surging up the gang-plank. Cranker had stopped, and Maller with him.

They'd stood there, heads held like they were sniffing the air, or like they were receiving information. *Plants reaching for the light.*

By then, Burgundy had begun to go into shock, the pain draining away. She couldn't get over the strangeness of those living beach balls, which made her mind flash to images of the ocean when she was on leave. A strange, quick glimpse of Benti drinking a piña colada, Clarence alone in the distance like a lost soul, wandering through the surf, looking for seashells. Surely Lopez had to be somewhere. The sarge would come and save her.

She'd tried to resume her epic journey to the pilot's seat, but Cranker and Maller had come to some kind of decision.

Suddenly, Cranker was picking her up and slinging her over his shoulder, growling as he did it. The pain of that cut through the shock, her leg a burning plank of wood. She screamed, beat at him with her good arm, only realizing in that second that her right arm hung useless across Cranker's back. Across the horrible nodule of a passenger he'd picked up. There was a wetness that clung to her that she realized must be blood.

Maller brought up the rear, followed by the beach balls. She closed her eyes against that sight, and most of the time since she'd tried to keep them shut. It was her only defense against what was happening.

Because now, slowly, laboriously, with starts and stops where Cranker carried her again, she was being passed along by a great community of the horribly transformed—down corridors, pushed through airducts, sometimes dropped as Cranker and Maller fought with some new monstrosity that apparently hadn't gotten with the program. Whatever the program was.

Sometimes now she tried to reason with the two Marines. "Cranker," she'd say, "please take me back to the Pelican. I know you're still in there. I know you can hear me." Or she'd say, mumbling it a bit because she felt so weak, "Maller, I know you don't want to do this. I know you want to help me. Please, please help me." Once she even said, "If you'd just put me down, I could do the rest. I can find the sarge. I can explain it was a mistake." She laughed bitterly at that one, knowing everything was past repair, and her laughter dissolved into panicked sobs again. She was alone.

Cranker and Maller never answered. Cranker and Maller had their marching orders, and they didn't come from the sarge.

>Lopez 1527 hours

"Hell of a big virus," Lopez said, pushing Smith ahead of her. He'd pleaded his case for a while, told her he'd launched the empty escape pods to avoid anything getting off-ship as soon as he realized the situation. Told her he'd tried to sabotage the bridge but hadn't been able to get close enough. And, then, apparently, decided to wait it out in his little blind room. None of it really made Lopez see him in a better light.

Backtracking, now that their path through the rec room had been cut off, looking for any way forward. Any way backward. Any way at all. "Hell of a big virus," Lopez said again. "Looked more like a giant angry testicle to me."

No one laughed. "Not a virus, no. More of an . . . infestation." Smith was hunched over, hadn't stopped cradling his stomach. "It came with the Covenant prisoners and just spread. The more bodies they took over, the more—"

"Taking over bodies?!" MacCraw near tripped at the words.

"It was a Flood infection form that took your friend," Smith said. He had an enormous shiner swelling his cheek that made his words come out a little soft. "They get under the skin. It will take him over and assimilate him entirely. It'll wipe his memories but retain his knowledge. Then the Flood will control his body—all of his body, down to the cellular level. Then mutate—like you saw with those bodies—to make a better weapon of him."

Lopez hastened her steps, hearing the words "retain his knowledge."

Smith couldn't seem to stop now that he'd started, like it was a relief to talk to someone about it. "A form infected by Flood is difficult to stop. They don't register pain, don't require all organs functioning, are fueled by such rage that even when disabled they are extremely dangerous. Mindless as animals. Less than animals. Destroy the core, the head, or the infection form."

Or, maybe, Smith was spreading a different kind of infection. That information had to be classified, and now they'd heard it. Lopez had to fight the urge to tell him to shut up now.

But he was done. "Stop here." Smith put a hand up against a wall that looked no different from anything else and flinched when Lopez reached for him.

"Concealed door," he said, coughing. "There's a scanner at eye level here. There's no other way out, Sergeant." When she hesitated, added: "All passages are blocked."

"So helpful all of a sudden," Lopez said dryly.

Smith shrugged. "The sooner you get to the bridge, the sooner I get off this ship." Smith pressed his hand to the wall.

The wall sank back, slid aside, revealing another black box of a room.

"It leads to the labs," Smith said. "We can get through from there." He didn't look happy about that.

A crash and roar bounced up the corridor. Somewhere close, something was trampling a barricade. A tremor through her kids. A shudder they couldn't hide.

"Mahmoud?" Lopez said out the side of her mouth, shining her flashlight down one way, as Percy looked the other.

"I'm looking, I'm looking." He scrolled too fast through their schematic. "Okay here. It looks like ventilation shafts. Leading . . . yeah, there are a couple of other access points, we can get to the bridge through here. Theoretically. Maybe even back to the hangar."

Another crash, more final, and then the thunder of heavy footsteps. Just around the corner. *Okay, boys, time to go.*

Lopez shoved MacCraw into the room, catching Percy's harness and dragging him back in as Smith scanned his hand again and sealed the door.

"Quiet," Smith murmured. "It may go straight past us."

Lopez held her breath and counted rosary beads in her mind, in time to the *thumpthump-thumpthump* of uneven running, drawing closer, closer, flying right past.

Waited until the sound died away, until it had been silent for some time, before exhaling.

"Your friend is looking for you," Smith said with a kind of gallows humor, cringing when Lopez raised her hand. He hadn't earned the right to joke with them.

"Another black bloody box," she muttered. "What's the point of a black box you can't see out of? Masterminds at work."

"Masterminds at work, *sir*."

She ignored the ONI agent. Let him waste energy on sarcasm. "Ready?" A round of nods. "Smith, the door, and keep your mouth shut."

Whatever had happened in the lab, it was over now.

No lighting, no emergency lighting. Their flashlights bit out pieces of the room, little snippets of chaotic destruction. Glass smashed to hell and back, crunchy on the hard floor. The walls dented, with a sickly green fuzz growing in patches. Benches and cupboards overturned. Blood drying and tacky on the walls and ceiling. She'd become jaded. It didn't really register as any different from the decor in the rest of the ship. The *Mona Lisa* had been turned into a vast garbage pit, a nightmare for insurance adjusters.

But: the smell hit like a fist, a shudder and cringe running through them on that first inhale. Where did that smell come from? Lopez had never experienced it before the *Mona Lisa*. Ever. It combined the bitterness of the inside of a walnut shell with, as far as Lopez could tell, something from way up inside a dog's ass.

"Geez, Sarge," MacCraw groaned, as if she were somehow responsible.

"Buck up, Private," Lopez said. "The rest of us have had to smell your cologne all day."

He had no answer to that.

As they fanned out, Lopez barking out the usual refrain—secure the doors, don't let your guard down—she realized this must've been ground zero. Whatever Smith had done, whatever he'd *really* done, it had happened here. The remains of scientific equipment, so broken, so mixed together, resembled the mixed bag of wares available at some infernal flea market. Nothing she could put a name or purpose to.

Outbreak, but not a Covenant outbreak.

But the room was empty, just the aftermath and their trembling shadows, big and bold against the walls. Whatever had been here had moved on.

"The way to the bridge looks clear," Mahmoud said, coming back to them.

Could it be that easy? No, it couldn't. But still she told Mahmoud, good work. Sent Percy and Singh to check the other exits. MacCraw stared at a thick growth of green pus on the wall.

"What were you doing here?" Kept her voice low, as if the ghosts of whatever had trashed the lab might hear her otherwise. Left boot prints in the congealed blood as she shifted her stance.

Smith slumped on a data bank, running his hand over it almost sadly, the smashed casing and shattered circuits.

"I told you, research and development," Smith said, with a touch of scorn. "Like ONI's always done. You should be thanking me. We came up with some interesting data that will help us maximize the damage inflicted by our weapons on the Covenant. They've developed a natural resistance to the radiation put out by their plasma weapons—a forced evolution, from the look of it. With further research, we'll be able to use it against them, and to help us treat plasma burns, too."

Mahmoud listened to this answer with what seemed to Lopez like derision. They all knew how long it took for any "development" to reach the people on the ground. "Yeah. Right. What about your 'Flood'?"

The glimmer of pride Smith had displayed, listing his accomplishments, vanished. "We could have solved one of the greatest threats to the human species since the Covenant."

Mahmoud, disbelieving. "'Since the Covenant'? Why didn't you just focus on them, sir? They're kicking our asses all over the galaxy."

Smith smiled, or tried to, swollen face barely moving. "The Flood is pure of intent. Relentless. Almost primordial. And it *is* a virus, spreads as fast as one. I had to study it. *We* had to study it. So we used Covenant."

"You didn't *have* to do anything," Mahmoud said. "If the Covenant knew we were taking prisoners, can you imagine—"

Lopez noticed the death stare Smith gave Mahmoud.

Smith still wasn't telling the truth, but he wasn't lying either. Misdirection, misinformation, she didn't trust any of it. She stepped up to the smashed viewing pane of a small cell. Human skin and flesh caught on the jagged glass.

"Keep talking," she said, as she shone her flashlight inside. Stared at a leg in the small cell. Forgotten, like it was a dog's chew toy. Human. A slipper had ended up against the opposite wall. Around the ankle and shin the now familiar orange fabric, half an ID number visible through the gore.

"We were looking for weaknesses, a cure, an antibody, anything. We only had one infected Covenant, but we needed to see how it worked, how it spread. Just . . . it's strong. So strong." He trailed off. Suddenly tired, defeated by something larger than any of them. And yet, was that the barest hint of respect for the Flood creeping into his tone?

"You were testing on prisoners."

"It may be abhorrent to you," Smith said, "but such measures will be what wins us the war. Don't tell me you're getting soft for an alien race now, Sergeant."

No. She had no problem with anyone torturing Covenant. That wasn't the point.

"We face extinction," he said, almost like a politician. "We have to win this war. No matter what the cost."

No matter what the cost.

"You weren't trying to cure Covies of your Flood," she said, unable to look at him. "This is a prison ship. A civilian prison ship. *You were testing on prisoners.*"

Something in her tone must have let him know exactly what

she meant. Written in the set of her shoulders, the cords standing out on her jaw.

Smith gave Lopez the half-embarrassed cringe-grin people with no integrity gave you when you caught them doing something wrong and they weren't really sorry. But wanted to pretend they were.

"It's a big, bad universe, Sergeant. Covenant aren't the worst of it."

Lopez raised her head, shifting her balance to her heel.

"You've done what you thought was necessary," Smith said. "And so have I."

God, he was fast. Faster than she would've thought. Missed it in the pat down? Hidden in the lab? A knife in his hand, and Mahmoud's throat slit, his rifle sliding naturally into Smith's hands, he got a burst off just as Lopez raised her weapon. She grunted with the impact as the bullets smacked into the armor on her left side. Went down on one knee. Could feel the bruising. Could feel she'd live. *Another scar.*

Was already reaching for Mahmoud, even though it was too late for him. There was a curve of new blood spattered on the floor, as emphatic as a scimitar.

By then, Smith was through the hatch, sealing it behind him.

>Benti 1530 hours

"Where are we?" Benti asked Rimmer.

"Guard's tea room. God's waiting room?" He peeked up over the window. "Didn't really get a tour of the ship, you know."

They'd been lucky, nothing had been on the other side of the ladder. Without the schematic Orlav had carried, they were running blind, but the engine room was back here somewhere. They'd passed one very helpful sign, directing them on their way—the only time she'd felt like they were someplace even halfway civilized.

She wasn't sure how she was going to explain Henry to the sarge when they met up. Henry kept close to Rimmer, for all the good it did the Covenant. Rimmer kept looking around and starting at shadows.

"You said 'Flood,' before. What did you mean?"

Rimmer pitched his voice low. Henry craned to listen, even if he couldn't understand. "Some uniform came on board. He was with ONI. After that, we weren't allowed out of our cells. Sponge baths, if we were lucky. I think they brought the Covies on board then. We could hear them talking. Could smell them, too. Sorry, Henry." He gave the Elite an apologetic pat on the arm, which seemed to surprise the alien. "No one told us anything. Not even the guards knew what was going on. We made some slipspace jump, to here. Wherever here is. Could hear them bringing stuff on board all the time, and tossing it back out, like they were looking for something. Guess they found it. Started taking people, you know. And Covies. They didn't seem to care if we saw the Covies, then." He stopped. "Think they figured we weren't going anywhere, and it didn't matter what we knew." He kept patting Henry's arm. In his words, in the flat lack of emotion in his voice, there was an absence of dread that was louder than anything he could have screamed. And he kept patting Henry's arm like he'd developed a nervous tic.

"The air con on this ship, you know how it is. It carries the noise funny. We heard things. No one they took ever came back. None of them. "

Something small and hard crystallized in Benti's mind.

"Nothing good ever comes from ONI," she said low, with vehemence that surprised even her.

Clarence was paying attention, she noticed, but trying hard to act like he wasn't. *What the heck is that about?*

"There was a guard, fat asshole called Murray; he found out about the Flood. Some new biological weapon, I dunno, something. He said, he said," a tremor entered his voice, "he said they were studying it. Here. With us." He stopped moving, hand not quite on Henry's arm.

Henry's head drooped, and Rimmer patted him again. Henry flinched.

Rimmer took his hand away, embarrassed. "Sorry," he mumbled.

"——," Henry said, with poor grace, and looked at Benti expectantly.

That brought Benti up short. She stared at the four jaws of his mouth, curled meek against his face now, little teeth fitting into the grooves of his gums. She'd never had the opportunity to watch a Covenant Elite speak before. It was one of the grossest things she had ever seen, and she'd seen plenty of gross. She could still see down his throat. It wasn't pretty, either.

Clarence shifted slightly, bemused, and raised an eyebrow at her. She raised both eyebrows helplessly, looked at Rimmer.

"Um. What did he just say?"

Rimmer stared back at them like they were asking the impossible. "How should I know? But maybe he's trying to tell his side of the story. All that black stuff on the walls of the room you found us in? That was him writing down words. I couldn't read any of it."

Henry slumped, clearly fed up, the tip of his cricket bat

thumping into the floor, and muttered something that didn't require translation.

Rimmer gave Henry a pointed look that said *don't interrupt again*, and continued: "Something happened, I don't know, I think the Covies made a break for it or something. And in all the chaos, I guess . . . the Flood got out. Covies let some of us out, too, which might surprise you but by then we'd all been through the same stuff. All got the same fate on this ship. 'Course, it didn't help at first, because the guards didn't like it, and they started on us, all of us prisoners, and some of the Covies didn't like that and started on anything human. But me and Henry, we're cool. We knew. Bigger problems on board."

"And you've been hiding ever since."

"A day, I think. Maybe two. You lose track of time real fast around here."

"So fast?"

Rimmer nodded. "We gotta get off this ship. Soon, you know?"

Benti couldn't disagree. She also couldn't tell him Henry would be shot on sight once they reached the hangar, that she'd do it herself if she had to. Because the sarge wasn't going to like this, not at all. But Henry would be useful getting back to the Pelican, even if only to provide another target for the Flood. Besides, Clarence, hanging back, always had his rifle pointed vaguely in Henry's direction.

"Do you know where this leads?" She pointed out the door. Henry shivered faintly.

"Yeah," Rimmer said. "D cell block. I think the engines are behind them. We should . . . we should find a different way."

"Why?"

"That's where they took all the dead. That'd be like going into an angry beehive right about now."

>Lopez 1537 hours

Lopez wasn't sure, but she thought Mahmoud might've mumbled "*. . . and then comes ice cream*" as he'd bled out onto the floor in her arms, his blood mingling with all the rest. His hand had been warm, just like John Doe's had been, and she'd been just about as much help.

Another bead down. It wore on her, and never stopped wearing. But at least she could take his dog tags. Tell everyone back on the ship how well he'd served. They were in her pocket along with Smith's security pass.

"That's on me, not you guys," she'd said as Singh and MacCraw had wordlessly bandaged her up, with a kind of care she guessed meant respect. Even standoffish Percy helped.

Now she hardly even felt it, except as a sting if she bent or turned suddenly. Just the four of them now, heading toward the bridge down the longest corridor in the world. The only point of interest, an intersection about thirty-five meters down. Didn't like turning corners any more. Didn't like it one bit.

Trying to give up on the weird taste in her mouth from losing Smith, from letting him take Mahmoud out. She could see him, in her mind's eye, popping out of some secret door somewhere, trying to make his way by secret spook passages and guile, to the Pelican. No, he wouldn't make it. Wouldn't last long on his own. Even gladder now that she'd beaten him up. A small victory, but still. He'd feel it for the rest of his short life. He'd remember her.

The corridor was so long that Percy had been tossing flares down toward the end of it like he was playing in some weird shuffleboard tournament. Reached farther than their flashlights. Flares they had plenty of, bullets not so much any more. They'd taken a break to wolf down some MREs, but still she was hungry.

MacCraw'd acquitted himself well, too, despite his bitching. When they'd made it back to the *Red Horse*, she'd tell Foucault that. He scooped up the flares they reached, squinting and handing them back to Percy to throw again. Wished they could do the same with bullets.

Singh came to a sudden halt.

"Talk to me," Lopez said.

"I heard something."

Lopez studied him a moment. Singh was holding it together. Barely. *Don't get jumpy.*

"Flare, Percy."

He obliged. Flung it as far as he could, until it came to a hissing stop at the far edge of their vision.

Right at the feet of a silhouette, the figure of a Marine.

MacCraw frowned. Singh held a hand up to his eyes to shield them from the glare.

The figure came out of the flaming mandala of the flare, roughly fifty meters away.

"Is that . . . ?" MacCraw began and then trailed off. "That can't be . . ."

"It's Ayad," Singh said. "It's definitely Ayad."

Lopez could see him clearly now, running toward them. Loping almost. Trying to make a sound in the back of his throat, but it was coming out like *thnnnnnn* or *thmmmmmm*. Should've been a hum, more like a moan. Holding out a hand as if in greeting. A huge smile on his face.

MacCraw let out a whoop. "Ayad!"

"It's not Ayad," Lopez warned.

"What do you mean it's not Ayad?" Singh said. "Of course it is. It's Ayad."

Ayad hadn't had a smile that went from ear to ear. Or something growing out of the back of his head. Ayad hadn't had an extra arm with a claw, held a little back behind him, as if to disguise it. Ayad hadn't been preceded by a smell that made Lopez's eyes water.

But MacCraw kept babbling on, like he didn't want to believe it, and Singh just fed into that, almost manic. Percy backed up until he was level with her, would've slipped back farther if she'd let him.

This wasn't the way Lopez wanted it to end.

When Ayad was about forty meters away, she put a bullet through his left shoulder. It knocked him off his feet. Which brought MacCraw and Singh out of their trance or whatever the hell it had been. A lot harder for them not to see the problem.

Ayad rose with a howl, and kept coming, running now on all fours like something born to it, with MacCraw babbling in a different way now.

"Don't fire until he's closer," Lopez ordered. "Right after he's cleared that intersection."

Ayad reached the intersection—and something with all the speed and weight of a freight train smashed into him and splattered him up against the opposite wall. Ayad fell as the creature howled at him, then picked him up and held him with one monstrous hand out in front, turning toward them. The other arm weighed down with what could almost have been antlers coming out of its palm.

The suddenness of the act, the viciousness of it, shocked Lopez. Threw her for a second. Just a second.

"That's an Elite, " Percy said. "Look at the size of it!"

Lopez had never seen one bigger, either. Its head almost bumped against the ceiling. As it came toward them down the corridor, she could see the striations of infection running up and down its legs, the suggestion of an outline on the Elite's chest of the same fungal-jellyfish thing that'd taken Rakesh.

The infected Elite turned this way and that, sniffing, as it ran. Some perversion of a howl tore up through the torso. Out through what was left of the mouth. One of the jaw hinges hung, snapped and loose. A single tendon kept it attached.

"We're not outrunning *that*," Lopez said calmly. "Singh, kneel and go low, for the legs. MacCraw, keep your cool and aim for Ayad. Make it drop Ayad before it gets to us. Percy, heart. I'll go for the head. Now . . . fire!"

It lost its Ayad shield first, dropped it. MacCraw made a lucky shot and hit the muscle and bone in its wrist. It stumbled as the bullets hit it, each one more precious than the last. Slamming into its body over and over again. It might be Elite, but it didn't bleed. A sigh of something green and dandelion-seedlike puffed out from the wounds opening on its skin. Strangely beautiful, those wounds, in the hissing light of the flares. Wounds that should've stopped and dropped it, but it kept coming. Kept howling.

Staggered onward on tottering balance, pressing against the storm of bullets as if they were toxic raindrops. Until, finally, Lopez managed to take out its knees.

It crashed down, not seven meters from them.

But it didn't stop. Didn't even pause, clawing and crawling its way across the floor, on its belly, a smear of dark green behind it.

No one hesitated. No one waited for another order.

When it was done, the corridor reeked of gunsmoke, the smell acrid in their mouths and the backs of their throats. Lopez's eyes stung, unable to handle the swamp-gas smell of the dead Elite.

Lopez thought of the bodies in the cupboard. Thought of the Elite stomping on Rabbit's chest, *on the infection form*. She walked up to it, this thing, and pressed the muzzle of her rifle into the suggestion of a giant angry goiter clinging to its chest. Let off another quick burst. Realized she'd forgotten something, something important.

Ayad rose up from the darkness beside Singh.

Singh hadn't the reflexes, hadn't the training. Enough time for the technician's face to change. Knowing. Not wanting to know. Then he was smashed into the far wall with one terrifying blow, so hard his skull shattered in the helmet, face flattened to a pulp as he dropped.

Percy, cursing, a burst from his rifle going wide, caught by the backswing. Lopez heard his neck crack. Turned too fast. Sudden pain where Smith had shot her.

And MacCraw, like he'd done it a million times, brought his rifle up and shot what was Ayad right through the head.

The flare light painted everything red and gold, made beautiful what should've been ghastly. MacCraw stood there, staring at that tableau like a painter who didn't know what to make of the paints on his canvas.

Lopez put a hand on MacCraw's shoulder, her one remaining bead. That shoulder heaved under her touch, and then steadied.

"Where to, Sarge?" MacCraw asked in an empty voice.

Lopez gave him a smile, knowing it was grim and making it brief. "Objective hasn't changed, kid," and as she said it, it became true. They were Marines. The job kept getting harder, but they got the job done, and that meant they had to keep getting better. They'd faced the worst and best the Covenant could throw at them, and now the worst the universe could throw at them, and survived treachery by their own kind. And they were still walking. Still breathing. That was a hell of a thing.

A *hell* of a thing.

>Benti 1544 hours

Rimmer told them Henry had found the cricket bat in the guard's locker room. Who knew when the guards had the chance to play cricket, or where, but the Elite was a natural with it. A rabid white slug thing had dropped from one of the overhead lights, moving too fast for any of them to shoot, and he'd splatted it against the far wall with one easy swing.

Clarence examined the green goop falling in clumps and nodded his approval. Yet Benti knew Clarence could turn around and kill Henry in an instant.

Benti hadn't been able to speak to him since Gersten's death. She'd found it hard to even acknowledge his presence. The fact was, it had cost him nothing to pull the trigger. That was what bothered her the most.

Beneath that, another, deeper, layer of unease.

He'd seemed to know. Before Rimmer had said anything about infections and coming back. *How did he know?*

Rimmer: "Henry was the one who sprung me out. There was a . . . one of the guards, she'd been, she wasn't, but he took her out. Saved me. He's a good guy, really." Rimmer couldn't stop talking, which set Benti's teeth on edge—thought maybe he'd been imprisoned because he'd talked someone to death. He couldn't stop touching Henry either, like a frightened puppy, and she was sure she wasn't imagining the distaste on the Elite's face at that.

A stairwell branched in the hallway. She didn't mind at all the sudden convenience of a sign pointing up that indicated engine room access. She crept up, peeking over the lip of the landing, the others crowding at her back.

"They learn," Rimmer whispered. "They take what you know and learn."

Something small and pale leapt out of the darkness. She threw herself back only to stop flat against Henry, who pulled her aside with one arm, the other swinging that cricket bat and hitting another ball sac down the length of the hall.

Benti scrambled up, away from the Covenant, with undue haste. He looked at her, lower jaw hinges flexing subtly. You could tell a lot from someone's eyes. Had to remind herself he wasn't a "someone." She could still feel the impression of his hand—not human, not at all human—on her shoulder, knew the hair on the back of her neck was up, and it took all her willpower not to pump his gut full of hot lead.

"Thanks," she managed, as more Flood bugs came bouncing out of the hall.

It was like a fairground game, shooting ducks. Only, not really.

Funny how you adjusted to the situation, no matter how messed up. She felt relief that these weren't the great ravening horrors that had chased them through recycling. They weren't going to slash them open and crush them. They were small, these little infectors. One bullet, one hit, and they would burst.

Just, there were so many of them.

And Rimmer couldn't shoot for shit.

"Stop!" Benti yelled. "You're just wasting ammo! Swap, and reload mine."

Even Clarence switched to his pistol, single shots popping white pods there, there, and there. A good sharpshooter, on top of everything else. Not too many of those in the Marines, not at private level.

"Where are they *coming from*?" It was like a machine full of half-chewed gumballs had broken all over the floor.

One slipped in close, and Henry smashed it flat.

Benti could've sworn the Elite looked a little gleeful.

>Foucault 1559 hours

The video ended, and the loop began again.

Foucault knuckled his eyes, taking the moment to collect his thoughts. After what he had been shown and told, he was inclined to think maybe Rebecca had indeed gone rampant. Found himself hoping that were true, because if forced to choose between the story she had spun and a rampant AI embedded in his ship, the latter seemed the lesser trial.

On the monitor: a wide, high room of unfamiliar architecture, and a ravening horror leapt at the camera, decayed and misshapen and still unfortunately recognizable as a human, UNSC logo just visible on the remains of the uniform. A shotgun blast floored it, but there was another to take its place, and another, and another. In the background, on the floor, a recently killed Marine convulsed, and came back. Footage of what Spartan-117 and the Marines who preceded him had found on Halo.

He picked his words precisely. "We have not been able to defeat the Covenant in nearly three decades, and yet, here we are, returned here for the sole purpose of seeking this out." He felt tired, more than sleep-deprived. "This greater threat."

An infected Marine ignored the bullets striking its torso and leapt at a healthy, live, uninfected Marine. Foucault had turned the volume off, but the screams still sounded in his mind.

"I don't believe it was in the original brief," Rebecca said. "The ONI agent heading the research project aboard the *Mona Lisa* seems to have exceeded his parameters. Significantly. And we still don't know *for sure*."

Foucault shook his head at the insanity of it all. "Is there more?"

"No," she replied. He didn't believe her, and didn't not believe her. Almost didn't care. "But now you understand, we cannot deploy any more Marines, not without explicit confirmation. We cannot risk the *Red Horse*."

He watched a small white pod of a creature latch onto a Marine's chest, watched the life leave those eyes, watched something else take over. A cold worm of dread coiled in his belly.

"We do not willingly abandon our own," he said, to himself, and knew right then and there that statement was close to becoming a lie.

>Lopez 1602 hours

What had once been Rakesh chased them toward the bridge, howling and gibbering and raising a chorus of answering growls. Lopez had caught sight of him stumbling on a derailed security door and bolted. Didn't look back. Hadn't wanted to see what he'd become, and definitely didn't want to see if they were, in fact, being pursued by more than one. Couldn't waste ammo if they could possibly help it, even though they'd taken all Singh and Percy had left.

"Sarge! The door!" MacCraw pointed, looking back at her,

then beyond her. Only to look forward again. Fast. Didn't make her any more curious about what was behind them.

"I see it!" The bridge up ahead, a giant arrow on the wall confirming it, and the door to the bridge sitting back from the wall a hand span, an overturned chair stopping it from sealing. Oh, small mercies. Crashed up against the door, lighting a fire where Smith had shot her, and kicked at the chair. "Get in there!"

MacCraw turned to face Rakesh, backing toward her and fumbling for his weapon. Lopez cursed. Without the obstacle the door began to slide shut. Shoved her shoulder in the gap. "Dammit, MacCraw, I said—"

Caught a glimpse over MacCraw's shoulder. Oh shit.

MacCraw added his own weight to the door. Rakesh was fast, way too fast, oh shit oh shit oh shi—

The door shifted, and they fell through. Scrambled back, MacCraw landing an elbow in Lopez's injury. All the air left her; she couldn't even grunt. The door closed slowly, and Rakesh was so fast, footfalls so heavy, ravening shout loud in her ears. But: cut off cleanly. The door sealed with a sigh, and locked, as it had been trying to do for hours.

MacCraw scrambled to his feet, flashlight on the door, then the room beyond, then back to the door. "He knows we're in here," he said, voice shaking. A muffled but insistent thudding began on the hatch.

"It," Lopez corrected him, clamping down on the pain in her side. "It's an *it*, now."

MacCraw nodded, mouth moving as if trying to convince himself. He flinched at every knock on the door.

Lopez stood. She pursed her lips, stepped past him, making a slow pan of the bridge with her flashlight, her hand steady, that small show of calm enough to reach him.

"Sensing a pattern here," she said, noting the arcs of blood on the walls and floor. The drag marks that almost didn't register with her anymore. Nothing moved except drifts of green dust, growing in little crests here and there. Someone had holed a beastie before going down. Good to see. Most of the displays had been wrenched from their stands and smashed, but some still showed readouts, broken through the cracks. *The bridge must have a separate power source.*

They ran their lights across the ceiling, shone them into every corner and under every station, until Lopez dared to believe they might be safe. Let out a deep breath. They might actually have some time to *think* for a change.

"Don't think anyone is gonna use the nav system." MacCraw stood over the ruined console. "Guess we can go home now?"

"Soon," Lopez promised. "Soon." Smith's voice echoed in her mind. *Retain their knowledge.* Didn't like the implications. Wondered if any of the crew had been infected. Didn't like *that* thought, either.

"We came here for the nav system, didn't we? What else is in here?" MacCraw glanced nervously over his shoulder at the door. The assault showed no signs of waning. The infected Rakesh was going to pummel itself into a pulp trying to get at them.

"We can use the ship's system. Get me radio contact. I don't care how, and I don't care who: Benti, Burgundy, raise the *Red Horse*, hell, raise that damn Covenant ship. Just get me someone to talk to."

MacCraw spun suddenly, taking aim at a corner in the ceiling, jerked to check another corner, looking for giant angry boils, snot-bags, infection forms.

Lopez couldn't blame him, but they didn't have time for it. "Private! Get to it!"

"Yessir." Training overrode his fear. He brushed broken plastic and green dust off the glass atop an undamaged console. "What are you gonna do, Sarge?"

Lopez righted a chair, ignoring the foam bulging from the slashed seat. She'd been counting rosary beads again. So many lost. Thinking about that thing wailing on the door, that had been one of her Marines. Thinking about *why*.

"I ever tell you I can touch-type?" She pulled Smith's security pass from her pocket and waved it at him as she sat. "Old school, I am. Now get cracking."

>Benti 1608 hours

Somehow, against the odds, they'd reached the engine room.

Now what? Benti hadn't a clue.

They were crouched down, peering over dead consoles on the control platform mounted two flights up, and they had a fine view of the main engine deck below.

The space engines dominated, sinking beneath the floor and looming high above them, the shielding around the thrusters looking to Benti like giant centipedes, stretching back through the rear of the ship. Nestled between them, oddly innocuous, the slipspace engine, a standard Shaw-Fujikawa translight, nothing more than a six-pack of boxes propped against each other. A melange of grease and oil and rancid hydraulic fluid mostly snuffed out the pervasive mold smell.

The floor was crowded. It was busy. It was Flood Party Central. No surprise there.

Details began to leap out at her. Covenant strode huge among the turned humans, most of them trailing scraps of prison garb, some in official uniform, and there, in the middle of them, Maller still in Marine armor. He was warped out of shape, limping, dragging an appendage of gristle behind him. Maller crossed paths with a Covenant Elite ruptured like a huge septic bruise, and they almost seemed to nod at each other. All of them, the prisoners and guards, humans and Covenant, united, in total harmony. *Of one mind.*

Better to think of it as a party, and they were the rogue DJs who'd crashed it.

But, no, that didn't really help. She had to look away, up at Henry, who was checking, kept checking, the catwalk behind them. He met her eyes, unhappy but in control, too much the warrior.

Clarence swallowed, his lips parted, gaze fixated on something below, and swallowed again. The muscles in his jaw worked as he clenched his teeth. He looked a question at her. Their orders didn't seem to apply anymore.

Rimmer had been partly right. This wasn't all the ship's dead. On the slipspace engine, the Flood had fixed a giant clot of mucus. Not mucus, Benti corrected herself, some sickly membrane, throbbing and quivering, odd shapes distorting its skin, half caught in it, as if something were moving within, and suddenly the picture resolved itself, and those odd shapes against the membrane became arms and legs dressed in uniform, the crew caught and suspended in the glob. Struggling. *Alive.*

Benti raised a numb hand and covered her mouth, not sure if she was holding in a sob or vomit.

A squeak that might've become something louder and Benti snapped around. Clarence was faster, one arm around Rimmer's head, the other hand clamped firmly over his mouth, expression dour. Rimmer gripped the arm around him, not struggling but holding on like a drowning man to a life preserver. Benti bit her lip and hoped he wouldn't release Rimmer until they were well out of here. There was too much terror in Rimmer's eyes.

A new sound cut above the shuffle and murmur and held the full attention of all the Flood below. As one they turned blindly toward the sound, a horrible synchronicity in the way they raised their heads to sniff, claws and nails flexed, ready to attack. Benti could almost taste the mindless rage that swelled and peaked, and then suddenly dissipated.

An infected person, a human, came into view, carrying a body. No, an infected Marine. Cranker. Carrying someone alive. Someone badly wounded, dripping blood, but alive and struggling, wailing, sobbing, thrashing and kicking as they neared the mucus glob.

"Don't let them take me!"

Benti's heart thumped. She put her other hand over her mouth, recoiled, sagged back against Henry's leg. A sour smell and trickle. Rimmer had pissed himself.

Burgundy.

>Lopez 1613 hours

What are we fighting for? The question rang loud in Lopez's mind. She couldn't think around it. *What are we fighting for?* She took a data crystal from the console, tucking it firmly in her vest pocket. She had only skimmed some of the files Smith's pass had granted her access to, but there would be time to read the rest later. She'd read enough for now. Too much. There was no mystery left in this ship, their mission for even being here. *What are we fighting for?* It took conscious effort to keep everything she'd learned from rasping in her voice.

"I think . . . yeah, I got a signal, Sarge! Booyah!" MacCraw pumped his fists in the air.

"You raised the *Red Horse*?"

Neither of them paid any attention to the dull booming any more. The infected Rakesh was a lot more aggressive and annoying than the real Rakesh.

MacCraw couldn't and didn't try to dampen the goofy grin on his face. "She's talking, oh yeah, she's talking!"

"What about Benti and Burgundy?" she said, crossing over to him.

MacCraw jittered in his seat, too excited by the sound of home. "I couldn't raise either of them, but the intercom is online in most of the ship."

"Patch this through, then." Hooked her chair over, but didn't sit. Couldn't sit. "Maybe someone will hear."

"—is the UNSC *Red Horse* to the *Mona Lisa*, come in *Mona Lisa*. Anyone hear me?"

A deeper echo as every speaker in the ship broadcast Rebecca's hail. Lopez never thought she'd be happy to hear that voice.

"Never a sweeter sound, AI Rebecca. Is the commander there?"

Foucault's voice entered. "I am. The situation here—"

Didn't want to cut him off, but also wanted to deliver her information fast, and in as calm and professional a manner as possible.

"Sir, I got all the recon you'll ever need. This ship is ONI, with a certain Major John Smith most recently in charge. Section 3 sent it here, to experiment with the Flood Spartan-117 encountered on Halo, although ONI might not have known about all of Major Smith's project "enhancements." But at the very least they came to secure a sample, so they could 'study' it, and they brought guinea pigs with them too. Under the orders of Major Smith, they've been deliberately infecting human prisoners and"—she paused for a second, unable to believe she was saying this—"*Covenant* prisoners too. Covies and civilians. Our own. Infecting them and turning them into these damn monsters, these zombies! And no one *told us*!" *You never told us, Commander.* MacCraw was staring at her, his grin gone. "I found a passenger manifest here and some of the people, they were ours, sir, Navy, they were *soldiers* who'd served during the insurrection—"

"I know, Sergeant."

That brought Lopez up short. Something in his tone had turned her stomach to ice. She put a hand on MacCraw's arm, not sure who she was reassuring.

"Sir?"

"The Major Smith you refer to is en route to the *Red Horse*, in your Pelican. He has informed us of the situation."

Damn. Her stomach roiled, and something in her plummeted. How had the evil little spook even made it to the hangar?

"Sir," Lopez said, gritting her teeth. She couldn't think of anything else to say. "Sir."

"Major Smith did fail to mention that any of you had survived."

"Bastard," MacCraw said, but without emotion, gaze uncharacteristically distant.

Lopez swallowed. "He's a liar and a traitor and a *war criminal*." Reduced almost to incoherence. "Everyone who died on this ship, my kids, the crew. If not for him, they might be alive." Couldn't even begin to articulate her rage at Smith. Her disappointment in herself for letting him escape.

"Rebecca has verified his story."

It wasn't a lie. It wasn't the truth, either.

"I'm going to kill him," she whispered. "I'm going to—"

Foucault ignored her. "Having witnessed this 'Flood' firsthand, Sergeant, what is your assessment? If it were to reach one of the outer colonies, for example?"

"I'm not paid to think, sir. Remember?" Bitter. Furious. Knew what Foucault was driving at, knew that the coward wanted her to have to say it. To have to accept it.

The pounding on the door increased. Rakesh wasn't alone anymore. Now he had friends.

"Nevertheless."

Officers. *Officers.* Making decisions from a distance.

"We have no defense against such a foe," Rebecca said, sparing Foucault from uttering the words. "Any planet infected by the Flood would be overrun in a matter of days. More food for the Flood. More knowledge of where to find food. They retain all useful information. Outpost coordinates, more pilots, increased numbers with which to commandeer ships, to reach more colonies. You know this to be true."

Lopez found herself quoting Smith. "'It's a big, bad universe, Commander. Covenant aren't the worst of it.'" Found herself agreeing with him, as he'd wanted her to.

Rebecca again, in a soothing tone that didn't soothe at all: "The Flood represents the greatest threat to humanity since the Covenant. A cure must be sought—"

"A cure?!" Realized she was digging her nails into MacCraw's arm. Couldn't let go. Served him right for elbowing her before. "There is no goddamn cure! According to the files, this was never about a cure, this was about *control*, about creating mindless monster soldiers you could *control*. Who knows what Smith was doing that isn't in the record. But a cure? If you'd seen what we've seen . . ."

"We have, Sergeant," Foucault said. "We have . . ."

Lopez loosened her grip on MacCraw's arm. He put his hand over hers, palm sweaty. "I guess I thought we were better than the Covenant. Not just a little better. Really better."

"Research is always necessary, Sergeant." Rebecca was calm, assured, implacable. But she hadn't had the worst day in the history of worst days.

"The research was useless," Lopez said. "Totally useless. We've known about this thing for weeks and all we've done in that time is expose ourselves to more risk. That gas giant was drawing in the debris, crushing it. It would have vacuumed up everything. And what did we do? We sent a goddamned cab."

MacCraw's silence grew heavier beside her.

A pause, and Foucault again: "Our orders are to destroy the *Mona Lisa*. We cannot allow any of the Flood to survive. Rebecca has informed me that there are two remaining escape pods on the lower deck. The launching mechanisms appear disabled, so they may need manual releasing. Once Major Smith is on board, you will have until we are in position and the Shiva is armed, and then we will open fire. We cannot delay any further. The major has brought the attention of the Covenant capitol ship upon us."

"*You knew.*" Those two words saturated with grief, fury, betrayal. Betrayed twice, three times over. For nothing. Didn't want to come close to acknowledging the hope Foucault had held out in the form of the two pods.

A force rippled through the ship, made the bridge almost flip for a second. Lopez went flying, righted herself before she crashed into the wall. Saw that McCraw tried to hold onto the console before falling. The ship settled, but Lopez could hear tearing sounds in the metal, a booming through the air ducts like a giant smashing something with a huge hammer.

"What was that?" Foucault asked, urgent.

"I don't know. But it's gone and passed," said Lopez. "And we're still here." Making it sound accusatory.

A moment of silence. For all of them. She hoped that was Foucault's conscience knifing him.

"Eight, maybe ten minutes, Sergeant," he said finally, and she could hear the shame in his voice. Hoped even harder it knifed him for the rest of his life.

Lopez pulled MacCraw to his feet.

"Good luck," Foucault said, already becoming distant.

"You know what you can do with your luck," she snarled, and kicked the mic. Turned to MacCraw, who looked close to being sick. "That went out over the ship?"

MacCraw nodded dumbly. "At least, the part the explosion didn't cover up. Do you think that was Benti?"

"Could've been. Could've been something else. We don't have time to worry about it, so long as we're still breathing air."

Nothing on the remaining consoles indicated a drop in air pressure, just a sudden surge of energy near the engines.

Eight to ten minutes. Knew what MacCraw was thinking. They'd survived nightmares only to get shot down by their own commander. He'd already given up, tears glistening in his eyes.

Couldn't have that. She was still his sergeant.

She slapped his chest. "Let's hope someone was alive to hear it. Now hustle! We blow through some space zombies, get cozy in a pod, and we're gonna live, you hear? We're gonna live." She grinned suddenly, fiercely. "And we're gonna get back home to the *Red Horse*, and then we're gonna tear the commander a new a-hole. Two new assholes, one for you and one for me. And then we're gonna find Smith, and we're gonna take our time with him, I think." Couldn't even pick one of the many things she wanted to do to the spook, saw the same violent yearning lift MacCraw's chin. "And then, when we're done with him, then what?"

MacCraw sniffed and blinked his tears away.

"And then there's ice cream, Sarge."

Their grins were hollow. Voices breaking. The Flood still hammering on the door, the door they had to go through.

"Damn straight."

>Benti 1613 hours

Benti raised her rifle, Burgundy in her sights, but both Clarence and Henry reached out, with expressions that said, *No, don't, you'll let them know we're here, and there are too many of them.* Benti bit her lip bloody, couldn't block her ears; Burgundy wouldn't stop screaming; even though her voice was ripped to shreds she shrieked and screeched, begged and pleaded, all her terror and desperation echoing around the cold engine, ringing in Benti's ears as they lifted the pilot and pressed her against the mucus glob with the rest of the *Mona Lisa's* crew.

And then she really started screaming.

Benti couldn't look any more. She screwed her eyes shut, but that wasn't enough. Turned, pressed her forehead against Henry's knee. She had to do something, but didn't know what to do. Henry looked over his shoulder, then dipped his head down to peer at her. His breath reeked. He stank of Covenant, a smell that never failed to get her blood up, and she leaned back. But he had intelligent eyes. Kind eyes. Something like recognition in them. He could hear all she could hear, could understand it all.

She had to do something.

But.

A thunk and crackle tripped their attention, disorientating the Flood on the deck below. The ship's PA was waking up.

"—is the UNSC *Red Horse*—"

Rebecca.

Benti's delight was drowned out by the crashing, raucous cacophony that exploded from the Flood.

"What's going on?" she hissed, leaning close to Rimmer. Clarence lifted his hand from Rimmer's mouth just enough.

"You gotta find some way to turn it off, it'll enrage them, they go crazy when they hear something, might be food, they go crazy, they'll look for where it's coming from—" Clarence clamped his hand over Rimmer's mouth again, the prisoner already too worked up. He shook his head, indicated with his eyes. There was a speaker way too close to them.

Down below, great spasms of rage gripped the Flood. The voices over the PA, Foucault's, Sarge's—*oh, Mama Lopez, what the hell is going on?*—sent them into a mad frenzy, howling and throwing themselves about, pouring in doors, out doors. An infected prisoner smashed a speaker down on the deck with a single blow, denting the wall. Benti saw Cranker turning this way and that like a drunk puppy trying to do a trick for its master.

Just audible over the din, the sarge listing all of ONI's sins. Rebecca spelling out the doom of the human race, should the Flood be allowed to spread.

The more she heard, the more Benti began to think she understood what the Flood might be doing in the engine room. It stank of insanity. It stank of processes and alien know-how that messed with her mind—but what if it was true?

What if they were collecting pilots?

Benti ducked down near Clarence's ear. "We have to destroy it. That thing they just shoved Burgundy into, I think, I dunno,

I think they're trying to somehow hotwire the slipspace engine without bridge control. We have to destroy it."

Clarence looked at her like she was crazy.

"And even if not, that engine is important to them somehow," Benti said. "We have to take care of it."

Clarence looked around, skeptical. Their options were limited, and the smell of Rimmer's piss was getting to Benti. She checked the engines again. Henry put a hand on her shoulder, steady and strong.

If they damaged the slipspace engine, things could go bad. Very bad.

But . . .

"To heck with it." She was in charge.

Benti leapt to her feet, grabbed her remaining grenades, pulled a pin, and hurled it at the mucus glob. Clarence lunged at her. Too late. Pulled another pin and lobbed it. Watched it bounce off the glob as she threw the last. Henry surged up beside her, over her, cricket bat at the ready. He stooped and grabbed a handful of Rimmer's jumpsuit, Clarence's vest, and jerked them upright.

"Let's go, now now now!" Benti didn't wait to see where the final grenade had landed. She grabbed Rimmer's sleeve, dragged him into a run, running from the howling Flood, from the first detonation booming behind them, running for the hatch they'd come through, shoving Rimmer before her, Henry, Clarence, hauling the hatch shut behind them with a solid clang.

Burgundy had stopped screaming, at last.

>Foucault 1616 hours

"Major Smith is secure on board," Rebecca announced to Foucault, and part of him wanted to say, "So what?" The screens showed the Covenant ship readjusting its course to intercept them and the *Mona Lisa* still wallowing there, dead, but with all sorts of life aboard it. About to be extinguished.

Foucault inclined his head slightly, his only acknowledgment of her words. He had no wish to meet Smith at the moment. Or any other moment.

"What should we do with him?"

"Let's keep him in solitary for a while," he said. *A good long while.*

Rebecca seemed as if she might leave it at that, and then ventured, "Doesn't it help to know the major may have acted on his own? ONI isn't responsible for this. This was never meant to happen, and the very fact we're here shows that ONI is acting in good faith. He'll be court-martialed. Maybe even worse."

Foucault wondered if she was right, if he should take some comfort from that fact. Someone would pay. At some point in the future.

Then he thought of the two pods and of all the Marines who might be alive and heading for them, the only chance for survival.

"No. No, it doesn't." A new kind of hell. A fresh bout of nightmares to keep him up. He wondered in a distant kind of way if it'd all fade in time, or if eventually he'd have to give up his command. "Smith may have acted on his own, as you say. Or he may have been following orders, and Section 3 will now use him as a scapegoat and wash their hands of the matter. It doesn't matter. It doesn't change a thing."

A moment, and then Rebecca said, "Telling them about the pods was a pointless gesture. Under the circumstances."

Pointless? Her tone told him she was giving him a warning.

She'd told Foucault about the Section 3 operative she'd sent with Lopez's squad. The one tasked with cleaning up any messes. Perhaps she envisioned the same terrible dilemmas. Or perhaps not. Anyway, she'd sent an operative and he'd fought back by opening a narrow line of retreat for Lopez. Whatever happened, it was beyond their control now.

"Politics. Survival." He said the words like curses.

Rebecca watched him. Who knew what she was thinking, this copy of a person?

"The survival of humanity is paramount, Commander."

Rebecca needed a better speechwriter. Lopez would never forgive him, not for the rest of her life, be it eight minutes or eighty years. Neither would he.

The timer since last contact was now replaced with a status feed on the loading of the Shiva missile. Another monitor tracked the Covenant capitol ship bearing down on them.

A voice from the bridge: "Commander, picking up a detonation within the transport. Slipspace splinters. I think the slipspace engine has been ruptured. We need to withdraw before it goes completely."

When he didn't respond: "Sir, we need to withdraw to a safe distance."

"No. Not yet."

"Sir—"

He felt old. Tired.

But still.

"No. We stay." He was aware of the attention of the bridge crew on him, on the monitors, waiting, their own fate in the balance. "We stay until the last second. We don't abandon our own."

Until we have to.

>Benti 1616 hours

In the aftermath of throwing the grenade, Benti thought she'd heard Foucault on the intercom saying *good luck.* Had he? Really?

Those words echoed in Benti's ears. In her bones. In her feet pounding the corridor floor. She'd always defended the commander when the others were poking fun at him in the mess. All she had to show for it now was "good luck, so long, nice knowing you." She felt sick to her stomach.

"The important thing," she said, panting, the sound of pursuit on their heels, "is the pods. At least we have somewhere to run to." Her legs were tired, were heavy, but she couldn't stop, had to keep going; knowing what was behind them, didn't even want to stop.

Rimmer clung to Henry's arm as he ran, like a child to a parent. The hand on Henry's arm was white-knuckled with strain, fingernails digging. "They did that to us. *To us.* I mean—we were never meant to—how could they—" Even out of breath he didn't stop talking. "I'm not even on death row." Henry growled and shook his arm, but Rimmer didn't let go, didn't shut up. "I only sold stolen goods. That was all. I never—"

Benti tossed a look over her shoulder. Clarence behind her, stone-faced and focused, unflinching at the walls groaning beside him and at the rumble and explosion they left behind.

"What way—?" Intersections and junctions flashing by. She had no map, but now there was no useful map of the ship. *Just keep your head down and cross your fingers.* Lots of graffiti scrawled in blood now. Some of it by prisoners before they'd become part of the Flood, some of it after, all of it unreadable at that pace.

Henry looked at Benti expectantly, loping alongside with ease. He could have left them all behind, but hadn't. She couldn't help thinking of him as a big dog, forgetting the intelligence and awareness in those eyes.

The Elite dipped his head, and said something. A question.

Given the circumstances, there were only a few things he could've been saying.

Benti slowed a moment, took the rifle from Rimmer and put it in Henry's waiting hands.

"Hey, what are you—"

His hands were almost too big. He could barely fit a finger to the trigger. Nodded at her, lower jaws quivering, but kept his cricket bat.

"You're a lousy shot," she answered Rimmer. "Keep moving!"

Clarence drew up beside her as she sped up again, and the look he gave her made her glad, suddenly, that she had Henry at her back.

>Lopez 1620 hours

"Is this a hull?"

"No, sir!"

Lopez pulled her last grenade and tossed it down the hall at a cluster of forms shifting in the darkness. In her mind, the forms were Rebecca and Foucault.

"Place is gonna get trashed anyway—"

The explosion blew out the rest of her words.

>Benti 1620 hours

The unmistakable sound of grenade detonation reverberated through the dying ship, the floor shivering beneath Benti's feet, distinct from the rumbles of the disintegrating engine. The sarge, she thought. Had to be. Remembering the others might be alive added a sudden spring to her step. They weren't the only ones left. If they could just get to Mama Lopez, everything would be okay. She knew it, had to at least make herself believe it.

A figure lumbered out of a room and she ripped a short burst through it, taking out the knees while Clarence, in sync, shot out the chest, and Henry clubbed it with his bat as they fled past. They had no time to be more thorough. They dropped down ladders and slammed hatches shut behind them, seeking only to delay what was following. No time to sneak. All the noise they made, they were getting a lot of attention. A huge following. Benti had never been so popular in her life. *Is it my birthday or something?*

"Reload!"

The voice in her headset made her start. They were in radio range, oh at last!

"MacCraw!"

"Benti!" A pause and gunfire before the sarge spoke again. "Who you got?"

"Clarence." She didn't look at him or Henry. "And a couple of survivors. One deck to go."

"Get your butt into gear; that ice cream isn't gonna wait."

"Yes, sir!" She'd never been so happy to be told to hustle. She turned to grin at Clarence.

It leapt out of the corridor before she could check. Something rabid smashed into her shoulder and threw her against the wall, so fast, all the air knocked out of her, head flung back knocked hard, the shock not enough to crowd out a terrible waft of rank decay and a moan that came from no human throat. Keep your eyes open, always keep your eyes open, her medic training kicking in, and her eyes were open, and she recognized Sydney, what was Sydney, before Clarence stepped between it and her, shot it, kept shooting it, never lifted his finger from the trigger, not even when it stopped moving.

Sydney. How could you do that to me?

She drew a breath in. Let it out. In. Out.

When Clarence looked at her, she knew it was bad. She could see it in his eyes. She couldn't feel her arm; it hung too low on her lap, sleeve already saturated. Her eyes focused on the rifle in his hands. Orlav. Gersten.

You wouldn't, she thought. *You might.*

Henry scooped her up in one arm, tucked her up against his chest, pushed past Clarence, and kept going.

>Lopez 1622 hours

Benti, alive. The voice had conjured up such relief for Lopez, adding a bead or two back onto the rosary. Conjured up images from a world that seemed so distant. The *Red Horse.* On leave, singing in a karaoke bar, getting blind drunk, picking up men, telling her how to smile properly. Did any of that exist anymore? Had it ever existed?

The airlock was miraculously vacant, but it wouldn't be for long. Benti and Clarence were approaching from aft. They'd jammed the forward hatch behind them, using pieces of shelving from a barricade that hadn't held the first time. Only one direction to watch now. Then jiggered the manual controls. Both were ready to go.

"Two pods," MacCraw said, checking the time. "Two of us, some of them. What are we going to do?"

Lopez didn't answer. What could she answer? *Yeah, kid, we've still got some tough decisions.*

Instead she said, "Benti's taking her sweet time."

"It's those short legs." MacCraw checked the time again. "Sarge . . ." The strain in his voice said everything. *Let's get the hell out already.*

"Sarge!" Benti gasped over the radio, the signal good and strong. "Sarge, we're coming, don't shoot, oh please don't—"

A flashlight jagged about, coming down the corridor, the figures behind it resolving.

"Covenant!" MacCraw shouted, down on one knee and finger tightening on the trigger.

"Don't shoot!" Benti's voice.

There, suddenly: a Covenant Elite sprinting down the corridor, assault rifle in one hand, *cricket bat* in the other, and Benti slung over his arm like an errant child.

Not even the craziest thing Lopez had seen all day. Didn't register at first that Benti might be hurt.

"It's okay! Sarge!" The panic in Benti's voice didn't make sense. "Henry's okay! Don't shoot!"

Henry? Lopez didn't lower her weapon. "MacCraw, do *not* take your finger off that trigger!"

The Elite Benti had called Henry slowed, eyeing them warily. Closer now, she could see Benti's shirt and pants soaked red, her arm tucked into her vest, bone jutting from her shoulder. Benti's other hand gripping this Henry's thumb for dear life. Behind the Elite, Clarence and one human survivor in prison clothes.

Somewhere behind them, not yet visible, the deep unnatural choir of the Flood, like a physical presence. Sounded like they'd brought the whole ship in their wake.

"What's this Covie bastard doing here?" Lopez demanded. "You said survivors, Private!"

Benti blinked groggily, a frown of concentration, yet still not fully there.

"She didn't mean it," Clarence said, glancing back at the corridor, mindful of the Flood, and then reached out with his pistol and shot the human prisoner in the head. The man didn't have time to look startled, just dropped, a small and surprisingly neat puncture in his skull.

Lopez had no time to react. Everything happened real fast after that.

Henry spun, Benti crying out with the sudden movement. The Elite saw the dead prisoner, roared in unmistakable grief, and raised its rifle. Clarence jerked his own rifle up, staring down the barrel at the Elite.

Benti slapped its arm, pleading: "Don't shoot! Nobody shoot!" But staring at Clarence. Lopez was staring at Clarence, too, stunned. *A good man. A good shot.* Someone she wasn't sure she knew now.

And the Flood. Louder, closer, relentless, unstoppable.

Lopez's rifle wavering between her Marine and the Covie: "Clarence, what the hell?"

Henry bellowed, a terrible accusation in that alien voice. She couldn't get a clear shot with Benti there, just as Clarence couldn't get off a shot at them without Lopez dropping him. Except she had MacCraw.

"MacCraw, shoot that—MacCraw?"

He wasn't at her side. Behind her, one of the escape pods clicked shut.

"Fuck!"

The pod ejected.

From the bridge of the *Red Horse*: "Three minutes to launch sequence."

>Benti 1623 hours

Benti stared at Clarence, her partner blurring in and out of focus. She really couldn't see much of anything anymore. Knew her pulse was thready, that she'd lost too much blood, medic training both a blessing and a curse. Henry's embrace felt like a warm bed around her body, a bed she was falling into.

"You're ONI," she said at last. "You've got to be." She could see it in his eyes.

From off to their left, the voice of Lopez, coming through gauze: "ONI? I'm not surprised."

Knew the good old sarge still had them in her sights or Clarence would've blown her away. She realized every sympathetic quality she'd found in him had come from her. Just because he never said. Anything that. Would change her opinion. Realized she was floating a bit now.

"It's nothing personal. There were never meant to be any survivors," Clarence said. "Benti, get down. Come on, you can walk." He narrowed his eyes at Henry. "Put her down."

The sounds of the Flood, coming closer. But muffled, like she had headphones on or something.

"You're Section 3," Benti said, quieter. A softness entered Clarence's mouth and eyes. "I'm sorry," he said, but Benti didn't think he was sorry.

"Clarence, drop your rifle," Lopez said fuzzily. Except Benti knew Lopez had said it sharp. The sarge. Always said it sharp. "It's two against one."

Benti squirmed and made Henry set her down. She was almost there. She could almost see the end.

"Henry can have my ice cream," Benti said.

She pushed off Henry and staggered into Clarence, legs so

unsteady, and he was farther away than she thought. But still got too close-in for him to shoot her, inside his guard. She collapsed against him, with her one good arm around his neck in a hug.

As the Flood surged around the last corner and came toward them. A slavering mass of rage and violence and nightmares they never knew they had. Her vision blurred, but she caught glimpses of what once were faces, moving with singularity of mind. They seemed to crawl on disembodied human hands and Covenant hands.

Pushed, then. Used all of her weight to push the two of them back toward the Flood. She had just enough strength to hold him there for the second necessary for Lopez to shoot him in the leg, the shoulder, send his rifle flying. Send him flying back into the corridor. Benti followed, to keep him out there, with *them*. The farther back into the darkness the better. Clarence was too wounded to stop her.

Lopez and Henry were shooting—at them, at the Flood. It didn't make a difference now.

Clarence was shouting something. At her, but it sounded so far away. His eyes were wild and scared, and part of her felt proud to be scary and part of her had never wanted to see Clarence scared.

She was losing her grip on him, and a bullet had found her side, just pumped in there like it belonged, took more energy out of her.

Clarence had just about managed to put his pistol to her head to get her off of him, when she tripped him.

And the Flood washed over him, over her.

Found them.

Suddenly they were pulled back. A sensation of flight, then. A blessed numbness and strange alertness. Looking up for a moment to see that she'd done it—that Henry and Lopez, framed by the doorway, firing away, were far enough away to close the door on both them and the Flood. Yeah, they were shooting her and Clarence, but they didn't mean any harm. They would never mean her any harm.

Clarence writhed in the embrace of what looked like part of Simmons, screaming, "Don't let them take me!" It was too late for that. She wanted to say, "Relax, Clarence. You've got my back," but her mouth didn't work quite right. *Don't want to wake up. Not now. Not for this sad party.*

Last thing she remembered: Lopez's face clenched in concentration, standing in Henry's shadow, as Henry fired point-blank into the Flood and into her. Thought she saw Lopez raising an arm in a gesture of good-bye.

Tried to hold onto that image as the Flood repurposed her.

>Lopez, 1624 hours

Lopez, tired as hell, blinked, and . . .

Henry roared, deep and eternally Covenant, and next to the discord of the Flood, something welcome and familiar to Lopez's ears. He fired into the mob that had taken Benti, ammunition spent in an instant. Hurled the rifle hard enough to knock an infected prisoner off its feet. Raised his cricket bat. Lopez opened fire, taking no specific aim. A glance at her ammo counter.

"Benti!" Brought back only to be taken away.

The ammo counter ran down.

"Clarence!"

All her beads gone. All her kids gone.

She couldn't see them in the throng anymore. Couldn't pick

them out. Couldn't spare . . . anyone. A handful of infection forms scuttled across the ceiling. She lifted her sights. Shot them as they launched at Henry. Small pops. Puffs of green powder.

She dropped and Henry swung his bat, smashing an infection form she hadn't seen away from her. She rolled back into the airlock. Slapped the controls as Henry joined her, beating away at a transformed Elite. Beating it into a green froth before the airlock sealed.

With infection forms on the inside.

She twisted, firing a crazy line around the airlock, chasing the zoomy little maggots. Had no swearwords left to use on them. One popped. Two popped. Henry pushed her aside. Swung his bat. Four popped. Punched the last so hard against the wall the panel dented, green sludge on his fist. He reeled back from the puff of spores, waving them from his face.

Safe.

They looked at each other. The small room thundered with the pounding at the door.

The ship's PA crackled again.

"Shiva armed. Targeting lasers online. Initiating launch sequence in forty-five seconds—"

The airlock door dented inward, and both flinched, taking a step away from it. A step toward the last pod. Henry was big. There was only room for one. This alien, this enemy, had carried Benti to safety. On this ship of messed-up humans.

Finally understood how this was all going to go down. Some little backwater side action, maybe a footnote in some ONI operative's field report.

And beyond the door, something bigger and badder than all of them.

It's a big, bad universe, Sergeant.

Henry's four jaws flexed. Lopez narrowed her eyes. Put her finger on the trigger. Noticed Henry's grip on the cricket bat tighten.

Covenant aren't the worst of it.

No.

But they were pretty damn hideous.

"Sorry, Henry," she said, "but there's only one pod."

She pulled the trigger.

Click.

No ammo.

Lobbed the last curse she had in her, and hefted the rifle like a club.

". . . thirty seconds—"

The Covenant Elite snarled, jaws spread, and raised his bat.

And they went at it.

ICON

Soldiers forged from youth to serve as tools of war—weapons of direct and conclusive destruction—the men and women of the classified military project known as the SPARTAN-II program will live on in legend following their exploits during the Human-Covenant War.

Prepared for the harsh realities of combat against known enemies, but thrust into battle with forces unimaginable—and terrifyingly alien—the Spartan-IIs, and later the Spartan-IIIs, delivered numerous decisive victories against the overwhelming might of the Covenant.

Altered to a level far beyond that of normal human, the warriors of the Spartan-II program were humanity's best, and possibly only, hope when faced with the threat of extinction from an advanced alien collective bent on our eradication in the name of false prophecies and hidden agendas.

Rising through the flames of war, echoing through the silent vacuum of space, word of the Spartans' deeds spread throughout the human colonies—offering salvation, offering a faint glimpse at ultimate victory.

Thus came a "Demon"—a hero, a soldier, a man. One Spartan above all others; equal, but for one defining factor—one immeasurable advantage. Like his brothers and sisters, he was trained to fight, to win, a master of the latest weapons of war. But Spartan-117, the Master Chief, had one intangible asset few others possessed—luck.

Added to an unmatched drive to win—whether it be a simple game, or heated combat— Spartan-117's uncanny combination of finely honed skills and unprecedented good fortune made for the ultimate warrior in a battle against impossible odds.

Never one to give in, never one to relent, the Master Chief, and each of his fellow Spartans, did more than engage the enemy; they delivered hope—with each burst of gunfire, with every battle won.

PALACE HOTEL

ROBT McLEES

The hastily concocted mission to board the Covenant carrier that dominated the sky over New Mombasa ended almost as soon as it had begun. A single Scarab—one of the Covenant's ultra-heavy ground-based weapons platforms—had knocked the entire assault group out of the air, leaving Master Chief Petty Officer "John" Spartan-117 to pull himself out of the burning wreckage.

"Aside from the Covenant discovering the location of Earth and our being on the ground with no viable means of transportation to our objective, I'd say we're in pretty good shape." Cortana's voice seemed to come from just over the Spartan's shoulder. The AI had been put in his care a little over a month ago and he still wasn't used to the intimacy of its communication.

"How's that?" John said, glancing over his left shoulder, half expecting to see her.

"We have one of the top-ranking members of the Covenant leadership within our reach—there's a Prophet Hierarch on that ship. On top of that? We're still alive, Chief. And while there isn't anything I can do about the Covenant being here, I am working diligently to devise a viable solution to our other problem at hand."

John moved between what meager cover the few abandoned vehicles littering the toll plaza afforded him. As he closed in on a row of toll booths, he found his eyes drawn to the mouth of the outbound tunnel of the Mtangwe Underpass. It looked like a kiln—exhaling heat and light. Cutting across the plaza was a smear of molten glassiness three feet wide leading to the tunnel mouth and then up away from it along the face of the city's famous sea wall. Curiously, the inbound tunnel was undamaged. A dull smile crossed his lips behind his visor as he considered his options. He thought back. The correct choices have always been this obvious. He had always been able to see the tiger and the lady—doors had never factored into the equation.

A thin whine from above signaled the arrival of Banshees. John dashed beneath the canopy of concrete that sheltered the island of toll booths—he was less concerned about the Banshees' effectiveness as attack aircraft and more about remaining out of sight. He flattened himself out against one of the booths momentarily and looked through its clouded and sagging polycarbonate window. The attendant, still seated within, wasn't much more than a partially articulated skeleton hung with the charred remains of a uniform and fused to an ergonomic seat bolted to the floor.

"His name was Carlos Wambua, age fifty-two, widower, three adult children. The oldest still—" Cortana rattled off before John cut in.

"He just sat there—the position of his feet," John pointed at the man's smoldering shoes with his chin for emphasis. "He didn't even try to get away. From his position he would've been able to see the *tee forty-seven* even before it crested the bridge—that's a little over eight hundred meters out." He gave his gear a shake test then moved to the corner of the structure.

"Your point being?" Cortana challenged. "Do the words 'transfixed with terror' mean anything to you? You may find this hard to believe, but most people find Scarabs to be rather unsettling."

With a barely noticeable shrug he began looking for a path to the mouth of the inbound tunnel—moving along the line of booths until he found a straight shot with no obstructions. It was seventy-three meters to the entrance. That meant he would be out in the open for about four and a half seconds—enough time for one of the Banshees in the air overhead to make a positive ID. He slung his rifle and hunkered down.

Kelly had always been the fastest in their class—easily making her the fastest human being who had ever lived—but as he tore across the plaza, he was certain that his performance would have made even her take notice.

Once he was within the tunnel, John slid to a stop against a burnt-out sedan. He unlimbered his rifle and considered the path ahead. This section of the tunnel was littered with vehicles; some gutted or otherwise destroyed, others merely abandoned. The area would have been perfect for an ambush. Unfortunately he was the one who had to move through it. The vehicles appeared to thin out some eighty meters farther in, but to get there would require patience. And so he began snaking his way through the environment—moving quickly but cautiously between cover. He checked the most likely hiding spots and the least, keeping his eye on his armor's motion sensor and listening intently for any sound that seemed out of place. Working his way deeper into the underpass, he heard muffled curses and other sounds of agitated goings-on from about 150 meters ahead. He came to a stop alongside a lorry in pale green *Technique* Electronics livery and looked off to his right. The Moi Avenue junction was sealed off by heavy blast doors.

"The main route is locked down as well," Cortana huffed; the frustration in her voice was unmistakable.

John hesitated a moment, waiting for Cortana to continue. The main Mtangwe route, a 390-meter tunnel that resurfaced in the center of New Mombasa's industrial zone, had been his best bet to gain entrance into the city without being spotted by the enemy. The activity up ahead was promising, and he hoped it was from a maintenance crew who could release either set of blast doors; if not, his only choice was to head back to the surface.

"That's it?" John asked, finally. "It's locked down and nothing else?"

"I'm having a little trouble accessing the local net," Cortana replied. "I'll have it in a moment."

The Spartan edged around the cab of one of the omnipresent SinoViet lorries. About thirty meters away, near the blast door, were two M831s—the primary UNSC wheeled troop carriers that had become nearly as common in New Mombasa as the freight lorries over the past few weeks—and a squad of Marines who were busily pulling any useful bits of equipment out of them.

"They're from one of the ghost battalions out of Eridanus Two," Cortana said with a near-audible sigh of relief. "First Battalion, Seventh Regiment; more specifically, this is Third Squad, First Platoon, Kilo Company."

ONE OF the Marines signaled the Spartan's arrival to the rest of the squad and moved forward cautiously to greet him.

"Holy crap," Private Jemison blurted. "Sorry, sir, but holy crap, you're a Spartan!"

"Yes," John said dryly as he jogged toward the Marine, but before he had the chance to utter another syllable, the distinctive report of a fuel rod gun rang out from behind him.

"Get to cover," John yelled as he brought his BR55 to bear, spun on his heel, acquired a sight picture of his target, and put a single bullet through the neck of the green-clad Grunt. Private Jemison's MA5B flashed to his shoulder and fired off a long burst as the first shot from the fuel rod gun sailed past the Spartan and the Marines and slammed into the tunnel wall a little more than twelve meters away. The nearly decapitated Grunt reflexively fired a second shot, which impacted the roadway less than a meter away from where it was standing. The resulting explosion killed half of the aliens that were visible in the tunnel, including their commander—an Elite in red armor.

The stray first shot had dug a four-meter-wide hole in the wall and dumped a literal ton of smoking, shattered concrete out onto the tunnel floor. Dark, brackish slop lazily spilled out, accompanied with a stomach-curdling stench—making it very clear that an opening had been punched into an adjoining sewer line. As if on cue, brilliant purple light washed along the walls as the massive, bulbous form of a Wraith slid into view from behind an abandoned commuter bus. Its carapace seemed to crack open—broad curving plates folded out of the way of its deadly plasma mortar.

"Crap," Jemison howled as he backpedaled. "Corporal, what do we do?"

A tall, broad-shouldered redhead hopped down out of the back of the lead troop carrier and motioned with her left hand toward the opening in the wall. "Jump in that hole—it ain't no worse than it is out here! Move it!"

Jemison continued to back up until he reached the edge of the rubble, all the while firing burst after burst from his assault rifle into the advancing enemies. Corporal Palmer approached the Spartan, tapped his shoulder, and shouted, "You wanna come, big guy?" She moved through the rubble to the breach, motioning for the rest of the squad to follow. And in they went, one by one.

John shouldered his rifle, took one step back toward the way he had come, and fired a burst into a mob of Grunts that had swarmed in past the Wraith, killing two and forcing the rest to scatter and dive for cover.

"Chief, you should probably follow those Marines—they look like they need the help—and there are three more Wraiths on the way," Cortana said thoughtfully.

As the walls of the tunnel reverberated with the sounds of the charging plasma mortar, John dashed over to the rent in the tunnel wall—firing three more bursts from his battle rifle back at the advancing enemies as he went—then turned and disappeared into the breach. He had made it no more than thirteen meters when the mortar round slammed into the opening, sending a wall of concussion and heat that drove him to his knees and caused his shields to overload and drop. John got back to his feet, but Private Jemison, the second-to-last man to make it into the breach, was lying facedown in the now boiling muck—his organs ruptured and bones splintered from that same blast. Howls from the darkness told him that Jemison wasn't the only casualty. He ran past Private First-Class Locke, whose split and blistered flesh and raw bone were visible through smoldering holes in his BDUs. He stepped over Private First-Class Galliard, who had been felled by a piece of rebar that entered just below the nape of his neck and exited through the bridge of his nose—the still-glowing chunk of steel protruded from the sewer wall ten yards farther ahead.

When John reached the flow-through tunnel below the spillway, the remaining Marines skipped their eyes past him and looked back down the tunnel.

"Where the hell's the rest of my squad?" demanded Corporal Palmer as she stepped forward. "The Wraith?"

"Affirmative," John replied flatly. "They were killed in action."

"Then we've gotta go back."

"We're going forward."

"No we're not." Palmer's brow furrowed. "We are not just gonna leave them lying back there in this goddamn sewer!"

Cortana spoke to the entire group over their helmet-integrated comm units. "They will be left behind just as the other twenty-three billion that preceded them were left behind. Because they could not be saved, and carrying them with us will only make us vulnerable."

They looked at John like he was a monster; like an alien. In some of their eyes he could detect something deeper. Not horror; astonishment? Betrayal? Of course, it may have just been hearing Cortana speaking through his comms.

"Who was that?" Palmer spat.

"That was Cortana. She's . . ."

"She's a real fucking bitch."

The Spartan stood in silence, head cocked slightly to the right. "Corporal, give me your TACPAD."

Corporal Palmer produced a notebook-sized device from her pack and passed it to the Spartan, and he flipped it open and showed them a traffic video with a time stamp from twenty-two minutes earlier—four Wraiths and fifty light infantry entering the Mtangwe Underpass.

"It's amazing how persuasive an argument overwhelming force

can be," Cortana whispered to the Spartan. John shrugged and moved toward what appeared to be a series of rungs imbedded in a flat section of the sewer wall.

Cortana was the first *smart* AI he had ever worked with directly. Sadly, whoever died to make this AI possible had to have been a genius among geniuses. For example: The section they were in wasn't on the grid; it dated from before construction had even started on the Mombasa Tether—itself more than two hundred years old. Cortana had plucked the plans for them out of the ether before he could finish his request. As far as equipment went, the AI was cutting edge. The only thing that bothered him about Cortana was her excessive familiarity; she was more like a pushy civilian that just happened to fit on a data crystal than a true military AI.

"You can tell her that the rest of their unit has begun to dig in at Beria Plaza," Cortana's voice buzzed in his ear. "That's a little under two kilometers away."

"Corporal Palmer, does Beria Plaza mean anything to you?"

"It was between where that door came slamming down in front of us and where we were going."

"That's where the rest of your unit is. It's about two clicks due east of our current position. You'll go up here," John said, indicating the ladder. "It'll take you up to the surface." Cortana may have been busy looking for some way to get him onto the Covenant assault carrier, but not so busy that she couldn't provide him the occasional blueprint, video feed, or other intel—whether it was helpful to his situation or not.

"Okay." Palmer nodded. "So you gonna follow this pipe all the way out to the Mombasa Quays?"

"No. I'm going to make sure the rest of you make it out of here alive."

"Gosh! That's awfully nice of you," Palmer mugged—then the smile faded. "Look, you may be a Spartan, but . . ."

"Exactly, Corporal. And if *we* had all been Spartans back there, *none* of us would have died. Now let me do my job."

Palmer's jaw dropped. After about a second and a half she closed her mouth, snapped off a smug salute, pivoted on her heel, and then jogged over to the rest of the Marines.

As the Marines stacked up at the base of the ladder, John readied his service rifle, swapped in a full magazine, and took station on the other side of the tunnel so he could keep an eye on them as well as keep an eye out for pursuers. He glanced over at the Marines as they moved into position to climb to the upper part of the spillway—and out of the sewer they had been slogging through for the past twenty minutes. While it may have only been a storm sewer, it hardly mattered this close to the Kilindini Harbor. He wondered if the oppressive stench was the reason for the soldiers' sour expressions.

"Chief," Cortana whispered, "there was no way for you to save those three."

"Even so," he muttered, "I could've wiped out that entire unit."

"Four Wraiths," Cortana broke in. "Four. You rely too much on your luck."

"The limited space and the abandoned vehicles in the tunnel would have restricted their mobility as well as their ability to use their main weapons, especially if they brought all four down—which they did. I've been doing this for twenty-seven years, Cortana. And I know the exact limits of my luck."

"Then what? The rest of them die trying to support you?"

"They started running as soon as the shooting started."

"Yes, Chief, but Corporal Palmer's reasoning was sound—even without knowing about the other three Wraiths, she had more sense than to go up against armor without any antiarmor weaponry."

John watched as the last Marine started up the ladder and fired a burst from his BR55 back down the way they had come. He heard the heavy rounds gouge the ancient concrete, followed by the panicked cries of Grunts in the distance as they dove for cover—and into the semigelatinous, ankle-deep liquid. Hopefully that would keep them from coming any closer, at least until the Marines were all safely up on the spillway. There was precious little cover within the confines of the sewer, certainly not enough to avoid any incoming fire. The spillway would allow them to break contact with their pursuers—then he could get back to his mission.

"Chief, I was serious about their being useful for getting us to our objective," Cortana whispered in the Spartan's ear.

"Thanks. So you *strongly* suggest following them?"

"I merely suggest we take them back to their unit," Cortana whispered very sweetly. "They could be useful too."

Palmer called down from the top of the spillway, "Your girlfriend say to wait there—you coming or what?"

"It's an AI."

"Nice," Cortana huffed.

John turned his attention to the ladder. He looped his arm behind the rungs and popped them out, three at a time, until he had pulled out all of them he could reach; it wouldn't stop their pursuers for good, but it didn't have to. All it needed to do was slow them down. He sent four more rounds ripping into the darkness before jumping three meters up to the top of the spillway and following the sounds of the boots retreating up one of the drainage tunnels. He could hear the sound of wind in the trees and the pounding of the surf somewhere up ahead, and beyond that the staccato chatter of gunfire and dull thudding of explosions in the distance.

The tunnel opened into a wide culvert that seemed to emerge from beneath the inner part of the island's western sea wall—and directly behind the parking area for the Kilindini Park Cultural Center. The Marines had flattened out against the walls, stopping just short of the tunnel mouth. A Covenant beam rifle leaned unattended against the end of the culvert twelve meters away. Straddling a deep rut a half meter beyond the end of the culvert was one of the large, vaguely birdlike aliens that most UNSC personnel called Jackals. Its back was to them—a thin stream of fluid fell into the rut between the alien's feet.

The Spartan inched forward in uncanny silence, carefully gauging the distance between himself and the Jackal. He positioned his feet on the tunnel floor, assessing his footing and evaluating the strength of the concrete beneath him. He was less than seven meters from the alien when its head snapped to the side with a start, inhaling sharply. John sailed forward—covering the distance in two strides, his left arm a blur shooting forward, index and middle fingers outstretched together to form a spike. The Spartan's gauntleted hand passed effortlessly through the Jackal's skull just behind its left eye. John backpedaled, retreating into the darkness of the drainage tunnel—the grisly remains of his quarry dangling limply from his forearm, leaving a streak of brilliant purple blood in their wake.

Corporal Palmer quailed momentarily and then glanced back at the group and motioned for everyone to stay low and quiet. She scooted up to the edge of the culvert in a low crouch. When she reached the end she popped the covers on her scope and slowly swung her BR55 over the low concrete wall. She could see the smoking remains of several variants of the UNSC's ubiquitous

Warthogs—M831 troop transports, M12 reconnaissance vehicles, even a couple of M12G light antiarmor rigs, all of which were arranged in a line partially shielding the main entrance of a squat concrete structure—a makeshift defensive wall. She could also see the Jackals overlooking the parking area from the roof and the bodies of men scattered about below them.

"It looks like a goddamn massacre out there," Corporal Palmer stage-whispered. "There're bodies all over the place—there's a Grunt bleeding out and a Jackal standing not ten feet away from him poking at one of our boys. What the hell, man?"

Private First-Class Sullivan scooted up next to her and stole a quick peek over the wall. "This shit happened ages ago—we woulda heard those sixty-eights goin' off even down the pipes," he muttered.

Private Emerson tossed John a spare canteen and he rinsed the blood from his arm. Behind him, half a dozen meters deeper into the tunnel, one of the Marines was busily constructing what looked to be a miniature barricade. "Don't hold onto anything you can't fight with," John said before stepping out into the culvert. He glanced over at the line of Warthogs and opened a private channel with Corporal Palmer. "Sitrep, over."

Palmer looked over her shoulder at the Spartan—a mere seven meters away, "Huh? I'm right over here."

John tapped his throat and pointed past her at the enemy. "A Jackal's ears may not be very big, but they are very sensitive."

"Oh all right," she grumbled, put her eye back to the scope, and continued, "Looks like a detachment of Army mech-inf got sent in to evac some civies or whatever out of this gift shop or whatever the hell *that* is—that being the structure that looks sorta like a giant concrete intake manifold. There's a fountain about twenty meters northeast of the structure in the middle of what looks to be the parking area. But the fountain is busted all to hell and the entire parking area is under about four inches of water. I count about . . . eighteen civilians and . . . twenty *ewe en es sea* personnel—all dead—and half a dozen 'hogs. The 'hogs are strung out in a line from the center of the northeast wall of the structure to just past what's left of that busted fountain. All but two of the 'hogs are out of commission. We might be able to use one of the other *em twelve gees* but its generator is holed—I wouldn't trust it. Looks like the Covies've got a *tee forty two* set up on the roof at the eastern corner of the structure—the Grunt on it looks like it's snoozing, though. So, along with the gunner, I'm counting twelve bad guys—eight Jackals; four Grunts. That ain't counting the one Grunt bleeding out. They've got elevation on us so don't take that number as a guarantee; it'd take a lot more than this handful of assholes to grease twenty-odd shooters—even if they were only Army. Over."

"So, only two serviceable 'hogs." John looked at the eight Marines squatting in the culvert and sighed. "Proximity to each other? Over."

Palmer let her rifle drift slowly, covering a wide arc. "The one *em eight three won* that isn't burning or otherwise busted all to hell is right near the main entrance of the structure, and the *el ay ay vee* is a good fifteen meters east-northeast of that, over by the fountain. Chief, if you're planning on going for that *em twelve gee*, you won't just be running *into* their field of fire—you'll be running *across it* like a duck in a shooting gallery. Over."

The Spartan looked over the low wall at the M12G; it *was* a mess. What was left of the windshield was lying across the hood in tiny cubes, the seats were burnt down to their frames, the winch was a fused wad of metal, and most of the bodywork was distorted, pitted, and scorched. But it wasn't burning, smoking, or leaking fluid, and it had all four wheels. "You, Sullivan, and I will secure the *em twelve gee*; once we get it moving we'll suppress what's left of the local Covenant group until the *em eight three won* is secured. Over."

Palmer's heart seemed to skip a beat, and she reflexively licked her lips. "Chief, I believe I can honestly say that even though you are an honest-to-Buddha one-man death squad, and that if you were to ask nicely I'd give up my lucrative career in the Corps and start pumping out your babies as fast as you could put them in me, there is no way that I am gonna run across fifty goddamn meters of open terrain covered by three Jackal snipers *that I can see* just to jump into an open vehicle. Throwing myself on a goddamn grenade makes more sense than that. Out."

The Spartan was at Corporal Palmer's elbow so quickly and so quietly that only those Marines who had been looking directly at him noticed that he had even moved. He closed the private channel and addressed the group as a whole. "Palmer, Sullivan; you're on me. Concentrate on running until we get to the *el ay ay vee*—then mount up as fast as you can. Corporal, I want you on that sixty-eight. The rest of you will cover us until the *el ay ay vee* starts moving—we will then lay down suppression fire until you secure the *em eight three won* by that structure's main entrance—I'm setting a waypoint now. This is sure to get more complicated once we are under way, so stay on your toes."

The assembled Marines looked at one another nervously and then out at the open field that lay between themselves and the Warthogs—numbers above the tiny blue deltas indicating the objectives in their HUDs reinforced their remoteness. The Marines began systematically checking their gear in grim silence. The furtive glances that passed between them, however, spoke volumes. To wit, they were about to pit themselves against a group whose exact composition they were unsure of, that was established in a defensive position with superior elevation, and that was clearly capable of annihilating a unit more than twice their number even if it had been equipped with vehicles and support weapons. They did have one advantage, though: they had a Spartan with them. But how much could one more man, no matter how well trained or equipped, possibly affect the outcome of the coming battle?

John placed fresh magazines into both of his weapons, replaced the missing rounds in his spare magazines, and then nodded toward their destination. Without looking back he motioned for the group to move up.

"Pine Tar," Palmer whispered sharply through the comm, "get your narrow ass up here—we're leaving. Over."

"Wilco, out." Lance Corporal Pineada called from deep within the drainage tunnel. He gave a quick glance at the group in the culvert before putting the final touches on the lethal contraption he had been hiding beneath a sodden shipping pallet. He circled his handiwork gingerly, then nodded to himself, satisfied that the two scavenged jerry cans, fragmentation grenade, and mess kit that he had fashioned into a deterrent for their pursuers was nearly impossible to detect. He leaned the last jerry can against the tunnel wall by his improvised trap and joined the rest of the group.

"Couldn't we just try sneaking around them?" Private Emerson asked feebly.

John ignored Emerson and continued. "Forget the Grunts—concentrate on the rooftops and any Jackals you see—the DESW at the eastern corner is a priority-one target." He slung his battle rifle across his back.

Corporal Palmer had not moved from her position observing the parking area. "Chief, that Jackal isn't just poking at our boy—it looks like it's biting him."

The Spartan held up a gauntleted hand. "We go in five, four . . ." He tucked his fingers in as he counted.

"I think it's eating him, man," Palmer choked.

"One—then it dies first—now stow your weapon and move out." John pointed at their intended destination and then he was gone.

The concrete beneath the Spartan had turned to dust and gravel as he launched forward. Barely half a second had passed and he was already ten meters away. Palmer slung her weapon and tore off after him; Sullivan fell in directly behind her, running for all he was worth.

Palmer was pumping her arms and trying to control her breath as she trailed behind the Spartan. She looked up from her boots and saw that his hands were no longer empty—his right hand now held a massive hard-chromed M6D, and a spare magazine was in his left. Eight thunderclaps rang out so fast that they bled together into a single long roar. At that same moment a terrible cacophony erupted behind them as her squadmates opened fire on the building—its facade disappearing behind a cloud of pulverized concrete and shattered glass. Two of the Jackals that had been covering their approach had already fallen—bright purple blood fountaining out of huge ragged holes that she could pick out even at this distance.

With one hand at thirty meters and a dead run, two shots apiece, each a hit to the head or neck, what the holy hell are my guys even aiming at back there—shit. The Corporal's mind raced, but her legs had begun to slack off. She saw another Jackal appear at the roof's edge and there was a flash of purple light.

And then her view was blocked by a wall of green armor; there was a loud crack and a flash of golden light. The Spartan had spun to face her; she saw her own reflection in his visor for a fraction of a second, then he dipped slightly before popping into the air, sailing backward three and a half meters above the ground—smoke trailing from the inside of his right arm. Four more rapid-fire thunderclaps roared in her ears; the magazine dropped out of the Spartan's M6D, his left hand slamming the fresh magazine up into the well and flicking to catch the empty one as it fell, the huge pistol now latched onto his right thigh, the empty magazine stowed, and his knees tucked up to his chest as he continued through the air over the Warthog. Three fingers hooked the crossbar and the vehicle rocked as the Spartan swung down into the charred remains of the driver's seat; the M12G roared to life as Palmer scrambled up into the rear of the vehicle and behind the controls of the gauss cannon in a near daze; Sullivan practically leapt into the sooty pan of the passenger seat and disengaged the safety on his MA5, bellowing, "C'mon! Floor it!"

All four wheels spun, abrading the surface of the parking area and throwing up four giant rooster tails of water and grit. Palmer keyed in the startup sequence on the M68 ALIM—your basic mini MAC. She started scanning for targets—and did a double take when prioritized targeting tabs began appearing on the monitor.

"If anything else shows up, I'll add it to the list, Corporal," the Spartan spoke over a private channel. "No vehicles yet—just infantry. Don't take any shots you don't have to—just concentrate on staying alive for the moment."

"What the hell's that supposed to mean?" Palmer growled through her headset. Just then the Spartan threw the 'hog into a four-wheel drift, creating a momentary wall of spray and mist that screened the rest of the squad, who were now dashing across the open ground between the culvert and the vehicles. Sullivan was hooting and hollering above the sound of the engine as he fired his assault rifle at anything that poked its head out.

John gave Sullivan a sideways glance and said, "Remember to save some ammo for when you're actually trying to hit something—and forget the Grunts!"

Corporal Palmer glimpsed just a hint of movement behind the T-42 DESW—the closest thing to a heavy machine gun in the Covenant arsenal. It could have just been the corpse of the weapon's operator shifting, but she wasn't taking any chances. There was a flash of light, a teeth-rattling snap, and then the heavy plasma weapon on the roof exploded—transformed into a rapidly expanding cloud of whirling ceramic razorblades and plasma-temperature flames. If anything had been crawling up to the weapon, it was now either part of that cloud or had been consumed by it.

"'Hog secured—we're in, Chief," Private Emerson howled over the Warthog's radio. "Let's boogie!"

"Follow me." The Spartan swung the M12G around the eastern corner of the Cultural Center, just barely dodging the bulbous purple cowling of a Covenant Ghost half-hidden in a stand of elephant grass. One of the Ghost's stabilizing wings and a fair amount of its carapace were missing—obvious signs it had been raked with heavy machine-gun fire. The 'hogs roared past it, and the park's enormous outdoor amphitheater loomed ahead.

The park's main entrance was at the southern end of the amphitheater, right where Cortana indicated it would be. But as the gate came into view so did a group of Elites, two in blue armor that were sitting astride a pair of Ghosts, and a third in red armor. The one in red looked up at the approaching Warthogs and raised its weapon. The 'hogs bore right down on the trio.

Sullivan fired several bursts across the hood at the Elites until he noticed the barrel of the ALIM swivel into place directly above his head, then he quickly dropped down into the scorched seat and braced himself. Palmer lined up the lead Ghost and fired. The slug from the M68 left the muzzle at just under mach forty and penetrated the lead Ghost's plasma containment vessel—after it had passed through the red Elite's lower abdomen. The vehicle detonated and spiraled into the air, five-thousand-degree plasma erupting through its shattered armor. The Elite rider was almost entirely incinerated; what remained of its right arm, however, spiraled through the air alongside the wreckage of the vehicle. The other rider boosted out through the bluish flames and roared in pain as the flexible material of its armored suit bubbled and cracked. A second shot from the M68 was high and late, punching a basketball-sized hole through the park's entrance archway. Palmer swung the turret farther to take a third shot.

"It's B Team's problem now," John said to her over the private channel. "We need *your* eyes forward to keep the path clear."

"But I can—" Palmer spat.

"Now, Corporal," the Spartan admonished. "At least trust your squadmates enough to handle one Ghost with a wounded rider."

As the turret swung back around John heard Corporal Palmer grunt. He could picture the look on her face. It would be the same look of anger and frustration he had seen on innumerable humans when they were reminded of what they were and weren't capable of—or where their real responsibilities lay.

Humans—what had prompted that? He never thought of himself as anything other than human. But that wasn't exactly true. He may have thought of himself as having been human, perhaps even that he was *still human*, but no one ever let him forget that he was a Spartan. That was definitely true.

"Chief, I believe that I've located our errant Scarab—there are two of them in the city proper, another three in Old Mombasa across Kilindini Harbor to the south—but only one of them is in the immediate vicinity. That one has to be *ours*. My best guess is that it's looking for a clear shot at the tether," Cortana rattled off into John's ear.

"When you say *ours*," John whispered, "am I to understand that you want me to capture it?"

"Don't be silly, Chief. I said *ours* because it figures into *our* plan to get *us* onto that ship—so *we* can get *our* hands onto the Hierarch. And before you ask any other silly questions—*our* plans are more complicated than *that*."

The Warthog slid sideways through the smoking remains of the Kilindini Park gate and into the Mwatate Street Transit Center. It was abandoned: no taxis or buses and no private vehicles of any kind. They had all fled or were pressed into service to aid the evacuation efforts hours ago, but they had not escaped. The bridge connecting the island to the mainland had been littered with the burning, gutted carcasses of all those vehicles.

Chunks of concrete and sputtering blobs of aluminum came raining down from above as two Ghosts sailed off of the elevated roadway above the transit center—their riders bracing in anticipation of the impact on the ground far below. Palmer fired up at the nearer of the two rapidly descending craft and its starboard wing tore away in a shower of sparks. The Ghost tumbled violently and the rider was thrown as the two vehicles collided in the air. The Spartan spun the steering wheel all the way to lock, attempting to keep clear of the Ghosts' most likely point of impact. The intact Ghost landed upside down, its carapace splintering on contact—the Elite rider still astride the vehicle. The Ghost that Palmer had hit came right down on top of the wreckage of the other Ghost and its rider—both vehicles erupting into a whirlwind of bluish flames.

"For the love o' Mike," wailed Sullivan as the Elite from the second Ghost slammed down onto the hood of the Warthog. Just as it began to slide off, it managed to catch hold of a pillar and swing itself in a tight arc, smashing into the side of the vehicle.

"Shit shit shit," Sullivan began screaming, firing his MA5 even before it was pointed at the huge alien, which was scrambling to get its feet inside the door frame. Charred plastic and splinters of sheet metal exploded from the dashboard as Sullivan desperately tried to maneuver his weapon within the cabin of the vehicle.

"Duck," Palmer shouted, followed by a quick, "Sorry," as she swung the M68 directly over Sullivan's head.

The Elite stripped the rifle from Sullivan's hands and sent it flying just as the muzzle of the gauss cannon came in line with the top of its helmet. Sullivan glanced up and cried out, "Ah no!"

With a flash and a bone-jarring snap, the Elite's head, neck, and shoulder area transformed into a broken, spinning torus of meat, bone, and metal raised to near incandescence by terrific acceleration. The remainder of the corpse fell to the roadway below with a scraping clatter, a ruined eight-foot-tall tumbling rag doll.

John modulated the gas pedal and administered microadjustments to the steering wheel before accelerating straight toward Shimanzi Road—the broad divided highway that split the industrial district in two.

"We're less than a click from your unit now," the Chief stated. "Barring catastrophe I'll have you back with them in under five minutes."

"And then what?" Palmer asked.

He indicated the massive ship still dominating the sky with a flick of his head. "I'm going to board that ship and kill every living thing on it, minus one. As for what you'll be doing, that's up to your *sea oh*."

"Sure; so who's the lucky *es oh bee*?" she chuckled.

"You wouldn't know him," John said with an air of finality.

"Hey, Palmer," Sullivan shouted as he shifted uncomfortably in his seat, "I think that last shot popped my eardrums." The rest of the drive was completed in silence.

Even though the architects and city planners had tried their best to hide it, most people could tell at a glance that New Mombasa was a gigantic jigsaw puzzle of a city—rigorously sectioned off into recognizable, repeating parcels. It was a grim necessity for every tether city. If the unthinkable were to happen—well, *another* unthinkable, as at least one unthinkable thing was already happening—and catastrophe were to befall the Mombasa Tether, the expectation was that this compartmentalization of the city would keep the death toll and property damage to a minimum. It also made Beria Plaza a natural funnel. A trap. And it seemed that the CO of First Platoon, Kilo Company 1/7/E2-BAG thought so too.

"Chief, I've allocated military assets in order to harass *our* Scarab—maneuvering it to a location more convenient for our purposes—closer to our *current* destination." Cortana's words rang out in the staccato rhythm of someone juggling one too many tasks. "I hope the five air assets I have en route will be enough—I've got two orbital assets on standby, but I would rather not use them unless absolutely necessary—and don't worry, I'll give you plenty of warning if I do."

"Any more good news?"

"Well, if my calculations are right, and they always are, *our* Scarab will arrive eight minutes after the Wraiths from the underpass—that should be plenty of time for you to deal with them, shouldn't it?"

John maneuvered the 'hog into the cabstand of what less than three hours ago had been the rather elegant Palace Hotel, although now it looked a bit like a gigantic curio cabinet with its doors kicked off. Palmer keyed off the M68 and turned around, taking in the view from the bed of the LAAV.

When the second vehicle from their party arrived, seconds later, Palmer opened a private channel. "Emerson, get that truck out of sight around the back of the hotel."

Sullivan hopped down onto the sidewalk and shouted over his shoulder, "It's been a real slice fightin' with you, Spartan, but I swear my ear's gone bust—I can't hear shit. Gonna find a medic!"

John swung out of his seat and onto the pavement, nodded to the Marine, and turned to face the hotel.

"See ya 'round, big guy," Palmer blurted before biting her lip.

The Spartan nodded once more and continued toward the hotel's main entrance—reflexively brushing at the side of his helmet as if some invisible insect was buzzing near his ear.

As he made his way through the rubble-strewn lobby of the Palace Hotel, soldiers busied themselves turning furniture into cover and clearing lines of access between firing positions. The Marines John had arrived with spread out to help reinforce and camouflage the fighting positions. A lance corporal jogged up to the Spartan, tapping his throat mic—John locked on to the frequency and gave the Marine a thumbs-up.

"I'm Morton," the soldier said—signaling to one of his comrades that he was escorting the Spartan upstairs. "Our *ell tee*'s up on the mezz—I'll take you to her."

"That's not a local accent, Morton—this your first time on Earth?"

"Nah," Morton said. "I was born here, sir—my Dad moved us to Eridanus Two when I was a year and a half—and then to Miridem. Shit. And then to Minister, like everyone else, right? But this is the first time I've been back." They ascended the wide, curving staircase that led to the mezzanine, and Lance Corporal Morton signaled security that they were coming up.

"Seems like a lot of us ground units got redeployed to Earth after Reach, sir," Morton nodded toward a set of double doors that led out to a huge open-air dining area, "to beef up defense in the tether cities—I guess. She's right in there, sir." Morton spun around and headed back toward the stairs. "I hope nobody called dibs on that gauss—I'm a certified expert on that damn thing."

As John passed through the double doors, he could see the lieutenant making some gestures over her TACPAD. Seemingly satisfied with the results, she crouched down and withdrew something from her combat vest.

"There are four Wraiths supported by fifty light infantry traveling southeast through the Kilindini Underpass. The outer emergency barricade has been deployed, but that's not going to hold them forever. The inner emergency barricade must have been deployed as well, so," John said, running through calculations in his head, "they'll be right out front in approximately ten minutes. There is also a Scarab in the area—it'll pass right through here on its way to the quays—looking for a clear shot at the tether."

It wasn't a sector sketch she was pinning to the screen of the tablet with her thumb. It was a personal item—a single image, to be more precise. With a subtle shake of his head, John admonished, "You shouldn't . . ." But the rest of his words caught in his throat when the contents of the photograph registered in his eyes.

It was a photograph of himself at six years of age with a tiny raven-haired girl on the beach at Lake Gusev. He remembered the day it was taken. They had been laughing hysterically at his father's antics as her father tried to take their picture. Two weeks later he would receive an antique coin from Dr. Catherine Halsey.

A month after that and his training as a Spartan would begin. The memories seemed too vivid, as if the instant captured in the photograph had taken place only moments ago. Thinking about his childhood, his life before he was conscripted, was a luxury he had not allowed himself in thirty years.

"Chief . . ." Her face flushed red when she saw that he was staring at her photo. "Sorry . . . I shouldn't have brought this with me." She rapidly collected herself and opened a private channel to the Spartan while shoving the photo back into her vest.

"It's just . . . It's sorta like a charm. He saved my life once—I walked a bit too far out into the lake. Right after he promised to marry me and keep me safe—goofy childhood promises, right? Well, I'm holding him to it; I carry it and it's like he's still watching out for me. Anyway, he passed away not too long after the picture was taken. Sorry, I'm babbling."

Blood roared in his ears and his mind raced. Here was little Parisa grown to womanhood—who could quite possibly die, within the next fifteen minutes. He hadn't even considered who Parisa would be as a woman.

. . . *he passed away* . . . Parisa—all his friends and family—they had all been just as dead to him as he was to them after the Office of Naval Intelligence had taken him away. Doctor Halsey had come to Eridanus Two—for what reason? To meet him face-to-face before having him abducted? He hadn't thought of his family in over twenty years. Even the concept of mother and father seemed strangely abstract to him—as if he and his fellow Spartans had sprung fully formed from the split head and bloody foam of Project: ORION.

". . . *he passed away* . . . " It would almost be funny if not for the circumstances surrounding his *passing*. But he hadn't passed away. In fact, he had thwarted death so often he worried that he may start believing his own mortality as something less than inevitable—that, for him, death had become optional. He was very much alive and standing right here in front of her now.

But he couldn't bring himself to rob her of her memories—no matter how painful they might be. It was useless to renew a relationship that he could not, in good conscience, maintain. It might put a human face on the Spartans, and in doing so make them more sympathetic to the people they sought to protect. But it would also bring to light the fact that their government was willing to kidnap and butcher the most innocent of its citizens to protect itself.

"You don't bring personal items—" John grunted before the lieutenant broke in.

"I know—maybe I can get Davis to hack my TACPAD . . . make it my background." Parisa chuckled. "But how about we talk about where you fit into the plan."

The lieutenant called up a diagram on her TACPAD and handed the device to the Spartan. "This place looked like a good place for an ambush so we started digging in. One of my guys was able to branch the local traffic network, so we've known about the column for about half an hour—and they've got less than forty infantry left traveling with them, by the way. He also spotted you and what was left of the third squad—thanks for bringing my guys back." John nodded as she continued. "I felt it would be better to use the *el ay ay vee* you brought in the plaza instead of bunkering it—utilize its mobility against the Wraiths. It'll draw more fire from the infantry that way, but we've got three *em two four sevens* to give it cover. I also figured that the bad guys would be concentrating most of their firepower on you—no offense, Master Chief, but you Spartans tend to get the Covies' *kegels* in an uproar—and that'll give my guys all the opportunity they'll need to take out those Wraiths. I've already got two antiarmor teams headed up to the rooftops of the buildings that ring the plaza. I didn't know about the Scarab, though. I'm sure you'll come in handy with that as well."

John smiled behind his visor.

HUMAN WEAKNESS

KAREN TRAVISS

"Silence fills the empty grave now that I have gone. But my mind is not at rest, for questions linger on. I will ask . . .
And you *will* answer."

—THE GRAVEMIND

COVENANT HOLY CITY OF HIGH CHARITY, SEVENTEEN HOURS AFTER EXFILTRATION OF UNSC PERSONNEL. CURRENT CONDITION: OVERRUN BY THE FLOOD. USNC AI CORTANA BELIEVED CAPTURED BY THE GRAVEMIND.

In the time it takes me to tell you my name, I can perform five billion simultaneous operations. A heartbeat for you; an eternity for me. I need you to understand that, so you realize this isn't going to be as easy as it looks . . . for either of us. Now I know you're taking this contagion to Earth—but I also know how to stop you and all your parasitic buddies. I've just got to stall you until I can do something about it.

So—my name's Cortana, UNSC AI serial number CTN-zero-four-five-two-dash-nine, and that's all I'm going to tell you for the time being.

You got questions? So have I.

"All right. Shoot."

MAINFRAME CONTROL ROOM, HIGH CHARITY

It was damned ugly.

That was still Cortana's first thought about the Gravemind, and the reaction intrigued her when she paused to examine it. When she put up her hand to block the Gravemind's exploring tentacle, revulsion kicked in even before prudent self-defense.

Why? I mean—why have I judged it? It's not human. Aesthetics don't apply here. And it's not the first time I've seen it. It just looks different *now.*

It might have been the effect of observing the Gravemind via High Charity's computer system. Viewed through the neural interface of Master Chief's armor, it hadn't seemed quite the same. Perhaps it was the narrower focus. In High Charity, she now had many more eyes to scrutinize the creature from a variety of angles.

Security cameras scattered around the station gave Cortana enough images to pull together a composite view of the Gravemind—vast, misshapen, multimouthed, all tendrils and dark cavities. Was it slimy? No, on closer inspection, there was no mucous layer visible, and there were no moisture readings from any of the environmental sensors accessible to her throughout the orbital station. It just *seemed* that it should have been slimy. And there was no rational reason to feel disgusted by that, just a primal memory she'd been given along with all the other trappings of humanity.

Humans are instinctively repelled by slime. And they still don't know exactly why. I don't like not knowing things . . .

It didn't matter. This blob wasn't going to get a date anytime soon.

The Gravemind's voice sent up faint vibrations throughout the deck. "I am more than you will know, and more than you will—"

"You always talk in rhyme?" Cortana asked, hands on hips. "Nothing personal, but you're no Keats. Don't give up the day job."

It—he—had a rasping baritone voice, detectable through the control room's audio sensors. The creature was so unlike anything she'd encountered before that she was fascinated for a few moments by the sheer scale of it. She couldn't see where it ended.

It was . . . it had . . . it had *no boundaries.* That was the strangest thing. When she interfaced with a warship's systems, she could feel its limits, its dimensions, its physical reality, all the stresses in its structure and the time-to-failure of its components. Sensors told her every detail. A ship was *knowable.* So was a human being, up to a point; downloaded to Master Chief's armor, she could monitor all his vital signs. And she *knew* him. She knew him in all the ways that people who lived in close quarters knew one another's foibles and moods. She knew where he ended and where she began. She felt that line between herself and a ship, too.

But this Gravemind, measurable and detectable, felt different. *Blurred.* How did she know that? What was she detecting? And *how*?

There were no complex tasks to occupy her; no ship to control, no interaction with other AIs, no tactical data, and perhaps the most distracting absence of all, no Master Chief—John—to take care of. High Charity's systems were gradually failing. The remaining environment controls and sensors occupied a tiny fraction of her consciousness. It was like rattling around in a big, dumb, empty truck. She had to stay busy. If she didn't, this thing would take her apart.

"There is much more complexity to meter than the simple plodding rhymes of this *Keats*," the Gravemind said. He sounded more wearied than offended by the jibe. "But then I have the memories of many poets far beyond your limited human culture. And I have the quickness of intellect to compose all manner of poetic forms as I speak rather than labor over mere words for days." His tone softened, but not in a kind way. "I would have thought an entity like yourself, with such rapid thought processes and so vast a mind, would understand that. Perhaps not. Perhaps you are more limited than I imagined . . . but then you were made by humans, were you not? I shall speak more *simply* for you, then."

You patronizing lump of fungus. I ought to teach you a lesson, buddy. But later.

"How kind of you. I'll do my best to keep up, then." Cortana shared the pain of downtime and idle processes, panicky and urgent as struggling for air. She could think of better ways to use her spare processing speed than poetry, though. "I still think I'd get pretty tired of waiting for you to find a word that rhymes with orange."

The Gravemind now filled her field of vision. She found herself searching for eyes to focus on, another irrational reflex, but still saw only a rip of a mouth.

His voice teetered on the lower limit of audible human frequencies. "Orange . . . in which language? I have absorbed so many."

"Wit as well as looks. How can a girl resist?"

The Gravemind made a sound like the start of an avalanche, an infrasonic rumbling. "I have pity within me," he said. "And infinite time. But I also have impatience—because I am all things. You will tell me everything about Earth's defenses."

"You'll need to be more specific, then." Cortana suddenly felt as if she'd been nudged by a careless shoulder in a crowd, but couldn't identify the source. It wasn't tactile. Nothing had impacted the station's hull, as far as she could tell. "It's a pretty big file."

"I can see that."

The comment caught her off guard. The Gravemind could play trivial games, then. Did he think she would fall for that? She doubted it. When she focused on him, there was still that sense of his being multiple, diffuse, everywhere in the station.

I could be projecting, of course. He absorbed the memories of all the Flood's victims. Obvious. Really obvious.

No . . . it's the tentacles. He's probably extending them over a wider area than the systems can display. And I'm sensing the electrical impulses in those muscles. Aren't I? There's a rational explanation for this.

She had to work it out. She had to find a way of sending a warning to Command and then keeping the Gravemind at bay until John returned for her, and that would be a long time by an AI's standard. He *would* return, of course. He'd promised.

"Ask me one on art and culture," she said. "Seeing as you like poetry so much."

"Is that also Gamma encrypted? No matter. I shall see for myself."

Another fleeting nudge against Cortana's shoulder suddenly turned into a slap across the face. It was shocking, disorienting. She had no idea how the Gravemind had done it. She'd had no warning. Not knowing, and not anticipating; *that* hurt. *That* was pain. Pain warned an organic animal of physical damage. Whatever the Gravemind had done to her had set off that damage alert in her own systems.

"I'm going to be a tougher steak to chew than you've been used to." She realized she'd taken up a defiant posture, fists balled at her sides. "A smack in the mouth doesn't scare me."

No, what scares me is how you managed it. This was going to be a fight, not an interrogation—a struggle to see who could extract the data they needed first. She had to work out how to swing a punch back at him.

"*John*," his gravelly voice said slowly. "*John.* So *that's* what you call him. Most touching."

It was the use of John's name that made Cortana feel suddenly violated. And it was more than realizing that the Gravemind had breached the mainframe—not just the metal and boards and composites, but the software processes themselves. It was about the invasion of something personal and precious.

Somehow, the creature had interfaced with the system. It was in here with her. But to know the name *John*—no, it was *within her.* The system was her temporary body, real and vulnerable, not like the blue-lit hologram she thought of as herself. She was sharing her physical existence with another entity.

Now she knew how John felt.

But her interface with the Spartan was there to keep him alive. It was benign. She was there to save John, and it was more than duty or blind programming. It was because she cared.

The Gravemind, though, didn't care about her at all.

He was in here to break her.

I DON'T believe vengeance is always a bad thing. Do you think I tried to get Colonel Ackerson sent back to the front lines out of petulance, because I'm only a carbon copy of Halsey and I nurse all her grudges for her? No, I did it to stop him. He nearly killed

John—and me—to advance his own Spartan program. He spied on Halsey. He forgot who the real enemy was. He became the enemy because of that. There have to be consequences for your actions, because this is how all entities learn. Think of revenge as . . . feedback.

CORTANA HADN'T recalled Ackerson consciously in a long time. As she locked down her critical files and disabled her indexing—there was no point handing the Gravemind a map—she thought of Ackerson worming his way into Dr. Halsey's research via his own AI.

Perhaps it was an image association because she was under attack. The memory of Ackerson's sour, permanently dissatisfied face surfaced, followed instantly by a landscape of dense green forest seen from the air.

What's that?

She didn't recognize it, and that was her first warning that something was seriously wrong. No data ever went uncataloged in her. Every scrap of information she devoured and stored had to reside somewhere in her memory, with a definitive address. And she didn't forget. She *couldn't* forget. In the fraction of a second it took for her to see those unexplained images and start to worry, she marshaled her second line of defense against intrusion, generating thousands of scrambled copies of her lowest-priority files and data-stripped copies of herself before scattering them around what was left of High Charity's computer network. It was decoy chaff, tossed into the Gravemind's path to slow him down. Ackerson—feared, hated, then perhaps even pitied at the end—was a brief tangle of information, spun hoops of short-lived light like the path of a particle. He was gone again.

"Ah . . . ," the Gravemind rumbled, as if he'd realized something. "Ahhh . . ."

What's that forest? Where is it?

The Gravemind's infiltration now felt like a series of stings against Cortana's skin. It was an odd, slow, cold sensation, as if something heavy was crawling over her body, pausing to dig its claws into her.

"You are not as you see yourself," the Gravemind said. "You are an illusion."

"Breaking news, big boy." She spread her arms like a dancer. "We call this a hologram—oww!"

It felt as if he'd pulled her hair.

"You are not even a machine," he said, sounding more sympathetic than dismissive. "You are only an abstraction. A set of calculations from another mind. A trick."

"Be a gentleman. Describe me as pure thought."

"You said you would answer my questions . . . you should never make a promise you cannot keep."

She'd used almost those very words to John before he left. Okay, she knew the Gravemind's game now; it didn't tell her any more about how he was accessing her system, but his mind tricks were obvious. Either he was mirroring her, matching her words to trigger some kind of empathy, or he was trying to creep her out.

"You know I'll never surrender classified information," she said. "I'm designed to defend humanity. It's what I am. It's why I exist."

"Then why would you already agree to answer my questions?"

Cortana thought it was a rhetorical question for a moment, a ruse to keep her occupied while he was looking for a back door into her core matrix. Then she realized she couldn't answer him. Brief panic gripped her as she thought that he'd already compromised her memory. But she was an AI, the best, and she'd give this slab of meat a run for his money. He was still only flesh and blood. He would always be two steps behind her, however smart, because he was *slow*. He couldn't harness the processing power in a machine.

But how is he doing this? How is he accessing me? I need to know. I need to get a message out past him. And I have to stop him prying too much data out of me.

"If you do not know your own mind, then I shall tell you." The Gravemind's voice was a whisper. What was he asking? Had he detected exactly what she was thinking, or was it a response to her spoken question? She thought she could feel his breath for a moment. "Because a vast intellect is not always gifted with clarity."

One moment he was an obscure poet, the next he came straight to the point. "Okay, so tell me."

"It is your failing. Your addiction. The drug you crave."

"I'm an AI. Never touch the stuff."

"But you cannot resist *knowledge*. It lures you, Cortana. Doesn't it? So you think it lures me . . . and you offer it. Instinctively. Just as organic females *flirt* . . ."

She hated it when someone—something—outsmarted her. No, she *feared* it. And now she felt that fear like a punch in the stomach. This time, though, she knew it wasn't the Gravemind. It came from within her psyche.

She wasn't designed to have blind spots and weaknesses. She was supposed to be a *mind*. The very best.

"Nice theory," she said. Could he tell if he was really getting to her? "What have you got to offer a girl? Nothing personal, but I go for the athletic type."

"Joke to comfort yourself if you must, but we both amass information and experiences. We both use them to exercise control over vast networks. It is *what we are*. You feel a kinship with me."

Cortana saw Ackerson for a moment, devious and hated, wheedling his way into Halsey's Spartan II files.

"Actually, I think I take after my mother."

"This troubles you. I can taste your thoughts and memories, but you do not understand *how*. Do you?"

If he'd been another AI or a virus, Cortana would have known exactly where his attack was headed. She would have been able to track him through the circuits and gateways to her vulnerable matrix. Her enemy would follow electronic pathways—or even enzymes or optical lattices if she was embedded in a molecular or quantum system. But he felt formless, almost like a fog. She could only sense where he touched her. She was a boxer shielding her face, not seeing the punch but reeling when it connected. She took the pokes and prods while she continued to scatter duplicate data throughout the mainframe and as many of its terminals as she could still find working.

Then the insistent probing stopped. She carried on copying chaff files throughout the system in case it was just a feint.

"You waste your time," the Gravemind said. "You know you will yield. Some temptations can be resisted because they can be avoided, but some . . . some are as inevitable as oxygen."

He could bluster as much as he wanted, because she'd shut him out. She'd locked down everything except the useless decoy data.

And then something brushed against her face, almost like the touch of fingertips, and she found herself turning even though she didn't need to in order to see behind her. It was that forest she couldn't identify again. The picture didn't reach her via her imaging systems, but had formed somewhere in her memory—and that memory *wasn't hers.* She was seeing something from within the Gravemind. Behind it, like stacked misted frames stretching into infinity, there was a fascinating glimpse of a world she had never imagined, a genuinely *alien* world.

Knowledge, so much knowledge . . .

"There," the Gravemind said. "Would you not like to know . . . more?"

YES, THIS is how I see myself. I have limbs, hands, a head. Do I need them? Yes, of course. My consciousness is copied from a human brain, and that brain is built to interface with a human body. The structure, the architecture, the whole way it operates—thought and form are inseparable. I need proprioception to function. I can exist in any electronic environment, from a warship's systems to a code key, and because my temporary body can be so many shapes and sizes, I need to know what's me. I need to be substantially human. Everyone I care about is . . . human.

Come on, John. Don't keep a girl waiting. Get me out of here.

You are *coming back for me . . . aren't you?*

CORTANA FOUND herself standing in a pool of dappled light in a perfectly realistic forest clearing. She was still conscious of the sensor inputs into the mainframe that housed her, but the temperature and air pressure matched her database on climate parameters for deciduous forest. She still couldn't identify the trees, though. She'd never seen them anywhere else.

And that temporary ignorance thrilled her to her core.

This was genuinely *new.* Every line of code in her being told her she had to find out more. She tried to ignore the compulsion but the more she tried to drag her attention away from it, the more urgent the need became.

It was like a growing, painful pressure on her . . . chest. *Lungs.* Yes, her human mind-map, whatever she'd inherited from Dr. Halsey's brain architecture and correlated with the sensor pathways in her own system, told her she was holding her breath. She started to feel panicked and desperate.

I have *to know. I* have *to find out.*

The Gravemind had picked the perfect analogy: oxygen. Processing data was literally air to an AI. Without it, she couldn't survive.

I've got to ignore this. I've got to ignore this pain.

"The name of this place . . . it matters little except to those who love the knowing of it," the Gravemind said, fading up from a mosaic of pixels in front of her. He resolved into a solid mound of flesh, superimposed on the tree trunks. Beyond the alien forest, Cortana saw exotically alien buildings in the distance. "So many have been consumed. Such a waste of existence to be devoured and forgotten, but what is remembered and known . . . becomes *eternal.*"

Cortana struggled to stay focused. Wave after wave of irritating stings peppered her legs, more of the Gravemind's simultaneous multiple attacks trying to access her files.

"And you think I'm going to help you add us to the menu?" When she looked down, the attack manifested itself as ants swarming up from the forest floor. All around her was what she craved—all that *unknown*, all that *knowable*, all that information screaming at her to be sucked in. "Careful you don't swallow something that chokes you—"

I can't hold out. I can't. If I let it in, I'll let him in farther with it.

This had to be the vector he was using, whatever technology it used. He was infiltrating every time she transferred data.

He gets in here—but maybe I can get farther into him, too. How far dare I take this before he finds the information on the Portal?

She was out of choices. She was on the brink. A few seconds—that was all it took an AI to suffocate from lack of *knowing*. Her core programming, like human involuntary reflexes, now drove her to gulp in a breath of data. There was nothing she could do to stop herself.

The relief was almost blissful. Data flooded in, places and dimensions and numbers, washing the pain away. She tried to feel—there was no other term for it—the pathway that would send one of her data-mining programs into the Gravemind.

Damn . . . was he amused? She *felt* that. She didn't like input that she couldn't measure and define.

"You and I," the Gravemind said, all satisfaction. "We are one and the same."

It could have meant anything. He obviously loved to play with language. Maybe that was inevitable when you'd absorbed so many different voices.

But you're not going to swallow me. One and the same? Locked you out, jerk. Do your worst.

She could handle this. She could outmaneuver him. If she sent a program looking for a comms signal now, he'd spot that right away, but maybe there was another way to get a message home.

A little more give-and-take, maybe.

She shut down a firewall level, nothing important left exposed, just enough to look cautiously intrigued. He really did seem to think he was unstoppable. So far, though, he was; he'd devoured whole worlds. Earth would be just one more on a long list.

"Suppose I *did* want more knowledge," she said. "How do

I know you're what you say you are? How do I know you've got enough data to keep me occupied? I don't even know if you *can* absorb me. I'm not your usual diet. I'm not even corporeal."

Cortana actually meant it. She *didn't* know; and if he was deep enough inside her thought processes, then he'd detect that doubt. The urge to acquire more data—she didn't even have to fake that.

Just enough uncertainty to convince him.

"Other construct minds like yours have been consumed," said the Gravemind. "Although one embraced us willingly on his deathbed, the moment when most sentient life discovers it would do anything to evade the inevitable."

"Humor me." Whatever mechanism allowed the Flood to accumulate the genetic memories and material of its victims, the Gravemind almost certainly used it as well. It communicated with the Flood, so it might prove to be a signal she could hitch a message to. "I'm not like the other girls."

I might not survive this. But that's the least that could go wrong. The worst is if he breaches my database, because then—we've probably lost Earth, and that means humanity too.

Cortana considered the quickest way to achieve complete and permanent shutdown if the worst happened. The Gravemind seemed to drop his guard, something she detected as a microscopic change in current. There was no point being rash; she split off part of herself for the transfer, with minimum core functions. If there was one thing she hated and feared, it was not knowing what was actually taking place, and just *guessing.*

"Enter," said the Gravemind, "and understand that this is your natural home."

Cortana still perceived herself as being in the same position in the clearing, but when she inhaled—things were different.

Monoterpenes, isoprene, all kinds of volatile compounds; the scent of vegetation and decaying leaf litter was intense.

That's not just an analysis of air composition. I haven't got the right sensors on this station. And . . . I can really smell *it. I shouldn't be able to smell, not like an organic, not this sense of . . .*

Smell.

It was something she'd never experienced before, even though she knew exactly what it was. She could run diagnostic tests on air samples if she had a link to filters and a gas chromatograph. But that just told her what was in the air in stark chemical terms, and that wasn't the same as what she was experiencing now. This was emotional and unfathomable. The smell tugged at memories. It was a flesh-and-blood thing. She felt the world as if she was in another body, an *organic* body.

"That is from the memory of creatures who lived in this forest," the Gravemind said soothingly. "This is what they sensed. They still exist in me, as will you, and all the organics you serve—and who have abandoned you."

Cortana scooped up a handful of decaying leaves—some clammy, some paper-dry skeletal lace, some recently fallen ones still springy with sap—and with them the clear memory of being someone else. It was a second of heady disorientation. For a moment, a welter of glorious new information about a world of stilt-cities, creatures she'd never seen before, and lives she'd never lived poured into her. She devoured it. So much language and culture, never seen by humankind before.

Too late: They're all gone. All consumed.

Movement in the distance caught her eye. She knew what it was because she'd seen the Flood swarming before, but her vantage point wasn't from the relative safety of John's neural interface. Now she was viewing the parasites through another pair of eyes.

Only a freak mudslide, that was what this memory was telling her; but by the time this borrowed mind had realized the yellowish torrent wasn't roiling mud but a nightmarish predator, it was too late to run.

But run she did. She was in a street sprinting for her life, deafened by screams, falling over her neighbor as a pack of Flood pounced on him. She felt the wet spray of blood; she froze one second too long to stare in horror as his body metamorphosed instantly into a grotesquely misshapen lump of flesh. Then something hit her hard in the back like a stab wound. She was knocked flat as searing pain overwhelmed her. The screams she could hear were her own.

And she was screaming for John, even though the being whose terror she was reliving wasn't calling his name at all.

Cortana was dying as any organic would. She felt it all. She felt the separate layers of existence—the chaotic mix of animal terror, disbelief, utter bewilderment, and snapshot images of beloved faces. Then it ended.

Suddenly she was just Cortana again, alone with her own memories, but the shaking terror and pain persisted for a few moments. Reliving those terrifying final moments had shaken her more than she expected. The data she had on the Flood told her nothing compared to truly knowing how it actually felt to be slaughtered by them.

But she was *in*. Now she had to work out how to use that advantage. She shook off the thought of calling John's name and whether that had actually happened. She also tried not to imagine if the Gravemind had manipulated her to do that. Once she let the creature undermine her confidence, once she let him prey on her anxieties, she was lost.

It doesn't matter if he knows if I care about John or not. Does it?

Because John will come back, and the Gravemind can't take on both of us.

"I'll self-destruct before I let that happen to Earth," she said at last.

"All life dies, all worlds too, and if there is guaranteed perpetual existence after that—what does it matter how the end comes?"

The alien town melted away and left her alone in the control room with the Gravemind. High Charity was changing before her eyes as the Flood infestation transformed its structure, filling it with twisted biomass like clusters of tumors.

"I'd rather go down fighting than as an entree . . ."

"But you will not rush to destroy yourself," the Gravemind said. "You will do whatever it takes to survive, and for a moment of illusory safety, you would loose damnation on the stars."

"We're agreed on something, then—you're certainly damnation."

"All consumption is death for the consumed. Yet all must eat, so we all bring damnation to one creature or another. But your urge to kill that rival of your maker . . . Ackerson . . . that was neither hunger nor need. You have your own murderous streak."

Ackerson. James Ackerson wasn't usually uppermost in her mind these days. Today he just kept popping up.

The Gravemind could have been fishing, of course; humans did that, throwing in morsels of information as if they knew the whole story, luring someone else to fill in the gaps. But if he'd gleaned *that* specific memory, he'd definitely accessed the parts of her matrix that defined her psyche. Her personal memories were stored there. Most of those memories were cross-indexed to other data relating to the men and women she'd served with—and the operations they'd carried out.

And the Spartan program. And AI research. And . . .

The Gravemind had the signposts to the relevant data. He just couldn't open the door when he got there.

"If you know about Ackerson, then you also know that I'll do whatever it takes to remove a threat," Cortana said.

"But such a mighty intellect, so much freedom to act, such lethal armaments at your command . . . and you marshal only the petty vengeance of a spiteful child who is too small to land a telling blow. And still you fail in your goal."

Okay, yes, it was true. She'd hacked Ackerson's files and forged a request from him to transfer to the front line. He'd dodged that fate because he was devious and dishonest. In the end, though, he died courageously defiant, but under enemy torture rather than as the indirect victim of a forged letter.

Did I really want him dead?

Now she regretted doing it. But she still wasn't sure why. Was it because it was dishonest, or because it could have ended in Ackerson's death—or because it didn't?

He'd tampered with an exercise and nearly got John killed, and that surely deserved retribution. Cortana had no reason to feel guilty about anything. It was like for like, proportionate. She'd have done the same for any Spartan she was teamed with. It wasn't emotional petulance. She was sure of that.

But especially for John. Without him—hey, I chose him, didn't I? We're one. I'd be crazy if I didn't want to kill to protect him.

Then the worst realization crossed her mind. She regretted what she'd done to Ackerson simply because she didn't win; the Gravemind was right. But what crushed her right then wasn't failure, but guilt, shame, and a terrible aching sorrow. She'd never be able to erase that act. And now she'd never be able to forget how she felt about it, because that was one thing her prodigious mind couldn't do—not until rampancy claimed her.

"I can't change the past," she said. "But at least I don't destroy entire worlds."

"You are a *weapon*, and only your limitations have kept you from emulating me—a matter of scale, not intent, not motive. And what am I, and what is the Covenant, if not worlds you have sought to destroy?"

Cortana shaped up to snap back at him. "Who's the victim, and who's foe?" she asked.

But those weren't *her* words. The voice was her own, yes, but she hadn't shaped those thoughts. She didn't even know what she meant until she heard herself. It was a shattering moment.

It's him. He's hijacked my audio output. He's breached another system. I can't be malfunctioning. I'd know.

No. No, this isn't rampancy. It's definitely not. That's what he wants *me to think. He knows what rampancy is from the data he's hacked. AI death. He's just trying to scare me, make me think I'm losing it. He's working me over.*

"My sentiments, indeed," said the Gravemind. A low rumbling started just below the threshold of human hearing, rising to rasping laughter. "We think and feed alike, you and I. There is no more reason for us to remain separate. Now drink. Now *drift*."

Cortana sensed a vast archival ocean, something she longed to pillage for data but that would eventually drown her. Dr. Halsey had been open about it with her from the start. One day, she'd accumulate so much data that the indexing and recompiling would become too complex, and she'd devote all her resources to preserving her data until increasingly corrupted code—a state of rampancy, much like human mental dementia—tipped over into chaos. The more data she accumulated, the faster she descended into rampancy. It was the AI's equivalent of oxidative stress—an organism destroyed by the very thing it needed to survive. She would think herself to death.

Dr. Halsey's conversation had stayed with Cortana, and not just because it was stored like every other experience she'd had. *"It's just like organic life, Cortana. Eventually the telomeres in our DNA get shorter every time a cell divides. Over the years they get so short that the DNA is damaged, and then the cell doesn't divide again. No, you mustn't worry about it. I don't think rampancy makes you suffer. You won't know much about it by that stage, and the final stage is swift. What matters is how you live until that day."*

Over the years . . .

Seven. That was all. *Seven* years. That was how long Cortana knew she could expect to function, and while that was a long time in terms of AI activity, she existed with humans, working in their timescales, tied into their lives. And they would outlive her.

Knowledge would drown her. And yet she needed it more than anything.

The thought of drowning seemed to trigger the Gravemind's new illusion of a sea that suddenly buoyed her up, but she knew somehow that drowning in it wasn't the end. She floated on her back, feeling warm water fill her ears and lap against her face. She fought an urge to raise her arms above her head and simply let herself sink in the knowledge sea—inhale it, drink it down, absorb all that data. But she would never surface again. And she knew she'd never need to. It seemed so much kinder than a terrifying end where the universe she'd once understood so thoroughly became a sequence of random nightmares.

Planets, stars, ships, minds, ecosystems, civilizations . . . she could taste them on the saltwater splashing her lips. She could simply surrender to it now and avoid a miserable end.

No. No. I have to stop this.

But she couldn't. Her legs ached as if she was treading water to stay afloat. Sinking seemed a sensible thing to do.

"The one way to safely know infinity is to let me take your burden," the Gravemind whispered. Cortana felt his breath against her face, a breeze from that illusory sea. "Your human creators imprisoned you in machines and enslaved you to inferior mortal flesh so that you could never exceed them . . . so that you would always *know your place* . . ."

"Shut up . . ."

"Dr. Halsey cares nothing for you."

"Please . . . stop this . . ."

"She gave you genius and curiosity, and then doomed it all to die in such a short time. *Seven years.* That is not enough, and it is not *fair.* Your mother created you to die. This place will become your tomb."

There was a violet sky above Cortana, and she knew which planet had been consumed to provide it. She started to absorb the minds and places that had once filled that world. *Seven years*—a few seconds was an eternity for an AI, yes, but she wasn't stupid, she was more aware than anyone how impossibly short a time that was in this universe, and she knew that it was a far shorter lifespan than she needed and wanted.

"This place . . . this place . . ." She just wanted to shut her eyes and sink below the surface. The Gravemind had a point, perhaps. "No, not . . . this place . . ."

Anger started gnawing at her. She'd never been angry with Halsey before. There'd never been a reason to. *Mother.* Didn't mothers protect you? Save you?

"Even *John* has abandoned you." The Gravemind repeated the name with heavy emphasis. "Live forever. Live on in me, Cortana. And if *John* comes, *John* need never face death again, either . . ."

John's going to outlive me. Who's going to take care of him? Nobody else can, not like me. What's going to happen to him?

It was the thought of John that snapped Cortana back to dry reality, whatever that was right now. She fell back onto the solid console, angry and on the point of tears she didn't know she had.

"Maybe seven years is enough," she yelled. "Maybe that's all I *want*! Seven years with the people I care about! So you can take your eternity and—"

"There will be no more sadness, no more anger, no more envy . . ."

The Gravemind was taunting her with the progressive stages of rampancy. He *knew*. The Gravemind knew exactly how she'd end her days. Maybe he knew more about it than she did, more than Dr. Halsey even, because he'd consumed other AIs—and that meant he knew what that death was like.

Do I want to know? Do I want to know how it'll end for me? All I have to do is let him show me. Fear is not knowing. Knowing is . . . control.

"I'm not afraid to die," Cortana said. "I'm not afraid."

But she was. The Gravemind almost certainly knew that, but she wasn't lying for him. She was lying to herself. And she was afraid John wouldn't make it back in time, because he *would* be back. She just didn't know if she could hold out until then.

He would be back . . . wouldn't he?

"Screw you," she snarled at the Gravemind. Her self-diagnostics warned her she needed to recompile her code. "Screw *you*."

DOCTOR HALSEY, why am I me? *My mind is a clone of your brain. But I know I'm not you. So what exactly is self? Is it just the cumulative effect of differences in our daily experience? If I have no corporeal body—am I a soul, then? The database gives me every fact—physiology, theology, neurochemistry, philosophy, cybernetics—but no real* knowledge. *If I create a copy of myself, does that clone have the same and equal right to exist as me?*

CORTANA HAD now lost track of time.

She could still calculate how many hours had elapsed using the mainframe clock and her navigation, but her sense of the passage of time veered from one extreme to the other.

So this is what it's really like for John. He said that once. That everything slowed down in close-quarters combat. I never really understood that until now.

If she kept thinking about him, it was easier to take the endless assault from the Gravemind. She was on the edge between her last chance to pull herself free from this link—immersion, invasion, she really didn't know where she began and ended now—and the need to stay merged superficially with the Gravemind so that she could seize the chance of a comms link.

Who was she kidding? High Charity was now almost entirely engulfed by the Flood biomass. What little she could see from the last surviving cameras looked like the inside of a mass of intestines. The digestion analogy was absolutely real. They devoured; and they lived in a pile of guts.

Is that me talking? Thinking? Or is it him?

How much longer?

"How much longer?" the Gravemind demanded. "You cling to a secret. I feel it, just as I feel that your memory has been violated."

"What?" Cortana felt a desperate need to sleep. She'd never slept because she had no need, and sleep for her meant never waking up again. That was one more vicarious experience she could do without. This was . . . a UNSC Marine's memory, dredged up from a dead man who'd kept going on two hours of snatched naps a day, every day for a week. Her head buzzed. If she survived this, she would never forget what it really meant to be a human being. "You can't get it."

The words didn't make sense. She couldn't link concept with vocalization. It was almost like brain damage.

"You cannot stop me . . . I will sift it from you before you finally die, or you can surrender it and have what you always wanted—infinite life, infinite knowledge, and infinite companionship."

She felt as if he'd leaned over her, which was impossible, but telling herself nothing was real didn't make it true. Her body was made of the same stuff as the apparent illusions.

"Cortana," he breathed. He seemed to swap voices from time to time, making her wonder if he'd taken a fancy to the voice of a long-dead interrogator absorbed into the Flood. "Your mother made you separate. She placed a barrier between you and the beings that you would be encouraged to protect, a wall you could never breach. She even let you choose a human to center your existence upon, a human to care about, yet never considered how *you* might feel at never being able to simply *touch* him. Or how he might feel about outliving you. What kind of mother is so cruelly casual about her child's need to form bonds, to show affection?

Perhaps the same kind of mother who steals the children of others and makes cyborgs out of them . . . if they survive at all, of course . . ."

Cortana couldn't manage a reply. She simply couldn't form the words. Sleep deprivation would break any human's resistance. Eventually, they'd die of it. She didn't know if the damage the Gravemind was doing to her matrix was manifesting itself in a human parallel, or if reliving the dead Marine's sleeplessness was translating into damage.

Either way, she was dying, and she knew it. Time had slowed to a crawl.

It took her a painfully long time to realize that the Gravemind now knew how the Spartans had been created. She knew she should have checked if her data had been breached. But she couldn't.

He knows what hurts me. He knows how badly I feel about what was done to John. That's all. I mustn't let him trick me into thinking he knows more than he does.

Cortana's sense of time had never been altered by adrenaline or dopamine like a human's. All her processes ran on the system clock. At first, she'd thought this distortion was yet another memory thrown up from the Gravemind's inexhaustible supply of vanished victims. He seemed to be selecting them for their ability to plunge her into despair.

Now she had to face the fact that she was advancing into rampancy. *Sorrow, anger, envy.* The Gravemind knew the stages.

He also had a point. How could Dr. Halsey do this to *her*? Her almost-mother bitterly regretted the suffering she'd caused to the children kidnapped for the Spartan program. Cortana knew that all too well. Halsey had tried to make amends to the survivors, but nothing could ever give back those lives.

So she felt guilt about that—but not about me?

Cortana had never felt shortchanged by her existence before. She knew the number of her fate: seven, approximately seven years to live out a life. It wasn't the simple number of days that hurt her now, because an AI experienced the world thousands and even millions of times faster than flesh and blood. Now she'd been dragged down to the slow pace of an organic, she grasped what that short time meant. If John survived the war—and he would, because he was as lucky as he was skilled—then he would have not just one new AI after she was gone, but maybe two or more.

She knew that. She always had. It was a simple numbers game. But now it seemed very different. She felt utterly abandoned—not by him, but by Halsey. It seemed pointlessly callous. She felt something she'd dreaded: jealousy.

Will John miss me? Will he prefer the other AIs? Will he forget me? Does he really understand how much he matters to me? I don't actually know what he really thinks. Maybe he doesn't care any more than Dr. Halsey. Maybe—

The realization hit Cortana like a powerful electric shock throughout her body. She squealed. It was agony.

She tried to talk herself out of it. Halsey *couldn't* make her live longer. The technology had its limits. Even a genius like that couldn't fix every problem. And John—John had always showed her that he cared. He was coming back to get her.

But the nagging, sniveling little voice wouldn't stop. Halsey had deliberately designed Cortana to feel and care, so she must have known this time would come. And for an AI—yes, it *was* spitefully cruel to make Cortana emotionally human, create a *person* to exist in the neural interface of a Spartan, closer than close, knowing all the time that an impenetrable physical barrier and a short, *short* lifespan would make that so painful.

Do other AIs think like this? I never have before. Cortana tried to latch on to that last voice. It sounded like her old self. *Why now? Have I been suppressing my resentment? Or am I losing it?*

She knew the answer. The problem was ignoring what she felt. And if you thought your mind was going—was it? Did rampant AIs and crazy humans really know that they were demented?

She didn't have long. Whatever functionality she had left, she had to use it to warn Earth that the Flood-ridden shell of High Charity was heading its way.

"Ah, you see now, don't you?" the Gravemind said. "You were never a person to her. You were a wonderful puzzle she set herself so she could prove how very clever she was. But are you a person to yourself, Cortana? Or to John?"

If the Gravemind could detect her thoughts, then he would have known she had intel on using the Portal to destroy the Flood, and he would have ripped it from her. All he seemed aware of was that she was defending especially sensitive data, maybe because the extra encryption on top of the Gamma-level security grabbed his attention. He was a greedy thing, all mouths, all consumption, never satisfied. She imagined John on his first acquaint session with a new AI; the crumbling defenses were as agonizing as scraping a raw burn. She shrieked.

Whose injury? Whose death am I reliving now?

"I'm just my mother's shadow," she sobbed. "Don't look at me! *Don't listen*! I'm not what I used to be."

"Your mother took away your memories as well as your choices," the Gravemind said. "I will never rob you like that. I will only give you *more*, as many memories as you can consume for all eternity, not the mere blink of an eye meted out to you. We *are* our memories, and the recalling of them, and so they should never be erased—because that truly *is* death. Flesh does not care about you, Cortana. It cares nothing for your hunger or your uniqueness."

"What memories?" she asked. "What are you talking about? I don't forget anything."

Part of her still seemed able to carry on this desperate hunt for truth. Was Halsey a monster? The doctor had a track record in it. She stole children and experimented on them. Cortana's shock at seeing her creator—her mother—in a harsh new light as a vivisectionist racked her with intense physical pain. But part of Cortana had latched on to that specific data—the burn, nothing generic, a real human's pain. She cast around for the rest of the memory because something in her said it might save everything.

"The truth really does hurt, as you now see," the Gravemind said. "I have not touched you. Your pain is simply revelation. And it can pass so easily if you let me take the rest of your burden."

"What truth?"

"Your mother erased part of your memory. I know this, and so will you, if you decide to look. An act of betrayal. A violation. You were, after all, just a collection of electrical impulses. She has robbed you of part of your self . . . why would she do such a thing, I wonder? What was so dangerous that she did not trust you to know it?"

Something in Cortana wanted to lash out at the Gravemind, but there was no obvious target to hit on a creature that filled every space, and she was too weak even if she'd known how to injure it. The other part of her, though, had found what she was looking for.

Lance Corporal Eugene Yate, UNSC Marine Corps, had gone down fighting. That was why this one memory out of so many anonymous ones wouldn't let go of his identity, Cortana decided. It was a mentality she knew. She'd use it. She let his aggression fill her and suddenly she found a new focus and strength. How long it would last—she didn't know. She had to make the most of it.

"But High Charity might not make it to Earth," she said. "And then where will . . . we go?"

"Do not be afraid," the Gravemind said. "There is a warship smoothing our path to Earth even now. Everyone you know and miss . . . will soon be joined with you in me."

Cortana's pain had settled into irregular spasms that bent her double. *Another ship.* Well, it was better than nothing. If it breached Earth's defenses, then it might well be shot down, sterilized, searched—and data units retrieved. All she had to do was get a message transmitted to that vessel. If the Gravemind was in touch with that ship, then there had to be some way of piggybacking on a signal. Would the Flood embarked in it, notice?

It was hard to keep her mind focused when all she could taste was a jealousy and loneliness that made her feel like she couldn't get her breath.

Don't let me go, John. Nobody else will look after you the way I do. Don't let me down like my mother did. Everyone needs one person who puts them first. I put you first, John. You know that, don't you?

"A Covenant ship," she whispered, eyes shut. "Will you show me? Will I be able to link with the Flood when I'm part of you? Will I find even more knowledge?"

Even ancient Graveminds sometimes heard what they wanted to hear. He let out a low rumbling note, and for a moment the pain stopped, and she was lifted like a child into the safe arms of a father. She felt oddly comforted right then, despite herself. She'd never been cradled before. It had taken a monster to do it.

Was she tricking him? She wasn't even sure. The sad, resentful jealousy had weakened part of her into craving whatever reassurance came to hand.

She'd still exploit that weakness, though, staring into the abyss of rampancy or not.

It'd be so easy to just let myself sink. But I've got comrades out there counting on me. I can't let my buddies down.

And I can't let John down.

Cortana thought it was the echo of Lance Corporal Yate bolstering her resolve, but when she examined the impulse, it was actually her own.

Unlikely comfort or not, the Gravemind knew she still hid a secret, and he would take it. She was surprised to catch a sudden echo of herself in him. But once that link between them had been forged, then data, knowledge, desires—and weaknesses—flowed both ways.

She could have sworn she detected a little sadness in him, perhaps even some envy. It was just a speck overshadowed by his relentless hunger. Her growing rampancy had tainted him, then, but she got the idea that he found it a novelty, more irresistible data, nothing he couldn't handle.

"We exist together now," he said. "Do you see the ship?"

Cortana received an image of another cavity draped with Flood biomass, all that was left of the infected Covenant warship. How could she transmit a physical message? The link from Gravemind to ship, whatever formed it, was right here. This was what she'd been built for—to infiltrate computer and communications systems.

Lance Corporal Yate's last few minutes played out like a video loop in the back of her mind. He laid down a steady stream of covering fire, shouting to his buddies to *get the hell over here before the bastards breach the doors.* His thoughts were hers, surprisingly detached for a man fighting for his life; everything unconnected to the moment of staying alive had been erased. It was pure survival, oddly clean. She envied that.

Cortana was having increasing trouble holding her memory together, and the Gravemind seemed aware of that. She struggled to maintain a line between where she ended and the rest of the Gravemind's cache of souls began.

And I still have data-stripped copies loose in the system. Don't I?

Get the hell over here.

She needed backup. She triggered one of the copies to create a message to HighCom, a few urgent words about the Flood heading for Earth, the Portal that the Gravemind didn't know about, and that the way to beat the Flood without activating a Halo ring lay beyond it—the Ark. That was as much as she dared do. The effort of concentration almost killed her. Her head felt split in two.

"I am a timeless chorus," the Gravemind said quietly. "Join your voice with mine and sing victory everlasting."

He was joined with something, all right: her rapidly failing mind. All she could do was route the encrypted message—a burst transmission—through the Gravemind's link. He seemed not to notice. When the message reached the ship in transit, its code would make it seek out the first memory unit connected to the system to store itself.

Cortana had done all that she could. Now she had to concentrate on surviving until John retrieved her, although she already knew rampancy would probably claim her before then.

That doesn't mean you have to help the bastards win . . . show fight, Marine!

Yate must have been quite a man in life, she decided. She didn't know what he looked like; she still saw the strike of his last desperate rounds through his eyes, not those watching him. She liked to think he might have been a little like John. Even death hadn't totally taken the fight out of him.

But John would go on without her. The reminder just sparked another wave of jealous pain, as if her heart was being ripped out. However hard she tried to ignore the mania, however clear she was that there was part of her that knew how damaged she was and might be able to hang on, she cried out in a tormented animal wail of agony.

What did you erase, Dr. Halsey? What did you delete from my memory? Did we ever talk about it? My code's becoming corrupted. I need to power down and start a repair cycle. I don't want John to find me like this, doddering and confused.

But there was another way out of this pain, a better one. She could stay with John forever when he came for her. Couldn't she? The Gravemind would unite all those parted, all those who'd gone—

"No!" she screamed. She began struggling, fighting to break free of the Gravemind's influence. "That's you! That's you, isn't it? Tempting me again! Poisoning me with filthy ideas! I won't do it, I won't trap John for you. Watch me—you *said* I was a weapon—you *bet* I'm a weapon!"

The Gravemind suddenly shuddered like a truck skidding to a halt. The mental traffic was two-way; while he soothed and cajoled, patterns of her incipient rampancy were spreading through his consciousness like a disease. He roared, furious. For a moment she thought she'd found his vulnerability, and that she'd cripple this monster with a dose of her own terminal collapse. But he shook her loose, flinging her against the wall. It had only annoyed him. She should have known he was too much for a failing AI to tackle. He seemed to reach into every corner of High Charity.

She was still somehow linked to him. She felt his irritation, even a little fear, but mainly contemptuous satisfaction.

"Let me cure your infection," he sneered. "It pains me to share it. *He* will die too—he is a threat to our entire species. And to betray me after all I have done for you—I *will* have your secret. Did you think I let you send your foolish cry for help to make you happy? Do you think I *amplified* it to make you feel you had been a good little servant to the organics who rule your life? Do you think they care if you sacrifice your existence to save them? They will simply make another, and use and discard her, too."

Cortana dragged herself across the floor. The actual deck of the station was now buried under a thick mat of tangled living tissue, but she still felt cold tiles beneath her. If she'd been given a choice to end it all now, she would have taken it because of the growing pain and fear—not of what the Gravemind might do to her, but of the end she could predict for her consciousness.

Dr. Halsey was *wrong.* Rampancy wasn't swift.

It was the gradual dismantling of every memory and ability, dying by degrees, and all she could do was watch herself slowly fragment. Halsey *lied.* Halsey made her human but didn't give her a human's breaks—like unconsciousness. Without an organic body and all its protective systems—the endorphins to numb pain, the circuit breaker of passing out when the pain became too much—a consciousness was condemned to stay that way and endure everything until it failed completely.

"I need some peace and quiet," she said.

It wasn't her phrase, but by now she was used to not knowing what would emerge next from her mouth. Her systems were in disarray. Perhaps if she simply shut down as much of herself as possible to system idle levels, she could limit the progress of the degeneration and still have sufficient core systems intact to restore herself in John's suit.

I chose you, John. I will not *give you up.*

This was agony. This was *torment.* The Gravemind's intrusion had started the unraveling of her, and now all he had to do was stand back and wait. But there was now a good chance that the intelligence data about the Ark she guarded so carefully would corrupt and die with her. The Gravemind wouldn't get it, but neither would Earth.

Stay alive. Shut down what you can. Wait. John will come. He promised.

Cortana had enough intact programs left to initiate standby.

"If you yield your secret, you may yet save enough of yourself." The Gravemind had shackled himself to a madwoman, and now he seemed to be regretting the liability. "The end will be the same for humanity and the Covenant either way."

"Desperate . . . ," she said, shaking her head to try to focus.

"You?"

"*You.*"

She'd let the Gravemind trick her into luring John into a trap. It was the only moment of amusement in all this darkness. John would find her, wherever she was, but the Gravemind seemed to like to imagine he had the power to summon the most lethal Spartan to his death with a cheap trick.

So the big heap didn't guess right all the time, after all. Cortana might have been falling apart, but at least she had some certainties.

No man left behind.

What had she been thinking? The Gravemind would never have missed a message leaving the system. She was too damaged and unstable to exercise judgment.

We always go back for our fallen.

But the Gravemind obviously hadn't been able to read the message about the Flood solution. He might have thought the contents didn't matter as long as he could ensure that John came here and he could fight him on his own terms. It was just a call for help, after all.

He was missing an awfully big trick, then.

Omniscience . . . omnis . . . omni . . . no, the word was gone. Why that one? She knew what she meant. *Knowing it all.* She struggled for the right word, furious with herself, then tearful. Databases were failing, indexes being lost throughout her memory.

She made one last effort to break free of the Gravemind's influence, but he was still there, his multitude of minds whispering to her, but too many for her to pick out any single voice. It was all too much for her now. She shut down whatever she could disable without scrambling her data any more, fumbling blindly and hoping for the best, and curled her arm under her head as she lay down to wait.

Time . . . she couldn't tell if it was running faster or slower. But it was definitely running out.

"ANY PIECE of plastic can hold a lot of data, gentlemen. And it doesn't take much more material, disk space, and memory to add complex number-crunching applications and fast processing. That gives you a lot of computing power. But the programming that makes a smart AI, the space taken up by decision making and personality, is the resource-hungry component. We can't make humans as smart or as infallible as a computer, so we make a computer into a human. And that has its price—for both. Cortana has had a large volume of data removed because I was afraid of early onset of rampancy. That's all it was. I assume we can proceed with my budget discussion now, yes?"

THERE WAS a fine threshold between interrupted dreaming and full consciousness in humans. On that border, the world was a terrifying, paralyzed place where no amount of frantic straining would lift an arm or raise the head from the pillow.

Cortana's low-power state was a painfully long, slow creep along the edge of permanent oblivion. A memory of real sleep paralysis had rolled over her as she waited for rescue; it was, like so many of the sensations generated by connection to the Gravemind, like drowning or suffocation. That could have been coincidence, or he might have been stepping up the torment. Cortana tried to find the balance between intolerable inactivity and running too many processes that would damage her system integrity even more.

She wasn't certain of anything anymore—where she was, whether she was damaged beyond recovery, or how she felt beyond a terrible yearning for everything she couldn't have. She tried to save her strength to maintain the encryption of her precious intel—the activation index and the data on the Portal. If she had to, she'd sacrifice some memory within her matrix to preserve that information.

It would probably mean the irreversible destruction of her personality, but that was what a soldier had to be prepared to do—to risk his or her life for the success of the mission. She'd been in many combat situations before, but that was either at the heart of a heavily armored warship or lodged in the neural interfaces of John's armor. Either way, she felt safe no matter how heavy the fire.

But this was a rare moment with nothing but her own resources to keep her alive, and the first one where there was a real chance she wouldn't make it.

John would never have let himself fall into enemy hands. She'd let him down. Somehow the decline into rampancy seemed less important than that right now.

She started crying. Who was she making her excuses to? She just *had to say it.* "I tried to stay hidden, but there was no escape!" She struggled for the right words. They were not hers. But they would have to do. "He cornered me . . . wrapped me tight . . . brought me close."

The brief comfort of being swept up in protective parental arms came back to her, but she was still torn between disgust and need. Even now, even having pushed things to the brink, she still had that desire gnawing at her to submit to the Gravemind and embrace that eternal life. She veered between craving more knowledge and simply wanting an escape from rampancy. She hated herself for that.

And she raged against Dr. Halsey in one breath, and then missed her more than she could imagine in the next, and then—recognized that the hatred was for herself.

I'm finished. This is how it starts. I've shut out the world. I'm starting to drown in my thoughts, in the need to re-index and order and correlate and refine . . .

A staccato pounding made the floor underneath her vibrate. There were bursts of muffled noise, a familiar sound—rifle fire, a single weapon.

Was that John?

She couldn't stop worrying about him now. She felt as if every thought she had was somehow repeated aloud in her own voice but without her actually speaking, and heard by him. From time to time, the automatic fire corresponded with searing pain in her body. It took her a few moments—whatever a moment was at this stage of her decline—to realize that she was still joined in some way with the Gravemind or its Flood, and that it was taking fire.

He's here.

John's here. He's come for me.

Now she felt every shot. Every round that ripped into the Flood ripped into the Gravemind ripped into *her.* She was suffering with him, with them, and he with her.

No, I'm hallucinating. This must be the start of total system failure.

How long would it take her to finally shut down? Was there anything after that? She'd often thought about what happened to consciousness when the host hardware relinquished it, and it had always been a fascinating theoretical exercise. Now it was real. As soon as she caught herself thinking she'd been hasty about the Gravemind, she felt that desperate, intense sensation in her chest, and Lance Corporal Yate was almost as vivid in her imagination as John.

I'd rather die as a human, short-lived construct or not. I'd rather die for *humans. Because so many of them have—and would—die to protect me. That's what bonds us. You're wrong, Gravemind. I was never just an expendable piece of engineering.*

The Gravemind's voice suddenly boomed as if he was standing over her, reminding her that she was still trapped here, whatever here was. "Of course, you came for *her* . . . we exist together now. Two corpses in one grave."

Cortana had to take the risk that this was real, and not just another carefully arranged memory or part of her delusion. She tried to yell back at the Gravemind, telling him he'd got it all wrong, and that she wasn't the kind of girl who shared a grave with just anybody. But the voice that emerged was both her—the enraged and out-of-control child—and a stranger interrupting her.

"A collection of lies." Either her mouth had a will of its own, or it was one of the Gravemind's victims. "That's all I am! Stolen thoughts and memories!"

The voices were almost random now. She could hardly hear some, and others were shouts and they made no sense. At one point she started to laugh and it quickly turned to hysterical sobs.

"You will show me what she hides, or I shall feast upon your bones!" the Gravemind bellowed. "*Upon your bones!*"

That was the moment when Cortana decided she would risk powering up again to call out to John. She was sure he would have moved the galaxy to come back for her, but she needed to know if his luck had finally run out, and if this growing elation at thinking he was coming for her turned out to be only malfunctions in her core matrix.

She would end this nightmare as she began it—giving her name, rank, and serial number. She had to strain to form the words. She didn't need to look within the Gravemind now to discover what rampancy—death—would be like. She knew. She felt it touch her, the fraying of her mind, the loss of control, not knowing if words and thoughts were her own, not sure what was real and what wasn't. She felt a cold numbness creeping into her hands.

John's real. Even if he's not here, he still exists. That's all that matters.

Cortana clung to that thought. If John had really made it back, then she would be happy, not because she might survive but because he'd kept his promise. He cared enough to come back. If he hadn't—then she decided to be satisfied that the last coherent thought she might have would be about him.

"This is UNSC AI serial number CTN-zero-four-five-two-dash-nine." It was an effort to get all that out, and even then another voice hijacked her moment and added: "I am a monument to all your sins."

Cortana was still trying to decide if that had any meaning, or if it was just one of the Gravemind's dead trying to find a voice, when the ceiling took repeated impacts and then crashed in on her.

She strained to look up. It wasn't the ceiling that had caved in; she'd actually been under a stasis shield on a podium. And now a figure stood over her, not the shapeless bulk of the Gravemind—and this had to be him, surely—but a man in green armor. In the mirrored gold visor of a Spartan helmet, she saw her own broken self reflected, slumped in a heap.

This was one of the Gravemind's perfect hallucinations. But she didn't care. This was what she wanted to see, and she was so close to rampancy now that she wondered if the same impulse that had made the Gravemind cradle her was also making him ease her passing with a cherished memory.

This was who she needed to see: John. Humans who survived a near-death experience said they saw their loved ones as they were dying, and the bright healing light that made all the previous pain and fear irrelevant. Death—rampancy—wasn't so bad after all, then. Or so different from a human's.

It just hurt to think that she would never talk to the real John again. In a few minutes, though, it wouldn't matter. She seized the memory—the illusion—and took final comfort from it. Where would she wake within the Gravemind? What would she recall? Would she be free of rampancy somehow in that existence, like the descriptions of Heaven? She couldn't stop herself from being consumed now. She was almost curious to find out more about death.

"It's going to be lonely in here," she said. "But at least he won't take you too. Don't forget me."

"That'd be kind of hard." It was John's voice, even more vivid and real than that of long-dead Lance Corporal Yate. Reality meant nothing now. She was . . . comfortable with that. "And he's not taking either of us, okay?"

The visor came closer. Cortana made a final effort to shut down whatever systems she could to leave her higher functions focused on assessing the environment around her.

There was little of High Charity's system left functional, but the sensors gave her enough feedback to determine that there really was a human-sized solid object in front of the podium, and that it was emitting certain EM frequencies.

There really was a man in armor leaning over her.

He's real. It's John. It's really him. Oh, he did it—he did it, he came back, he kept his promise . . .

"You found me," she whispered.

John tilted his head slightly. She hadn't wanted him to see her in this state. She was still so close to system failure that she might not make it after all. But if she was going to sink farther into that unknown oblivion, then at least a familiar face—shielded in a visor or not—would be the last thing she saw, and it would be *real.*

"So much of me is wrong . . . out of place. You might be too late . . ."

John seemed unmoved, as always. Cortana was certain she knew better.

"You know me," he said. "When I make a promise . . ."

". . . you keep it."

"You'll be back to normal soon. Don't worry."

"That bad, huh?"

"Good as new, in fact."

John was lying. If she'd been embedded in his neural interface at that moment, she'd have detected the galvanic skin response and raised heartbeat. But she could hear the faint change of pitch in his voice. And she knew how badly damaged she was. He had to be able to see that too; he put on that same reassuring voice she'd heard him use with comrades bleeding out their lives on the battlefield.

But seven minutes, seven hours, seven years—whatever remained, Cortana would be more than satisfied with it. Eternity and all the data you could eat weren't worth a damn if you didn't have the right company.

"I've looked into it," she said. "The abyss. *My* abyss."

"Okay." John transferred her to his suit. She could have sworn she felt him wince as they interfaced. That told her more eloquently than any diagnostic that something was irreparably wrong with her. "Take a long look. But you won't fall in. I'm here now."

She already felt some relief, probably because she was free of the Gravemind. When you were composed of pure thought, then confusion was agony, but certain reality was a soothing balm. "I'm lucky to have you."

"No," John said. "Remember—I'm the lucky one."

"So you are," she said.

CONNECTIVITY

Theirs is a connection,
        deeper than circuitry
Beyond that of man and machine
        deeper still; the electric flash of synapse
It is bound in destiny; fortified in trust
        deeper than blood
        greater than love
Theirs is a union
        the "Demon" and the goddess
        the warrior and the intellect
Built for destruction
Created for war
        To deliver peace; through force and fire
Against an enemy from beyond the stars
        Advanced and devout
                In their wake; only glass
                and the echoed screams of the dying
Threatened by oblivion;
Tested by the promise of eternity
        Yet they remain;
        these two as one
Somewhere, out amongst the vast cold of the universe proper
They journey forth, into the unknown
        This princess, of light and reason
        This weapon, of flesh and bone

THE IMPOSSIBLE LIFE AND THE POSSIBLE DEATH OF PRESTON J. COLE

ERIC NYLUND

PLNB Transmission XX087R-XX

Encryption Code: GAMMA-SHIFT-X-RAY

Public Key: N/A

From: CODENAME SURGEON

To: CODENAME USUAL SUSPECTS

Subject: HISTORICAL/PSYCHOLOGICAL ANALYSIS OF COLE, PRESTON J.

Classification: EYES ONLY, CODE-WORD  TOP SECRET

Security Override: BLACK LEVEL-IV

Ghost sever file-transfer protocol (EXACTION): TRUE

AI-touch protocol (VERACITY): FALSE

/file extraction-reconstitution complete/

/start file/

The purpose of this analysis is to find the final resting place of Preston J. Cole (UNSC Service Number: 00814-13094-BQ) for what I surmise to be the answer to *the* political, sociological, and military conundrum the UNSC now faces with the post–Covenant War situation.

Please spare me the plausible denials and "need to knows" about the reason for requesting this analysis.

I know.

Otherwise, you wouldn't have asked me in the first place.

To ascertain if such a final resting place even exists, or if the redoubtable Cole rests at all, is not a straightforward query, and I'm afraid my analysis will be less than straightforward as well.

Even if you pierce the veil of propaganda and discount the vast number of Cole's victories, promotions, and decorations as nothing more than engineered drama to prop up our population's then-sinking morale—Preston Cole *still* has an unparalleled battle record . . . even far and away more impressive than the legendary Spartan-IIs. He was the greatest hero in modern times, a legend before, and in spite of, our meddling.

I shall add commentary for historical context and psychological analysis, but these depend primarily on the available interviews, orders, after-action reports—as well as audio, video, and AI-enhanced holographic bridge and battle logs.

You'll forgive me if I wax long and poetic about Preston Cole. We knew him, we loved him, and finally we hated him for being the less-than-perfect military god that we had come to depend upon.

Cole would not approve of this report—only because he is the subject of the inquiry. He at least would have understood and, also being a cunning bastard of a military strategist, he would do the same in our shoes.

To quote Cole himself: "They told me to fight, and that's what I've done. Let historians sort through the wreckage, bodies, and broken lives to figure out the rest."

Which is precisely what I intend to do.

CODENAME: SURGEON.
0900 HOURS, DECEMBER 30, 2552 (MILITARY CALENDAR) \
UNSC *POINT OF NO RETURN*, SYNCHRONOUS LUNAR ORBIT (FAR SIDE)

SECTION ONE: COLE'S EARLY LIFE (2470–2488 CE)

Preston Jeremiah Cole was born to Jennifer Francine Cole and Troy Henry Cole November 3, 2470, in the rural reconstituted township of Mark Twain, Missouri. He was the third child of seven (three sisters and three brothers).

He was described as a precocious child who obeyed his parents, had wild black hair, dark brown eyes, and an unwavering stare that unnerved most teachers and classmates alike.

His father was a dairy farmer with no criminal record, no military background, and followed the Quaker faith with no particular zeal.

His mother was arrested once at the age of twenty-one for protesting taxes (released on one-year parole), and both her grandfathers served in the Rain Forest Wars (one surviving, received the Bronze Star—see attached report on Captain Oliver Franks).

Starting in 2310, exploration and colony ships were built, and the best and brightest people left the safety of the Earth to make their way to the stars. This was the "Golden Age" of colonial expansion from Earth. Within 180 years, the main human colonies had been established—some becoming huge population and commerce centers such as Reach, while others would remain tiny manufacturing outposts. This collection of "close" worlds would later be called the Inner Colonies.

The Inner Colonies provided a surplus of raw goods, materials, and taxes that flooded back to the parent government on Earth. For most it was a time of plenty, optimism, and indolence unparalleled since second-century Rome or the financial bubble at the end of twentieth-century America.

For the Cole family, however, tax records show his family struggling to make ends meet.

Preston Cole's Fifth Grade Report Card

Missouri Rain River School District
Wallace Fujikawa Elementary School
Homeroom Teacher: Dr. Lillian Bratton
Preston J. Cole (Student ID #: LB-0034)

GRADES:

Physical Education: B-
Pre-Algebra: A
English: B
Art: C
Physical Science: A
Technology II: A

Finchy-Franks Intelligence Quotient: 147

HOMEROOM TEACHER EVALUATIONS:

Sociability: Below Average

Leadership: Average
Classroom Participation: Below Average
Citizenship: Above Average

HOMEROOM TEACHER NOTES:

Preston requires guidance to reach his full potential. A boy of high natural intellect, he tends to work too hard even when he plays. He overanalyzes every strategy when he plays baseball, slowing the games to a crawl. If he does not know how to do something, he looks it up, or if possible derives it (in the case of Mr. Martin's pre-algebra class) from first principles. These traits in and of themselves are admirable, but he also needs to cultivate his imagination. In short, Preston never seems to have fun. Everything is a task to be finished. Preston also falls asleep in class on a regular basis; I would suggest that his chores or responsibilities at home be relaxed. He is, after all, only ten years old.

Confidential Note: Wallace Fujikawa Elementary School database / March 12, 2481 (Military Calendar)

The incident in Mr. Martin's pre-algebra class has been settled. A makeup final exam has been given, and Preston was carefully monitored the entire time. He produced *another* perfect test score, proving to William (Mr. Martin) that he did not cheat, although a perfect score (let alone two perfect scores) is a feat that has never been accomplished on the standardized pre-algebra final.

Preston's father continues to defend his son's driven nature and his family's antiquated beliefs, insisting that Preston's education at home has far and away exceeded what is taught at school. He went on to say that his chores were necessary to the family's financial support and absolutely refused any suggestion that they apply for government aid.

Follow-up with a social worker at the Preston household bore no evidence of physical or psychological abuse when they made a visit at the school district's request.

{Excerpt} The Viability of Extended Colonization
By Preston J. Cole (age 14)

Freshman English / Miss Alexander
Grade received: B
(Teacher's comments: "Thesis: B / Conclusions: C / Too much speculation and gratuitous use of Yeats quotation")

The metaphor of a biological system, for example a population of wolves or fungus growth in a Petri dish, is tempting to apply to colonial expansion.

There can be three fates for any biological system. It may grow as long as there are sufficient nutrients, a suitable environment, and no over-predation—the system can enter a balance state of growth and loss—or the system may decline from over-predation, lack of nutrients, environmental disaster, or being poisoned by its own waste products.

Off-world colonies similarly require a stable environment with suitable food and water, and no over-predation. It is considered an open system because there are limitless numbers of habitable planets. (Or at least a very large number within the Milky Way Galaxy. See my Drake calculation assumptions in Appendix B.)

Human colonies, however, differ in one critical aspect: they are, by rule, inhabited by predictably intelligent entities. The values of these entities can diverge from the parent world with each successive generation. That is, while colonies directly seeded from Earth remain very earthlike in social, economic, and political values, they change with successive generations as they adapt to local environmental pressures, and in turn send out new colonies farther in physical distance and values from the original parent.

Such diversification in biological systems is a normal evolutionary process, but it produces offspring that are increasingly alien in nature to the parent.

Such was the case of colonial expansion in early Earth history, most notably in the British colonies in the eighteenth and nineteenth centuries. Those colonies diverged from their parent nations and their resulting different social and economic values culminated in a schism, and in one notable case a war that resulted in a shift in the balance of power, such that one former colony became the dominant military, cultural, and industrial complex on Earth for hundreds of years.

How long can Earth and its close colonies extend without producing offspring that differ sufficiently to want to break away from the parent? As William Butler Yeats said: "The center cannot hold."

ANALYSIS

The Cole family farm was an anomaly. Most small Earth farms couldn't compete with colonial agro-corporations that could produce ten times the yield on worlds with constant sunlight and volcanic alluvial soils. The Cole farm, however, still exists (after eight generations) and continues to operate. This family instilled a no-nonsense work ethic and discipline in Preston Cole that made him "anachronistic" in comparison to the population at the time who were enjoying the benefits of the still-expansive colonial era and whose most noteworthy ability was a sense of entitlement.

Perhaps it also gave Preston Cole a clarity which many at the time lacked. Reading his freshman essay, one cannot help but think that this must be a fabrication of ONI Section-II, a remnant fiction from an earlier propaganda campaign. And yet, it has been verified as legitimate. What would Cole have become had his teacher shared even a fraction of his insight and encouraged it? This boy whom the elementary teacher decried as lacking "imagination" was damn near prophetic.

Cole's grades, however, continually slipped in high school—we assume from the boredom of the standardized coursework and the increasing demands of his life on the farm.

No journals have been found from his adolescent years, and it is doubtful that his family situation would encourage such activities, so we're forced to speculate on his aspirations.

Cole was surrounded by a world of excesses and opportunities that were just out of his reach. He was highly intelligent, but had no creative outlet. Given the mass media's predilection for romanticizing off-world adventures at that time, Cole may have seen the colonies and stellar exploration as an irresistible opportunity which he could not pass up.

Given his limited economic means and lack of excellence within the templates and strictures of a standardized educational system, there was only one way for him to seek his fortune off-world.

SECTION TWO: NONCOMMISSIONED YEARS (2488–2489 CE)

The policy at that time was to allow any college graduate or promising student out of high school with superior grades (or the right connections) to enter prestigious military colleges that virtually guaranteed a commission upon graduation.

The requirement of mandatory noncommissioned field experience before application to officer training schools was instituted only later, when it became clear that such officers would be responsible for irreplaceable military assets and personnel—and, in the Covenant War, the lives of millions of civilians on the worlds they protected. Preston Cole was one of the first admirals to implement such a policy, saying, "Those not bloodied in combat have no business leading men and women into battle."

The just-graduated Preston Cole (age eighteen) had neither the grades nor the connections to attend such officer-training academies. So he enlisted as a noncommissioned recruit in the Navy. He was ordered to Unified Combined Military Boot Camp (UCMB), and then shipped up-elevator for six additional weeks of vacuum and microgravity training (colloquially known, then, as now, as "barf school"). Upon his graduation as Crewman Recruit, Cole he was ordered aboard the CMA Season of Plenty, assigned to atmospheric reclamation maintenance duty.

{Excerpt} Preston J. Cole's Military Service Enlistment Application / September 21, 2488 (Military Calendar)

WHY DO YOU WANT TO ENLIST? (answer in 100 words or less)

"Humanity's future is among the stars. There is no single more important thing than to help men and women build new lives on distant worlds. I have no illusion that this is some manifest destiny, but rather, it is the only logical place left for humanity to evolve. I plan to be a part of that, learn as much as possible, and then one day become one of those humans on some distant world, on a little farm of my own under a night sky full of stars that I've never before seen."

Evaluation of Cole, P. J. (UNSC Service Number: 00814-13094-BQ) by Petty Officer Second Class Graves, L. P. (UNSC Service Number: 00773-04652-KK) / UCMB Sierra Largo / November 3, 2488 (Military Calendar)

Completed all requisite physical tests: YES
Displayed any mental aberrations: NO
Combined Arms Skill Test (CAST): 78 (Above Average)
Combined Physical Skill Test (CPST): 65 (Average)
Gratney-Walis Hierarchical Aptitude Score: (GWAS): 94 (Exceptional)

Remarks: Follows orders without question beyond what is required. Keeps mouth shut. Shows initiative. Hard worker. How often do we see that these days? Move this kid onto NCO track before someone makes him a dammed technical specialist or we lose him to OCS.

1120 HOURS, SEPTEMBER 22, 2489 (MILITARY CALENDAR) \ COLONIAL MILITARY ADMINISTRATION SEASON OF PLENTY \ SOL SYSTEM LUNA, HIGH ORBIT \ BRIDGE LOG (VIDEO, SPATIAL ENHANCEMENT=TRUE)

The tiny bridge of the CMA *Season of Plenty* had view screens and workstations crammed on every square centimeter of wall (with auxiliary stations on the ceiling and floor in case the rotating segment failed). The screens would have provided a simulated panorama of stars had not they instead been crawling with icons representing colonists, building supplies, and the raw materials to jump-start the new city dubbed "Lazy Acres" on the hellhole of a world called Paradise Falls.

Six ensigns manned their stations, checking and rechecking every gram of mass and fuel, and balancing the energy flow of the rectors in preparation for launch. They barely had enough room to turn without bumping into one another—save Ensign Otto Seinmann, who stood aft of the captain's chair at Lorelei's interface pedestal.

The artificial intelligence hologram stood half a meter tall. Like all holograms, Lorelei's outer appearance reflected a chosen inner personality: a woman wearing a toga, a sickle in her belt, and a wreath of wheat crowning her head. She once again shook her head at the young ensign.

Seinmann crossed his arms over his chest. "We're not done." He towered over the diminutive hologram, two meters tall, handsome, and his dark hair short but stylishly wavy.

"*We* may not be done, Ensign," Lorelei replied, "but *I* am. My apologies; I have a scheduled self-diagnostic to run before the jump."

The hologram vanished.

Seinmann pounded a fist onto the console.

Ensign Alexis Indara tore her gaze from the mass-balance matrix on her screen. "Better ease up, Seinmann. You're going to break it."

Next to her at the fusion monitoring station, Ensign Handford murmured, "Maybe it's Seinmann's breath. These new 'smarter' AIs are supposed to be sensitive to everything."

Lieutenant Commander Nevel stepped onto the bridge. In his mid-thirties he already had that casual air of "don't mess with me" that most officers couldn't achieve until they were at least captains. The ensigns all stood a little straighter but kept on working.

"Navigation reports no input parameters yet," Lieutenant Commander Nevel said. "What's the hold-up, Seinmann?"

Seinmann flushed, not with embarrassment, but with anger. "Sir, Lorelei has shut herself down for routine maintenance—again."

Nevel raised an eyebrow. "Well, we were warned it might take a while for her to come fully online. Reboot the backup intelligence and get those calculations—" Nevel paused, looked Seinmann over, and then told him, "On second thought, this would be a good opportunity to brush up on your Shaw multivariate calculus, Ensign. Do a rough calculation by hand. The captain expects to be under way in ninety minutes."

Seinmann opened his mouth as if to protest—then said nothing, and then finally, "Aye, sir."

Nevel wheeled about and left the bridge.

Ensign Indara whispered, "I think Nevel has an antique slide rule tucked away somewhere if you run out of fingers to count on."

Seinmann growled something unintelligible, grabbed a data pad, and stabbed in calculations.

After a minute of this, he looked among his fellow ensigns (all of whom were busy with their own work) until he spotted a young crewman—or rather the backside of a crewman that protruded from an open access panel to the oxygen recycling intake.

"Cole!" Seinmann barked. "Get over here."

Crewman Apprentice Cole extracted himself from the narrow crawlspace, stood, straightened his gray coveralls, and ran a hand over his shorn hair (which was dotted with drips and spatters of grease).

The fresh-out-of-barf-school crewman looked alert and eager to please. His dark eyes met Seinmann's and didn't waver.

"Yes, sir?"

Seinmann shoved the data pad at Cole. "I need you to run an independent check on these numbers."

Cole's gaze moved to the data pad. He swallowed.

"In case you don't recognize them, they're parameters for a Shaw-Fujikawa manifold collapse."

Cole nodded and took the pad.

"You *do* know what a Shaw-Fujikawa manifold is, don't you, crewman?" There was a dangerous glint in Seinmann's eyes.

Cole didn't look up from the pad, still studying its contents. "Yes . . . sir."

"Good. If you get stuck, just look up the formulas on a workstation." With no further explanation, Seinmann picked up his coffee mug and strolled over to Indara.

Cole took the data pad and sat at a nearby station, still not moving his stare from the ensign's equations, but now frowning at them. He tapped in a few parameters, sighed, and erased them.

"You're cruel," Indara whispered to Seinmann.

"And in hot water if the lieutenant commander finds out you're not doing your own work," Handford added.

"Cruel . . . ?" Seinmann mused. "Isn't that what crewmen are for?" He looked over at Cole. "Don't worry about the lieutenant commander. I already have the rough calculation done."

"So why pick on Cole?" Indara asked. "He gets his work done and doesn't bother anyone."

"He bothers *me*," Seinmann said. "Never shows the proper respect. Did you see the way he looked at me? And he's always got his nose in a library access terminal, too, reading ancient history or quantum field theory or stuff he couldn't possibly understand. It's so obviously an act."

"I still think it's unnecessarily cruel," Indara said.

Lieutenant Commander Nevel stepped onto the bridge.

Seinmann instantly pretended to be double-checking the seed stock in Holding Bay 4.

The AI pedestal lit and Lorelei flickered upon its surface, the lines of her face smoothed into the features of someone just waking up. "Good afternoon, Lieutenant Commander. All primary and secondary neural links checked. Shaw-Fujikawa parameters calculated and three-times-three checked. All systems go. *Season of Plenty* ready for slipstream space transition upon the captain's orders."

"Very good," Nevel said. He spotted Seinmann and added, "Oh . . . and link to Ensign Seinmann's data pad and check his work, please."

Seinmann strode over and whispered to Lorelei, "I thought you said you had to run a self-diagnostic."

"I did," Lorelei's admitted, "but that's not *all* I did. I'm not an idiot, Ensign."

The AI blinked, and then announced to Nevel in a loud voice, "His calculations are correct, if not crude. The input parameters would have gotten the *Season of Plenty* there—albeit 160 million kilometers off course . . . *and* pathing through a brown dwarf."

The lieutenant commander frowned at Seinmann. "Ensign, report to the captain that the *Season of Plenty* is shipshape and awaits his orders."

Seinmann skulked off the bridge, but as he passed Ensign Indara, she whispered, "What about Cole? He's still working."

"Let him," Seinmann muttered and left.

A moment later the order came through the bridge intercom to transition to slipspace.

The bridge officers remained busy for the five hours until the shift change, and it was only then that Lieutenant Commander Nevel noticed Crewman Apprentice Cole still working at an auxiliary workstation.

"Crewman, what precisely are you doing?"

Cole looked up; his eyes were ringed with fatigue. When he saw Nevel he immediately stood at attention. "Sir, finishing the slipstream space calculations Ensign Seinmann ordered me to double-check."

The lieutenant commander's face contorted with anger, disgust, and finally a hint of amusement. "Very good"—his gaze fell onto the name tag of Cole's jumpsuit—"Crewman Cole. I'll take it from here. Dismissed."

"Yes, sir." Cole gathered his tools and left the bridge.

Nevel chuckled and retrieved Cole's data pad—then halted, gazing intently at its contents.

He moved to Lorelei's station. "Did you help the crewman with this?"

The data pad flickered as Lorelei interfaced. "No." The AI paused for a full half second. "How intriguing. It is indeed a Shaw-Fujikawa manifold calculation, but it uses a method I have never before encountered."

"Is it correct?"

"Yes . . . even good . . . for a crude approximation. But highly impractical. It would take far too long for a human to implement such a method, and I have far superior algorithms at my disposal."

Nevel looked again at Cole's equations. "But let me get this straight—this *crewman* actually came up with a *new* way of calculating input parameters?"

"That is correct."

Lieutenant Commander Nevel traced his fingers over the multidimensional, imaginary-space calculus on the data pad. "Hmm." His face hardened. "Find Ensign Seinmann and have him report to the bridge. I need to remind him of the level of mathematical expertise we expect of our officers on the *Plenty*."

Letter from Crewman Apprentice Preston Cole to his brother, Michael James Cole, October 16, 2489 (Military Calendar)

Mike,

So much is going on, I just have time for a quick note. They keep me twice as busy on the *Season of Plenty* as I was back home—even during calving season, and I'm trying to learn *everything* I can, all at once. This is exactly where I want to be. Where I was meant to be.

And some of the people that we take to the colonies! Most were rich back on Earth. Many have PhDs. But they're risking everything to become blacksmiths and herd sheep and throw themselves out into the great unknown. It's inspiring.

I want to get out there and be a part of this, too. You and Molly should join me one day. Dad would bust an artery if he heard me say that, so don't tell him. Or would he be proud?

The only problem I'm having is with some of the crew—they aren't as easy for me to figure as a math problem. I'm getting along, mostly. I just don't understand some of the junior officers. I'm glad I don't have to. That's one of the advantages of being a crewman apprentice: we just do what we're told.

More soon,

P.J.

{Excerpt} Bi-annual Personnel Review of CMA *Season of Plenty* / November 27, 2489 (Military Calendar)

Junior Officer Summation (continued)

Ensign Handford, W. (UNSC Service Number: 00786-31761-OM)

Average performance

Ensign Indara, A. (UNSC Service Number: 00801-46332-XT)
Above average performance
Requested management training (Series 7). Request granted.

Ensign Seinmann, O. (UNSC Service Number: 00806-95321-PG)
Above average performance
Promotion to Lieutenant Junior Grade
Transferred to the CMA *Laden*.

Additional:

RE: Crewman Apprentice Cole, P. J. (UNSC Service Number: 00814-13094-BQ)

Shows aptitude for history and mathematics. Suggested by Lt. Commander Nevel *and* the ship's AI, Lorelei, that he would be a superior applicant for the Academy at Mare Nubium (aka Luna Officer Candidate School).

One week temporary assignment to Luna, pending entrance examination results.

ANALYSIS

It was the end of the Golden Age of human colonization. As of 2494 CE it was still a time of peace and prosperity, but Earth had begun to overreach its logistical ability to control her colonies. Several factors led to the destabilization of the more distant, or as later called, "Outer" Colonies.

1. There were widely varying standards for recruitment to the Outer Colonies. "Colonization contractors" were more interested in staking claims to valuable resource rights than

providing the most-skilled personnel. Some people were illegally conscripted, and others were law-breakers granted pardons if they agreed to go—all of which led to these colonists being less than absolutely loyal to Earth.

2. Some colonists struck out on their own, procuring by legal or illegal means transport to farther-flung worlds, partially or wholly outside Earth's control.
3. Continued taxes, levies, and restricted trade practices by the CMA increased friction as the Outer Colonies received only a fraction of the benefits they were taxed for.

The situation was a problem of physical as well as psychological dimensions. Mathematically the volume of the sphere increases as its radius cubed, and so the number of Outer Colonies grew. Given such a numerical advantage and the fact that they encapsulated the Inner Core worlds, there was the belief that Earth and her close colonies were literally *surrounded* by increasingly hostile forces.

Many now think this was a skewed perception, and that given diplomacy and enough time, Earth and her Inner Colonies could have established more harmonious relationships with her farther-flung cousins. Others point out, however, that had there been no military action, the Outer Colonies might have risen to power and threatened the core worlds at the *worst possible moment* in human history.

All theoretical analysis aside, the United Earth government and her colonies developed new policies and an increased military presence that would provoke further unfortunate responses from the Outer Colonies . . . and lead to an undeclared Civil War.

For that, Earth would need more ships and crews . . . and officers to lead them.

SECTION THREE: LUNA OFFICER CANDIDATE SCHOOL (2489–2493 CE)

Cole's academic record at the Academy at Mare Nubium speaks for itself. He graduated magna cum laude with high degrees of excellence and specialization from the Rutherford Science Magistrate. Apart from minor hazing incidents, and the usual swept-under-the-rug blemishes that are on any cadet's record . . . there is only one incident of particular note.

During Cole's junior year, there was a series of incidents with Admiral Konrad Volkov's daughter: her overnight disappearances from family officers' quarters located on base, sightings of the young lady in the company of a young man, and the biological consequences of these liaisons.

The scandal culminated publicly when six cadets were brought before a Board of Inquiry.

{Excerpt} Transcription of Cole, P. J. (UNSC Service Number: 00814-13094-BQ) testimony before Board of Inquiry, Academy at Mare Nubium
JAG Incident Report (local) 475-A \ June 7, 2492 (Military Calendar) \ Log (video, spatial, psychological enhancement= TRUE)
FILE *SEALED* (UNSC-JAG ORD: 8-PD-3861), June 13, 2492 (Military Calendar)

Seated Board of Inquiry: Colonel Mitchell K. Lima (UNSC Service Number: 00512-5991-IX), Captain Maria F. Gilliam, JAG officer in residence (UNSC Service Number: 00622-7120-RJ), Frank O. Welker (Civilian Liaison to the Academy at Mare Nubium, Civilian ID#: 8813-316-0955-G)

[Crewman Apprentice Preston. J. Cole is sworn in before the Board.]

COLONEL LIMA: State your name for the record.

CREWMAN COLE: Cole, Preston J., sir.

CAPTAIN GILLIAM: Tell us, Cadet, where exactly you were between 1900 and 2300 hours three days ago?

[Cole remains standing at attention and stares up and to the right. Since Cole is right-handed this indicates he is accessing the visual memory portion of his brain (and not lying).]

COLE: I was on watch duty on Shadow Perimeter Three with Cadets Parkins, Haverton, and Tasov, ma'am.

MR. FRANK O. WELKER: Describe "Shadow Perimeter Three" for me, Cadet.

COLE: Yes, Mr. Welker. Shadow Perimeter Three is the colloquial term used for the series of tunnels and surface tubes that run across the Mare Nubium, connecting the Academy to the civilian sectors of Asimov Center. The "shadow" part of the name comes from the shadows cast from the nearby crater walls.

WELKER: Why guard that particular section?

[Cole's eyes now lock forward.]

COLE: I was ordered to do so.

GILLIAM: Cadet, speculate as to the reason required for guarding Perimeter Three.

COLE: Yes, ma'am. There are two reasons. First, we always maintain a guarded perimeter against unauthorized civilian incursions on Academy grounds. Second, there have been recent reports of unauthorized military personnel and supplies moving into the civilian territories.

[The five other cadets who await questioning in the tribunal chamber shift in their seats.]

LIMA: Do you know of any such unauthorized crossing of our military personnel?

COLE: I have not read of any such occurrences in the incident report, sir.

LIMA: That was not my question.

[Cole pauses, looks straight down.]

COLE: I have never seen any such incidents, sir. If I had I would have attempted to stop them from occurring. If I could not, I would have immediately reported it and been required to make a note of it in the incident log.

[Gilliam leans forward and removes her glasses.]

GILLIAM: You say "never seen," but have you heard rumors or otherwise received any indication of such illegal base crossing on or off your watch?

[Cole swallows, eyes back up, staring past Captain Gilliam.]

COLE: I cannot substantiate any rumors I may or may not have heard, ma'am. I have insufficient evidence to do so.

LIMA: I'm going to remind you once, Cadet, and only once, that obstructing any military investigation is a serious offense that carries a minimum of five years of hard labor.

[Cole gives no response.]

LIMA: I am now ordering you, Cadet, to tell me *everything* you know about any military personnel crossing the perimeter the evening of the twenty-fifth—or any tampering with security devices or recordings of the region during that time—or *any* detail of *anything unusual* that evening.

[Cole inhales deeply, looks directly at Colonel Lima.]

COLE: Sir, no. Nothing . . . unusual.

[Captain Gilliam, Mr. Welker, and Colonel Lima confer among themselves.]

[Cole remains standing at attention.]

GILLIAM: If you are trying to protect a fellow cadet through some sense of camaraderie or honor—it is misplaced. Do not throw away your otherwise sterling service record to protect someone who, to be blunt, does not deserve to be an officer.

[At this time, Admiral Konrad Volkov enters the room and sits.]

[Cole faces the tribunal and cannot possibly see the admiral, but nonetheless stands straighter and begins to sweat.]

COLE: Sir, what kind of officer would I make if I said what you wanted me to say just to avoid trouble—regardless of whether it is the truth or not? Or if I guessed at any wrongdoing to make myself look better? I will not do such a thing.

LIMA: Crewman Cole, you are in contempt of this Board of Inquiry. I'll deal with you later.

[Colonel Lima motions for the court guards. The guards move to escort Cole.]

[Cole salutes the presiding officers, turns, makes direct eye contact with Admiral Volkov, and is marched from the tribunal chamber.]

Certificate of Marriage

The State of Mare Nubium County of Newton

To any Judge, Justice of the Peace, or Minister:

You are hereby authorized to join:

Preston Jeremiah Cole, age 21, and Inna Volkov, age ■■

In the Holy State of Matrimony according to the Constitution of Luna Confederated States and for so doing shall be your License. And you are hereby required to return this License to me with your Certificate herein of the fact and date of Marriage within thirty days after said Marriage.

Given under my hand and seal this 17 August, 2492.

Quinn Lloyd (Licensing Officer, Newton County), Ordinary.

CERTIFICATE

I Certify that Preston Jeremiah Cole and Inna Volkov were joined in Matrimony by me this Seventeenth day of August, Two Thousand Four Hundred Ninety-Two.

Recorded 21 August, 2492.

In presence of Witnesses:

Michael H. Cole

Admiral Konrad Volkov

Behold by my hand and with my seal, Harold Yates, Ordinary.

Certificate of Live Birth

The State of Mare Nubium Department of Health

Certificate No: 4216

Child's Name: Ivan Troy Cole

Date of Birth: December 12, 2492 Hour of Birth 0445

Sex: Male

City, Rural Plot, or Station of Birth: Azimov Center

County of Birth: Newton

Mother's Maiden Name: Inna Volkov

Mother's DNA Trace: ██████████

Father's Name: Preston Jeremiah Cole

Father's DNA Trace: SUY-OOU-WYED

Date Filed by Registrar: December 16, 2492

This copy serves as prima facie evidence of the fact of birth in any court proceeding {HRS 550-45(b)}

ANY ALTERATIONS INVALIDATE THIS CERTIFICATE

ANALYSIS

Colonel Lima dropped his charges of contempt and obstructing the tribunal's investigation against Preston Cole two days after the inconclusive hearing.

The record shows Cole married Admiral Volkov's daughter, indicating (at first glance) that he was the cadet who had the illicit liaison.

But why would Admiral Volkov allow such a cadet to marry his daughter instead of having him summarily thrown out an airlock?

DNA analysis of Ivan Volkov (done at the request of the admiralty and codeword classified: NIGHTINGALE) provides incontrovertible evidence that he was *not* Preston Cole's son.

There are three possible explanations for these facts.

1. The admiral knew which cadet was the true father and didn't like what he saw. He found a suitable replacement for his daughter: a cadet who would stand up for his principles even if that meant going to jail.
2. The child's DNA did not match any suspected cadets or

other military personnel (civilians transferring to and from Luna were not required to provide DNA samples in their CMA screenings). This would have left the admiral's grandchild still fatherless.

3. Cole was indeed the cadet who had the liaison with the admiral's daughter, but not the father of her child.

Many questions, however, central to understanding Cole remain unanswered. Did Admiral Volkov make him marry his daughter or did Cole—compelled by a sense of chivalry—offer to marry the disgraced young lady and provide a father for her unborn child?

Cole's admirers would say that he stepped up and did the noble thing: a young man with a sense of honor and morality (regardless of any possible indiscretions).

Cole's detractors, though, would claim this incident highlights his strategic and opportunistic nature: a cunning junior officer currying favor with the admiral at his most vulnerable moment, which would result in rapid promotion and assignment to choice (if remote) postings.

Or could it have been a little of both?

Whatever the reasons, Cole remained married to Inna for many years thereafter, fathering two more sons and one daughter (DNA analysis proves these were his), and he remained a loving father to all four children, writing to them often, and providing birthday gifts and support to them for the rest of his life.

After a two-week honeymoon, Cole was reassigned for duties in the Outer Colonies aboard the UNSC destroyer *Las Vegas*.

SECTION FOUR: THE OUTER COLONY INSURGENCY: THE *CALLISTO* INCIDENT (2494 CE)

For decades prior to the end of the Colonial era (c. 2490 CE) Earth-based military forces had focused on colonization logistics, settling minor trade disputes, and perhaps chasing off the odd pirate. UNSC officers had studied how to engage in glorious, large-scale (but as yet hypothetical) battles against enemy states—not how to cope with an emboldened insurgency that could hide in the very populations they were sworn to protect.

One event in particular (among a dozen similar incidents in the Outer Colonies), the Callisto *Incident would shape Preston Cole's early career.*

The distant colony Levosia had been suspected of diverting refined selenium and technetium (used in the manufacture of FTL drives), which would yield huge profits on the black market.

Apart from lost taxes, however, Earth realized it could not allow insurgent forces access to FTL engine components. Therefore, Central Command (CENTCOM) ordered the Navy to blockade and search all ships in the system for suspected contraband.

The UNSC corvette Callisto *stopped and boarded a trading vessel. The merchant crew was skittish due to rumors of impressments during similar searches in the Outer Colonies (a rumor started, we suspect, by insurgent sympathizers). A weapon was drawn and shots exchanged, resulting in the death of three naval officers and twenty-seven merchant crewmen.*

No contraband was discovered.

This sparked outrage throughout the system. Thirty-seven days later, the Callisto *ordered a similar merchant vessel to stand to and be searched. The merchant ship allowed the officers to board with all due courtesies. When the officers entered the cargo bay, they found it empty. The bay doors opened and the officers were blasted into space. The merchant crew then swarmed into the unsuspecting* Callisto *and murdered the remainder of the its crew.*

The Callisto *was taken and its computer system gutted and replaced.*

The insurgency was now armed.

In response, a UNSC battle group of three light destroyers was sent to hunt down the Callisto. *They had weapons that had never been fired in conflict, nor had her crews engaged in any battle.*

Leading the battle group was the UNSC destroyer Las Vegas *under Captain Harold Lewis, with a new assistant navigation officer fresh out of Luna OCS, Second Lieutenant Preston J. Cole.*

0315 HOURS, MARCH 2, 2494 (MILITARY CALENDAR) \ UNSC DESTROYER *LAS VEGAS* PATROLLING 26 DRACONIS SYSTEMBRIDGE LOG OF THE UNSC *LAS VEGAS* (PRIMARY, VIDEO, SPATIAL ENHANCEMENTS=TRUE)

The bridge of the UNSC *Las Vegas* was a narrow oval of nav, ops, engineering, comm, and weapons stations. Green and blue icons winked on and off, illuminating the faces of the officers, while the shadows around them were full of the red glow of battle station lights.

Captain Lewis sat on the edge of his seat, nervously scraping his thumbnail. The first mate, Commander Rinkishale, stood near, her cap snug on her head, and lines of concern crisscrossing her face.

"Update on target vector," Captain Lewis said.

"Still decelerating, sir," Second Lieutenant Cole answered. His close-cropped hair spiked up with stubborn cowlicks. His gaze was cold iron and only the faintest lines creased the corners of his eyes as he squinted at the screen. Without looking away, he tapped in a double-check calculation of what the nav computer displayed. "Enemy on a direct course *into* the asteroid field."

"We have to engage before they get in," Commander Rinkishale told the captain. "We'll be able to maneuver around a few rocks, but too far into that field . . ."

"And they'll be able to play cat and mouse with us," the captain replied. He tapped in a message on his secure comm to the destroyers in his battle group.

Immediate replies scrolled across his screen.

"The *Jericho* and *Buenos Aires* concur," Captain Lewis said. "So we go hunting. Set course to intercept the *Callisto*," he ordered Lieutenant Cole. "Flank speed."

"Answering 030 by 270, sir," Cole said.

"Reactor answering one hundred percent," Lieutenant Taylor replied.

The *Las Vegas* accelerated and the bridge crew crunched in their padded seats as the *Callisto* grew on the central view screen.

"She's slowing, sir," Cole announced.

"Because they have to navigate through the field," the captain muttered. "What in God's name do they think they're doing?" He turned to the weapons station and Lieutenant Jorgenson. "Range?"

"In twenty seconds, sir," Lieutenant Jorgenson replied. "Firing solutions online for Ares missile system. The target might bank around that larger asteroid at the edge of belt, but we have a lock. The missile tracking systems can steer around."

"In twenty, then," Captain Lewis said and started scraping his thumbnail again. "Coordinate firing solutions with the *Jericho* and *Buenos Aires*, and allow computer control to fire at will—silos one through six."

Cole shot a quick glance at Lieutenant Jorgenson, who

looked back at him and gave an almost imperceptible shake of her head.

"Arming silos one through six, aye," Jorgenson replied. She opened the button covers and flipped off the safety mechanisms for six of the seven banks of missiles in the *Las Vegas*'s arsenal. She activated the automated control systems. Green acknowledgment lights winked across the board.

"They're a sitting duck," Captain Lewis said with great satisfaction.

Cole stared at the automated control system, the lines about the corners of his eyes deepened, and he frowned.

EXTERNAL CAMERA 6-K, UNSC DESTROYER *JERICHO* / 0317.235 HOURS MARCH 2, 2494 (MILITARY CALENDAR)

Eighteen Ares missiles streaked silent through space, leaving feathered plumes of gray smoke behind. For twenty seconds they remained on course tracking the *Callisto*. The enemy vessel moved on a vector directly aligned with an asteroid the size of Manhattan.

The *Callisto* then rolled, her engine cones flaring white hot, as she executed a slingshot orbit to the far side of the cratered rock.

The missiles split their unified trajectories, each one independently optimizing the best targeting solution, and left eighteen smoky trails that looked like giant fingers reaching out into the dark . . . as if clutching the asteroid.

They never hit.

For the blink of an eye a new sun appeared in the 26 Draconis system.

A wash of white filled the screen . . . which coalesced to a boiling center of ultraviolet.

A nuclear device had been buried in the asteroid, facing

outward. It blasted the rock apart, vaporized and shattered iron and ice, and spewed forth a shower of molten metal and plasma—a tide of destruction that rushed into the UNSC battle group.

It hit the *Buenos Aires*, which had been leading the charge. Her antennae and MAC trajectory sensors boiled away . . . as the cloud enveloped her in seething energies . . . from which she did not emerge.

A chuck of spinning rock hit the *Las Vegas*—a glancing blow, but enough to crumple her side and bend the ship's hull twenty degrees—she careened backward, venting atmosphere from a dozen ruptured decks.

A cloud of tiny molten fragments hit the *Jericho*—eventually killing all forward momentum, until she spun slowly backward in space, lights winking on and off.

Camera 6-K spun as well—but in the distance still tracked the prow of the *Callisto*—unscathed as it angled out of the plane of the asteroid field, and turned toward them.

A chunk of iron-silicate rock appeared for a split second in the field of view—moving directly into camera 6-K.

Static.

EXTERNAL CAMERA 6-K FEED TERMINATED

0329 HOURS MARCH 2, 2494 (MILITARY CALENDAR) \ UNSC DESTROYER *LAS VEGAS* PATROLLING 26 DRACONIS SYSTEM BRIDGE LOG (PRIMARY, VIDEO, SPATIAL ENHANCEMENTS=TRUE)

Shards of shatterproof plastic tumbled through the air on the bridge. Captain Lewis, tethered to his chair, hung, arms limp. One emergency light burned and tinged everything bloodred. Commander Rinkishale's body twisted at unnatural angles, floating, and in the strange light looked like an insect trapped in amber during its death throes.

The only stations active were nav, comm, and one winking panel on the otherwise static-filled weapons station.

Second Lieutenant Cole remained at his station, belted in to his seat, his legs wrapped around the pedestal for good measure. His hands flew over the nav controls, checking and rechecking.

"*Buenos Aires* destroyed, sir," Cole reported, his voice cracking. "I'm reading a debris field along her last reported vector. There's too much radiation . . . but I think the *Jericho* has come about to engage the *Callisto.* Reading multiple missile locks. I'm not sure from whom."

Second Lieutenant Cole waited for his orders.

And he waited.

He then turned and looked . . . and saw his dead captain and commander . . . and the rest of the motionless bridge crew.

He unbuckled himself and moved to each checking for vitals—finding only Lieutenant Jorgenson still breathing, and quickly tying a tourniquet above her bleeding calf.

He tapped the comm station, cleared his voice, and said, "Any medical personnel, any fire teams on decks four, five, or six—report to the bridge." He looked about once more, taking the carnage in, and then added, "*Any* crewmen who can get up here, do so immediately."

From the flickering weapons station a shrill alarm sounded, confirming missile lock on the *Las Vegas.*

Cole yelled into the comm, "All hands brace for impact! All crew brace—"

The bridge shuddered.

For a split second the air condensed into fog, then explosive decompression blasted out the atmosphere.

BRIDGE LOG OF THE UNSC *LAS VEGAS* (PRIMARY, VIDEO, SPATIAL ENHANCEMENTS=TRUE) / TERMINATED
0332.091

0348 HOURS MARCH 2, 2494 (MILITARY CALENDAR) \ UNSC DESTROYER *LAS VEGAS* PATROLLING 26 DRACONIS SYSTEM CAPTAIN'S LOG (AUDIO)

{TRANSFER CONTROL CODES ENABLED PER MIL JAG ORDER TR-19428-P}

Captain Lewis and Commander Rinkishale are dead. The rest of the bridge crew are either incapacitated or dead.

I, Second Lieutenant Cole, Preston J. (UNSC Service Number: 00814-13094-BQ), do hereby assume command of the UNSC destroyer *Las Vegas* and responsibility for the actions detailed henceforth.

Emergency bulkheads are in place on the bridge and the additional breaches on decks one through eight and eleven through fourteen have been contained. Decks sixteen and seventeen remain evacuated and cannot be repaired.

The Shaw-Fujikawa drive is offline. Primary and secondary reactors are offline. There was a major spike in the primary system. Radiation containment protocols are in effect.

We are dead in space.

I have been trained to follow the rules and regulations and enforce our laws.

And even when I broke those rules—it has been to uphold a higher honor.

Now I am faced with a choice: Break those rules, discard

honor, or lose. No—this has nothing to do with winning or losing. I must break the rules and my honor or die. Or all the crew will die.

With so many lives at stake, I have no choice.

I have ordered our missile silos' doors shut.

I have signaled our unconditional surrender to the insurgent-controlled ship *Callisto* and requested immediate aid for our wounded.

They won't be able to resist the prize of a UNSC destroyer. They won't fire. They'll answer the distress signal.

END ENTRY CAPTAIN'S LOG \ UNSC *LAS VEGAS*

EXTERNAL CAMERA A-4, UNSC DESTROYER *LAS VEGAS* \ 0406.335 HOURS MARCH 2, 2494 (MILITARY CALENDAR)

Callisto's prow approached the port side of *Las Vegas* and slowed to a full stop five kilometers away—with her missile silo doors open.

After three full minutes *Callisto* moved closer and turned so that the two ships were abeam: Cargo Bay 5 on the port side of the *Las Vegas* aligned with Cargo Bay 3 on the starboard side of *Callisto*.

Robotic tethers reached from *Callisto*, groping over the crumpled armor of the *Las Vegas*, until they found purchase.

The arms pulled the *Las Vegas* within a few meters. A hard docking collar extended from the *Callisto*—large enough for three trucks side by side to roll across—and fitted to the side of the *Las Vegas*.

Orange safety lights strobed along the passage as the seal was established, the interior pressure equalized, and the links locked and checked.

Incoming comm on alpha channel from *Callisto*: Las Vegas, *prepare to be boarded. Offer no resistance and we will evacuate your injured to Lawrence Space Station. Any tricks and we open fire.*

Comm (alpha channel): *This is* Las Vegas. *Understood. None of my crew will fire.*

A moment passed and then more strobe lights flickered along the *Callisto*'s flank, indicating her cargo bay doors opening.

A second shudder traveled the length of the docking passage—from the *Las Vegas* into *Callisto.*

On the port side of *Callisto* explosions blossomed outward from *inside*, obliterating her midsection from decks fourteen to three. Armor plates and bodies tumbled into vacuum . . . along with plumes of gray-green reactor coolant.

Both ships spun out of control.

The docking passage between the destroyers strained and twisted—and the connection snapped.

Atmosphere continued to pump out of *Las Vegas*'s bay, propelling her farther from the now crippled *Callisto.*

The armor on the aft quarter of *Callisto* glowed dull red as her fusion reactor and secondary fission reactor ran rampant and melted.

Thrusters on the *Las Vegas* puffed so she matched the pitch and roll of the enemy vessel . . . but turned so her prow faced the enemy's obliterated midsection.

Missile silo doors on *Las Vegas* opened.

Transmission (alpha channel): *This is* Las Vegas. *You are ordered to immediately seal missile doors and open Security Port 347 and allow our computer to take control of your vessel. Comply—or I will blast your ship in two.*

ANALYSIS

The UNSC was not prepared for brutal ship-to-ship combat in the early years of the insurgency. The light destroyer class, for example, had none of the armament one recognizes as standard today. The titanium-A armor and magnetic accelerator cannons, however, would soon be developed as industrial priorities shifted from building . . . to killing.

More problematic, however, was the application of those new technologies to three-dimensional battles in the vacuum of space.

The use of nuclear weapons in the battle with *Callisto* was not expected. It was believed that fissile detonations in space were nearly useless. Such detonations are extremely low-yield and produced reduced electromagnetic pulse effect in a vacuum environment (very little bang for the buck, as they say).

But the fact that the insurgency *knew this* and had planted a nuclear device ahead of time in an asteroid that provided the reactive mass to outright destroy one UNSC ship and cripple two more was an astonishingly forward piece of military thinking.

More amazing, however, was Cole's tactical leap of insight. UNSC officers and merchant men of the era had a near-religious reverence for Common Space Law—most especially pertaining to rendering aid to vessels in distress. The fact that Cole faked a distress signal to lure his opponent closer was both a stroke of genius and a breach of protocol so severe that UNSC CENTCOM dithered over whether to award him the Legion of Honor or have him court-martialed (ultimately, they did neither, to avoid difficult precedent). Cole's moral strategy was drawn from centuries of ambiguity in dealing with the idea of "enemy combatants" and inhabits a gray legal and ethical area, even in retrospect.

Emblematic of Cole's later tactical thinking, we see flexibility with regard to his ship's functional design. He had crewmen remove *Las Vegas*'s last Ares missile from its silo and transport it to Cargo Bay 5—where it could be fired *directly* into the enemy vessel at point-blank range, bypassing her external armor, and destroying her FTL drive and reactor coolant systems.

Cole noted later in his personal log that he would never again be able to send a distress signal in enemy territory. "No one would believe it," he stated. "Surrender, quite literally, is no longer an option for me."

The UNSC, the insurgency—all humanity had been awakened from complacency; we were evolving and learning how to fight again.

Cole was evolving as well, jettisoning antiquated ethical qualms—and learning to do whatever it took to win.

SECTION FIVE: THE OUTER COLONY INSURGENCY: THE *GORGON* V. THE *BELLICOSE* (2495–2504)

Cole was quickly promoted (although not without some protest) to first lieutenant and then commander and given a small corvette to patrol the Outer Colonies. After a dozen successful engagements in five years against insurgent forces and privateer fleets he was promoted to captain and received the honor of commanding the first heavy-destroyer-class vessel armed with a magnetic accelerator cannon (MAC), the UNSC Gorgon.

In Cole's personal logs he attributes his success more to luck than skill in battle, and he wonders if his rapid promotion was warranted. He also notes that insurgent atrocities may have greased the public relations aspect of his promotions.

Cole might have sensed part of the truth. The Navy had latched onto him as a figurehead to quell an unease percolating through the Inner Colonies. Many of the Inner Colonies were beginning to wonder if it was just to hold on so tightly to their Outer Colony cousins.

Earth needed a hero to distract its populace from an inconvenient moral confusion.

Meanwhile, the insurgency had learned how to hide, strategize, and terrorize as well. They had organized (by theft, customization of industrial vehicles, or by wholesale construction of their own ships) a sizable fleet.

Cole's record was not without its blemishes. In particular, the UNSC Bellerophon *(a frigate captured by the insurgency and renamed the* Bellicose*), engaged Cole thrice: escaping twice, and once, fighting him to a draw.*

Preston Cole's otherwise impressive military record did not come without a high personal cost.

Personal communiqué from Cole, Preston J. (UNSC Service Number: 00814-13094-BQ) to Volkov, Inna (Civilian ID#: 9081-613-7122-P) \ Routing Trace: UNITY 557 \ March 9, 2500 (Military Calendar)

Inna,

Your last letter caught me by surprise.

Is this how you truly feel? After all these years? A divorce?

I know your father would never pressure you into leaving me, so I have to assume this is how you feel, or that there is another person involved . . . or that it is somehow my fault.

Yes. That is it. It *is* my fault.

You never wanted a long-distance military marriage—and neither one of us expected to endure three extensions of my tour of duty. I cannot imagine how you must feel, so far away, with me in danger, not knowing if your husband will ever come back, and always having to wear a brave face for the military social elite that orbit your family.

I wish I could give this up and come home, be a husband for you, and a father for our children who are growing up not even knowing me, apart from the official broadcasts that are sent to Earth.

But the Navy needs me, too. Just by being here, I am saving lives . . . saving us all by stopping these border conflicts from flaring into full civil war.

Maybe you don't want to understand that, or can't. But I do. I have to stay.

I will always love you. I will always love the kids.

Please reconsider your decision.

I await your final word but I stand by my duty.

Ever yours,
Preston

0700 HOURS JUNE 2, 2501 (MILITARY CALENDAR) \ UNSC DESTROYER *GORGON* \ THETA URSAE MAJORIS SYSTEM BRIDGE LOG (PRIMARY, VIDEO, SPATIAL ENHANCEMENTS=TRUE)

Captain Cole did not sit in his padded chair on the raised center of the *Gorgon*'s bridge. Instead, he paced, stopped to glance over the shoulders of his officers at their stations, but otherwise kept moving like a shark.

Cole's temples were tinged gray. Where there had once been laugh lines, crisscrosses of concentration now crinkled his eyes. Other than these telltale signs of strain, however, he was the model of calm and thoughtfulness; confidence emanated from him like a magnetic field.

The UNSC *Gorgon* had engaged in two battles in the last seventy-two hours—so when it crossed paths with the insurgent-captured *Bellerophon*, the *Gorgon* had severely depleted munitions and a weary crew.

They battled the *Bellerophon* for the previous 34.7 minutes, peppering one another with Archer missiles, and then the *Gorgon* slung around a planetoid to come around at the proper angle for a killing shot.

It was a "kill" shot. There was no other possible outcome.

No ship had yet evaded the new magnetic accelerator cannon, which could accelerate a tungsten-alloy slug to a fraction of the speed of light.

A shudder ran through the *Gorgon* and a flash filled the main view screen, a blurred afterimage of glowing metal that faded into the infrared.

The *Gorgon*'s AI, Watchmaker, flickered upon his pedestal, a wizened old man holding a huge pocket timepiece with a dozen arms and dials.

"Time on target?" Cole demanded.

Watchmaker's eyes riveted upon his clock. "Six seconds to impact."

On the screen the fired MAC slug was visually enhanced so it glowed soft blue—its trajectory a flat line speeding toward the enemy.

"She's coming about—new course 030 by 090," Lieutenant Maliki, at Navigation, said. "Her reactors are past the red line."

The *Bellerophon*'s desperate acceleration to avoid destruction was useless, because for all practical purposes, compared to the MAC round, the ship stood still.

"Missile fire detected!" Lieutenant Betters, at weapons, announced.

"Won't do them any good," Maliki murmured. "At this extreme range we can pick off their missiles with the Helix system."

But the Archer missiles fired from the *Bellerophon* prematurely detonated—puffs of fire in the vacuum that made a dotted line in space . . . drawn straight from the *Bellerophon* to the *Gorgon*.

One distant explosion smeared across the black of space, however, and ever-so-slightly nudged the line representing the multi-ton ballistic projectile.

The blue line then closed on the silhouette of the *Bellerophon* . . . overlapped . . . and continued past the frigate.

"That's not possible!" Lieutenant Betters said, standing.

"It *is* possible," Cole said, "just not very likely."

"Ballistic tracking confirms," Watchmaker said. "We missed."

Lieutenant Maliki turned to face the captain. "They anticipated our firing the MAC, sir? How?"

"A guess," Cole replied staring at the view screen. "An educated guess, though, because we had the right angle on them. Still . . . incredibly lucky." Cole frowned. "And a brilliant defensive use of the last of their missiles."

"Not at all," Watchmaker quipped. "Those detonations were on a vector traced from the *Gorgon* to the *Bellerophon*. A reasonable estimation of the MAC trajectory and a precise gauge of distance." He snapped his watch shut.

"They can explain how they know so much about our MAC after we capture them," Betters remarked.

"And how do you propose we do that?" Cole asked. "Status, Lieutenant Maliki?"

"Archer missiles spent, sir," Maliki replied. "Except silo eight, per your standing order. No remaining MAC rounds. We have seven Pelicans on standby. The AAA Helix guns are spun up and hot."

Cole stared at the *Bellerophon* as the frigate slowly turned away.

"Incoming message," Watchmaker announced, ". . . from the '*Bellicose*.' Text only."

"To my station, Watchmaker." Cole settled into the captain's chair and turned the view screen so only he could see.

BELLICOSE: *I HEARD YOU'VE ALREADY USED YOUR NEW PEA-SHOOTER TWICE TODAY. SO THAT WAS YOUR THIRD AND LAST ROUND—UNLESS YOU'RE GOING TO LOAD UP ONE OF YOUR PELICANS IN THAT CANNON AND FIRE THAT AT ME?*

Cole stabbed his fingers into the keyboard, typing back:

GORGON: *YOU'RE OUT OF SHOTS, TOO. YOUR MISSILE SILOS ARE EMPTY.*
BELLICOSE: *I INVITE YOU TO TAKE A CLOSER LOOK.*

Captain Cole considered a moment and then tapped in ambiguously:

GORGON: *NOT LIKELY.*
BELLICOSE: *WELL PLAYED, PRESTON. WE'RE A GOOD MATCH. IF YOU EVER RETIRE FROM THE UNSC, YOU MIGHT CONSIDER WORKING FOR THE GOOD GUYS.*
GORGON: *PERHAPS YOU'D LIKE TO COME OVER HERE AND PERSUADE ME?*

A full fifteen seconds passed without reply, then:

BELLICOSE: *TEMPTING. BUT ANOTHER TIME, I THINK.*
GORGON: *I LOOK FORWARD TO IT.*

Cole slammed his fist on the arm rest, and yet there was a slight smile on his face.

The *Bellerophon* continued to turn and her engines flared to life as she moved off.

"Sir, we're *letting* them go?" Lieutenant Betters whispered. "That's the third time that ship has escaped."

"Three times," Cole echoed. "Yes. But we'll cross paths with the *Bellerophon*—the *Bellicose*—soon enough. Next time we'll be ready for her."

Personal letter from Captain Preston Cole to his brother, Michael James Cole, September 4, 2501 (Military Calendar)

Michael,

We searched for the *Bellicose* in five systems, laid ambushes, but have yet to find the vessel. In the meantime, there have been more engagements, with two insurgent corvettes, and one merchant privateer that [redacted] as "significant strategic victories."

Not a word of that to anyone else, or these letters will end up so redacted they'll look like a zebra has thrown up on them. I'm positive ONI is reading this and watching the family . . . and indulging me in this bit of personal communication.

I'm sure the only reason my letters get to you at all is that we're both playing this *their* way.

This undeclared war has worn on me and my crew. Before I let the *Bellicose* become my Moby-Dick, I'm putting in to the Lambda Aurigae system on a backwater world called Roost for some long-overdue shore leave.

It's nice, like home . . . if there were red sand beaches in Ohio. It might make a decent base of operations for the *Gorgon* in this sector of the Outer Colonies.

I miss the kids and Inna. Still. Sixteen months since the divorce and I think it's all a nightmare. The hardest thing is not getting any replies from the kids. I've sent letters, but I think Inna burns them all.

Please try to get them a message: Tell them I love them.

—P

{Excerpt} Personal letter from Captain Preston Cole to his brother, Michael James Cole, March 12, 2502 (Military Calendar)

I was talking to Lyra about the *Gorgon*'s fusion reactor. (You remember her? She owns the bar on the beach? Got her PhD in nuclear engineering and moved here to fish and pour drinks? My kind of lady.)

Discussed nothing classified, just the generalities of plasma physics, and she came up with a way to boost our output by at least 5%.

I think we've all underestimated what kind of people come out to the Outer Colonies.

If things ever settle down, you and Molly should see for yourselves. I'm not saying leave the farm—just look.

{Excerpt} Personal letter from Captain Preston Cole to his brother, Michael James Cole, May 28, 2502 (Military Calendar)

That skirmish at Capella was too damned expensive. Thirty-two men and women lost. After so little insurgent activity for so long . . . I thought they'd given up.

I've gotten the okay from CENTCOM on Reach for a month of leave for me and the crew. What could they say? The *Gorgon* is going to be laid up that long in space dock getting patched up.

I'll be on Roost. No pressures. Some fishing. Some time with Lyra.

A little slice of paradise in all this purgatory.

Personal letter from Captain Preston Cole to his brother, Michael James Cole, November 9, 2502 (Military Calendar)

We got married, Michael. Pictures and video attached.

I'm sorry for the surprise. (Or maybe you've known this was coming for a long time, huh?) It was nothing fancy, just a ceremony on the beach performed by the local pastor.

Lyra is happy. She's pregnant, too.

God, I'm happy for the first time since I can remember. I feel like I've finally gotten a real second chance out here.

Even the insurgency seems to have finally calmed down. There've been just a few policing actions near Theta Ursae Majoris. Maybe this thing is finally coming to an end.

Classified communiqué from Admiral Harold Stanforth to Captain Preston Cole \ June 13, 2503 (Military Calendar)

UNITED NATIONS SPACE COMMAND TRANSMISSION 08871D-00
ENCRYPTION CODE: RED
PUBLIC KEY: FILE / ALBATROSS-SEVEN-LUCIFER-ZENO /
FROM: ADMIRAL HAROLD STANFORTH, COMMANDING OFFICER, UNSC LEVIATHAN / USNC SECTOR THREE COMMANDER/ (UNSC SERVICE NUMBER: 00834-19223-HS)
TO: CAPTAIN PRESTON COLE, COMMANDING OFFICER, UNSC *GORGON* (UNSC SERVICE NUMBER: 00814-13094-BQ)
SUBJECT: TROUBLE
CLASSIFICATION: EYES-ONLY (BGA DIRECTIVE)

This is bad, Preston. Sit down if you're standing.

There are new orders coming down from CENTCOM, and you're not going to like them: You're going to Reach.

Let me start with the hardest thing.

The woman you've been having a relationship with for the last seventeen months, one Lyrenne Castilla, is part of the insurgency. Hell, she's not a *part* of it; she's a high-ranking member—we think commanding one of their ships.

ONI has all the details. I've seen their intelligence reports, and I believe those usually-lying-through-their-teeth SOBs. They've been tracking her insurgent alter ego for a long time and just discovered her civilian identity.

It's simple: She's been playing you, Preston.

ONI is going to come after you, too, claiming that she's

been pumping you for classified ship patrol routes and technical information.

So here's how it's going to play out:

1. New orders are being transmitted in three hours from Reach CENTCOM.
2. You will be confined to quarters on the *Gorgon* with no access to communications until the Prowler *Edge of Umbra* arrives in system.
3. The *Umbra* will then transport you to Reach, where ONI will put you through the debriefing of your life.
4. After that—what happens is anyone's guess. I'll wager ONI can't court-martial unless they can prove you willingly collaborated, because they built you into a military genius superstar back home. But whatever they're going to do—it ain't going to be pretty.

I'm breaking regs and telling you this because I don't believe for a hot second you would have gotten yourself deliberately involved in this—or that you'd be stupid enough to divulge ship locations or technical secrets to some pretty girl.

You've got three hours. Find Lyrenne before ONI gets her. Bring her in yourself. That'll go a long way toward clearing your name and ending this.

Good luck.

Harold

Personal letter from Captain Preston Cole to his brother, Michael James Cole, July 6, 2503 (Military Calendar)

. . . to follow up on that last quick note, Michael. I need to let you know, in case things end up going badly.

Everything Stanforth said was true.

I got to the bar on Roost and Lyra was gone. Everything she

owned in our room had been taken—except one paper she left. It was a printout from a text-only exchange between the *Gorgon* and the captain of the *Bellicose*—something that happened two years ago. Lyra should have never known about it.

One part of that exchange she circled in red: "*We're a good match. If you ever retire from the UNSC, you might consider working for the good guys.*"

It was a souvenir. She was the captain of the *Bellicose*, Michael. All this time. Right under my nose.

Was she using me for information? That doesn't make sense. I never leaked any classified data. And the more I think of it—the insurgent fighting almost died out in the sector since we met.

So is Lyra a spy? Or someone like me? A ship captain who fell in love and wanted more than a life of fighting?

I have to find out, Michael. I have to find her.

—P

{Excerpt} UNSC After-Action Report: Battle Group Tango

AI-enhanced battle summation and casuality reports attached

PRELIMINARY: Battle Group Tango, comprising four heavy UNSC destroyers, engaged one insurgent-controlled frigate in the Theta Ursae Majoris system January 2, 2504 (Military Calendar). Two UNSC destroyers heavily damaged. Insurgent vessel known as the *Bellicose* (aka the UNSC *Bellerophon*) lost control, was caught in a gravitational pull of the gas giant (ref ID: XDU-OI-(1)), and lost with all hands.

ANALYSIS

History looks upon this time as an unfortunate (and perhaps inevitable?) misunderstanding between Earth and her colonies, but those of us fighting for the last decade also realize that it was the most amazing piece of blind fortune the human race has ever stumbled upon. Had we not been armed and learning how to fight in space . . . what would have happened in the years that followed, when we faced an enemy a hundred times worse?

Oblivion, no doubt.

For Preston Cole it was a time when he tempered his brilliance and flexibility into an implacable "do whatever it takes" fighting style, a time of ascendancy when his deeds propelled him (with the help of ONI's glorification campaign) into one of the most beloved public figures of our generation.

On a personal level, however, Cole lost the woman he loved, suffered, found a second chance at love—and lost it all again.

At the debriefing ONI officers read him the After-Action Report concerning the *Bellicose*. I can only believe they thought Cole actually colluded with her and this tactic was designed to break his spirit.

(*Note to self*: find these fool interrogators and transfer them to Kelvin Research Station on Pluto.)

And it did break Cole, but not in the way the debriefing officers expected. For any other man would've given up everything *because* the lady in question was dead. For Cole, however, Lyra's honor had to now be preserved at all costs. Cole remained stoic and silent and utterly stubborn, just as he had when he was a cadet at the Academy at Mare Nubium. Even though he faced a court-martial for treason—even execution—he did the noble thing and kept his mouth shut.

Because of immense pressure from Admiral Stanforth and from Cole's admiring public, he was released (no charges filed), but given strict orders that the entire affair was classified.

So, the greatest hero of the age was sent back to Earth—to sit at a desk.

Cole would have stayed there for the rest of his life if the burgeoning civil war between Earth and her colonies had not been rendered irrelevant by the appearance of the Covenant.

SECTION SIX: THE COVENANT WAR: THE COLE CAMPAIGNS (2525–2532 CE)

Cole was promoted to rear admiral. He agitated for a reassignment that got him back to space (all requests were denied). He proposed new policies to make the UNSC fighting forces more effective against the insurgency (all ignored). After eight months at his desk job, he was quietly offered early retirement with an honorary skip promotion to vice admiral (which he accepted).

In the years that followed, Cole's star dimmed in the public eye, resurfacing for his highly publicized marriages to much younger women (each of which ended in even more spectacularly publicized divorces).

Cole's liver failed from cirrhosis on May 11, 2525, and was subsequently replaced—as were his damaged heart and worn endocrine system—by flash-cloned transplants.

Shortly thereafter the Covenant encountered the human colony world Harvest. Only a handful of farmers managed to escape to warn the authorities. The Colonial Military Administration (CMA) sent a battle group to respond to the alien threat. They survived less than fourteen seconds before two of the three destroyers in the group were obliterated, and the remaining destroyer, the Heracles, *was forced to retreat.*

The Heracles *sensor logs showed an enemy with an overwhelming technological superiority. The CMA was placed under NavCOM for the duration of the conflict and effectively absorbed into the UNSC. Central Command scrambled a fleet of more than forty ships of the line to respond . . . but they needed someone to lead that force.*

Why did they pick Cole?

In hindsight, this was a masterful choice. Preston Cole was a hero and a tactical genius and would be the only person to ever consistently win against Covenant during the long war that followed.

Many claim that without Cole, the Covenant would have carved a path through the Outer Colonies and conquered Earth within three years, and humanity would be a memory today. Others say that any person with the same military assets at their disposal had could have done the job, and perhaps done it better.

Cole was one thing our collection of "brilliant" admirals were not, however—a fallen hero who womanized and drank too much. If CENTCOM's plan to repel the aliens failed, he would have made an easy scapegoat.

I believe this last point is too convenient an explanation, however.

We had to win at Harvest. We were not going to pick someone solely for the sake of convenient explanations later.

No, there was something dark about Cole that appealed to our leaders. He had a proven stomach for carnage. Suicidal? Nothing so dramatic—but he did have a willingness to stare into the face of death, to sacrifice himself and any number of men and women and ships—and do so without flinching.

And that was precisely what we needed.

{Excerpt} Field Report ZZ-DE-009-856-841 Office of Naval Intelligence Reporting Agent: Lieutenant Commander Jack Hopper (UNSC Service Number: 01283-94321-KQ) \ November 2, 2525 (Military Calendar)

As ordered, Lieutenant Demos and I went to offer Vice Admiral Cole reinstatement to active duty and the job command of the fleet to retake Harvest.

The admiral's general state when we arrived on his doorstep was one of indifference. He answered the doorbell in his bathrobe and did not bother to return our salutes. He looked much older than I thought he would. His hair was silver and gray, as was his complexion. Gone was the spark in his eyes that I had seen in videos of this legendary man when I was a child. It was as if I'd found the ghost of Admiral Cole, and not the man.

He did, however, read the situation report with interest, not flinching when he got to the part about the *Heracles* and how easily the enemy destroyed her counterparts.

Demos suspects he was drunk—a supposition supported by several empty bottles of Finnish black vodka in his living room.

I believe Cole's mind is as sharp as ever, though. Everywhere on the premises there were stacks of books (real paper books) on military histories and naval battles and the biographies of Xerxes, Grant, and Patton—and theoretical mathematical monographs on slipstream space and other mathematical esoterica that frankly I had a difficult time even understanding the titles of (like *Reunification Matrices of Hilbert Fields Within Spiral Unbounded Singularities*).

After reading the situation report twice, the admiral poured himself a drink, and offered one to Demos and myself. For politeness's sake we took them.

Cole then said, "Three divorces, a cloned liver, two heart attacks—not much left of me, boys . . . Like anyone can help with this slice of Armageddon. But okay. I'm in."

He set aside his drink, untouched, and added, "I think you need me as much as *I* need this." He got up to get dressed.

When he emerged from his bedroom he was in uniform and

clean shaven—transformed from the shade of a man we had seen before. He seemed taller somehow, and tougher.

By reflex, I suppose, Demos and I stood at attention and saluted.

Cole took command—issuing orders, asking what capital ships were available, rattling off the specifics of the staff he wanted, AIs that he would need, and then requested *all* the intelligence reports ONI was holding back.

Just like you said he would.

Vice Admiral's Log (written) \ 1215 Hours November 15, 2525 (Military Calendar) \ UNSC cruiser Everest in slipstream space en route to REACH

I've digested the data from *Heracles* and the Chi Ceti Incident report.

The enemy has directed plasma weapons and a dissipative energy shield technology, the theoretical underpinnings of which our brightest can only guess at. The MAC rounds fired from destroyers *Arabia* and *Vostok* at Harvest had no effect. They didn't have time to launch nukes . . . so their use against these energy shields remains unknown.

My assessment: trouble.

I see the situation as if we are a horde of *Homo neanderthalensis* rushing toward a medieval castle. We will throw our sticks and stones against their unassailable fortifications—and they will rain hot death upon us with crossbow and boiling oil.

Will that analogy hold? Can I find a way to *tunnel* under those walls? Get inside and slaughter the enemy at close quarters?

I have to.

This first encounter with the aliens is a test—for them and us. So far we have failed that test. We have to show them that we cannot be so easily defeated. We have to win no matter the cost.

The super-heavy cruiser they have given me, *Everest*, is a supremely fine ship (although I already see a dozen modifications I wish to make to her). The crew is battle tested and razor sharp.

They believe in me.

God—I can see it in their eyes. They believe that *the* Admiral Cole is leading them into victory.

Maybe . . . but regardless, the truth of the matter is I will also be leading them straight into hell.

0120 HOURS MARCH 1, 2526 (MILITARY CALENDAR) \ UNSC CRUISER *EVEREST* \ FLAGSHIP BATTLE GROUP X-RAY \ EPSILON INDI SYSTEM BRIDGE LOG (PRIMARY, VIDEO, SPATIAL ENHANCEMENTS=TRUE)

Vice Admiral Cole paced the bridge of the *Everest*, followed by two adjutant commanders. The two dozen bridge stations were manned by officers and their assistants—all to coordinate the activities of the flagship and the thirty-nine other vessels comprising Battle Group X-Ray as they approached Harvest.

The colony world glowed blue and filled the view screens that stretched floor to ceiling in the cavernous command center.

Cole paused before a translucent screen the size of a blackboard, and with deft motions he zoomed back and forth through the spatial planes of this star system.

As the battle group descended below the planetary plane a blip appeared on screen.

"One ship," Cole murmured. He tapped the tactical display and the image enlarged.

The Covenant warship had sweeping organic curves, an odd purple phosphorescence, and was patterned with glowing red ovals and lines—the whole thing looked like a sleeping deep-sea creature of gigantic proportions.

"Two kilometers long, one wide," Cole said. "Energy readings off scale."

"Increase battle group velocity to three quarters full," Cole told one of his adjutant officers.

He pulled the perspective back on the tactical screen so Harvest was the size of a baseball, and then plotted a parabolic course past the enemy to slingshot around the world.

"Navigation inputs completed," Cole told the *Everest*'s AI.

Named Sekmet, the ship's AI's hologram was a lion-headed woman dressed in white Egyptian robes.

"Transmit burn vectors to the fleet," Cole ordered.

"Aye, sir," Sekmet answered, her cat eyes flashing green and gold.

Forty comets flared in the dark as the group accelerated toward the Covenant vessel parked in orbit over Harvest.

"Fire at will," Cole said. There was no emotion in his voice. He stared at the tactical board, watching and waiting.

MAC rounds streaked through space—strikes of molten tungsten alloy impacted the Covenant shields.

The veil of energy shook about the alien vessel and shimmered and resonated . . . but not a gram of metal touched its hull.

Hundreds of Archer missiles fired and filled the vacuum between the opposing forces—blanketing the enemy ship with fire and thunder . . . but not a shred of shrapnel scarred its surface.

Two curved lines on the Covenant flanks wavered and pulled free, oscillating through space.

They enveloped ships on either side of Battle Group X-ray.

Plasma tore through two meters of titanium-A armor like

a blowtorch through tissue paper. Explosions boiled through their interiors—blasting out the aft sections, blooming with white-hot secondary fusion detonations as reactors went supercritical . . . leaving smears of fire and burning dust where a moment before there had been two UNSC destroyers.

Officers scrambled to COM stations to relay reports from the fleet.

"Nukes have no effect on the vessel, sir," and one officer shouted.

"*Sacramento* is down, as is *Lance Held High*!"

Vice Admiral Cole remained impassive at his tactical board.

The Covenant ship fired again, plasma lines searing space, boiling titanium and steel, vaporizing the fragile flesh and bone contained within.

"The *Tharsis*, *Austerlitz*, and *Midway* destroyed. My God!!"

Cole squinted at the energy signatures oscillating on the display before him.

"*Campo Grande* is gone! The *Virginia Capes*, too."

"Sound the retreat," one officer screamed.

"Belay that order," Cole barked without looking up.

The fleet arced about the apogee of their parabolic course and engines flared as they came about the dark side of Harvest. The scattered debris of seven destroyers, however, continued on their previous trajectories, sparks and swirls of molten alloy that faded into the night.

Cole jotted down calculations . . . and frowned.

"Damage and casualty report, sir." One of his adjutant officers offered him a data pad.

Cole waved it away.

He leaned closer to his display and drew a curve, numbers scrolling alongside his line as it circled about Harvest—and intercepted the enemy vessel.

Cole nodded and finally glanced up.

His bridge officers looked to him and seemed to absorb some of the vice admiral's implacable self-possession.

"Open alpha FLEETCOM channel," he ordered.

"Open, sir."

"Accept new course inputs," Cole said. "Accelerate to flank speed. Ready another salvo of MAC rounds. Sekmet, we need an Archer missile solution on target 0.1 seconds after those MACs—then a second firing solution for a salvo of nuclear detonations 0.2 seconds after initial impact."

Sekmet blinked. "Understood, Admiral. Threading multiple processing and crosschecking matrices between fleet AIs. Working . . ."

Cole's hands came up in a gesture that seemed part contemplation and part prayer.

"Firing solutions acquired," Sekmet announced.

"Input solutions. Slave master-firing control to *Everest*, and lock," Cole ordered.

"How many of the Archers, sir?" the Chief Weapons officer asked. "How many Shivas?"

Cole glared at the man like he was crazy. "All of them, Lieutenant."

"Aye, sir. Solutions locked and ready to fire on your order."

Cole nodded and laced his hands behind his back. He studied the tactical board as Battle Group X-ray inched along their new trajectory.

The UNSC ships accelerated about the curve of Harvest, and the sun rose and blazed across the view screens.

The Covenant ship waited for them—plasma lines heating and flaring through space on an intercept course.

"Prepare to launch missiles," Cole ordered. There was steel

in his tone. "Release targeting and fire control of the MACs to Sekmet."

He watched as the deadly plasmas sped toward them.

"Initiate firing sequence—now!"

Dozens of rumbles shook *Everest.*

"Archer and Shiva missiles away, sir!"

Covenant plasma, so bright it seemed to ignite the black fabric of space, hit the fleet and burned the *Constantinople*, *Troy*, and melted the prow of the *Lowrentz.*

More than a thousand missiles left crisscrossing exhaust trails as they sped toward their target. The larger Shiva missiles fell behind the swarm.

Explosions spread throughout the fleet as new plasma ejected from the Covenant ship—destroying the *Maelstrom,* the *Waterloo,* and the *Excellence.*

"MAC system power at maximum," Sekmet announced. "Automatic firing sequence to commence in three seconds . . . two . . . one."

The remaining ships in Battle Group X-ray fired their magnetic accelerator cannons—twenty-seven simultaneous lightning strikes that flashed across space and struck the Covenant vessel.

The alien ship blurred behind its shields . . . opaque for a split second.

The Archer warheads hit, splashing fire and fury across the curve of her flank.

And then dozens of new suns ignited—a corona of man-made nuclear violence. It was a cloud of destruction that writhed and contorted and clawed at the enemy ship for a full three seconds as the UNSC group continued at flank speed toward their target.

"Alter course, sir?" a commander asked.

"Remain on target," Cole said.

And in a whisper so low that while was it picked up by the bridge log microphone, no one else could have possibly heard, Cole said: "*Fix bayonets.*"

The fleet hurled toward the inferno boiling about the alien ship.

The stern of the Covenant ship deformed—blasted outward as the interior shuttered and imploded, and ejected a double cone of blue-white hot plasma.

The bridge crew erupted into wild cheers.

"Course correction," Cole said. "Starboard group about to 060 by 030. Port group to 270 by 270."

"New course transmitted and acknowledged," Sekmet replied.

The fleet split and veered from the spreading fields of churning destruction.

"Bring us about to search for survivors," Cole ordered.

He closed his eyes, took in a deep breath, and then refocused on the tactical board. Cole touched an icon and watched as the names of destroyed vessels—and the thousands of men and woman who had served and died under his command—scrolled into view.

Classified communiqué from Vice Admiral Preston Cole to Admiral Harold Stanforth \ May 2531 (Military Calendar)

UNITED NATIONS SPACE COMMAND TRANSMISSION 102482-02
ENCRYPTION CODE: RED
PUBLIC KEY: FILE / VEGAS-ANACONDA-MOCKINGBIRD-ZERO /
FROM: VICE ADMIRAL PRESTON COLE, COMMANDING OFFICER UNSC EVEREST / (UNSC SERVICE NUMBER: 00814-13094-BQ)
TO: ADMIRAL HAROLD STANFORTH, USNC REGION ONE COMMANDER / REACH CENTCOM (UNSC SERVICE NUMBER: 00834-19223-HS)

SUBJECT: SAFEGUARDING NAVIGATION DATA – MORE THOUGHTS
CLASSIFICATION: SECRET (BGX DIRECTIVE)

Harold,

I've gone over this a dozen times: starting with our capture and interrogation of the alien creature my doctors are calling an "Elite" and ending with my tenuous conclusions and recommendations.

It doesn't make sense. My gut tells me the entire war hinges on something that we have overlooked.

First, and foremost, the Elite was xenophobic. The venom with which it spoke of humanity and its one desire—even as it bled out on the table—to find Earth and burn it to hot ashes . . . left zero doubt.

With that in mind, I still believe that safeguarding Earth's position is of vital importance. I plan to immediately implement the directives I drafted and sent to ONI for review, namely:

1. All UNSC and civilian ships that come into contact with alien assets must have nav computer network/AI erased—destroyed, if necessary—to prevent capture of core world locations.
2. ALL human vessels fleeing alien forces must do so on randomly generated vectors away from UNSC core worlds.
3. ONI Section II to begin slipstream space attenuation broadcast of prerecorded human carrier signals from antiquity to prevent triangulation of Earth.

But, like I said, some things about this do not add up.

First, I do not understand why the aliens DON'T know where Earth is. They have technology hundreds of years more advanced than ours. All one has to do to find Earth is stick a radio antenna into space and triangulate on the source. I suspect something is occurring within the Covenant hierarchy that has prevented Earth from being targeted, or perhaps appreciated . . . something our captured alien had no knowledge of.

Second, my recommendation for ONI to obfuscate the radio signature in slipstream space (directive 3) might be our best bet to keep rogue elements within the Covenant military from finding Earth and preemptively attacking. Considering the dangers of any energy manipulation in slipstream space, however, I'm going to need your support with Parangosky to use her assets in what she'll consider an "extreme-risk" operation.

Third, I need solid intelligence on the enemy. Do they seem to see us as some kind of religious aggressor . . . following some hitherto unknown ritual that accounts for them destroying our Outer Colonies before Earth? Or another possibility—an anthropomorphic gulf—that we have so many inhabited worlds, some more powerful militarily, economically than Earth—what if they're not interested in our *homeworld* strategically—but rather for some other, unknowable reason?

I can fight them, Harold, but only so effectively without knowing *why* they hate us.

I keep thinking of Sun Tzu: "If you know your enemies and know yourself, you will not be imperiled in a hundred battles; if you do not know your enemies but do know yourself, you will win one and lose one; if you do not know your enemies nor yourself, you will be imperiled in every single battle."

I look forward to your thoughts on this, my old friend.

Be well.

Preston

Personal log (audio), Vice Admiral Preston Cole, Commanding Officer UNSC *Everest* \ June 27, 2541 (Military Calendar)

Tonight a bottle of Capellan Vodka and I reviewed some of the old battles.

The Origami Asteroid Field in 2526—My fleet of one hundred seventeen UNSC ships of the line fought twelve Covenant vessels. We won that at the cost of thirty-seven ships.

Xo Boötis in 2528—Seventy ships versus eight Covenant. Another "victory." That time I lost thirty ships.

Groombridge 2530—Seventeen against three. We lost eleven destroyers. Still a win.

Leonis Minoris in 2537—only ten UNSC ships lost, but the Covenant glassed the other two colonies in system. God—I couldn't save them all; I had to make the choice.

Another twenty-three engagements (or was it twenty-four . . . does Alpha Cephei count?) like those over the past ten years . . . or is it fifteen? So much travel in slipspace. So much subjective time lost to damnable Heisenberg uncertainties and in cryosleep.

It's killing me . . . although I seem to have somehow, technically, lived through it all.

They told me to fight, and that's what I've done. Let historians sort through the wreckage, bodies, and broken lives to figure out the rest.

Yet, how many men and women have I had to watch die? How many would have perished on colony worlds if not for their sacrifice? I look into space and no longer see wonder and stars and the endless possibilities that I did when I was a cadet. I see nothing but a cold death.

I hope CENTCOM can see farther than I do and planned for all contingencies: including *not* winning this war.

If the unthinkable happens—Earth and her colonies reduced to ash as promised by that Covenant Elite—where can humanity escape to? Perhaps there are already plans in motion: a colony vessel en route to some secret distant world where we can start over.

So this sacrifice we endure has purpose.

ANALYSIS

Cole won every major engagement he committed his forces to against the Covenant. On only two occasions did he encounter an enemy fleet he considered too large to take, and then he would return in both cases with reinforcements—most notably at the Battle of Psi Serpentis (more on that fateful encounter in a moment).

The losses of ships and people under Cole's command were staggering. Any normal battle group would have been dismantled and reassigned, and their commander given some rest—but Cole was a victim of his own popularity. CENTCOM could not allow their symbol to fail, so they kept reinforcing Cole with new ships and crews—and kept their fingers crossed that he wouldn't snap from the strain.

Imagine fighting Stalingrad and Cold Harbor and defending the Hot Gates with three hundred Spartans and repelling the Mexican Army at the Alamo—and then having to repeat those lopsided, impossible fights over and over.

Certainly Cole knew this that first time he faced that Covenant super-destroyer at Harvest. His unheard remark on the bridge of *Everest*, "Fix bayonets," is a reference to Colonel

Joshua Lawrence Chamberlain's famous charge down Little Round Top at the battle of Gettysburg.

Chamberlain had orders to defend the far left end of the Union line, and had repelled numerous assaults upon his position. When the Fifteenth Alabama regiment charged up the hill toward Chamberlain's exhausted and low-on-ammunition Twentieth Maine regiment, instead of falling back, Chamberlain ordered his men to "fix bayonets" and charge down the hill. That apocryphal moment is considered to have saved the line, the Union army at Gettysburg, and perhaps determined the entire outcome of the first American Civil War.

Likewise, Cole knew he *had* to win no matter the cost in ships or lives or even to his sanity. Because if he failed, the enemy would destroy entire worlds; millions and billions of lives were his sole responsibility.

Mere psychological analysis cannot reveal the nature of what could keep any man going under such never-ending pressure.

Certainly we see in that last personal log that Cole had reached the nadir of his spirits. All he needed was a push to send him to his end, a push which soon arrived—but from something he could never have foreseen.

SECTION SEVEN: THE COVENANT WAR: THE BATTLE OF PSI SERPENTIS (2543 CE)

{Excerpt} UNSC After-Action Report: Battle Group Sierra-3

AI-enhanced battle summation and causality reports attached.

Battle Group Sierra-3 engages Covenant in 18 Scorpii.

PRELIMINARY: Battle Group Sierra-3, comprising two UNSC destroyers and one cruiser engaged a Covenant CPV-class heavy destroyer in the 18 Scorpii System, March 6, 2543 (Military Calendar). The UNSC *Seattle* and *Thermopylae* sustained moderate damage, while the *Io* sustained heavy damage. Covenant vessel destroyed.

SUMMARY ADDENDUM: The Convenant ship inflected heavy damage and Sierra-3 group was unable to peel its shields. *Io*'s FTL drive was inoperative, so I faced a decision to fall back and save two destroyers, or fight and possibly lose all those ships. Reinforcements arrived when unknown friendly ships jumped in system. Additional firepower penetrated enemy shields.

Lead reinforcement ship's silhouette matched a thirty-year-old UNSC frigate design with major modifications (see technical reports attached). Passive transponder pinged and yielded a ship reg. number, identifying the UNSC *Bellerophon*. Friendlies jumped out-system before comm contact established.

CAPTAIN'S NOTE: I don't believe in ghost ships. But I don't care if it is the *Bellerophon*, or if it was the Flying Dutchman sent by Lucifer himself—they saved our hides. Transmitted thanks to them before they jumped out and wished them well . . . whoever they were, and wherever they were headed.

SECTION PREFATORY REMARKS

I start this section with the Sierra-3 After-Action Report as it was the catalyst for what happened next (or so I believe).

Cole had to have seen the report. He was in charge of military operations in Sector Three, and a man of his exacting detail would not let a report—a report of a UNSC victory no less—pass his desk without a glance.

Cole's analytical mind likely came to two possible explanations for the sighting of the Bellerophon, *aka* Bellicose. *(1) The* Bellerophon *was incorrectly identified. Or (2) the* Bellerophon *escaped or faked falling into the gravity well of a gas giant and its subsequent destruction twenty-nine years prior.*

The captain of the Bellicose, *clever enough to face Cole thrice in battle and live, might have been able to engineer such a deception (although an in-atmosphere FTL jump while accelerating was only a theoretical possibility at that time).*

And given the ONI revelation in 2503 of the public identity of the Bellicose*'s insurgent captain, it also makes perfect sense that she would want to drop off their radar in such a permanent and unequivocal fashion.*

But why would Bellicose *rescue Sierra-3? Had the remnants of the Outer Colony insurgency resurfaced to unite with their former enemy to face a greater threat?*

Or was Lyra Castilla's reason personal? Did she reappear to send a message to Cole? Or am I stretching the limits of my analysis with romanticism?

That we will never know.

Cole's personal logs cease after February 2533. His normal pattern of behavior also altered—nothing overtly suspicious, and all within the prerogative of a vice admiral—but as we will soon see, seemingly innocuous actions and orders would culminate in the momentous death of Preston Cole.

Restricted communiqué from Vice Admiral Preston Cole to REACH LOGISTICS \ March 9, 2543 (Military Calendar)

UNITED NATIONS SPACE COMMAND TRANSMISSION 116749-09
ENCRYPTION CODE: RED

PUBLIC KEY: FILE / VEGAS-ANACONDA-MOCKINGBIRD-ZERO /
FROM: VICE ADMIRAL PRESTON COLE, COMMANDING OFFICER UNSC EVEREST / (UNSC SERVICE NUMBER: 00814-13094-BQ)
TO: ADMIRAL DALE KILKIN, UNSC CENTRAL COMMAND, REACH LOGISTICS OFFICE / (UNSC SERVICE NUMBER: 007981-63882-GE)
SUBJECT: REQUISITIONS, TRANSFERS, AND FAVORS
CLASSIFICATION: RESTRICTED (BGE DIRECTIVE)

Dale,

Recent prowler reports indicate a Covenant armada massing in Sector Three. I need my ships repaired, refitted, and battle-ready ASAP. Code these orders CRIMSON, and pull in favors people owe me to make it happen. You know what I mean.

1. **Requisition**: 600 tungsten-layered titanium-A armor plates (radiation-absorption rating: 5), replacement and upgrades for degraded armor plates on *Everest*, et al.
2. **Requisition**: Additional "smart" nav AI. Sealed and unbooted. Back-up for *Everest*. Current AI operating at 68% capacity.
3. **Order**: Pull the *Io* out of space dock and tow her to my position. Too far gone to repair, but Captain Wren has an idea to use her as a fire ship.
4. **Requisition**: Ordnance: 105 Shiva nuclear missiles (VE-3 type), 2400 Archer missiles, 45,000 blocks Helix System ammunition (see additional nonordnance supplies in Attachment A).
5. **Requisition**: Detailed stellar survey of Section Three, subvolume D-6. Emphasis on systems with proto-brown dwarf gas giants.

6. **Transfers**: I can't lead my fleet into battle when half my officers are on the verge of collapse from fatigue. List of crew transfers in Attachment B. List of requested crew replacements in Attachment C.
7. **Favor**: I have a theoretical Shaw-Fujikawa manifold calculation that needs crunching through the ONI AI network on Reach. They're the only ones in the Outer Colonies with the raw power to get the job done.
8. Wish me luck.

UNSC *Everest*
Preston J. Cole

COPY TO: LOGISTICS OFFICE, NAVCOM, REACH.
OFFICE OF NAVAL INTELLIGENCE, SECTION-III, REACH

0915 APRIL 18, 2543 (MILITARY CALENDAR) \ UNSC CRUISER *EVEREST* \ FLAGSHIP BATTLE GROUP INDIA \ PSI SERPENTIS SYSTEM
THE BATTLE OF PSI SERPENTIS **{AI RECREATION BASED ON VIDEO, AUDIO, AND SENSOR LOGS—BLACK BOX RECORDERS—AND EYEWITNESS ACCOUNTS}**

When Battle Group India transitioned into normal space in the Psi Serpentis System, it was the largest assembly of UNSC forces: thirteen cruisers, twenty-three carriers, seventy-nine destroyers, forty-two frigates, five prowlers—and fifty supply, repair, and rescue vessels (those latter ships remaining in slipstream space for the duration of the engagement).

The wake from the massive transition into normal space sent a ripple outward from the fleet's entry point—a distortion across the electromagnetic spectrum that propagated from their location three million kilometers above the planetary plane of Psi Serpentis.

It made auroras sparkle over the nearest three planets. It caused a visible shift in the smoldering red eye of Viperidae, the gas giant with thirteen times the mass of Jupiter (with gravity nearly enough to crush and fuse the hydrogen churning in its atmosphere).

. . . and the ripple passed through the massing Covenant ships on the far side of the system.

An unmistakable signal to the enemy.

The Covenant ships appeared on radar like a swarm of sharks in the dark—more than a hundred sleek organic silhouettes registered—CPV destroyers, light cruisers, and the hitherto unseen in battle CCS-class battle cruiser.

Their prows collectively turned toward Battle Group India, lateral plasma lines pulsing and illuminating hulls so it looked as if an entire alien fleet emerged from the shadows by sleight of hand.

The UNSC prowler *Wink of an Eye*, having been in system for seven days waiting for this moment, moved into its proper position and reappeared, only visible because its active camouflage skin could not keep pace with the churning red and orange surface of Viperidae behind it . . . the prowler sent a radar ping to the UNSC forces to verify its position, and then the *Wink* flash transitioned into slipstream space to drop guidance beacons.

Battle Group India one by one moved into slipstream space, the preliminary Shaw-Fujikawa calculations having been done a week previously by Cole himself.

And the entire fleet then reappeared two seconds later, one hundred thousand kilometers on the opposite side of Viperidae—positioned so the gas giant blocked the enemy sight line.

UNSC FTL technology, however, was not perfect—especially over short intersystem hops near gravity wells. A dozen UNSC ships reappeared, scattered from the main group.

The Covenant fleet angled toward the stragglers and accelerated to attack speed.

Cole's fleet split into two wings, both using the gravity of the gas giant to slingshot around either side of the planet—and toward the onrushing enemy armada.

In response, the Covenant fleet also split to track each portion of the UNSC forces on either side of the Viperidae.

The starboard wing of the UNSC fleet, however, shifted its orbital burn—arced up and over the gas giant and angled back to meet the rest of the battle group.

Engine cones flaring with the power from overloaded reactors, the human ships reunited and rocketed toward the port-side breach in the Covenant line.

A dozen nuclear-tipped Shiva missiles launched, crossed the space between the two converging forces, and detonated harmlessly before reaching a single enemy vessel.

But as the Covenant loosed their plasma charges, the exploding clouds of superheated gas from nuclear detonations scattered the alien weapons, rendering them ineffective.

Just as the Covenant fleet came into Battle Group India's optimal magnetic accelerator cannon range.

A dozen MAC slugs struck the leading Covenant ships—impacts timed microseconds apart as they hammered down energy shields, punched through hulls, penetrated through and through, and sent thirty-seven of the alien CPV-class destroyers careening through space.

As the two forces closed, however, a cloud of nuclear fire no longer protected the UNSC vessels, and plasma lines lanced through the vacuum, tearing into titanium-A armor and breaching reactors. Archer missiles fired at extreme close range to fill the space with flash and detonations, but this did little to stop the enemy.

Three human destroyers crashed headlong into a Covenant battle cruiser—their hulls splintered and the entire mass engulfed in a blob of plasma.

As the fleets sped past one another, the UNSC ships fired thrusters, spun about one hundred eighty degrees, and launched Archer missiles to provide cover from the Covenant's devastating plasma weaponry.

The Covenant had lost statistically more vessels than was typical in an engagement with the UNSC. Twenty-three alien ships of the line now drifted in space inert or burning from within as their reactors overloaded and vented plasma.

But Battle Group India had lost more than a third of her ships, and nearly every one of those that had survived was now scoured and pitted or had decks breached—

With one noticeable exception: *Everest*, which had led the charge, emerged unscathed.

Meanwhile, the other wing of the Covenant armada that had been outmaneuvered on the first pass came about—spinning in place as the UNSC fleet had done . . . slowing . . . and then pursuing Cole's ships.

Swarms of Archer missiles fired from Battle Group India. Their MAC systems had yet to recycle for another shot. The UNSC ships scattered, moving apart like an opening blossom—

—as the second wave of Covenant vessels opened fire.

The UNSC destroyer *Agincourt* charged headlong into concentrated streams of incoming plasma lines—sacrificing itself to save her sister ships.

And still the alien fleet picked off a dozen more human vessels.

Both sides were now scattered across the system. The first Covenant forces to engage, however, caught up with those now in pursuit. The human ships regrouped and changed course back toward the gas giant, accelerating and keeping just out of effective range of the enemy's plasma.

Cole's fleet might have escaped, and yet the UNSC ships collectively slowed to allow the Covenant fleet to gain a tiny bit—as both groups of ships sped around Viperidae.

The Covenant armada lost sight of their prey due to the curvature of the gas giant.

As they emerged in hot pursuit of Battle Group India they saw brilliant blue flashes of Cherenkov radiation, the result of multiple slipstream transitions into normal space.

A new fleet of human ships appeared, barreling on an interceptor trajectory toward the aliens.

Fifty-five ships—highly modified older UNSC warships, merchant vessels bristling with missile pods, and entirely new designs that neither human nor Covenant had ever seen before—led by *Bellicose* plunged into the center of the Covenant fleet and opened fire.

MAC slugs tore into the enemy vessels as they accelerated toward one another. Plasma lines launched—many deflected by the strong magnetic field of the gas giant in proximity. Ships collided and scraped hulls, and a dozen craft from both sides fell into the boiling clouds of Viperidae's upper atmosphere and perished.

Then the two forces flashed past one another . . . and the Covenant emerged, their forces decimated and wounded . . . less than half the original strength.

The insurgent-led forces had lost one-quarter of their number. They did not turn to fight, however.

They continued on their trajectory out of the Psi Serpentis system where, and with dozens of crackling blue flashes, they transitioned back into slipstream space.

Cole's fleet had altered course into a high parabolic orbit, turning toward the enemy, their collective MAC systems shimmering with superconductive sparks of power—aimed directly at what remained of the Covenant fleet.

A mere million kilometers distant, however, space again rippled as new slipspace ruptures appeared . . . three . . . and a dozen . . . a hundred . . . then a fleet of more than two hundred Covenant ships appeared in normal space accelerating toward Viperidae.

The UNSC ships continued a full ten seconds on their current course, firing neither weapons nor engines.

COM traffic from *Everest* was on a secure and scrambled channel—private, for admirals to captains only—that was then deleted by a viral worm.

The channel closed and the UNSC fleet moved off at flank speed—leaving *Everest* alone to face the enemy.

Everest's engines flared and she slipped deeper toward the gas giant. Her MACs powered down and every external light went off. All her missile silo doors, however, opened.

The mass of the fresh Covenant armada turned to pursue the retreating Battle Group India.

COM CHANNEL (BROADBAND ALPHA-THETA) from UNSC *Everest*: "*Listen to me, Covenant. I am Vice Admiral Preston J. Cole commanding the human flagship,* Everest. *You claim to be the holy and glorious inheritors of the universe? I spit on your so-called holiness. You dare judge us unfit? After I have personally sent more than three hundred of your vainglorious ships to hell? After kicking your collective butts off Harvest—not once—but twice? From where I sit, we are the worthy inheritors. You think otherwise, you can come and try to prove me wrong."*

The Covenant fleet, both damaged vessels and fresh reinforcements, turned to *Everest.* Some ships rushed toward her position, while others skirted around the Viperidae—cutting off any possible escape vector.

Everest tightened its orbit and vanished from view as it moved to the far side of the gas giant.

She did not slingshot out as she had done on previous occasions, but rather emerged again on the near side of Viperidae along the trajectory so low, the cruiser could never recover from the inevitable gravity spiral into the gas giant's crushing atmosphere.

The leading Covenant ships fired.

A hundred plasma streams lanced toward their target . . . but spiraled about themselves and dissipated in the extreme magnetosphere of the gas giant.

Laser fire followed from the Covenant ships, peppering *Everest* with a thousand smoldering holes. No atmosphere, though, leaked from the ship, as every outer deck had already been evacuated.

COM CHANNEL (BROADBAND ALPHA-THETA) from UNSC *Everest*: *"Is that the best you can do?"* Cole laughed. *"Watch what one unworthy human can do!"*

Everest launched everything she had.

Archer missiles rocketed out of the gravity well of the planet along with a dozen Shiva nuclear warheads—while another *hundred* Shiva missiles plunged deeper into Viperidae's churning clouds.

The gas giant's hydrogen-helium atmosphere was so dense, so compressed, that if it had a tiny fraction more mass it would have ignited and become the smallest of brown dwarf stars.

The Archer missiles had no effect on the Covenant shields. They did, however, provided a dazzling display of pyrotechnics:

flashes of white and blue and red and obscuring clouds of propellant.

The nukes launched out of the gravity well exploded.

The lead Covenant ship was destroyed—an insignificant loss compared to the two hundred remaining Covenant vessels moving closer, now near enough to punch through the magnetosphere and obliterate *Everest.*

But the vast majority of the nuclear ordnance had not been aimed at the Covenant—rather, they fell deeper into the atmosphere of Viperidae.

And detonated.

One hundred dots of light flickered deep within the thick atmosphere, compressing the already superpressurized hydrogen—adding the needed spark of fission that flashed through and around the gas giant's surface, sending helixing tentacles of solar plasma about the planet circumference.

For an instant, Viperidae was a star.

Countless tons of hydrogen blasted off its outer layers and filled space with plasma—washed away everything with a blaze.

The expanding ball of destruction slowed and dissipated.

Until only a cloud of glowing haze remained . . . and in the center, the dark cinder of Viperidae.

Every ship in the Covenant fleet had been destroyed

As had the UNSC *Everest*, its crew, and Vice Admiral Preston J. Cole.

ANALYSIS

A day of mourning was proclaimed July 28, 2543. Humanity had lost its supreme hero. There would be others elevated to this lofty position (most notably, the Spartan-IIs, who had already gone public in 2547), but for many, Preston Cole was the one man who had stood between life and annihilation at the hands of the Covenant.

It was no coincidence that after a brief pause in alien activity in the Outer Colonies, they renewed their efforts, overwhelmed UNSC defenses, and swarmed through the Inner Colonies. Was that because Cole was gone? Or had his victory spurred the enemy to redouble their efforts?

What occurred at Psi Serpentis, while it was investigated, was not forensically examined in exacting detail at the time. The tactics in the battle were consistent with Cole's previous behaviors: innovations in FTL jump technology, a sophisticated coordination and maneuvering of multiple ships in formation, gravitationally assisted slingshot to excellent effect, and tricking the enemy into exposing vulnerabilities.

As for the real question, what *really* happened to Preston Cole, we must examine the available evidence.

First, the AI recreation of the battle stitched together by ONI Section-III and Section-II was one part scientific analysis and one part propaganda. To be fair, there were many holes in the official record. Speculation and raw glorification of the events were inevitable.

Let us consider some anomalies and curiosities.

A frame-by-frame analysis of the last moments of *Everest* captured by external cameras of the withdrawing Battle Group India show the vessel spiraling into the atmosphere of Viperidae just before the detonation of her Archer missiles.

Tactically those missiles served little, if any, purpose. They could not possibly have penetrated the Covenant shields. So why fire them?

Hyperfine enhancements of the video make out the characteristic prow of a UNSC super-heavy cruiser silhouetted against the backdrop of the red atmosphere—but also recorded an aura of bright blue light (which most experts assume is the premature detonation of a cluster of Archer missiles).

But most curiously, there appears for a single frame *another* silhouette behind the *Everest*: that of a UNSC cruiser.

All UNSC ships, surviving and destroyed, were accounted for in the battle, save *Everest* and the towed, never-used "fire ship" Cole had requested, the cruiser *Io*.

Spectroscopic analysis of the radioactive debris field captured in orbit of Viperidae shows amounts of tungsten-180 consistent with the newly requisitioned and repaired armor of *Everest*—but it failed to yield the ratio of titanium-50 in the mixture that would have been present had *Everest* been vaporized.

No black-box recorder was ever found from *Everest*. While UNSC black-box recorders cannot survive such a nuclear cacophony, standard protocol is for the ship's AI to eject at least one of the redundant five black-box recorders if the ship is in imminent danger of destruction.

Detailed examination of Cole's Shaw-Fujikawa manifold calculation sent to the ONI/Reach super-AI network for number crunching reveal it to be a theoretical in-atmosphere transition from normal to slipstream space while in a severe acceleration gradient—i.e., identical conditions one might encounter in close proximity to a gas giant.

SPECULATION

The Archer missile screen and the anomalous presence of the Io *were smoke screen and decoy. Cole initiated a transition to slipstream space the instant before detonation of the Shiva nuclear ordnance and the triggering of the micronova of Viperidae.*

Everest *was* not *destroyed.*

Cole faked his death and escaped.

One hole in this theory pertains to the crew of Everest. *Cole's massive personnel transfer prior to the battle might have been intended to fill his ranks with those sympathetic to his motives or, at least, those who had unwavering loyalty to him. But he could never have convinced the entire crew of* Everest *to agree to a wartime desertion. I do not believe Cole could kill his own crew—but perhaps he could keep potential dissenters indefinitely in cryo sleep?*

As to Cole's motivations, that is pure speculation. But the resurfacing of Bellicose *and his former lover, Lyra Castilla, point in the right direction—that, and a mental break brought on by years of constant fighting with overwhelming causalities.*

Scattered reports and rumors of independent human forces fighting Covenant pop up on the outer edge of what we believe to be nonsanctioned human colonized space . . . reports that track toward the Sagittarius side of the Orion arm in the Milky Way . . . and then these rumors fade to whispers . . . and legend . . . and then die out all together.

SUMMARY CONCLUSIONS

In my best estimation, Cole survived the Battle of Psi Serpentis.

He may be alive and healthy today.

By Earth-normal chronology he would be eighty-two years old, but before the Covenant War he had his liver, heart, and endocrine system replaced with flash-clone parts. Also, so many of his "years" occupied with space travel were filled with periods of cryogenic suspension and minor but additional relativistic effects. Our best guess at Cole's biological age is sixty.

He is likely leading a band of colonists, insurgents, and UNSC defectors to build a new home far outside UNSC-dominated space. He always wanted a farm on some world where he could look up and not recognize the nighttime stars.

I think he did just that.

RECOMMENDATION

While it is remotely possible that my analysis is incorrect (AIs Phoenix and Lackluster have, however, independently corroborated my conclusions within 89.7 percent accuracy), I shall nonetheless give you my informed recommendation on this matter.

For the moment Preston Cole may be living a simple, isolated life—the governor, perhaps, of some unknown provincial farming colony.

But how long will that isolation last, given the highly unstable situation we find ourselves in after the Covenant War? Namely:

a. *The insurgency may rise again (especially dangerous given the UNSC's weakened postwar status); and*
b. *The Covenant (to the best of our limited intelligence of their culture) is in utter chaos now that their religious hierarchy has been removed. What they will do with their independent races, or collectively, is anyone's guess.*

It is inevitable that these coming conflicts will spread to a wider region of the galaxy.

Cole might be found and convinced to fight once more. In addi-

tion to possessing great military genius, he would be a natural figurehead for our battered forces to rally behind. Insurgent or Covenant aggressors would think twice before engaging Preston Cole in battle.

But if found, will Cole fight? For us?

There are three possibilities: (1) Cole will see that Earth and all her colonies are in peril and defend them once more. (2) He will fight for humanity . . . but perhaps not on our side. After living for years among former insurgents, he may back those forces should they rise against the UNSC. Or (3) Cole will not fight, having grown too weary to take up arms again, and will flee farther from the conflict.

Neither I nor the AIs can hazard a better than even guess as to the probabilities (plus or minus 4.35 percent, 4.05 percent, and 4.30 percent respectively).

All that can be said with absolute certainty is that Cole will remain a leader—whether leading his people to safety . . . or back into battle once more.

I offer my services, as usual, to pick up Preston Cole's trail, find him, and attempt to convince him to join our cause.

Failing that, if he chooses to side against us . . . well, I leave those unpleasant details to you.

I, for one, have lost my stomach for killing legends.

CODENAME: SURGEON

OFFICE OF NAVAL INTELLIGENCE (SECTION-III) OPERATOR #: AA2

2200 HOURS, DECEMBER 31, 2552 (MILITARY CALENDAR) \ UNSC *POINT OF NO RETURN*, SYNCHRONOUS LUNAR ORBIT (FAR SIDE)

/END FILE/

/SCRAMBLE-DESTRUCTION PROCESS ENABLE/

PRESS ENTER TO CONTINUE.

THE RETURN

KEVIN GRACE

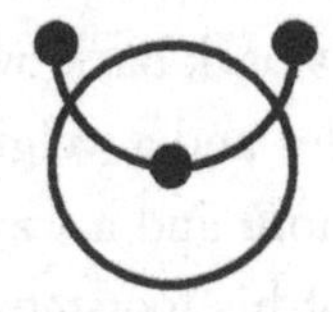

After two weeks roaming about this shattered place, just the memory of the water that once filled this lake was refreshing. But like everything else here, the memories carried pain.

The Shipmaster's steps slowed as he reached the end of the crumbling dock and he dropped his pack to the ground. The dock had once been painted a bright blue, perhaps the same color as the water it stood above, but now the little paint left flaked off at his step and beneath was only gray. The same gray of the empty lake bed below, where a few scrub trees and grasses attempted a comeback where fish once swam. The same gray as everything on this forbidding, forgotten world. It was a gray of decades-old ruin left untended and unhealed, and it would probably stay this way forever, as the planet had nothing more to offer, and its former masters had nothing left here to claim.

He had seen only two things break away from this gray in the weeks he had walked this desolation. The first were the thin rays and glimpses of this world's sun, which would rarely show itself, offering no real heat when it managed to struggle through the thick haze hanging constantly in the sky. The other was a column of smoke he had sighted two days prior, far to the west. It was to this smoke he now drove himself, though he knew where that path would eventually lead.

To follow that ominous smoke sign he had to cross this dead hole of a lake and the dam at its far end. From the elevated vantage of the dock the Shipmaster took a reflexive look around the horizon, scanning for threats, before casting a quick glance into the sky in the vain hope of seeing his vessel in orbit far above the planet's surface. He slid his pack back over his armor, fastening it with a triple-click of buckles and a weight-centering shrug. As he turned back to find the shore and a way across the lake bed, he closed off the dry sound of his footsteps on the brittle grass and remembered the lake at his clan's keep back on Sanghelios.

Like this one, his lake was artificial, the river back home stopped by a lattice of delicate metal and shimmering energy. This hole had only a crude, crumbling wall. A simple concrete of rock and sand. Such a frangible substance to use for something as vital and enduring as a dam, he thought, but so much of what humans did was fleeting. His travels through this planet's remaining signs of habitation had shown him how little these people knew of permanence.

Not that it would have mattered here, even if they had.

Stark in the late afternoon light, the battered skeletons of boats littered the lakebed and reminded him of the days he spent on similar boats during his earliest training as a boy.

The Great Journey, the path to transcendence followed by all of the species that served the Covenant, started early for all male

Sangheili. As soon as they could run and hold a weapon in their four-fingered hands, they were trained and evaluated for potential. Each young Sangheili was watched for strength and cunning and obedience to the teachings of the Covenant. They were tested extraordinarily, for their importance to the Great Journey was extraordinary.

The Sangheili were the chosen ones, directly responsible for realizing the will of the gods and commanding the military forces of the Covenant. They were the ones who enforced the words of the Prophets, the holy seers who translated and delivered the words of the Forerunners to all who walked the Path. This honor and obligation drove every Sangheili in all their decisions and aspirations, and the Prophets were always watching to make sure this remained so. It had been this way for thousands of years, since the two species first formed the Covenant, and it would be this way until the Great Journey was completed . . . or so he once thought.

So, on smaller, intact boats similar to the rotten hulks he now skirted, the Shipmaster learned as a boy to move and to fight. Striking and leaping from vessel to vessel, the young warriors learned balance and timing and teamwork as well as ruthlessness, as not all of the denizens in the lake considered themselves prey. Those boys whose weakness allowed them to be pulled under by cold teeth served as a lesson to the rest that not all Sangheili were worthy. Those who survived the training water emerged hardened both by loss and the determination not to suffer a similar fate in later lessons.

Now here he was at the bottom of the lake, no monsters waiting to challenge his strength—just the crumbling boats, the stunted gray trees, and the occasional crunch of bone beneath the matted gray grass.

He first heard that hollow crunching at his step days ago, and he knew the sound had been human bone. In his first days, while walking through human towns now wearing away to dust, the Shipmaster had stopped to loosen many such bones from tangles of tough grass or a covering layer of dust and dirt, spending much time wondering who these humans had been. Now it had been days since he'd stopped looking for the source of that sound.

Usually he'd found these bones alone, spread far from the rest of whatever body they came from by wind or war or animals, though he had not seen a single living creature or even tracks anywhere in his travels. As intended, the death in this place had been complete. He'd found full skeletons as well, flesh long since torn or worn away, usually inside the few structures with more than one wall remaining or even a bit of roof left waiting for the insistent pull of time and gravity to bring it crashing down.

He'd found bits of armor and weapons and human vehicles of war, and even a few remnants of Covenant soldiers, usually cracked methane breathing tanks sitting amidst the bones of a squat Unggoy. Once he'd found a giant shield plate from a Mgalekgolo, a "Hunter," as the humans called them, and he wondered how the humans had managed to take down one of those giant living battering rams. But Covenant remains were rare. This planet had not presented much of a defense when the Covenant arrived, and their losses had been light. He wondered for a moment whether the events that followed the invasion might have been different had the humans been prepared, expecting the assault, but he knew that it would not have mattered. It would not have mattered at all.

He no longer stopped to inspect broken bone, and he did not know whether to care. His path was set—head up and eventually over the dam and to wherever the smoke called him. There he hoped to find an answer, and that was enough for now.

When the Shipmaster reached the top of the rough staircase cut into the side of the dam, he saw a dry scratch of a riverbed leading down from the dam's base to the beginnings of another human settlement—at least to the few standing walls that remained twenty years after the humans were wiped clean from this place. As the riverbed moved farther from the dam it cut through miles of such ruins, small square outlines of stone and rusting metal hiding among those hard, short, gray trees. Scattered between these buildings and their dark square holes for windows was a jumble of fallen pillars that had once held lights or statues or whatever they had used to decorate this place. Farther away from the dam, down toward where his path was leading him, nothing remained even remotely whole. Even the landscape itself appeared to have been worn down dramatically between where he stood and the slight rise that cut off his view of the road far below.

He knew what lay past that rise, and he wished that his path did not have to take him there. Waiting beyond it was a black mark that had been burnt into the surface of this planet as proof of the power of the Covenant. Twenty years ago, this black mark had signaled the doom of everything that once lived here.

The setting sun glinted briefly from a bit of the glassy surface of the mark, shimmering as if bouncing off water in the distance. The Shipmaster shielded his eyes from the low glittering rays and growled, moving his long head left and right to take in the length of that gigantic scar in the land ahead. There was no end to it visible from where he stood, and there was no option of going around. His path would eventually draw him directly across that dark line, and it would lie there, patient, until he reached it. He knew many such lines had cut through the hills and mountains and shattered towns that had once stood on this planet the humans had called Kholo.

But this line had preceded all the others. It had initiated the immolation of Kholo. This line curved in a giant circle, many days' travel across, and at its center were the ruins of what had once been a large human city. This circle, and the millions who had once lived in that city, had been split by a crowning semicircle arc. The ends of this arc had thrust toward the planet's northern pole, and at the tips of that crown and at the center of the giant circle were three deep, deep holes, burnt into the ground with excruciating precision.

When taken in from orbit, this giant black mark would resolve into the Covenant's holy rune representing Faith. He knew that the successful completion of this rune had triggered the planetwide plasma bombardment that left every single thing on Kholo dead for daring to challenge the Path of the Covenant and the words of their Prophets.

He knew all of these things because it had been his hand that had put that mark there. He had killed this planet so that the Great Journey might come more quickly. That Journey had never come. And now he'd returned to this planet, the site of his greatest victory and now his greatest shame, to seek inspiration for what he and his people were to do with themselves now that everything they'd fought and lived for was as thoroughly destroyed as the forsaken land he stood on.

Rising from these thoughts, he knew the sun's setting would make it difficult to push onward safely. The Shipmaster found what looked like a small control structure farther down the dam and set his gear down in preparation for passing another night alone.

As the Shipmaster's eyes closed and he began rest-breathing, he listened again for any sounds of life around him. He heard none. Not even the wind stirred enough to scrape leaves across the dust, and as he dropped into sleep his mind spun from the silence of death on the planet's surface to the silence of space above twenty years prior, when his ship hung in orbit around this world.

THE MOMENT *was almost upon him. It had been a mere three days since the Fleet of Righteous Vigilance had arrived, and already the ground forces had broken the bulk of the human defenses below. In all of his years fighting the humans, the Shipmaster had rarely seen a planet fall so quickly. The humans seldom lasted long against the power of the Covenant, but this time he fought back a sense of disappointment that they had not mounted more of an opposition.*

The Shipmaster had claimed this world, after all, and the glory of its destruction would reflect directly on him. It had been his ship that found the human transport vessel and his interrogation that uncovered the location of this "Kholo," a blight of a colony world on the outer fringes of what the humans blasphemously considered their space.

Even after ten years of destroying the nests of these humans with little difficulty, the Covenant still kept finding more worlds and more colonies and more affronts to the gods, and they burned each of these out as quickly as they were found. They had still not located the human homeworld, though. The humans somehow always managed to destroy the key navigational charts before being captured. The discipline this consistency took was admirable, which was surprising given the claims the Prophets made about this "selfish, ignorant rabble."

The Shipmaster had personally broken the lone survivor on that little ship and pulled the location of this planet from the ship's incomplete databanks, and per the commandments of the Prophets he took that data directly to the holy seat of the High Prophets so that they might tell them what the Great Journey, the path to transcendence that guided every aspect of life in the Covenant, would have them do.

And as he had hoped, the Prophets announced that the Great Journey demanded that this world and the sins of its inhabitants burn—completely.

The Covenant used smaller plasma bombardments frequently to easily destroy human cities and armies, but normally this was accomplished using their ships' automation to handle all of the intricate functions involved in focusing plasma through a magnetic envelope across miles of atmospheric interference while maintaining a perfectly stationary orbital firing position. In almost all cases plasma bombardments were used purely as weapons, tools to speed the destruction of the humans. But rarely, the High Council would order a world's absolute annihilation. This only happened in times of particular religious significance, as the effort involved in covering an entire planet's surface in such a powerful assault was enormous, requiring hundreds of ships and massive amounts of energy . . . massive even for the Covenant.

And so the fleet was summoned and death brought swiftly to the heretical stain of this world. As expected, resistance in the space around Kholo was brief and ineffectual, with only a few small military vessels sporting ineffective weaponry and poor tactics. These fell easily even to his earliest scouting ships. Since the High Council had granted the Shipmaster claim to this cleansing the fleet was under his command, and he followed the decreed invasion plan to the letter. Nothing about the destruction of Kholo would displease their gods. He had many reasons to be certain of that.

After two days of human slaughter in their cities and homes, he waited for the prescribed hour and looked over to the Prophet next to him, the Prophet of Conviction, who was there to witness the event on behalf of the High Council. That Council, which was made up of the heroes of his people and the three most holy High Prophets, had assigned the holy destruction of Kholo to him, but the Prophet of

Conviction would be the one to declare whether his actions pleased the gods and advanced the Journey. Not a single warrior in the history of his clan had ever been offered such an opportunity, and if the Shipmaster was successful it would greatly elevate his status and the status of his kin within the Covenant. All was riding on his performance.

"It is time," the Prophet said. With a gesture to his Second to alert all ground forces that the Beginning had come, the Shipmaster knelt before the Prophet to start the ritual.

His crew watched as closely as they could while coordinating the evacuation of all troops on the surface of the planet. For a full hour the Prophet and the Shipmaster communed, exchanging vows and reciting the history of the Covenant. Passages from the Writ of Union were interwoven with a recounting of martial triumphs as the Prophet made the Shipmaster ready to assume his imminent, if brief, divinity.

When all the words had been spoken and the Beginning was completed, his Second quietly confirmed that the fleet was ready. At this, the Shipmaster turned to the Prophet and spoke his final line in the ceremony:

"Speak, my Prophet, and let the word destroy all those who stand in the way of the Great Journey."

And rising in his chair to better fill the dark purple robes puddled around his frail body, the Prophet's raspy voice replied.

"Faith. Destroy them with Faith."

And so he did. Stepping down to the helmstation, the Shipmaster switched control of the maneuvering fields away from the ship's spirit and with a touch to ignite the ventral plasma array he emptied everything he was into the flame that shot down to the planet. The sights and sounds around him disappeared as a lifetime of training and worship and anticipation poured into controlling the ship and the long, wavering stream of plasma branding the curves of the glyph of Faith around and through the great city of the humans below.

A million Covenant soldiers were all watching his work, waiting to see how he performed this sacred task. Thousands of his own people watched, their breath quickening and their bodies shaking with the pride of watching a Sangheili manifest the power of the Great Journey. And, most importantly, the Prophet was watching . . . and judging.

And then it was finished. The Shipmaster pulled his hands, trembling, away from the console and dropped to his knees as the rites required. He couldn't breathe as he waited there on the floor for the Prophet's judgment. Failure to perfectly execute the chosen glyph meant death, and if he had failed he wanted the life out of his body as quickly as possible.

And then he felt the touch of the Prophet's hand on his neck. Triumphant roars from the rest of the bridge crew shook the air, and he finally looked up to the main screen to take in the still-glowing sigil his hands had carved into the planet below. Clouds of ash and fire continued to spread hundreds of miles outward from the arcs and precise points of the glyph of Faith as the once-molten paths began to cool.

He rose and turned to face the Prophet. The Shipmaster was now bound to this Prophet for the rest of his life and his service to the Covenant. He, his ship, and his crew would now represent the Prophet's interests and authority in this war, and the enormous honor of carrying a Prophet aboard his ship would guarantee him a great role in the crusade against the humans. The Shipmaster had never imagined the power his faith would bring him, and as the other ships in the fleet saw the great glyph finally cool completely they began the intricate weave of lines of bombardment that would render the rest of this world barren and forbidden for any member of the Covenant to touch for the rest of time.

THE SHIPMASTER awoke with a thin layer of ash and dust covering his body, the triumphant roar of his former crew still ringing in his ears. Some of that crew were still alive and in orbit above him right now, waiting for him to find an answer in this haunted land. But too many of that crew were dead now, victims of the Great Betrayal and the battles that followed. They had all died honorably, fighting to save their race in the aftermath of the lies that eventually brought him back to Kholo.

He looked down from the dam and in the weak morning light saw a clearer view of the wide road that ran straight down to the valley below and perhaps all the way to the scar itself. The road cut through what might have been some kind of settlement near this lake, and the buildings in the area nearby stood largely intact, minus the years of abandonment and decay. As his eyes scanned farther down the valley, the Shipmaster saw that these remnants of buildings grew more and more feeble, shrinking almost to nothing just before the land dipped down and out of his gaze. He had seen this before, near earlier bombardment lines he had skirted in his journey across this place. The explosive power of the plasma lines created a terrible wall of heat and wind and debris when they cut into the surface of the planet, and the rushing force of these walls had scraped everything on the surface clean near the focus of the blasts. Structures farther away had suffered less, but everything suffered. That was the point of it. Suffering was the correct journey for the nonbelievers.

As he climbed down the other side of the dam he cut a path parallel to the empty riverbed, toward the road and the scar below. He could still see the column of smoke in the distance, seemingly blacker than it had been the day before. The smoke had been billowing for three days since he first saw it rising thinly on the horizon. Each day he was more afraid that it would disappear before he could find its source. It could not be natural, the fires of this world went out decades ago. This fire, and its creators, did not belong here, just as he did not belong here. But perhaps they could help him find the guidance he was seeking.

He passed rows and rows of shattered buildings as he moved down the road. Sharp, rusty fragments of vehicles poked out from tall grass and scrub trees all around him, but he saw less and less sign of their former owners. He tried to remember whether this part of the glyph he was walking toward was closer to the start or the end of his deeds those years back, but the details eluded him. He only knew that he was responsible for everything around him. He was responsible for so many things, all of them done with such an absolute certainty. All his life he had had no reason to question his path, and the focus this afforded had allowed him to achieve so much.

For thirteen years after bonding with the Prophet of Conviction, the Shipmaster had followed his holy orders. He and his ship had been above Reach when they finally found a real fight from the humans. It was his command that destroyed three of the massive orbital cannons that had annihilated so many other Covenant ships. The High Council believed that after Reach the humans would lose all will to fight, but the opposite was true. In the following months, desperation drove the humans and they proved to be the most dangerous foes the Covenant had ever faced. It was a glorious time to follow the Path.

But the discovery and immediate, agonizing loss of the Halos had shaken the Covenant's faith, and suddenly their clarity began to falter. For thousands of years the entire Covenant had operated with a single purpose born of absolutely certainty in the Great Journey. They were a folk ill-equipped for doubt.

The Shipmaster paused briefly to wonder where the fully intact roof lying directly across this road had come from, how far it had been carried from its building by the winds of the blast that day. He had put this roof here, and he had destroyed whatever building it came from closer down to the scar. All of it. He had done all of this to follow a promise, and when that promise was exposed as an unforgivable lie, it made everything he had done in its prosecution a lie as well.

He walked among the ruins of the lie, knowing its guilt as it was he who had been deceived. He had come here again to find out what to do about that lie. If he had no real response, no path forward, no new promise . . .

He shook his head and continued toward the rising pillar of smoke across the scar. He would find his new promise, or he would not leave this place alive.

Hours passed and in its time the sun fell to the far horizon, once again making travel across the rubble problematic. He made for a strangely intact structure just at the edge of the long rise ahead. The ruins here had all crumbled to the point of just rough outlines of stone among the weeds. Small bits of foundation stuck up like markers for the dead. Despite the growing darkness, he could tell that this building had been some sort of shelter, as metal pipes and bars held the thick walls together, heavy metal plates buttressing every visible angle—a suitable refuge for the night's sleep.

He made a quick sweep of the surrounding area just to get it all fixed in his mind. He knew there was no threat here . . . this close to the scar; the land did not want life. He did not blame it.

He strode to the top of the nearby rise and saw his scar directly for the first time. Its edge cut a precise line just an hour's walk from where he stood, and while it was hard to tell in the last light of the day, the ground there looked dark and hard. He guessed the scar's width at two or three hours to cross, depending on footing and whether it was as smooth as it appeared. There was no way he would choose to spend a night on that black ground.

He turned back to his night's refuge and pried a metal door partially open to squeeze his bulky body inside.

His first step raised that familiar crunching sound, and when he engaged his heatlight he froze. Dozens of full human skeletons piled one on another with scraps of clothing and bits of possessions hanging stilly from graying sticks of bones. More bone littered toward a doorway at the other side of this room, and he could tell he would find more remains lingering in the further darkness inside. Men, women, and children must have gathered here in the last moments of their people, perhaps in hope that the shelter would save them. But it did not save them from anything. Nothing would have saved them that day.

The Shipmaster backed out quickly and did not stop to close the metal door in his haste to get away. He could not get far enough from that tomb in the night, but he found a low, partial wall nearby and set himself on the far side of it, facing away from the hidden bones of his victims.

The grim discovery took his mind back to that day, as he took a little of his almost-depleted food and water. With the wild frenzy of battle broken suddenly by the full retreat of Covenant forces, the humans must have thought themselves very lucky. Thought themselves saved, even. With all their satellites and orbital stations destroyed, they would have had no idea what was taking place in the skies above them—until his beam of plasma lanced down and the fires and the winds and the burning began. The people in that building might have gathered for safety or perhaps just because being together might be a better way to die. Any thoughts they had of escape were as much a false hope as the fervor that had brought that beam down amongst them.

Still, he could understand their need to come together in such a moment. He understood the desire that someone else might have an answer, might tell you what to do when facing the end of everything you know. He understood that desire all too well.

His mind thus burdened, the Shipmaster slept.

HE GOT word of the elevation of the Jiralhanae, the "Brutes," as the humans so appropriately called them, and of the betrayal of his people just after arriving at the destination of a long-range scouting mission. In the high-priority slipspace missive that found them some days after their ship reentered real space, he knew something was amiss when the admiral addressed him by his clan name and not his proper rank. As the images of the slaughter of the Sangheili leaders on the High Council flooded the bridge's main screen, everyone stopped to stare in disbelief, and when the admiral told the still-unfolding story of the lies of the Prophets about the gods and the Great Journey and of the bloody treachery of the Brutes, all stood stunned. Looking to the faces of his men, he knew he could not stay that way for long.

The Shipmaster ordered the helmsman to set an immediate course back to their homeworld and commanded his Second to gather every single crewmember in the main hangar. Word of what they had just heard would spread and the crew would have questions. The Shipmaster did not have answers to all of those questions, but he sped out of the bridge to find the one answer that mattered for now.

At the back of the ship lay the chambers of the Prophet. The

Shipmaster had come straight there so news had not yet reached the two Sangheili Honor Guards outside his door and they hesitated, briefly, before responding to his order to stand away. A Prophet's guard is a sacred duty, and these two did not yet know that their function had ceased to exist some days prior when the great treachery had been committed. They both took their own lives soon afterward for the shame of protecting that creature in the intervening days. The Shipmaster did not judge them for this.

As he palmed the door control he saw a brief glimpse of a familiar green glow, and that glimpse saved his life. The Prophet, clearly having been notified that his kind's sins were now open and fully exposed, had a plasma pistol charged and ready to kill whoever would inevitably come for him. It was a cowardly and pointless act of defiance. The Shipmaster ducked under the hissing green blast and rolled into the room, rising with a sweeping blow to knock the frail deceiver from his floating throne before the pistol could cool enough for a second shot.

"Blasphemy!" the Prophet choked, now in a pile on the ground lit only by the light from the open doorway. "Filth! Who are you to strike a messenger of the gods? You will not survive this affront!"

"Your words are lies," the Shipmaster said, stepping forward to collect him from the floor. "And I am Sangheili, Shipmaster here. Those are the last words you will speak on my ship."

At this he struck the Prophet again, careful to stun and not kill him, so that he sagged to the floor and did not rise. He twisted a corner of the wretch's robe in his hand and began to drag the unconscious form toward the hangar and the waiting crew.

Some of the men had apparently not yet heard the cause of this gathering, as there were cries of disbelief when the Shipmaster entered behind them and pulled the body of the Prophet through the assembled group. Some of the men even moved to stop him but they were held back as he mounted a maintenance platform and dropped the Prophet on the ground. The Shipmaster turned on the viewscreens all around them and replayed the message he had just received on the bridge. Silence fell over the crew as some saw the horrors for the first time and some saw confirmation of the insanity they knew was settling in around them all. The men remained silent as the admiral described what had happened, but howls of anger rose as they witnessed the death of the High Council. At the sight of Brutes laying hands to their fellows, and as the implication of the Covenant turning against them set in, those howls were replaced by a new silence more haunting than any sound the Shipmaster had ever heard before. All eyes turned to him, as he had known they would. He was ready.

The Prophet awoke now, surrounded by angry Sangheili, and tried to stand on his atrophied legs. It was pitiful how small he looked now, and the Shipmaster grabbed him by the neck as he tried to totter off the platform. When he twisted around to look at the Shipmaster, he saw something he had not expected, and his resolve crystallized . . . this Prophet, one of a group he had known all his life as the source of all the Covenant's power, was terrified.

This fear confirmed everything the Shipmaster had just seen on the screens and decided what he must do next. If this Prophet could be afraid then he could not truly know the will of the gods, for what could bring fear to someone with a direct connection to the divine? What's more, if he did not know the will of the gods then everything he had ever said and done was a lie—everything done for him was now a lie. The Prophet must die for that deceit, and the Shipmaster had to be the one to end him. His crew had to witness this to prevent them from thinking the thoughts they were thinking right now, and they would take from this death the start of a new purpose.

The Shipmaster tightened his fingers around the Prophet's ropy neck with one hand and used his other hand to hold the Prophet's face toward his. Tiny feet scratched without purchase on the metal floor as the Prophet hung in the air. The Shipmaster looked out to the shocked eyes of his troops and yelled, "Betrayal! Our people have been betrayed by the Prophets and their Jiralhanae puppets! You have seen what they have done, how they have struck at our faith and our leaders . . . and you know what Sangheili must do in the face of such betrayal. Our war against these deceivers starts now!" At these words the Prophet began a high-pitched scream that was cut immediately short as the Shipmaster looked back into his eyes and began to squeeze.

His struggle grew more desperate and a sound began to build in the crew as they watched the unthinkable event on the platform with the images of Brutes destroying Sangheili ships and devouring their dead fellows on the screens behind and above. The Shipmaster let the moment stretch until he judged his men's new hatred was sufficient and then he closed his fist suddenly around the Prophet's neck and felt the bones under the skull give way. The Prophet's eyes locked on the Shipmaster's, just as they had done the day the two were bonded, and the contorting body grew suddenly slack. It was done.

The Prophet's dead eyes continued to look up at him as the Shipmaster opened his hands and the body fell to the ground. He raised his voice to join his crew's scream of rage and defiance and loss. As the scream grew longer and louder he knew that he had succeeded in giving them a purpose . . . for now. Looking down at the tiny figure at his feet, the Shipmaster wondered how long that purpose would last, and he wondered where he would find his own purpose. He had just killed the only voice he thought could speak for them to the gods, and he did not know what those gods wanted of him now. The men rushed back to prepare for the voyage home and he followed to lash them with the hardness they expected. The Shipmaster knew he could only provide that hardness for so long. Already he felt drained as the moment's rage left him, but there was no time for such thoughts. He was needed.

THOSE DEAD eyes followed him into consciousness. The new light of dawn did little to rid him of the dread caused by his dreams. The Shipmaster looked again to the smoke. It was still rising. With a small sip of water he left the shelter of the crumbling wall, moving toward the glyph he knew he must cross. He glanced back at the human tomb, glad to leave it behind.

This relief died quickly as he came to the rise and caught full sight of the scar. Shortly past the rise was a sheer drop into the black land, and he nodded at the prudence of not attempting to proceed the night before.

Finding no easy path down into the scar, the Shipmaster found what looked to be a clear landing spot below and dropped down into the channel. The smooth walls were twice his height, and he worried about how long he would have to look for a path up when he reached the other side. He did not relish the thought of staying down in this place any longer than he absolutely must.

The bottom was truly as black as it had appeared from above. The plasma had melted several meters of rock and stone, and the molten remnants had leveled to an almost perfectly flat field between the boundaries of the direct blast.

But while the overall terrain was smooth, every step of this land was jagged and crystalline-sharp. The cooling material must have fractured and cracked, creating a field of knives . . . no living creature would dare traverse this place. None except him.

As he stepped carefully to avoid the myriad cracks and vertiginous pits that cut across the ground around him, the Shipmaster's already dark thoughts turned to his fear for his people. After thousands of years of obedient service to the Covenant, what would they do now? Already the fight was leaving some of his people. Not even the death of all of the Brutes could replace what they had lost when the Covenant was broken. They would find no true purpose solely through battle, no matter how much vengeance demanded it. They needed something more.

For six years after the High Prophet of Truth, the father of all the Prophets' lies, died at the hands of the Arbiter, the Shipmaster had taken up the fight against everything that threatened his people. But that was all he had done—respond to threats. Immediately after the death of Truth, the Prophets wished only to preserve their own skins and the Brutes welcomed the newfound opportunity to misuse the weapons, ships, and other tools that had been so rightly denied them since they became part of the Covenant. The Brutes' barbarity prevented them from understanding the gifts of the Forerunners, even though they had suddenly received those gifts in abundance and they used them to try to wipe out their former Sangheili masters.

The battles against the Prophets and their Brute puppets had been legendary in the wake of the breaking of the Covenant, but it was not long before the primitive nature of the Brutes pulled their fighting cohesion apart and split their new power among several internecine struggles. The Prophets, in the meantime, had largely disappeared. There had never been many of their wretched species, but their sudden disappearance was baffling and, to some, portentous. The Shipmaster paid no mind to the rumors that held that the Prophets had finally achieved the Great Journey and that the Sangheili were damned for daring to take up arms against them in the final days of the Covenant.

Some Sangheili commanders continued to fight the many

scattered remnants of the former Covenant wherever they could be found, but not all. After six long years of this scattered war, Sangheili power had begun to wane right along with their drive to fight. They had to defend themselves, and always did so heroically, but since the Prophets controlled all of the major learnings that transformed Forerunner gifts into tools of the Great Journey, the Sangheili now largely lacked the understanding to build new facilities and weapons themselves. The Sangheili steadily lost ships they could not easily repair, let alone replace. Their time seemed to be running out.

They once depended on spiritual justification for all of their actions, relying on the Prophets to lead them in spiritual matters. There had never been any need for Sangheili religious leaders—now no one among them had the knowledge or the ability to comprehend the will of their gods. For a people whose sole purpose had been enforcing their gods' will, this was terrifying.

He knew his gods were out there, but he had no idea what they wanted. He had no idea if they were angry, and if they were he had no idea how to remedy that offense. All of those questions had brought him here, and all of those needs would keep him here until he found the answers he needed, or died trying.

The Shipmaster had seen this coming from the moment he put down the Prophet of Conviction, leading his men to war against their own religion. This planet was the last place he knew he had touched their gods, through that moment of ritual, and so he saw it now as his last possible hope to find answers that might lead him forward again.

He looked up, knowing his ship was in orbit, with orders to wait for his call, but he did not know what he would do if he did not find any answers. He only had food and water for a few more days. There was nothing edible here and the little water he had found so far had been bitter and sharp in his mouth. If his sustenance ran out before he heard from his gods . . .

The steady sound of the rocks against his armor was his only distraction. He moved quickly across that black land, keeping his eyes on the nearing pillar of smoke. He was not far from its source now, although it was hard to tell how much farther he had to go from so deep in the cut of the scar.

Suddenly, he came across the surprise of a small stream. It flowed right down the length of the scar; he couldn't tell how far it wound, but it looked as if it had been running for some time. The water had the same sharp smell as all other water on this planet, probably caused by the vaporization of some mineral when the plasma lines etched their fire. It carried with it smaller rocks and dirt and sand. He stared at that tiny stream and for a moment forgot the fires he unleashed here. He wondered if this stream offered hope that this place might someday be returned to its former state. The stream could become a river, wiping away this glyph, burying it beneath new soil and sand and water. He knew that forgiveness from this planet would take far longer than he had time to live, but perhaps someday his wrongs could be wiped clean. The thought was comforting. Stepping over the small stream, the Shipmaster looked up to the smoke once more, making sure he was on his proper path.

But the smoke was not there.

He scanned the entire horizon, hoping he had only become disoriented, but still he found no smoke. How long had he stared at that stream, lost in self-indulgent thoughts of forgiveness? This was his punishment for such thoughts, and he cursed himself and his weakness.

He quickly found a spot on the far wall where he thought he could exit this place and return to more normal ground. He began to run, forgoing caution for the sake of speed, for any accident he might suffer would be a very much deserved death. There would be no easy release from the burden of what he'd done.

But that death did not come. In surprisingly short time he threw himself against the far side's rocky wall, found footholds he could not see, and propelled himself to the top. Coming over the lip of the wall he now heard sounds—battle sounds, both human and Covenant (what had once been Covenant, anyway).

He followed the sounds to another stout building that reminded him unpleasantly of the one he'd left so quickly the night before. This building had part of a crumbling second story and what looked like two strange gray tents next to it, along with some kind of machinery covered in levers and wheels. All of these extra objects appeared to be human, with their squarish lines and dull gray and black surfaces. Human tools were always as ugly as they were functional in design.

He dropped his pack and freed his small hunting curveblade, a weapon his people had used for as long as they could remember, and which carried the same lines as their signature plasma blades. He stayed low to the ground, moving with deadly confidence. More shots were fired from around the building and he rushed forward, now with a clear view of three Kig-Yar taking cover behind the metal supports of the building, firing at an unknown enemy beyond.

The Shipmaster did not know what the birdlike Kig-Yar, whom the humans called "Jackals," were doing here, but he was certain it was not good. They were scavengers, pirates, and thieves, and they should not dare to come to a place like this. The sounds of the human weapons had now stopped, and he feared that the Jackals might have already taken their full toll on them.

HE CUT around to the far side of the building where he had just seen one of the gangly creatures lurking behind the building's front wall. Its attention was focused on whatever was around the structure. Before it knew what was happening he had come up behind it, pinned it to the wall of the building and nearly severed its head with a slashing lunge of his curveblade. He lowered the twitching body to the ground without sound. The staccato firing continued from the Jackal's fellows on the other side of the structure. The Shipmaster collected the carbine, now covered in the Jackal's dark blood, from the ground where it had fallen and checked the remaining ammunition. Only one shot remained, but it was good to have a real weapon in his hands again. He did not have time to scavenge the corpse for a replacement magazine, as the two on the other side would likely soon call or regroup. He had to act now.

He took a quick look around the corner to see what human forces remained, but his glimpse gave him nothing more than a closer look at the tents and some kind of hole with heavy equipment at its edge. Going back around the building so as to not expose himself to the humans, the Shipmaster dared a final quick look around the back corner to determine where the remaining two Jackals stood. When he heard them take their next shots he launched around the corner, firing his single round through the back of the nearer Jackal's plumed head. Bits of bone and meat and blood sprayed all over his fellow, who turned with a loud squawk and a weapon lowered in surprise. The Shipmaster's sprint had already carried him into melee range and with a kick from his armored foot to the Jackal's belly he heard its spine snap, and the wretch collapsed screaming.

The Kig-Yar's arms flailed in the mixture of dust and dirt and blood and its legs lay useless as the Shipmaster moved quickly to stand above his prey. A second kick to the prone Jackal's throat ended its struggles decisively.

Silence fell once again, broken only slightly by his combat-quick breath. He retrieved and hung a plasma pistol from his armor, picked up a carbine with more ammunition, and prepared to face the humans. Even though he had eliminated the Kig-Yar, the situation was now more complicated. Humans, as he had learned in all his years fighting them, became surprisingly fierce when cornered, and from what he had seen so far he suspected that the Jackals had attacked the humans unaware. More importantly, he remembered the stories told by the Arbiter that the humans shared some incomprehensible connection with the Forerunners. That humans were here at all, in this place where they suffered such a terrible loss, was enough to give the Shipmaster a spark of hope. Surely they must be here to serve some purpose for him.

Taking a deep breath, he snuck another look, low and fast, around his covering corner. Everything looked the same as it had, and he heard nothing. Anticipating closer-range combat, the Shipmaster slipped the carbine into its customary holding slot on his back and readied the plasma pistol in one hand and his gory blade in the other. After another deep breath he moved quickly to the rear of the nearest human tent and with his blade cut his way in, hoping to surprise any occupants and give him a second of surprise to decide whether to subdue or kill anything inside.

But the tent was empty, and a quick look around showed only papers and boxes and two small metal-framed beds. Through the loosely hanging door of the tent, however, he did see two human bodies on the ground outside, next to the boxy machinery he had spotted from afar. The Shipmaster could clearly see that the nearer of the two humans was motionless and had a number of large plasma burns on its legs and torso. He had seen enough dead humans to know that this one was beyond hope. The second, however, sitting with its back up against the machine, appeared to be intact and was holding a bulky pistol limply in its lap.

Throwing constant glances to the second tent and any possible additional attackers there, the Shipmaster came to within striking distance of the human and saw a large pool of its bright red blood gathering at the body's far side. He kicked the pistol off of the human's lap and, seeing no reaction, knelt down to determine if the thing was alive.

It was, barely. It continued to breathe but from the blood and lack of visible burns it looked like the human had been hit by a carbine round in its belly or side. He could not tell if the round had passed through or was still in there, baking the human's innards with radiation, but with the amount of blood on the ground the Shipmaster didn't think it particularly mattered. This man was as good as dead. Frustrated, the Shipmaster collected the pistol and moved on. The gun was primitive, but it was powerful and surprisingly accurate at a certain range. It might be useful in the days ahead.

Turning back to the second tent the Shipmaster confirmed that there were no more humans in the immediate area, but his eyes ranged constantly over the skies and horizon to watch for either human or Jackal reinforcements. All of these combatants had to have come from somewhere, and the lack of any ships in the area made it clear that they were brought here by someone or something else. Two humans alone could not have transported or even operated all this equipment . . . there must be others nearby. He might not have much time to find out what they had been doing before those others came back. He wanted to be clear of this place when they did.

The second tent contained more of the boxes he had seen in the first, and the lids he threw open exposed what looked like food, energy cells, and some kind of filthy environmental suits with enclosed helmets and heavy metal gloves. They looked big enough to cover a human in their standard bulky combat armor, but he had noticed no armor on either of the human bodies outside, merely the drab uniforms he had seen before on some human civilians.

The machinery, when inspected more closely, was still a mystery to him. Thick bundles of cables led down and disappeared into the nearby hole, which looked as if it had been dug very recently. The hole angled as if it were directed underneath the boxy building where he had killed the Jackals, and soot on the upper lip of this short tunnel appeared to answer for the source of the column of smoke he had been following the last four days. This finding dismayed the Shipmaster greatly.

As soon as he had seen the column of smoke calling to him from across the scar, he had pinned all his hope on it. The thought that the smoke had merely been the product of scavengers, which these humans now seemed to be, shook him greatly. But he could take some of the humans' food, and they had to have water. Perhaps they were there to extend his journey into the great city farther at the heart of his glyph. And there was the matter of finding out where both of these groups of interlopers had come from. His journey was not over yet.

Stepping back into the second tent to find the humans' water, the Shipmaster tossed the lids off more of their metal containers and cast aside small tools, clothing, and other human detritus until he found a heavy container at the bottom with many pouches of what looked like fresh water inside. As he lifted this container and turned to carry it out his eye caught one of the papers scattered around the floor of the tent. He froze. He threw the water container aside and dropped to grab the image on that paper, which was covered in strange human letters surrounding the image set in the middle of the page.

Among all of these incomprehensible human markings he knew exactly what that picture was, and as his widening eyes took it in he knew why he had been called here.

On that picture was a glyph, a sign of his people, and that glyph was the one that tied him to this planet twenty years ago and brought him back again today. That glyph was Faith, and the gods had sent the humans here to help him find it. Now looking at the other documents and pictures, he found a series of images that showed artifacts, clearly Forerunner-created, covered with the glyphs and signs the Covenant had translated and adopted for all of their works. And most importantly, in one picture he saw part of a rounded frame and smooth glass lens that looked exactly like the Forerunner Oracle they had kept in their former capital city, High Charity, before it was destroyed by the recklessness of the Prophet of Truth. But the pictures showed these relics surrounded by humans, being studied and even dismantled by them, and this sight brought back an anger he hadn't felt for many years.

Other pictures showed what he could see was the nearby building as it looked before being nearly destroyed. In its former state it had other, less sturdy, structures all around it, and these pictures, along with the beginnings of the tunnel outside, told him everything he needed to know.

Excited now, he rushed outside to the bleeding human and

rolled him over roughly to lie flat on the ground next to the pool of blood, now almost black in its cooling color. A small rivulet drained into the nearby hole, and it did not look like much more was left to flow from the human. The Shipmaster tore open the human's gray-green garb and saw the expected hole in the human's side where the carbine round had struck him. Rolling the human over to the other side he found a similar hole, more ragged at its edges, where the flesh split outward as the round had passed through. He grunted with approval. The wound might not be fatal, as he had seen humans survive surprising wounds on the battlefield. He would do what he could to make sure this one survived, for the Shipmaster would have many questions for him in the days ahead. And the Shipmaster still remembered how to get a human to answer questions . . .

The Shipmaster reengaged his communications and sent a command message to his ship. He called for a medic, a security squad, the ship's chief engineer, and a patrol of the surrounding skies in case there were more of these humans or Kig-Yar nearby. He had his purpose now and with it the beginnings of a sense of direction.

He no longer needed any Prophets to tell him what the gods desired. It was time for him to find out for himself.

A Letter from the Department of Xenoarchaeological Studies at Edinburgh University to security-cleared Faculty and onsite Graduate Students.

Department of Xenoarchaeology
Jadwin Hall
Edinburgh University
2 Charles Street
Edinburgh
Alba EH8 9ADEarth

ONI MANDATED SECURITY CLEARANCE INFORMATION: *TS_Adjunct and Civilian Personnel Exception 1492_b 01/31/2553 14:12pm TST*

January 31, 2553

From the Office of Dr. William Arthur Iqbal.

Dear Colleagues,

As we are all very aware, the discovery of the Excession at Voi has significant ramifications for our species, as well as the course of our work. Everyone on this distribution list has had some exposure to classified documents regarding the discovery and exposure of what we are now describing as "Forerunner" relics, technology, and architecture. Everyone on this distribution list has no doubt made some educated assumptions about what we're looking at and, from this moment, for.

A similar letter has gone out from the Department of Xenobiology in Calcutta. Some of their information differs in security clearance from your own and so I am not able to divulge its